The Westwood Mystery

A Chief Inspector Pointer Mystery

By A. E. Fielding

Originally published in 1933

The Westwood Mystery

© 2015 Resurrected Press
www.ResurrectedPress.com

All rights reserved. No part of this book may be used or reproduced in any manner without written permission except for brief quotations for review purposes.

Published by Resurrected Press

This classic book was handcrafted by Resurrected Press. Resurrected Press is dedicated to bringing high quality classic books back to the readers who enjoy them. These are not scanned versions of the originals, but, rather, quality checked and edited books meant to be enjoyed!

Please visit ResurrectedPress.com to view our entire catalogue!

ISBN 13: 978-1-937022-88-4

Printed in the United States of America

Other Resurrected Press Books in *The Chief Inspector Pointer Mystery* Series

Death of John Tait
Murder at the Nook
Mystery at the Rectory
Scarecrow
The Case of the Two Pearl Necklaces
The Charteris Mystery
The Eames-Erskine Case
The Footsteps that Stopped
The Clifford Affair
The Cluny Problem
The Craig Poisoning Mystery
The Net Around Joan Ingilby
The Tall House Mystery
The Wedding-Chest Mystery
The Westwood Mystery
Tragedy at Beechcroft

RESURRECTED PRESS CLASSIC MYSTERY CATALOGUE

Journeys into Mystery
Travel and Mystery in a More Elegant Time

The Edwardian Detectives
Literary Sleuths of the Edwardian Era

Gems of Mystery
Lost Jewels from a More Elegant Age

Anne Austin
One Drop of Blood
The Black Pigeon
Murder at Bridge

E. C. Bentley
Trent's Last Case: The Woman in Black

Ernest Bramah
Max Carrados Resurrected:
The Detective Stories of Max Carrados

Agatha Christie
The Secret Adversary
The Mysterious Affair at Styles

Octavus Roy Cohen
Midnight

Freeman Wills Croft
The Ponson Case
The Pit Prop Syndicate

J. S. Fletcher
The Herapath Property
The Rayner-Slade Amalgamation
The Chestermarke Instinct
The Paradise Mystery
Dead Men's Money
The Middle of Things
Ravensdene Court
Scarhaven Keep
The Orange-Yellow Diamond
The Middle Temple Murder
The Tallyrand Maxim
The Borough Treasurer
In the Mayor's Parlour
The Saftey Pin

R. Austin Freeman
The Mystery of 31 New Inn from the Dr. Thorndyke Series
John Thorndyke's Cases from the Dr. Thorndyke Series
The Red Thumb Mark from The Dr. Thorndyke Series
The Eye of Osiris from The Dr. Thorndyke Series
A Silent Witness from the Dr. John Thorndyke Series
The Cat's Eye from the Dr. John Thorndyke Series
Helen Vardon's Confession: A Dr. John Thorndyke Story
As a Thief in the Night: A Dr. John Thorndyke Story
Mr. Pottermack's Oversight: A Dr. John Thorndyke Story
Dr. Thorndyke Intervenes: A Dr. John Thorndyke Story
The Singing Bone: The Adventures of Dr. Thorndyke
The Stoneware Monkey: A Dr. John Thorndyke Story
The Great Portrait Mystery, and Other Stories: A Collection of Dr. John Thorndyke and Other Stories
The Penrose Mystery: A Dr. John Thorndyke Story

The Uttermost Farthing: A Savant's Vendetta

Arthur Griffiths
The Passenger From Calais
The Rome Express

Fergus Hume
The Mystery of a Hansom Cab
The Green Mummy
The Silent House
The Secret Passage

Edgar Jepson
The Loudwater Mystery

A. E. W. Mason
At the Villa Rose

A. A. Milne
The Red House Mystery

Baroness Emma Orczy
The Old Man in the Corner

Edgar Allan Poe
The Detective Stories of Edgar Allan Poe

Arthur J. Rees
The Hampstead Mystery
The Shrieking Pit
The Hand In The Dark
The Moon Rock
The Mystery of the Downs

Mary Roberts Rinehart
Sight Unseen and The Confession

Dorothy L. Sayers

Whose Body?

Sir William Magnay
The Hunt Ball Mystery

Mabel and Paul Thorne
The Sheridan Road Mystery

Louis Tracy
The Strange Case of Mortimer Fenley
The Albert Gate Mystery
The Bartlett Mystery
The Postmaster's Daughter
The House of Peril
The Sandling Case: What Would You Have Done?

Charles Edmonds Walk
The Paternoster Ruby

John R. Watson
The Mystery of the Downs
The Hampstead Mystery

Edgar Wallace
The Daffodil Mystery
The Crimson Circle

Carolyn Wells
Vicky Van
The Man Who Fell Through the Earth
In the Onyx Lobby
Raspberry Jam
The Clue
The Room with the Tassels
The Vanishing of Betty Varian
The Mystery Girl
The White Alley
The Curved Blades

Anybody but Anne
The Bride of a Moment
Faulkner's Folly
The Diamond Pin
The Gold Bag
The Mystery of the Sycamore
The Come Back

Raoul Whitfield
Death in a Bowl

And much more!
Visit ResurrectedPress.com
for our complete catalogue

FOREWORD

The period between the First and Second World Wars has rightly been called the "Golden Age of British Mysteries." It was during this period that Agatha Christie, Dorothy L. Sayers, and Margery Allingham first turned their pens to crime. On the male side, the era saw such writers as Anthony Berkeley, John Dickson Carr, and Freeman Wills Crofts join the ranks of writers of detective fiction. The genre was immensely popular at the time on both sides of the Atlantic, and by the end of the 1930's one out of every four novels published in Britain was a mystery.

While Agatha Christie and a few of her peers have remained popular and in print to this day, the same cannot be said of all the authors of this period. With so many mysteries published in the period, it is inevitable that many of them would become obscure or worse, forgotten, often with no justification than changing public tastes. The case of Archibald Fielding is one such, an author, who though popular enough to have a career spanning two decades and more than two dozen mysteries, has become such a cipher that his, or as seems more likely, her real identity has become as much a mystery as the books themselves.

While the identity of the author may forever remain an unsolved puzzle, there are some facts that may be inferred from the texts. It is likely that the author had an upbringing and education typical of the British upper middle class in the period before the Great War with all that implies; a familiarity with the classics, the arts, and music, a working knowledge of French and Italian, an appreciation of the finer things in life. The author has also traveled abroad, primarily in the south of France, but probably to Belgium, Spain, and Italy as well, as portions of several of the books are set in those locales.

The books attributed to Archibald Fielding, A. E. Fielding, or Archibald E. Fielding, are quintessential Golden Age British mysteries. They include all the attributes, the country houses, the tangled webs of relationships, the somewhat feckless cast of characters who seem to have nothing better to do with themselves than to murder or be murdered. Their focus is on a middle class and upper class struggling to find themselves in the new realities of the post war era while still trying to live the lifestyle of the Edwardian era. Things are never as they seem, red herrings are distributed liberally throughout the pages as are the clues that will ultimately lead to the solution of "the puzzle," for the British mysteries of this period are centered on the puzzle element which both the reader and the detective must solve before the last page.

A majority of the Fielding mysteries involve the character of Chief Inspector Pointer. Unlike the eccentric Belgian Hercule Poirot, the flamboyant Lord Peter Wimsey, or the somewhat mysterious Albert Campion, Pointer is merely a competent, sometimes clever, occasionally intuitive policeman. And unlike, as with Inspector French in the stories of Freeman Wills Croft, the emphasis is on the mystery itself, not the process of detection.

Pointer is nearly as much of a mystery as the author. Very little of his personal life is revealed in the books. He is described as being vaguely of Scottish ancestry. He is well read and educated, though his duties at Scotland Yard prevent him from enjoying those pursuits. In an early book in the series it is revealed that he spends a week or two each year climbing mountains, his only apparent recreation. His success as a detective depends on his willingness to "suspect everyone" and to not being tied to any one theory. He is fluent in French and familiar with that country. He is, at least in the first two books, unmarried, and sharing lodgings with a bookbinder named O'Connor, in much the manner of Holmes and Watson, though this character is absent in later works.

One intriguing feature of the Pointer mysteries is that they all involve an unexpected twist at the end, wherein the mystery finally solved is not the mystery invoked at the beginning of the book. *The Westwood Mystery* is no exception. Fielding introduces numerous red-herrings and subplots to confuse the reader while still largely playing fair with the reader. When Fielding wrote *The Westwood Mystery* the series was already eight years old, the book being the thirteenth novel to feature Chief Inspector Pointer. The author's style had matured and been refined over that period. Gone are the over reliance on disguises and other dramatic gimmicks that mark some of the earlier books. There is much more reliance on solid detection, the interpretation of clues, and judging the validity of the testimony of those involved. Yet, the Pointer mysteries have a certain flair that separates them from the "humdrum" school of mysteries that were starting to appear at the same time. Stylistically, they fall somewhere between the works of Christie and those of Ngaio Marsh or E. C. R. Lorac.

The Westwood Mystery involves the case of a well known barrister, Sir Adam Youdale, K.C. who is found murdered at his home, Westwood, having been drugged and then suffocated by a pillow while he lie sleeping. Early in the investigation, suspicion falls on his wife's uncle, who may or may not have been involved in a stock fraud case that Youdale was investigating on behalf of the shareholders. Yet the clues in the case begin to point in another direction. Pointer's task is made more difficult by the fact, that several of those close to the case have secrets of their own unrelated to the murder, causing them to withhold information.

In typical Fielding fashion, there are plenty of plot twists and turnings in *the Westwood Mystery*, more than enough to keep a mystery fan involved trying to solve the puzzle. Yet from the very beginning, the author supplies the reader with all the information needed to crack the case, all the information that is, except for the name of the murderer.

As a clue to the background of the author, many of the characters in *The Westwood Mystery,* have spent time in Tangier, leading one to suspect that Fielding had a personal familiarity with that North African city.

Despite their obscurity, the mysteries of Archibald Fielding, whoever he or she might have been, are well written, well crafted examples of the form, worthy of the interest of the fans of the genre. It is with pleasure, then, that Resurrected Press presents this new edition of *The Westwood Mystery* and others in the series to its readers.

About the Author

The identity of the author is as much a mystery as the plots of the novels. Two dozen novels were published from 1924 to 1944 as by Archibald Fielding, A. E. Fielding, or Archibald E. Fielding, yet the only clue as to the real author is a comment by the American publishers, H.C. Kinsey Co. that A. E. Fielding was in reality a "middle-aged English woman by the name of Dorothy Feilding whose peacetime address is Sheffield Terrace, Kensington, London, and who enjoys gardening." Research on the part of John Herrington has uncovered a person by that name living at 2 Sheffield Terrace from 1932-1936. She appears to have moved to Islington in 1937 after which she disappears. To complicate things, some have attributed the authorship to Lady Dorothy Mary Evelyn Moore nee Feilding (1889-1935), however, a grandson of Lady Dorothy denied any family knowledge of such authorship. The archivist at Collins, the British publisher, reports that any records of A. Fielding were presumably lost during WWII. Birthdates have been given variously as 1884, 1889, and 1900. Unless new information comes to light, it would appear that the real authorship must remain a mystery.

Greg Fowlkes
Editor-In-Chief
Resurrected Press
www.ResurrectedPress.

CHAPTER ONE

"What does it feel like to be foreman of a jury?" The parson spoke with an air of mingled distance and patronage, of which he was quite unaware. True, he only saw Fox at the golf club—the fellow was the rankest outsider, but he played a good game, and that after-noon, when it was pouring, any arrival made a welcome break in the desultory conversation that had run dry around the club-house fire.

Fox laughed a little under his breath. He never laughed aloud. He was a small man, but so well made that he looked the average size, and there was a hint of unexpected strength about his shoulders and arms, narrow though the former were. He was said by some women to have the face of a Greek god, but his blue eyes were modernity itself. They belonged to a machine age. Indeed they had an effect at times as though they themselves were of glass, instead of flesh and blood. His voice was harsh with an unpleasant twang.

He met the rector's tolerant look with a contemptuous flicker of his own lids. The parson's manner might be patronizing, but Fox's bearing was always arrogant, a certain conscious conceit in it. It said that not only was he, Fox, as good as any man, but a great deal better than most.

"Feel like?" he repeated, cocking his small, sleek head on one side. "Rather like being an intelligent collie put in charge of that peculiarly stupid sheep, the average juryman."

"Yet the average juryman is the average Englishman." The rector had the air of opening a debate in a workingman's club.

"You've said it!" Fox replied with a sneer.

"You're an Australian, aren't you?" a man asked from the other side of the fire.

Fox fixed his eyes on him for a moment. You found it difficult to wrench your eyes from his full-on gaze. A few people liked this, most disliked it.

"I was born in Yorkshire, and lived there all my life until I came to London." Fox spoke almost defiantly. "But about juries—what I meant was that you can make them believe just what you want to. A jury doesn't reason, doesn't think, it only feels." His tone told what his opinion of feelings was.

"Especially when Sir Adam Youdale is defending," another man struck in.

"Youdale? We didn't have him. Two quite unimportant men were for the defense," Fox said wonderingly.

"I wasn't thinking of the case you were on." The man who had mentioned Youdale picked up a paper from his knee. "I see here that he's got his client off again. Yet the verdict was a foregone conclusion. Of course she drowned the kid in order to marry that other man!"

"Youdale's a marvel," some one else joined in warmly.

"I can't think why he's considered such a genius," Fox said slightingly. "It's the people he defends who are clever. He couldn't do anything if they had bungled. Matter of fact, I think he often misses points he ought to make. My belief is that half the time when he scores, it's the accused himself who puts him up to it."

"I don't agree," the man with the paper spoke with asperity, "and, as it happens, I heard him once. His first murder-defense moreover. I was out in Tangier, of all the funny places! I was there for the day on a trip from Gib, and being a barrister, and hearing that there was a case on before the Mixed Tribunals, I stopped over. As far as I could make it out it was a simple, sordid affair. I know there wasn't the shadow of a doubt as to the prisoner's guilt. It wasn't even cleverly done. Yet Youdale got him off. As to any idea of his 'leading' Youdale, the chap sat with his head buried in his hands all the time I was

The Westwood Mystery

there," the talker went on reflectively. "The only thing I recall was his name, Honesty."

The men laughed. Fox for once came near to an audible burst of merriment.

"Honesty, did you say?" asked another man who had been looking through the front page of his own sheet. "Not this fellow who's being advertised for, Charles Oliver Honesty?"

"Hardly likely," yawned the man addressed, "but it was catching sight of that name made me think of the affair. It must be five years ago or even six."

Another man bent forward and asked if the paper were by chance a later edition than the ones that he had seen. "Anything fresh about the Rubber Trunk shares? I don't know whether to sell or average."

"Ah!" breathed the broker, "we're pretty well all in that boat." Every face looked grave. This really concerned most of those present. This was different from idle chatter. A year ago Rubber Trunk shares were considered practically gilt-edged, then they had begun to shake. Selling could no longer be explained away even by the press, as "on deceased account," it was too persistent. Whispers ran that a certain chartered accountant had sold his shares, smaller fry followed. There had been a company meeting. Followed by another. And another. The upshot was that the two directors had been arrested as they were on the eve of leaving England, and after a short trial, which had shown up the company as rotten beyond belief, had been sentenced to penal servitude. But the question now agitating every one was whether Mr. Sturge, of the big, though rather mushroom firm of Sturge and Company, Chartered Accountants, knew to what he had put his signature, when he had allowed the former misleading and optimistic balance-sheets to be issued with his name below the figures. There were rumors in the City... plenty of them, for and against him. The golfers around the club fire were fairly divided in their sympathies according to whether each had suffered a loss or had made money out of the recent switchback of the share price. All agreed that a month from today would tell the real facts. On that date, an extraordinary meeting of the shareholders had been convened. Sir Adam Youdale, the famous K.C., who had just been discussed from one point of view, himself interested financially in the concern for providing travelers with elastic-sided trunks, had been chosen to represent the shareholders. He had gone thoroughly into the company's finances with a well-known chartered accountant—other than Mr. Sturge—and the result would be made known at the meeting. It would determine whether Sturge would come out an honest man, or eventually join the two directors in their fall. The betting was about even. But they were all agreed on one point. Youdale would find it out if there had been anything crooked.

Fox threw back his head, and laughed, his soft, jarring laugh.

"Think so?" he said, and again he laughed. "What? When he's married Sturge's niece?"

"Well, what of that?" several voices asked. "That won't make any difference to Youdale."

"True! It may make him all the keener," Fox agreed, with a smile that showed pointed teeth. "He never goes anywhere with her."

"Do you know him?" some one asked coldly.

"No. I've only seen and heard him at public meetings," Fox explained, rather in the tone of a man who had been boasting a little too much. "I've never met him personally. As you all say, he's an awfully clever chap. One who never makes a mistake. You're right!" The tone made the words a jeer.

The talk went back to the Rubber Trunk Company. Under cover of it, Fox picked up the newspaper of the man who had spoken of an advertisement for Charles Oliver Honesty, and looked through the front page thoroughly. There it was:

The Westwood Mystery 5

"CHARLES OLIVER HONESTY—In accordance with directions in the will of the late Henry Trevor, the above-mentioned, as his sole legatee, is requested to communicate with the undersigned."

There followed the name of a solicitor's firm in the City. Fox read the item a second time. Then he hastily turned to the stock exchange page, and seemed to be hunting up some quotation, after which he folded the paper up and, as though absent-mindedly, tucked it under his arm, before saying that he thought it was slackening a bit, and he was going home; the ground would be too sodden to be pleasant.

"That's a good riddance," one of the men cocked his head in the direction of the closing door. "I mean the blue-eyed merchant. Fox is his name, isn't it? It certainly is his nature."

The club secretary nodded.

"His handicap is plus two," he murmured with a sigh.

"And his manners minus the limit!" snapped the other.

"It isn't even his manner," threw the barrister who had spoken of having heard Youdale at Tangier. "He's a wrong 'un, if ever I saw one. What's his line? Cheap share pushing? Or find the pea?"

"He goes in for jams," another man said lazily.

"Wanted to sell me a ton of his stuff while going around the course with me. Nearly pushed it down my throat. Business evidently sticks a bit—like jam." The talk left Fox and went to the Oxford and Cambridge boat race that was being rowed that day.

That young man, or rather young looking man, had hurried back to his house in Paddington, spent the evening rummaging through a locked trunk, a very securely locked trunk, and early next morning took a taxi for the firm who had inserted that advertisement. There he sent in a name penciled on a card. It was that of Charles Oliver Honesty. He was kept waiting rather a long time, then shown into a dingy office—the firm was evidently not a wealthy one—and asked to show his credentials.

"Here's my passport," the man known as Fox produced it. "Here are some letters from my solicitor to me during my trial. You know, of course, that I was most iniquitously tried for the murder of my wife, this same Henry's daughter. Of course, I was acquitted. That was a foregone conclusion. It was only my father-in-law's spite that rigged up a fake case against me. That's why he's left me his money in belated remorse. Well, I'm not one to bear malice. Is it a large sum?"

"About a thousand pounds." The solicitor looked over his spectacles at the man with a measuring, meditative look.

"Is that all?" Fox looked vexed. "Still, something's better than nothing, especially these days. Well, when can I have it? When did he pop off?"

"The death certificate is about six months old now. As to when the money will be paid you? I'm afraid we shall want additional corroboration of identity. Something personal. You might merely be a man who bears a strong resemblance to the Honesty of this passport, and who got hold of his letters."

Fox looked a little perturbed.. "I've changed my name. Call myself Fox. No one knows me as Honesty."

"Still, there must be some one who knew you in the old days—not as far back as your Sydney days, but some one since you went to Tangier, say. I may tell you, Mr. Honesty—"

"Fox!" snapped the man.

"—that my partners and I have talked this difficulty over, and we are agreed that we should only feel justified in parting with the money, if you were to have an interview before us, with Sir Adam Youdale. He defended you in that trial, which was only five years ago. He, better than anyone, would be able to assure us that you are the man in question. In fact, I may tell you that Mr. Trevor's

The Westwood Mystery 7

private letter which accompanied his will, directed us to do this if in any way possible, and suggested a test question which, if answered to Sir Adam's satisfaction, would indisputably prove your claim beyond any chance of mistake."

"Huh!" snarled Fox bitterly, "and how many hundreds do you suppose Youdale would ask to come and have a chat with me in your office? Why, he gets at least forty pounds a minute!" Judging by Fox's tone, every penny of that sum came out of his pocket.

"And how long after this precious identification do I get the money?" he demanded roughly.

"By the terms of the will, three calendar months must pass between Sir Adam's acknowledgment of you as the husband of the late Mrs. Flora Honesty, the daughter of Mr. Henry Trevor, and the paying over to you of your legacy."

"But, of course, in the meantime, you'll let me have something on account," Fox suggested more pleasantly.

"By the terms of the will, that is expressly forbidden. Here is a copy of the document in question."

Fox snatched it, and read avidly.

"Because of my acquittal—I see he gives this as the reason for leaving me his money. Better late than never. Old devil! Well, I'll set about this ridiculous farce of being identified by the most expensive chap to do it," he began truculently. But he had met his match, and finally, with but the thinnest veneer of civility over his anger, he promised to call with the solicitor at Sir Adam Youdale's chambers in Brick Court at as early a date as could be arranged with the barrister.

"It won't take five seconds to identify me," Fox said. "You have the papers all drawn up for him to sign. I don't intend it to be questioned again, as to who I am, I mean. Even Youdale ought not to charge an enormous fee for doing that. If he can't see me in his office hours, why not out of them? I've looked him up in your *Who's Who* here and see he has a house called Westwood somewhere out at Wimbledon. If need be, we might meet there."

"I doubt if he would consent to arranging an interview at his private house," the solicitor said frostily. Fox said that probably he was right, these fellows put on such airs, and that if he did, he might charge for the honor, so that, on the whole, he would prefer the meeting in the office. So saying, he thrust out his hand to say good-by, but Mr. Alderley was bending over some papers in a drawer, and did not seem to see it. Fox gave his bending figure a look that suggested a kick, and went out, slamming the door behind him.

The afternoon of the next day was appointed by Sir Adam Youdale's head clerk for the interview with Mr. Alderley and Mr. Alderley's client, Mr. Fox.

Solicitor and client did not arrive together. Fox had suggested sharing a taxi, but Mr. Alderley had made it quite plain that, though professionally he might have to meet Mr. Fox, the necessity did not extend to their private lives. Fox arrived in good time, and spent quite three minutes walking up and down in the Temple Gardens.

Mr. Alderley, when he arrived, promptly rang the bell. He had no nerves to quiet, no "attitude" on which to decide. He was shown at once into a noble room, dark because of its linenfold paneling, but warm and pleasing on that very account, where Sir Adam was standing by the big fireplace.

The famous pleader was a tall, well-made man in the early forties with a handsome, hawklike face, and big, rather weary dark eyes with very sharply-cut drooping lids. He had the true flexible, thin, barrister's lips, yet with a I certain sweetness about them that gave a hint of his almost uncanny charm at his best. He did not know the solicitor, but he wasted no time in small talk.

"This the paper you have drafted for me to sign?" he asked, reading it through in an amazingly short time. "I

The Westwood Mystery

9

suppose the will isn't a forgery? In confidence, Mr. Alderley, I should make very sure of it if I were you before parting with the money, even if I identify your client as the Honesty of that trial in Tangier."

"It's not a forgery," Mr. .Alderley said with certainty.

"Then it stands for an amazing change of sentiment. You say this money is left Honesty because of his acquittal?"

"So the will says, and so a covering letter says that reached us at the same time."

"No other explanation?" Youdale's dark eyes probed the other's face keenly.

"None whatever," Alderley said truthfully. "The covering letter suggested the following question to be put by you as a test."

Youdale took the slip of paper as Fox was shown in. With a swagger the latest arrival came forward as though to shake hands, but Youdale was reading the paper just handed him, and the solicitor was blowing his nose.

Youdale raised his head and looked at the man calling himself Fox. Something about the barrister's glance: suggested eyes that could see at a swoop all there was to be seen, yet he kept them a long moment on his visitor.

"Yes, you are the Honesty of Tangier. You call yourself Fox now, I understand."

"I changed my name after the trial," Fox replied briefly.

"Having identified you by sight, to the best of my ability, I am further required to ask you to repeat what I said to you when you came up to me after that case was over, and you were leaving the courthouse."

Youdale let his eyeglass fall, and looked blandly, down on the smaller man with his large but at the moment rather wicked eyes. As for Fox, he went scarlet, then white.

"What's the need for this sort of thing?" he asked angrily, "you recognized me. You see that I'm the man that was acquitted without any debate, merely on the evidence, at that old trial."

"Nevertheless, in accordance with the late Mr. Trevor's request, I have asked you that question. We were alone in the room. You came in, leaving the door open behind you, and saying, 'Well, that's over. Of course, I knew how it would be!' Now what was my reply to your effusive thanks for my efforts on your behalf? Even if you can't remember the exact wording, you will, I am sure, not have forgotten the gist of my sentence. Mr. Trevor happened to be passing at the moment and seems to have overheard us." Youdale looked at the big clock against the wall, swinging his eyeglass in time to the ticking.

Fox, after biting his lip for a second, said hoarsely: "You said I should do well not to forget that, if any fresh evidence turned up, of sufficient importance to have altered the verdict had it been known at the time of the trial, a second trial could be ordered. You"—Fox swallowed—"you suggested that I should bear that in mind."

Youdale nodded. "I was thinking of the Arab servant," he murmured, as though to himself. "Well, Mr. Alderley"—he turned to the silent solicitor—"the answer is quite correct. I am prepared to sign." He touched a bell on his desk. His head clerk glided in.

Another followed. Youdale put his bold signature to the document that Alderley had prepared, the two clerks witnessed it. Youdale handed it to Mr. Alderley, and with a pleasant nod to him and after a "I think that's everything, isn't it?—then I'll say good afternoon," left the room. He had not glanced again at Fox, whose small hands, that no manual toil, or games, had ever broadened, were tightly clenched at his sides. Mr. Alderley, too, left the room without looking at him. Fox realized that he was alone, kicked the wastepaper basket out of his way, opened the door, found a cat leaning against the sill as though eavesdropping, aimed a savage blow at her with his umbrella, which that nimble animal

The Westwood Mystery

avoided dexterously, and then rushed downstairs as though the furies were after him. As for Sir Adam Youdale, when Fox had gone, he listened with rather an absent mind to his head clerk's suggestions to what line they could, and what they legally could not take in a coming case. He nodded once or twice, but his thoughts were on the man who now called himself Fox. How he had writhed at having to repeat those words of his, Youdale's!

True words, too. Suppose that Arab servant, the one whom the defense insisted had run off with the money, had floated up out of the harbor where, privately, Youdale was sure that he had been hurled, or suppose that he had been picked up by a dredge... granted that the man was alive, and would have known enough to turn to the British consul, then Honesty would have found himself in a very awkward position indeed. Unless he had got to the servant in time! He, Youdale, in his position, would have looked to his safety with the greatest care. Chain-mail, two bulldogs, and a private detective, he told himself with a whimsical grin. Then he dropped the old case from his mind, and gave his attention to what his clerk was saying, for after five years Honesty was quite safe. It was most improbable that after five years anything would rise up from the past to hale him again before a jury to be tried for that murder which Youdale was as sure he had committed as though he had watched it being done.

Another hour saw Youdale on his way out to his home in Wimbledon. It was a comfortable house which he had bought on his return from the East. So far, he had refused to be nagged by his wife into moving into anything bigger. Hurrying into his library, his arms full of papers and books, he saw that someone was sitting by the window. A young and very smartly dressed woman came forward with outstretched hands.

"I was too upset last week to thank you as I wanted to! I collapsed when I was taken from that terrible dock, and I've been in bed ever since, but oh, Sir Adam, thank you a thousand times! No one but you could have saved me!"

It was Annabelle Luton, the young woman who had been accused of murdering her illegitimate child, and in whose defense he had made the brilliantly successful speech which had been referred to at the golf club as a proof of his power.

He shook her extended hands with a pleasant smile.

"Now you must forget all that," he said in his easy way; "forget it so completely that when you meet me next you say to yourself, 'Youdale . . . Youdale, surely I've heard that name before... or haven't I?'"

She shook her head at that, and her face grew grave. It showed its strength then, with its wide arching brows and high cheek-bones. The complexion was so lovely, in its geranium and cream tones, that it gave an air of mere prettiness to a face that was made of very firm, perhaps hard, material. He had dropped his books with a bang on the table when he saw her, now he wheeled up a chair and sat down with an air of having any amount of time to spend.

"What are you going to do now? Marry, eh?" She shot him a measuring glance.

"In due time. Not immediately, of course." She spoke very slowly.

"That's right," he said heartily. "Start a new life. I hope you'll be happy, my dear, and you must let me brow how you get on. Now, what about tea? I never take cocktails myself, but if you prefer them—"

His finger stretched itself out toward the bell. A well-shaped long finger.

"Lady Youdale was kind enough to give me tea," she said to that. Instantly his face froze. She was not looking at him as it happened, but at her gloves. She was thinking of what she wanted to say, and how best to say it.

"I was not aware that you knew my wife," he said quietly.

The Westwood Mystery 13

"I don't, Sir Adam. But she found me waiting in here and very kindly offered me tea."

He looked at her sharply. It was most unlike his wife to offer hospitality in that casual way.

She glanced up at him, sensible of the chill in the air. "You don't mind, do you, Sir Adam?" she asked a little uncertainly.

"Frankly, I do," he said to that, a haughty look now on his face, haughty and unapproachable. "My clients do not come here as a rule except on invitation, and when they do come they usually wait for me to introduce them to my family."

It was said with perfect ruthlessness, an utter disregard of her feelings, with the intention of putting the matter in the clearest and most unmistakable light.

Adam Youdale would have laughed had you called him a snob. But, though he did not know it, he would not have spoken in quite that tone to a woman of his own world, whatever her failings had been.

Her face went quite white. Her eyes began to glitter. Fine, large, bright blue eyes they were at all times. She rose to her feet. She had a charming figure, very graceful, very full of what is called sex-appeal, which might be better defined as sex-consciousness. Putting her two hands on the table, she bent forward to speak, in her face the look of a woman who feels herself master of the situation.

Youdale did not look at her face, however. Putting his eyeglass into his eye, he stared first at the one hand and then at the other. Then he let the eyeglass drop with a lift of his boldly marked eyebrows.

Now Annabelle Luton's arrest and danger lay in the fact that a laborer, passing through a copse near her father's farm, swore that he had seen her kneeling by the edge of the stream holding something down under the water with both hands. She said, or rather Youdale said for her, that it was a flat water-flask she used when picnicking with the child, but the laborer, when the child was found drowned next morning in the same stream, insisted that it was her four-year-old child that she had been holding under the water.

Annabelle knew what the barrister meant by that look at her hands, and knew that he meant her to know. Her face seemed to change into something carved, graven out of stone.

It was quite an hour later that Youdale stood waiting in his wife's drawing-room for a word with her. Lady Youdale joined him with some words about trying or a dress for the ball to which they were going.

He replied rather curtly that she would have to make his excuses. A case was coming on in the courts on the following morning in which he was appearing, and he wanted to have his head at its best.

She agreed, with her usual tepid amiability, that that meant fairly early hours, and a silence fell. One of those silences that was constantly falling between them, the silence of mutual boredom.

"By the way," he said in a negligent tone, "Miss, Luton was here when I got in this afternoon. She said you gave her tea. I didn't know that you knew her."

"I don't. I went into the library to speak to you—I thought you had come in. She got up and introduced herself, said you had just saved her life. As, of course, you had. I wanted to see her from the first day of the trial. I knew she was innocent. I never doubted that. It must be a dreadful ordeal."

"Dreadful," he agreed in rather a dry tone. His gaze was ironic. It struck him afresh as really comic that he, of all men, should have chosen this woman to be his wife.

He who admired wit, and brain's, and personality, to have endowed a flaxen haired doll with them, whereas inside the doll was only the equivalent of sawdust.

"Should she speak to you again," he said now, lighting a cigarette, "I think I should freeze her off. She might make herself rather a bore, I fancy."

The Westwood Mystery 15

This time it was her gaze that was ironic as it just swept over him, but she only murmured one of her usual conventional agreements before returning again to her maid. As she went, Lady Youdale smiled to herself—a rather curious, not very pleasant smile.

CHAPTER TWO

Honesty himself, or Fox, as he was now called, had left the K.C.'s chambers in Brick Court frowning heavily.

How much would be left of that thousand when that shark Youdale and that other smaller shark, Alderley, had been paid? Then there was the accursed legacy duty which there was no dodging. Still, he ought to get five hundred clear. Useful sum. Not in itself, but added to, say, another five hundred. Fortunately, he was a clever chap who meant to get on in the world, however much the damned universe banded itself together against him, curse it! He glanced at his watch. He would be in plenty of time for his appointment with someone who wanted to put a little money into his business. Fox would have gladly arranged to meet the devil if that ancient had suggested anything to his profit. But so far from it being the devil, it was a young and guileless thing who had answered an advertisement that he had inserted a few days ago. "Wanted—a lady partner. Well established home-made jam and preserving business. One with knowledge of cooking essential. Salary according to investment. Particulars at interview only. References."

That had brought him a long letter from a Kathleen Drury, now teaching cookery in a school in Somerset. She wrote that she might be prepared to put five hundred pounds into some such business, provided, of course, that the business, etc., etc. Fox decided that it should not only be in 'some such,' but in his. He could do quite nice things with five hundred pounds. But he must not rush matters. He had written asking for an interview in town, and had been given an appointment at a hotel in Bloomsbury for today. Within the next hour he met a pretty girl who told him that she was an orphan with no living relatives, and

18   *A Resurrected Press Mystery*

that the five hundred she was prepared to invest in a really sound business represented about half of what she had left of her parents' money. She was over twenty-one, though she looked under it, and her guardian was dead.

A more ideal partner Fox could not imagine, except that he wished the amount at her disposal had been a great deal larger. Still, Heaven helps those who help themselves, he often remarked, and he intended to do his best in the preliminary part. It was finally arranged that she should come for a month and try it. At any time she could either withdraw entirely if not satisfied, or she could make the investment, and take half the profits as well as the salary of five pounds weekly that he offered. Meantime, fifty pounds was to be paid in immediately as an option.

Fox seemed very frank. He said that he had been frightfully "had" over the business, which was represented to him as being a very flourishing one. He had sunk all his money into it. He was a late naval commander, he modestly murmured, and not up in business matters. Too late, he had found things quite different from what they seemed.

"That's why I want to be so careful with you, Miss Drury," he had said, and Miss Drury, and Miss Green, the principal of the school, who had accompanied her, thought what a frank and sailorly way of talking he had. His mother lived with him, he went on to say, and Miss Drury could count on having a quiet but pleasant home. As for the business, it offered every chance of doing really well with hard work. He had had excellent machinery installed, and went into technical details which were followed attentively and approved. The two women were quite up in this part of the talk. He had a good trade and private connection, and hoped to increase this as the quality of his products became better known.

Altogether, it was a most satisfactory interview to both sides, and the result was that within the week little Miss Drury said good-by to the school where she herself

The Westwood Mystery 19

had been first pupil, then pupil-teacher and then full-fledged mistress, and was on her way to Fox's house, there to meet Mrs. Fox and to make jam. She was trembling with excitement as she set out. It was so wonderful this venture of hers. To have a business bringing in five pounds a week for certain, and the prospect of ten times that with hard work, according to the carefully compiled figures of Fox. Both she and Miss Green had agreed that this sounded most promising, and secretly, each had also thought that Fox looked promising too. Not merely as a business partner. Miss Green, gentle, kindly, unbusinesslike, as only a woman of her type can be, privately thought that dear Kathleen's dead parents were taking a hand in things, and were going to provide their child with something quite extra nice in the way of a husband.

Kathleen's eyes were shining as she took her seat finally in the train that was to lead her to Royal Oak. She had never been to town but the once, and then only for two hours. The name of her station sounded fascinating, suggested the Stewarts and the gallant games of hide and seek an unfortunate monarch and his people played together over several pages of her history book.

The reality struck her dumb. Behind the public-house, that gave the corner its name, stretched streets and squares of most respectable and most dreary-looking houses. One of these was Tollard Road, the address to which she was bound, and her taxi finally drew up at a house in a row where each was as like the other as the sections of a caterpillar.

A neat little maid opened the door and in a second Oliver Fox came out into the narrow passage, seeming to broaden it by his hearty greeting.

"Come in and have some tea first of all. Mrs. Goodge just brought it as the taxi set you down. I think she must have second sight." There came a chuckle from behind him and he stood aside. "This is Mrs. Goodge herself," he said, and Kathleen looked into a very pleasant, middle-aged face. "The housekeeper," Fox added, "and now for tea." He showed her into a little drawing-room. It was shabby and somehow depressing. Perhaps it was the blue curtains over the window. But the table looked inviting.

"Will you pour? My mother—but that's a story for after you've had a cup," and he chatted of her journey and asked after Miss Green to whom he said he had taken "quite a romantic liking." Such magnetic eyes, Kathleen thought, and such a magnetic voice.

Quite the handsomest man she had ever seen. And with such charming, gay, friendly manners, too, though perhaps not as young as his way of talking would make you think.

"The first cup drunk?" Fox asked hospitably, "then I'll tell you my bad news. My mother has had to rush away to a great friend of hers who's very ill in Rome. She went by air this morning and hadn't a moment to let you know. So I dashed around and got hold of this Mrs. Goodge to come at once and stay here. She's a splendid woman, well known in the neighborhood as a most respectable soul and will run the house nicely for us until my mother gets back, as well as make everything—well, all right, eh?"

Kathleen said nothing for a moment. Was this all right? Mrs. Goodge was only a servant. What would Miss Green say? But it made the position ever so much easier. She had been keen on her first business venture, but not so keen on living with an unknown old lady.

"I hope you won't mind," Fox was saying earnestly. "I don't see how you can. Mrs. Goodge strikes me as a sort of ironclad duenna. Would you like a talk with her before deciding?"

His anxious, worried air completed the conquest.

"Of course it's all right," Kathleen said joyously, and is this where you cook the jams?"

Mrs. Goodge came in at that moment. He was wanted on the telephone. Kathleen looked at the room more closely. It was the usual kind of a room for that sort of a

The Westwood Mystery 21

house, except that over the fireplace hung a picture which looked rather more violent and forceful than was usual.

She got up and went closer. It was a battle scene. In the foreground were some bodies without heads, and heads without bodies, and a few arms and legs. It struck her as quite horrible. She heard a little sound beside her. Fox had returned and was looking at it with parted lips, his teeth showing a little. He had bad teeth she noticed.

"Fine, isn't it?" he said appreciatively. "The father of the chap I bought this house from went in for pictures. Some of them are pretty good. Know anything about such things?"

Kathleen did not. Personally, nothing would have induced her to let that horror stay on her wall.

She was shown over the house and the kitchens. The silver-plated cooking pots looked very neglected. She had understood that Fox had put them in. He told her that that was a mistake on her part. "But the point is that everything works, and the fruit is coming in tomorrow, just a few baskets at first till you get into the way of it. Milly here is to do the actual work, of course, and obey orders."

Kathleen smiled at Milly and then talked business with Fox. The talk wound up with the usual grumble at Davies, "the chap from whom I bought the show. Perfect pirate."

"If you had put your money into Rubber Trunks," she suggested, "you might have been worse off yet." They were back in the drawing-room. "Where I come from no one talks of anything else. The rector has some shares, and so has Miss Green, and heaps of other people."

"I have a few, as it happens," he said to that. "Then you can attend the meeting next month. How awfully interesting." Fox said he had no time for meetings. "Just what the rector and Miss Green say. The rector says he's quite content to leave everything in Sir Adam Youdale's hands. They say he's awfully clever."

A curious smile crossed Fox's thin lips.

22 *A Resurrected Press Mystery*

"There are probably people in existence who are cleverer still," he said.

"Let us hope Mr. Sturge isn't!" she put in, and laughed.

By the end of the first week she felt as though she had known him for years. She wondered how she had lived her life so cheerfully without him. She worked hard, and found that, as he claimed, the business was one that could, with care, be made into something quite good.

"Davies came a cropper, through some mortgage being foreclosed," he said one day, "and I got it awfully cheap."

She opened astonished eyes.

"I mean compared with what he would have asked for it otherwise," he corrected himself hastily. Fox was constantly correcting himself, as an older woman would have noticed.

His mother, he said, did not write of returning. On the contrary, she was going on with her friend to some spa.

"Of course, it's good for my mother too," he said soberly, when speaking of it in the beginning of the second week. "But it presses a bit hard on me just now. I had some money put by for the business, but she must have it instead."

"Is she dependent on you?"

"Entirely!" he said. "And unfortunately she's used to being well off, and doesn't—can't, you know—fit herself into the change." He sighed. "That last fruit grower is getting a bit impatient, but he must wait. Must!"

"Oh, let me advance the money," Kathleen said at once. "Or why not let me come into the business now? I'm quite satisfied. I am really. I'd like to."

He refused to consider the idea. Or seemed to at first. But in the end she had her way. And then it appeared that he had a deed of partnership all drafted ready, lying in his bureau. Kathleen read it through. He insisted on her doing this. And as it chanced—so he said—that he was lunching that very day with a solicitor, she lunched

The Westwood Mystery 23

with them too, and after a very pleasant meal the deed was signed, and the money, her money, paid into a joint banking account.

That evening he was in the highest of spirits.

"I shan't be living here much longer, he said confidently to Kathleen at dinner, "I'm not going to stay poor always." That last refrain became insistent in the days that followed. At the beginning of the third week he had asked her to marry him, and Kathleen, head over heels in love with him, consented, though after a little demur.

"Known each other too short a time?" he scoffed, "who cares? We've no one to think of but ourselves."

"But your mother—" she suggested.

"Oh, my mother will love you, for my sake," he grinned. And so they became engaged. Miss Green, to Kathleen's relief, did not disapprove of the hurry.

"You know as much, or as little, of each other as though you had met a year ago," she wrote. "I lost the best happiness of my life because I refused to go to the colonies with a man I'd only recently met." The letter wound up with promises to be at the wedding, which Kathleen thought she would like in August, as she and Fox could best take a holiday then. It was now only May.

Fox thought this a sensible idea. He looked rather grave this morning. The first, after their engagement.

"An insurance chap was talking to me yesterday," he said in explanation, "and he rather put the wind up me. Some of the things he said were so true. I hadn't thought of it, but if anything should happen to me, how would you carry on? No, no, I must insure myself at once! It's not fair in a partnership of this kind to leave anything so vital to chance. I can't think how I forgot it."

"I'll make a will at once. And you can too," she suggested.

"For a couple of hundreds? Not worth it, darling. I think, now that you've mentioned it, that each of us ought to insure our lives for the benefit of the survivor. We can, for each being partners, each has a monetary interest in the other remaining alive. The law doesn't pay attention to love, as I said."

"How does one set about it?" she asked.

"Let me see..." He seemed to have no idea for moment, and then to have it all quite pat. "Oh, yes, that man who called at the office—I'll phone him and we can settle it today. His firm is one that doesn't bother about a doctor's certificate."

She went regularly to his office in Elizabeth Street twice a week, and today was one of her days. The agent came and both insured their lives. That afternoon, when she had just got back to Tollard Road, a telephone rang. A man wanted to speak to Fox on the 'phone.

She said he was out. That his secretary was speaking. She and Fox had agreed that this name sounded better than "partner" when she spoke for him.

"Secretary? What does he want a secretary for, when he can't pay what he owes? I'll ring up again. I'm going to see him. None of his vanishing tricks for me today."

Kathleen hung up indignantly. The idea of speaking like that of her Oliver. About an hour later Mrs. Goodge said that a gentleman wanted to see Mr. Fox. Name of Davies. Said he would wait.

Kathleen and the little maid were deep in some cookery operation that could not pause. Besides, the man must be mad or drunk. Just as well that she should keep out of his way.

"Does he look violent at all?" she asked Mrs. Goodge.

"Oh, no, miss. Poorly dressed, but quite the gentleman."

Kathleen was surprised, but went on with her work.

About half an hour later Fox arrived, and the two men were together for some ten minutes. Then Fox beckoned her to come into the room that he called his den. It was the most comfortable room in the house.

The Westwood Mystery 25

"Darling, could you draw out some money from the bank and let me have it for a week? I'm frightfully sorry, but that man Davies got me. Unfortunately I signed a paper, thinking it was just part of the usual thing when taking on the lease, and there's a clause in it, saying that besides the thousand I must pay up another five hundred premium after six months. That's up now. He's got me on toast. Can't go back on my word."

Kathleen was horrified.

"Of course you mustn't pay," she said sensibly. "Take him and the papers to that nice solicitor who witnessed our deed of partnership."

"I sent Davies to him. He's just back. Sullivan writes me that he can do nothing. I signed and must abide the consequences."

"We shall have Viney's check and the payment from Levy and Moth come in next week," he murmured, running his hands through his hair, "we can put it back then. It's just for the moment—for the month, rather. I'll give you an I. O. U. for it, of course." He look quite distracted.

"But the five hundred I've just paid in," she minded him. He always seemed to be forgetting that, to her, a vast sum.

"Can't touch that, darling. That's our backing for the new agency from those northern fruit growers. They asked for a deposit as a guaranty of good faith. It can be called in after a month, but if we do it now we terminate the agency. No, can't touch that."

"But I haven't five hundred left," she expostulated. "I can scrape together four hundred, just scrape it together..."

"Oh, you mustn't run yourself out of every pound," he said lovingly. "Say three hundred and fifty and I must get the rest somehow... settling day's when?" He flicked open a paper. "Yes, you can just do it this settlement day, if you 'phone the brokers at once and confirm it in writing, of course."

Hurried, flurried, anxious, she did as he asked. He thanked her, and again mentioned that it was only for a month. He retired to the drawing-room and Davies. The two came out, and the voice that she had heard over the 'phone said, "Well, I'll wait till then. But mind, no tricks! You'll find they won't be quite so successful this time!"

She rather expected there would be a row. But apparently Fox made no answer. He came into the room where she was making calculations on her blotting pad. That northern agency promised well. They ought to make four hundred profit this year... if things went on as they were doing... and double next year...

"Poor chap!" Fox looked very pleased with the world. "I mean Davies. He was hit in the head during the war and has never been right since."

"He was right enough to swindle you!" she retorted indignantly at such an unnecessary amount of good nature.

"True," he agreed, looking gloomy at once, "but it's a sad fate." And he suggested going to a theater that afternoon. To the pit or gallery, he was a careful man. They would stop at Woolworth's for some chocolates—he was a thoughtful man.

The shares were sold. The money paid in to her bank and drawn out by her, leaving some thirty-five pounds. All that she had of ready money in the world. The next day Davies called again. This time the interview with Fox was shorter still, and she heard Davies say as he left, "— yes, and a hard enough time I've had to wring it out of you. Men like you ought to be scragged at birth. You'd have swindled me if you could—or dared. I won't wait a day beyond the month for the next installment" And the front door banged. Even for a head wound, Davies had a horrid nature, she thought.

Fox came in looking vastly pleased with himself.

"I got ten pounds back from the money," he said, laying the amount down. "Made Davies wild, but I insisted on it. Just for luck."

The Westwood Mystery 27

Kathleen eyed it without enthusiasm. Either it belonged by rights to Davies, or Oliver should never have paid it over. He read her thoughts. He had an almost uncanny gift of it. Because he loved her so dearly, he told her. But he could do it with Mrs. Goodge and the maid.

"Don't forget, darling, that Davies was injured in the head. You can't treat such a man as though he were normal."

How splendid he was at bottom under all his surface defects. And how handsome! Kathleen would have been indignant if anyone had pointed out to her that he was the first man of whom she had really seen much.

"I shall have to leave you tonight," he went on cheerily, "got to see a man down in Kent. About the forward sale of some of our jellies. I shall be away a week. So don't get into mischief. Suppose—" they plunged into business. He had a good head for figures. She had not. But she did a tremendous amount of work both in the office and the kitchen.

"Seems to me that when the week is over, I shall need a holiday," she said ruefully, when she had finish taking notes of what must be seen to in his absence.

"We'll get married then, Kit. Why not? Possibly I may be going to pull off something quite nice. No. I won't say more. Nor what it's about. But when I'm back, why not get married quietly at a registry office instead of waiting till August?"

"I'll think it over," she said lightly, but she asked self why not. She loved to look into his eyes that always held her own so that she had to fairly wrench them away, loved to hear his voice which sounded merely virile and masterful to her, loved to watch his nimble white hands. He was good at everything he did. And he was devoted to her.

"I shall make my will while I'm away," he said suddenly, "and you do the same, Kit. Nowadays we shan't have to make another after marriage. Get your bank manager and a clerk of his to witness yours. You ought to, you know. So ought I." So he had changed his mind about there being too little to leave.

Kathleen agreed. Death was a long way off from both of them. Wills were but words. He had left that evening, and she made her will next day, but at the office, though she sent it for safekeeping to her bank.

CHAPTER THREE

The Rubber Trunk Company meeting was over. The hall that had been packed from wall to wall emptied itself. On all the faces was a look of relief, almost painful in its intensity. Sir Adam Youdale had been able to assure his fellow shareholders that the affairs of the company were much better than had been feared, that there should be quite a large balance over at the end of the working year, and that with a little hard work, the company ought yet to fulfil its initial promises.

The audience, which had come prepared to tear the company's chartered accountant limb from limb actually sang "For, he's a jolly good fellow," as shareholders will, if they are given the smallest chance. Sturge and Youdale were cheered as they drove off together. Even Sturge looked comparatively cheerful. He was a tall, thin man with a long cadaverous face and an air of settled melancholy that had done much to ease the minds of the shareholders. Such gloom must surely be founded on principles of the most rigid kind they argued. His cold eyes, too, suggested severe honesty, as did his upright carriage and unbending bearing.

The two men did not talk much together. This drive down to Westwood was really only, a politic "gesture". They were not friends, though the one had married the other's niece. All their interests lay poles asunder. For Sturge they turned on figures. In return for this life service, figures were his servants to a really remarkable extent.

Lady Youdale met them in the square lounge that lent Westwood such an air of space and dignity. She was a tall, handsome woman, but with a singularly blank face. It was one that rarely showed any emotion whatever, not, people thought, because of self-control, but because of an entire lack of strong feeling. She had been a pretty girl but a silent one, and Youdale, endowing that young head with all the ideal virtues, had married what, he now sometimes thought, was a barber's block. Young, ardent, intensely in love with his wife, he found to his amazement that she did not love him at all. Every effort on his part to break through the wall of ice between them was unavailing. Soon he saw that on the other side of that wall was nothing worth his striving. He learned too late that she was a dull egoist to whom nothing but herself mattered.

"Well?" she asked. "Neither of you took the trouble to 'phone me. Well?"

"You sold your shares too soon," her uncle said icily. "They'll be up tomorrow morning."

Youdale looked at her with distaste, his lips curled, but he passed on without speaking. She turned to her uncle.

"He was on your side, then?"

He nodded. He was drinking his cocktail as though he really needed it. "Never heard him to better advantage," he said, when she was mixing him another, "that gift of carrying his hearers with him is simply priceless."

"I wish I had sold only half my shares," she said crossly. "I'll buy them back tomorrow."

He glanced at her with a sudden foxlike gleam of eyeball. They were quite alone. The lounge was large. "I shouldn't," he said in a low murmur. "On the contrary, sell the rest."

"Tomorrow?" she asked in an equally low tone.

He nodded. "As soon as the stock exchange opens. Send in the order tonight, tell them to do it at the best opening quotation—and to keep the matter confidential."

"He holds about ten thousand shares"—she moved her head in the direction of the stairs up which her husband had passed—"had I better sell a bear against them?"

The Westwood Mystery 31

Again he nodded. "Remember to ask me to stay the night," he went on in the same tone, "I don't want to ask myself. And it is essential."

She looked inquiry.

"It's just possible that a package of papers may be sent to Adam—from Godwind and Bulkly of Manchester. The firm's name will probably be on them."

"Solicitors?" she asked.

"Stockbrokers."

She was watching him intently now.

"They sent him a note just before his speech, asking him to mark time or even postpone a definite statement if possible, as some papers had just reached them that they wished him to see. I got the message by the merest lucky chance, the messenger didn't know who I was, and I passed on to Adam a betting slip instead which I happened to have on me!" He gave a thin smile. "But the papers will be sent on, of course. I must get hold of them. If they come by post it may be quite simple. I shall walk about in the gardens so as to intercept them. But if a private messenger brings them it will all depend..."

"What is in the papers?" she asked coldly.

"Figures," he replied with a sudden baring of his teeth. "Well tucked away ones, I fancied... It's too long and intricate a story. You couldn't follow... but had Adam got them in time, he would certainly not have spoken this afternoon as he did."

He stopped. A car had whizzed up. Out jumped a man who rang the bell as though on an errand of life and death.

Instantly Sturge had the front door open. He appeared to be just going out.

"Well, good-by for the moment, Imogen," he called back, then, as he seemed to see the young man facing the top step for the first time, he held out his hand.

"Something for Sir Adam? From Brick Court, I suppose."

"To be delivered to him personally," came the reply, quite civil in tone, but without any relaxation of the grip on the thick envelope. "May I come in, ah, there he is!" And catching sight of the owner house, who had just stepped out of one of the French windows, the young man hurried forward. He evidently knew the K.C. by sight. Sturge returned to the hall and closed the door. The butler, seeing that his services were not needed, vanished. Sturge stood staring ahead of him for a second, gloomier and more pious looking than ever.

"That settles it," he said almost in a whisper. "Well— there are other ways." He turned to his niece. "Has he any big case on just now? So that possibly he won't open that envelope this evening?"

"As a rule, he never glances at financial matters in the evening. In ordinary times he wouldn't open that envelope till around ten o'clock in the morning. Will he know that these papers concern you—concern the Rubber Trunks case?"

"Depends on what the young man said who brought them. As far as I could judge he merely handed them to Adam." Sturge's face for an instant showed in the light, it gleamed with sweat, his yellow, discolored teeth were bare. He recovered his look of composure with as evident an effort as though he had picked it up from the floor and forced it down over twitching muscles.

"I shan't forgive you if there is any open scandal," she said in low even tones.

"It's not me, but him, you oughtn't to forgive in that case," he retorted. "I suppose there isn't any chance of getting those papers away from him?"

"Not the slightest," she said to that. "He'll lock them in his safe, the key is on his ring." Something in his expression made her add: "I shan't see him from dinnertime until lunch tomorrow."

"Why do you put up with it?" he asked idly.

"I won't divorce him," she said briefly, "he's headed for big things." He was not listening as he stood, making his

The Westwood Mystery 33

cocktail glass into a ringer. Finally he looked up, and something cornered and dangerous looked up with him.

"I shall go to bed early, and shall pin a paper on my door to say that I don't want to be disturbed till eleven."

"You're not—" She looked at him with a real uneasiness for the first time in her fine, empty eyes.

He chuckled as though the idea amused him.

"Oh, dear no! Not that! Now listen—" But the telephone bell in a built-in cupboard beside them began to ring. She went to it. He heard her say in a surprised tone:

"I don't understand. It was the day after tomorrow, the twenty-ninth. Not today! No, I'm sure I made no mistake. Look at the date again. My nines are rather like sevens, but—I don't see how I can manage it today. I'm sorry. Yes, I see it's very awkward for you," Lady Youdale went on after some minutes of listening to the voice at the other end. "You're already in Wimbledon? Well... perhaps I can manage it, but it's awkward... let me think a moment..." There followed a second silence, then her voice came again. "Very well. As I say, I wasn't expecting you till the twenty-ninth, but as you're here..." Lady Youdale had closed the sliding door of the cupboard and shut the little ventilator panel in it, but Sturge was sitting with his head against the door. "You know that outside staircase that leads straight to my room? Come up by it. I'll be in the loggia. In half an hour, then." She came out again. Sturge looked at her.

"Mysterious visitors? I couldn't help hearing most of the talk."

"Woman to make me some loose covers," Lady Youdale said curtly, "she's mistaken the date. However, it doesn't matter much. Now, then—" and uncle and niece talked for half an hour in low tones. Suddenly Sturge said in a louder voice, "What about a round of golf before breakfast tomorrow?"

Youdale was walking toward them. His face was very grave. He held a bulky envelope in his hand.

"Young Godwind, of Godwind and Bulkly in Manchester, just handed over this," he indicated it with his glance, he was speaking only to Sturge; "said the papers inside concerned the Rubber Trunks inquiry. Seemed to think I was expecting them. Know anything about the probable contents?"

Sturge seemed uninterested. "They can't be anything new," he said easily, "or rather, they can't be anything important. You've had every paper put at your disposal which is of any moment. But I asked Godwind to send you a full copy of the insurance brokers' agreement. You have seen the abbreviated one, I know, but I had an idea you might want to go into that again. I told him to be sure and get it to you in time for the meeting. That's why he sent it on by hand evidently." Sturge was the perfect liar, he never seemed interested in what he was saying, never appeared to care whether you listened or not.

"That's all right, then," Youdale looked relieved, "as you're in a hurry, I'll open the envelope directly after dinner, and we can go through the documents together."

Sturge shook his head reluctantly. "I don't think I shall be up to even the simplest of papers tonight, Adam, I'm feeling too fagged. But how about ten-thirty tomorrow morning? I want to catch the twelve forty-three on to Canterbury, but that will give us plenty of time."

Youdale said that ten-thirty would suit him perfectly and Sturge followed the butler up the stairs with that ponderous gait of his that always suggested the head verger in a cathedral showing the bishop to his throne.

"I expect Nicholson for dinner, and the night," Youdale said to his wife. "I would have let you know sooner, but I wasn't sure if he could manage it. He's just 'phoned again to say he can be here by eight if you will excuse his not dressing for dinner. I told him to be as he was, that we should be quite by ourselves."

She made some uninterested assent, and moved away. Youdale drew out his watch. He had asked Nicholson, his solicitor and also a close personal friend, to come down this evening. He hoped Nicholson would not be late. He had a lot to say to him. But Nicholson never was late. The solicitor had started in plenty of time, and now as he drove, he speculated on the motive behind Youdale's request that he should come prepared to take instructions for a new will. Nicholson was just off for his own holiday, but he could spare a night and a morning, since the K.C. had added over his Brick Court telephone that the matter was urgent, since he was off for the Hague at noon.

Nicholson was a man around fifty with a rather saturnine face that belied a warm, impulsive temperament, and he was deciding that Youdale must be meditating something foolish. In Nicholson's experience, people never talked over the wise steps that they contemplated taking. Nicholson hated foolish things. He feared that Youdale was going to leave some indiscreet, or unnecessary, codicil or legacy, yet surely a fresh will and a talk would not have been necessary in that case... amusing that a barrister couldn't, or wouldn't, draw up his own will. But then, Youdale's law was—Nicholson shook his head sadly—distinctly weak. It was his forensic gifts that had put him where he was, among the leading men at the Bar. More than ninety per cent of his acquittals, Nicholson thought, with warm professional admiration, were miscarriages of justice, which in itself was the highest tribute to his powers of eloquence. Though the last case, the Luton case, was different. There innocence had been vindicated, of that Nicholson, one of the solicitors for the defense, had no shadow of doubt. Nor had Lady Youdale, as he happened to know from some words of hers. Lady Youdale . . . he rather liked her, or at least did not dislike her. She was quiet and inoffensive. Perhaps the quietest woman whom he had ever met. Yet her eyes were intelligent... or no, that was not the right word. Intelligence implies reflection, the power to pass what is observed through the crucible of the mind and turn it into something—experience or wisdom—whereas Lady Youdale's eyes merely suggested that she would see all that went on around her. If she reflected on what she saw, it was never to be read off her face... her oddly blank face... she ought to make a good poker player... The contemplated change in the will probably concerned her. Ever since their return from Tangier, about a couple of years ago—Youdale had been one of the three British members of the International Legislative Assembly, and they had lived there for years—things seemed strained between husband and wife.

The car drew up at Westwood. Youdale met him at once, and carried him off into his library. The dressing bell had gone sometime before.

"Sturge is spending the night with us," he said, opening a cocktail cabinet in a cupboard. Casually, like a man making conversation, as he was, Youdale told of the arrival just now of more papers, not yet looked at by himself, which he and Sturge would wade through in the morning.

"They're merely extra copies of the insurance brokers' contracts he tells me. We're both sick of the name Rubber Trunks."

"Sturge is going to forward his resignation, as soon as he's well away on his cruise."

"I heard on all sides that the shares will spurt tomorrow," Nicholson said, making his choice of the bottles.

Youdale nodded. "I can't sell mine of course for some time, so let's hope they'll continue to rise."

"You do intend to sell?" Nicholson asked with interest. Youdale did not heed the question; his tone had changed entirely and become alert and alive as he said now rather abruptly.

"What I got you to sacrifice some of your holiday time for, Nicholson, is this: I'm rearranging my life. I want you to have a talk with my wife. I empower you to offer her another five hundred a year for life, besides the settlements. I'm afraid she'll find it a tight fit, even so.

The Westwood Mystery 37

I've had to refuse only last week to pay some preposterous gaming debts of hers, but it should be sufficient." He paused.

Nicholson guessed what was coming. The equivalent for this. "You are to tell her that this added income will only be hers if she consents to a divorce. I shall let her get it, of course. I want you to put things very clearly before her. She will be troublesome—oh, not from affection, but because she feels sure I'm down for something good in next year's Honors."

"Well, aren't you?" Nicholson asked.

Youdale shook his head with a curl of his lip.

"I intend to cut the whole thing, and start life some where else. In different surroundings. Date growing or sheep farming in North Africa probably. But that's only in the air. First I want my freedom."

"Probably in order to lose it immediately," Nicholson reflected.

"You want to marry again?" he asked, after a pause.

Youdale nodded. "Yes, I've met my dream woman rather late in life, but not too late."

"Out in Tangier?" Nicholson asked. The other was in the mood for confidence. The solicitor had long fancied that there was some engrossing interest connected with North Africa.

Youdale looked dreamily at him. "Good guess. Yes, my Dark Lady of Romance. With a soul as beautiful as her face. A man's intelligence and a woman's heart." His voice was moved. "Now, to go back to Imogen—. she'll think my offer very inadequate. But we spend pretty well all I make. I don't say I haven't been extravagant too. But Baccarat was about all I had to interest me. If I were to retire immediately, I should have an income from all my investments of roughly two thousand, and I am offering her half. That's my best offer. Make her see that, and make her realize that whether she sees it or not, I do intend to retire, and start afresh—differently. Quite differently. If she refuses to divorce me, I shall simply disappear, an she'll have to live on two hundred and fifty. I shall sink every penny of my own capital in some wild region. Make her realize that I'm in earnest."

"I suppose you won't go alone in either case," Nicholson said. He had to know where he stood.

Youdale shook his head again. "I wish I could tell you 'yes.' Or no, I don't know that I do. Anyway, there's no question of the lady I want to marry coming with me except as my wife."

"I suppose you've considered the step from every point of view?" Nicholson deeply regretted it. "You are just on the threshold of reaping what you've sown in these years of work," he added.

Youdale looked at him and smiled, a light in his usually rather weary eyes.

"What shall it profit a man if he gain the whole world and lose his soul?" he asked in a ringing voice. "My chance to save mine is to get away."

Nicholson did not agree. Most emphatically not. His face said as much.

Youdale looked at him.

"You think position and money can make up to a man for the atrophy of all the spiritual part of him?" 'Of no one else would Youdale have asked that question, but he and Nicholson had had many a talk before. "Look at Sturge! He's the type of man who thinks the soul well lost for the world. There isn't anything he wouldn't do for more money." He flung his cigarette away as though he disliked the flavor.

"Still—to leave your life-work just now—" Nicholson spoke with real regret. "After this Luton Case too— that final speech of yours was one of your best. You're booked for a High Court Judgeship, Youdale."

The barrister gave one of his amused half smiles.

"And it saved an innocent young woman's life—" Nicholson went on warmly; "frankly you don't always appear on the side of Justice, you know—"

"If you're going to bring in the Absolute and the Real—" Youdale shot his friend a glance from eyes that positively danced, "I don't claim any standing in those courts. But there's the gong!" And he led the way upstairs.

Sturge was not at table. Lady Youdale said that her uncle asked to be excused, as his liver was troubling him again.

Youdale's secretary, a Mademoiselle Le Brun, whom Nicholson had often met before, sat beside him. She was a young Frenchwoman with a plain, but interesting, face, and very intelligent, dark eyes. The only guest was a friend of hers, a Monsieur Gaudet, who, it appeared, was also spending the night at Westwood. He mentioned that he belonged to the French Colonial Service "in a humble capacity," and, being home on one of his rare leaves was "doing England." He seemed to have been to the house several times before, but not to stop. Knowing what Youdale had in mind, Nicholson could understand his host's interest in the latest news from North Africa, where France has such a wide hold. Gaudet was a most interesting talker, since he could use his own language, which all at the table spoke fluently.

Nicholson was no Francophile, rather the other way but he had to admit that they think with a sharpness of outline, and put what they think, and why they think it, with a clarity rarely, if ever, found in an Anglo Saxon.

Listening to Gaudet, Nicholson felt as though he himself were living among the Moslems out there, now an Arab, now a Berber, now off hunting with the treacherous Touareg to give them a name which he learned from Gaudet was sheer nonsense. Gaudet turned often to the solicitor, and insisted on drawing him in. He seemed to court his opinions at times, as of special value, because it was unprejudiced. So did Mademoiselle Le Brun. Nicholson was flattered in spite of himself. Had he met the two in a hotel, he would have wondered what they wanted from him, but in the present case, in a friend's house, it was very agreeable.

Lady Youdale took no part in the talk except, by monosyllables, when a reply was absolutely necessary. Any allusion to Tangier found her woodenly unresponsive, but Gaudet never forgot that she was his hostess, though her husband, like his secretary, addressed her rarely.

Gaudet finally tried to draw the lady of the house out with some pretty compliments about the Youdale's villa outside Tangier, a villa which Youdale had bought when he first went to the town.

Lady Youdale said she never wanted to see Tangier or the house again.

"Then you must persuade Sir Adam to sell it to me," Gaudet laughed lightly. "My mother adores it. It is just the position she wants, high on the cliffs, outside the town proper."

Youdale curtly refused to discuss the idea, and while saying as much chanced to drop his lighted match. While he was extinguishing the little flame on the carpet, Nicholson happened to be glancing at mademoiselle. She and her French friend were looking across the table at each other. 'I told you so!' her eyes said, and he gave a half shrug as though to say *tant pis*, but he looked with very lowering brow. Then Youdale's head rose again, and the Frenchman pressed the point once more. "Why keep a house in which one never lives?" he asked.

"One never knows what may happen," Youdale replied, his eyes on the ceiling, as he blew a smoke ring, his face lit as though by a ray of sunlight. And again the two French people, the man and the woman, exchanged a glance. Hers a warning as though to caution him against continuing along that line, his reluctantly agreeing with her, as he switched the talk back to the Atlas range.

Some illuminating correction that he made of a sentence, which Nicholson had quoted from a recent book of travel in those mountains, made the solicitor stare.

The Westwood Mystery

"What a knowledge of native affairs, monsieur!" he exclaimed "I was talking only last night at dinner to one of our consuls in that part of the world, and he didn't know a tithe of what you have just told us."

Something—some curtain—went down in the intelligent dark eyes looking at him through rimless pince-nez, and with a laugh Gaudet said that he hoped he had not been showing off. As for talking shop—he had nothing else to talk about.

After dinner, Lady Youdale said that she was going on later to a charity ball with some friends who were coming for her. Nicholson asked her if he could have a word with her first. She promised to let him know when she was ready, before her friends could arrive. Youdale himself carried off Gaudet to admire a Koran which he had recently acquired, and the solicitor and secretary were left to entertain each other. She went out of her way to be amusing, it was almost as though she were laying herself out to please him this evening, to win that liking that he had never quite given her. He turned the talk to Monsieur Gaudet, and his really wonderful knowledge of Moroccan people and customs.

"Yes, he has always taken a great deal of interest in the people out there quite apart from his own work." She spoke lightly, but he had an impression of deliberate belittling of the man's knowledge. Nicholson, rightly or wrongly, always had a feeling about Mademoiselle Le Brun that she said nothing without a reason, or a purpose, though that reason or that purpose might not be easy to see.

This idea of his was really the cause for his not caring much for her. But one thing was certain. She was no gossip. He had hoped that she might talk about Tangier and give him some hint of the identity of the Dark Lady for whose sake Youdale intended giving up his life in England, which meant life as he had made it. But she was not to be drawn, even if she saw the drift of his questions, and so he noticed it all the more when she brought the talk around to the Tangier villa that Monsieur Gaudet wanted to buy.

Had she ever seen it? Nicholson asked.

She had lived in it! She, like Lady Youdale, did not care for it, or for Tangier. Unlike old Madame Gaudet who had so set her heart on the little place with its superb views over the sea. She herself was very fond of Madame Gaudet, who had been a friend of her own dead mother's, and she would like the old lady to have the house, seeing that the Youdales never went near the place, never lent it to a friend. Nicholson, since his talk just before dinner, had an idea that the house might well be connected with Youdale's romance; if so, either mademoiselle knew nothing about such a connection or she was indifferent to it. Yet it was not the kind of thing to which women, as a rule, are indifferent. He decided that she knew nothing of this side of her employer.

Lady Youdale now sent word that she would see him in about ten minutes in the Chinese room. Mademoiselle went off with Gaudet, who asked her to show him a short cut to the nearest post office. Nicholson, too, stepped out into the gardens, and sat down under a grand old beech, thinking over how best to open his coming talk with the wife.

Meanwhile, mademoiselle was talking swiftly to the Frenchman in her level intonation with *n'est ce pas* interpolated every second. They drew no answer from him. Gaudet reserved approval or correction for the end of the sentence. He, as Nicholson had seen at once, had a logical mind, and a logically-minded Frenchman is the most unemotional thing on earth. He was listening to Léonie Le Brun just now, not because of his own feeling for her, but because of her reasoning powers and her application of them to something that interested them both very greatly. They were not going in the direction of any post office as they talked, but rather in under the trees that rounded off one corner of the garden.

The Westwood Mystery

"And so finally, my dear Lucien, what do you suggest? You have already tried to move him each time you have been down here—that is, three times in all—and have failed. From the point of view of argument then, there is nothing left for me to say. No new way to present the facts. Of that I am sure." Here her *n'est, ce pas* obtained a reply.

"He loves you. It should be quite easy to get what you want from him"

"I want marriage, my dear Lucien," she said coldly and proudly. "I do not stoop to less. But as to getting this villa... Mr. Nicholson will not help. I am now sure of that."

"I believe that Sir Adam keeps the place on because it was there he first met you. So that, if you ask for this villa to be settled on you, before you even consider— appear to consider—other things?" he asked interrogatively. "Then you could pass it on to me secretly. I have told you the sum that would be paid you for it, Léonie. It would be the equivalent of a magnificent *dot*..."

"Oh, la, la!" She made a contemptuous gesture of her slim hand. "Do you think Sir Adam would let it run like that? Smoothly, without a hitch? You do not know him. He is in some ways cleverer than either of us."

"No man is clever where the woman he loves is concerned," Lucien replied rather grimly.

"Could a woman trick you, my friend? She could not. Neither could any woman trick Adam Youdale successfully. For the passing moment, yes, either of you could be blinded. But the passing moment—passes."

She gave a mischievous smile that made her dark eyes, sparkle like black diamonds.

"What could he do?" he asked coldly.

"Many things," she retorted. "You would be surprised to find out how many. You see, Lucien, you have not lived in England and with the English people as I have. You think they are stupid. Not always, not even the women."

"They have no logical sense," he said firmly.

44 *A Resurrected Press Mystery*

"Most of them have not," she agreed, "but when they have it, look out! For they have at all times a power of intuition that is startling. And intuition and reason together are formidable. Sir Adam, for instance. He knows by instinct, quite surely, how I stand. That I will not run away with him, because he would not be worth marrying afterwards. He would have no career. And a man without a career is not a man for me. And if you think that he would not at once suspect the truth, if I asked for that villa as a gift, however roundabout the request, you do yourself injustice. Besides—no—it is quite hopeless. I see no way to get it. It is exasperating. I feel like the little child who regards the jam pot on the shelf just too high to reach. We must think of something else."

"You said the villa is left to you in his will?" Gaudet asked thoughtfully.

"In a codicil. But to get a gift after a man is dead is easy. It is while he is alive he will not part with it," and Léonie led the way back into the house, where Gaudet went on up to his room for a French revue that he had brought down with him.

Nicholson saw them pass his tree on the way in. He glanced at his watch. The ten minutes were nearly up, but Lady Youdale was the most unpunctual person that he had ever met. "Ten minutes" with her meant thirty at least. He rose finally, and decided that he would have just one more word with Youdale first. He walked through a glass door that led into the back of the square central hall. He had a step that was naturally light. At any rate, Lady Youdale did not seem to hear, it. She was standing with her hand on the knob, closing the library door, as he turned the corner. Her expression stopped him half-way in his stride. This was not the face that he had thought quite pretty but wooden. She looked like a cat about to spring. For a second she stood there with a light full on her, her two hands clasped together, the fingers balled like claws, her shoulder hunched a little forward, under the gorgeous brocade cloak she had on, her neck and head

The Westwood Mystery 45

outthrust. Then her expression changed. Slowly the look that had so surprised the solicitor passed. She smiled, and still smiling, turned up the stairs behind her.

In a trice, Nicholson had opened the same door. Mademoiselle Le Brun and Youdale were standing side by side staring at the door. There was only the one. Nicholson's expression said that he too had seen Youdale's wife, for the barrister said something quickly to his secretary, and, with a nod of agreement, she left the two men alone together.

"What on earth, Youdale—" Nicholson began as the door shut.

"She knows! Imogen knows! She found me begging Léonie to come away with me. I had her hands in mine. She guessed, of course, before, but now she knows. And I wish to heaven it hadn't happened yet. Before you had had your talk with her."

"Who's Léonie?" Nicholson asked, bewildered. Had the Dark Lady appeared then? Where was she?

Youdale stared at the lawyer as though at a half-wit. "Léonie Le Brun, of course!" he said impatiently. "Good God! don't waste time in meaningless questions. There's only one Léonie in the world for me."

But not for Nicholson. He clasped the radiator near him as though it had been a raft and he out in the ocean. Mademoiselle Le Brun the Dark Lady! Impossible! Absurd! And yet—

Youdale went on, still in the same passionate undertone, his beautiful voice like a deep organ note.

"She was refusing to come away with me. As she always has refused. She isn't the kind to go off with a married man. But for the first time she's promised at last that if—when!—I am divorced, she will come. I lost my head a bit on that—I was urging her—"

"Look here," Nicholson said. "Sit down, and, since you've told me so much, tell me everything."

"There isn't anything more to tell—" Youdale objected, but he sat down. "I've loved her ever since I saw her standing under the porch in Tangier, framed in the bougainvillea, a white figure among flowers."

He talked on. Nicholson got a clear idea of Léonie Le Brun as seen by Youdale, and hardly, recognized one part of the portrait. But there were other parts. She had frankly told the K.C. that love counted for little with her. That she held all her emotions in a grip of steel, and would always so hold them. Apparently she laid claim to no moral scruples whatever. Her goddess was Reason, and on that altar, one to which every French man and woman bows, she was prepared to sacrifice anything. To be unreasonable was, she had said, to put yourself among the animals. To reason well, and to act accordingly, was her guiding line.

"What can one say to a girl who really means that?" Youdale asked. Nicholson felt that the other would not have minded her refusal to run away with him had it been based on morality, however discordant he might call it. But to have her resist him, because her reason told her to, that, Nicholson thought, rankled.

"Just now she too is furious with me," Youdale finished "She has a really awful suspicion that I wanted to get her into a position she can't get out of. Compromise her, before my wife." He spoke angrily, and yet sadly. "I think she would never forgive me if I let her name be dragged into a divorce court."

"You can hardly blame her," Nicholson said dryly. "I always thought she was just your secretary. I had no idea—"

Youdale flashed him a scathing look. "Past praying for!" it said. Then he went on: "We were just talking of the villa I have outside Tangier. She wants it as a gift. Well, why not? I wouldn't let anyone else have it. The place where Romance entered my and life when I thought my heart was buried. Evidently it means that for her too. Oh, yes, in spite of her repression of herself, it must mean that for her too. I said as much, and on that the door

The Westwood Mystery   47

opened and my wife looked in." Youdale stopped and lit
his pipe.

"Well?" Nicholson prompted him. The solicitor liked to
imagine how people would act under any given
circumstances and then measure it up afterwards with
what they really did do. In that swiftest thing on earth, a
flash of thought, he had decided that Lady Youdale had
told mademoiselle to leave the house at once—had
insulted her probably.

"Imogen said nothing whatever." Youdale stared hard
at the other. "Her face was—well—unpleasant. But she
only looked at me, then at Léonie, and then closed the
door quite gently."

Nicholson rubbed his glasses. It certainly sounded
rather awkward. But things would not improve by his
keeping Lady Youdale waiting. For the first time, as he
hurried up to the Chinese room, he was aware that he
had no idea of what the real woman was like. She still
might be what he had always thought her, but if she was
like that face that he had seen shutting the library door,
then she most certainly was a complete stranger. But
there was nothing catlike about the woman whom he saw
standing in the big room with its overpoweringly
handsome carpet and black and gold enameled furniture.

"Mr. Nicholson!" She came forward indignantly. "I've
been outraged in my own house. That girl and my
husband— I've known it for years and borne it... But
tonight—!" She stopped as though choked by emotion,
and Nicholson could not blame her.

"I'm exceedingly sorry for the situation," he said
genuinely enough. The trouble was that he must not
minimize it. Youdale wanted his freedom. This might be a
way to it. An unpleasant way, but still, the only one.

"You will divorce him, of course," he said calmly.

"Certainly not!" She spoke positively, and with a
certain look of hard satisfaction. "That would be to play
her game. Adam is down in the coming Honors List. Mr.
Cohen-Levi told me that confidentially. If she thinks I've

lived through the lean years with my husband in order to let her have the fat ones, she's much mistaken!" The smile reminded him strongly of her Uncle Sturge.

"Then what do you propose to do?" he asked.

"I shall think things over," she said, and smiled a little as she gathered her full skirts around her. The front door bell had rung, but he detained her for moment. In moments of crisis Nicholson could speak well, just because his words were dispassionate and sensible. But he made no headway with this.

"I'll think over what's best to be done," was her final word. "I'm afraid I must go now. The ball's in aid of the blind. Really, Mr. Nicholson, I feel I ought to share in the profits. Only my blindness is cured."

They walked together down into the lounge. The front door was just opening and Reggie Youdale stepped in. Reggie was Adam Youdale's nephew. His only one. He too was reading for the Bar. Nicholson and he were rather by way of being friends. Seeing his side face, the solicitor thought, as often before, how little the young man showed of the outdoor life he led. Reggie always looked washed out, even when he had spent hours swimming in the sea. But tonight his face looked more than usually sallow and puffy. He greeted his aunt by marriage without any warmth. She on her side, after a momentary frown at sight of him, came forward with a smile such as her face rarely wore. Nicholson wondered at it.

"Reggie! How unexpected, but how nice! Coming down to stay the night, of course! What about dinner?"

He muttered a refusal to the last, and went on to say that he had dropped in for a word with his uncle, before the latter left for The Hague.

"But he can't see you tonight. Not possible! He can't see anyone tonight," she said hurriedly. "Now, don't try and see him. Just go off to your room. I call it yours. It's the one you usually have, you know, and have a talk with your uncle in the morning. He's not leaving until noon.

The Westwood Mystery 49

He's upset tonight. Not himself at all." She fairly swept Reggie up the stairs.

It was like Reggie to allow himself to be put off, Nicholson thought. The young man had not that soft cheek and full, babyish mouth for nothing.

"Oh, by the way," Lady Youdale called after him in her flat voice, "if there's a seamstress in there taking measurements for some covers, don't mind her. She'll only be a minute." And Lady Youdale's smile broadened. She rang for her own maid and said something to her in a low tone. The maid looked very sly, Nicholson thought, but she ran upstairs after the heavy footed Reggie, who had gone on up, head sunk between his shoulders, feet appearing to find it hard to rise to the next tread. He had barely nodded to Nicholson. What had happened to Reggie? Something was wrong. Evidently something which he wanted to see his uncle about. It certainly was an unfortunate time for the young man to have chosen. Nicholson felt sorry for Youdale's coming morning. What with his wife, his secretary, and now his nephew, Adam Youdale would have a wearing time. But Nicholson's thoughts went to Lady Youdale again, as she turned and smiled good night to him now. An artificial smile, and yet it suggested somehow concealed exultation. The solicitor went into the morning room and paced the floor. He was vexed with himself. He loved conundrums, as a rule. The crossword puzzle with the most intricate clues had no terrors for him. But here—here in this ordinary problem of husband, wife and Other Woman, he could not see one step ahead.

What would Youdale do? What his wife? What the Frenchwoman? Thinking over the three of them, he was suddenly aware of the importance which he found himself attaching to the character of the last of the trio. Quiet, reserved Mademoiselle Le Brun would dominate the situation he believed. As for Youdale, so accustomed to settle matters for himself and for others, having given his heart to the French girl, he was a defenseless man.

Bound. Tied. He, Nicholson, must of course tell him at once of the lack of success he had just had. Not that Youdale expected anything else. And he himself wanted to ask a question about that promised gift to mademoiselle of the villa off in Morocco. He was certain of one thing. She was back in the library with Youdale by now. It would not be like any woman, however calm, he thought, to go off for the night on that scene without some clearer understanding with the man who had brought it about.

He was right. Léonie had returned to the room, and, her back against the door, was saying:

"It is more than 'unfortunate,' my friend. It may be a disaster."

"Oh, come, Léonie! Besides, why not tell her—"

She interrupted him. She had the power of talking and listening at the same time that all Latin races have.

"Tell her what? She knows how things are. She knows you. She knows me. The position might become insupportable if we talked it over. As it is, it can stay for a day or two."

"You are not going away? I couldn't face life without you." And he meant it.

"It all depends," she said to that. "I do not intend to act in a hurry. As for Lady Youdale, she will not do anything stupid, I think. And so long as people do not do stupid things there is always hope that matters will arrange themselves."

Youdale looked at her half in admiration, half in anger. She was always so practical. She would take up her position with care and then refuse to budge from it. It maddened him. Yet he loved her as he had never loved his wife, not even before he married her.

"Well, witch," he laid his fingers over hers on the table, "if she falls in with Nicholson's proposals we may yet come through without trouble or fuss. And start off for the little white house high up on the cliffs with old Abdul and his staff of office waiting for us."

The Westwood Mystery 51

"Ah, that villa," she said slowly.

"It shall be my wedding gift to you," he said in a voice that shook with his emotion.

"I don't know that I want it." Had he heard her, she would have given Nicholson more than ever the impression that she was carrying out some plan now. "I have a growing feeling about that house. A feeling that it is unlucky."

"It will always be to me the house where I first met you," he said in low tones of passion. She smiled at him, and there was sweetness in that smile."

"It is that to me too. But I keep it for my dreams. Aren't you confusing the things of the spirit with those of the material world? If you try to mix the two, you risk great disappointments. Live in memory in the dream house, dear friend, but do not try to live in it the body." She picked up a pencil and played with it. "Why not let Monsieur Gaudet have it for his mother. He offers a price a little higher than you paid. His mother is a dear old lady. She wants it badly. And I have that feeling so strong that trouble will come if you keep it. Come, Adam, I asked for it as a gift without thought. Now I have a definite feeling that I do not want it, nor want you to keep it either."

He smiled at her fondly. "Not even your terror can make me part with it. You shall have it on our wedding day, but not to sell—to live in with me."

They both heard, it was meant to be audible, a step outside the door. In his determination to be heard, Mr. Nicholson was walking like a heavily-laden elephant with wooden legs.

Léonie said good night as soon as he came in. Said it with complete composure and dignity. Nothing in her face or tone suggested that she had passed through a most trying evening. Again Nicholson felt the steel in the fiber of her.

Before he could speak, the door opened. Tukes, the butler, came in.

"Gentleman of the name of Manning asks if he can see you, Sir Adam. He asked first for her ladyship, but she's not here. Then he asked if you could spare him a minute. Said he wouldn't detain you but that long..."

"Manning?" Youdale was so deep in his own concerns that for a second the name meant nothing to him. Then he tossed the card into the fire as he remembered.

"Show him in!" he replied curtly, and as the door closed: "You know him, Nicholson? It's Manning, that Luton girl's lover. Can't think what he wants with me. But he said 'a minute,' and he struck me as a chap who means what he says."

Even as he spoke, James Manning was shown in. Tall, thin, angular, he looked a farmer of these modern days when a man's wits must till as well as his hand. It was a resolute face with that hint of capacity for great violence in it that Nicholson had noted when the man was called in the Luton case as a witness for the defense.

Manning stood a moment looking hard at Sir Adam, then he came forward and greeted both men civilly enough.

"It's about Miss Luton that I've come. May I speak to her at once? I wasn't sure under what name she was staying here."

Youdale stared. "Miss Luton isn't here. I wonder what makes you think she is?"

"I went out to Brixton to see her this afternoon. Her aunt has a furnishing shop there, you know, and Annabelle's stopping with her just for the moment. Well, she wasn't there. Her aunt says she had gone on here to do some work, take some measurements and bring some patterns—said that Lady Youdale had asked her to come for a week. She showed me the letter. Annabelle had left it with her for the address."

Nicholson was surprised to see that Youdale had gone quite pale. A sign with him, as a rule, of anger.

"To the best of my belief Miss Luton is not here. Wait a second, and we'll clear this up." He rang the bell.

The Westwood Mystery 53

Tukes appeared.

"Is there any lady stopping in the house, except her ladyship and mademoiselle, of course?"

"None, Sir Adam," Tukes said positively.

"Miss Luton hasn't come down again by any chance?"

"No, Sir Adam." And Tukes was allowed to go.

"Well, Sir Adam, I'm sorry to've troubled you." Manning 's face had not lost the grim look that it had worn since he entered the room. "I thought the date in the letter was a nine not a seven, but her aunt would have it that it was a seven, that's today, and that Annabelle was off here."

He drew something out of his pocket. "I took it with me so as to be sure of the house—" he explained as he handed Sir Adam a letter written on a sheet of blue linen paper. It was Lady Youdale's paper, headed with the address of Westwood. The date was three days old. It ran:

Dear Miss Luton,

I would like you to take the measurements for a new set of covers for the furniture as we arranged. If you are free on the 29th, I shall expect you on that date for a week, unless I hear to the contrary. I should very much like to continue our talk as to your future plans, in which, as you know, I am sincerely interested.

Faithfully yours,

Imogen Youdale.

The date was written in figures, not in words, and though Youdale knew the last figure for a nine, it might easily have been read as a seven.

"May I keep this?" Youdale asked easily. "I had no idea the two knew each other, or rather, that they had more than met once by chance. I can only repeat, Manning, that I know nothing about it, and that Miss Luton is not at the moment here, and will not be staying here in the future."

54 *A Resurrected Press Mystery*

The two men looked straight into each other's eyes. Nicholson would have left them together, but they both chanced to stand between him and the door.

"I can count on that?" Manning asked abruptly, his mouth tightening.

"Absolutely."

Manning's face flushed a little at the other's cool tone, but he said with what looked like genuine feeling:

"Quite apart from the debt we—anyone who cares for Miss Luton owes you, Sir Adam, I'd take your word any time. Sorry I troubled you, but hearing she had come to Wimbledon..." He bowed to Nicholson, and made for the hall.

Youdale went with him—it was but a step to the front door.

Half-way across the lounge Manning stopped as though a wire had been stretched across the parquet.

"She is here! Or was! Those are my roses!" he said, his face all one flame of passion. His big brown hands were actually trembling as he stretched one out to a bowl of crystal which stood on a malachite topped table. The bowl was crammed with yellow roses.

"Those are my roses!" Manning said again. "I sent them to her this morning. Not all. But those four there are mine, and so are these two in front. It's my new rose... called it after her."

"Well, she isn't here, Manning," Youdale said very patiently. "She must have sent those roses to my wife in return for that order for new covers which, I think, we shall find she has refused to superintend. I told you I'll inquire about it as soon as I see Lady Youdale—which will be tomorrow morning. Tukes!" The butler was hovering about with that air of seeing nothing and hearing nothing which marks the type.

He came up at once.

"When did those roses come? I mean these largish ones here?"

"I don't know, Sir Adam, but I saw her ladyship add those to the others herself just a little before dinner."

Manning looked as though the answer satisfied him. The post came in around seven-thirty. Youdale's suggestion that Annabelle had sent some of the roses on to his wife in return for the offered work struck Manning as very likely, and this time he reached the door and his car without further incident.

"Now what the devil does it all mean?" Youdale asked as he came back into the library. "That letter of my wife's to Miss Luton. Why on earth! What on earth!"

Exactly what Nicholson was asking himself. Why this surge of passion, this veiled hostility,—it had almost looked like suspicion—on the young farmer's part toward Youdale, toward the man who had saved his fiancée, for Annabelle Luton and Manning had been engaged to be married when she had been arrested. The prosecution maintained that it was because he objected to having her illegitimate child in his house that the mother had made away with it, as a preliminary to marrying him. Why should Manning mind her being at Westwood? What if those had been her roses? And Youdale's manner too, and pallor as of great anger restrained?

"Anything wrong?" Nicholson now asked.

"I'll tell you about it in the morning." Youdale said with compressed lips. Before turning, he began to discuss a painting behind him or rather to talk about it, for Nicholson had no pretentions to any knowledge of art, and unashamed preferred a neat oleograph to most of the paintings he saw.

CHAPTER FOUR

Nicholson was awakened by someone shaking his shoulder. It was Tukes, the butler.

"Wake up, Mr. Nicholson, sir! Wake up! Sir Adam's lying dead in his bed!"

Nicholson rushed as he was with the distraught butler to where Youdale was lying in his bed, a pillow on the floor beside him. He was cold to the touch, his whole blue-white face flattened in some horrible way as though it had been ironed.

"I found this over his face," Tukes whispered, pointing to the pillow. "Pressed over his mouth. I don't see how he could have done it himself..." Tukes was shaking. "There's the telephone, sir." He answered Nicholson's searching look around the big room. Nicholson told him to stand by the door, and picking up the instrument, asked for the Wimbledon police station. He was put through at once. Superintendent Claxton told him that he was listening from his bedside 'phone. Nicholson replied that he was speaking from Westwood, that he had just been fetched from his bed to find Sir Adam Youdale dead. Apparently smothered. He, Sir Adam's solicitor, happened to be staying the night in the house, and wanted the superintendent to come at once.

"Time's just gone six," came Claxton's firm voice. "You're quite sure a doctor can do nothing?"

"Oh, quite!" Something of Nicholson's shudder got into his voice.

"Then will you please lock his door and wait for me outside, keeping the key yourself until I come. I'll send for our police surgeon, and be there inside of five minutes."

Nicholson hung up. What a blessing the police were.

"What time is it by your watch?" he asked the butler.

"Just three past six, sir, and I set it by the B.B.C. every evening.

"The superintendent wants me to lock the room and hand him the key when he comes. He'll be here almost at once with the doctor. You shut those windows."

This was done, Nicholson going out behind the other and making sure that the door was properly fastened. Then, being a lawyer, he suddenly remembered Youdale's safe. Telling Tukes to carry on as usual, and keep the dreadful happening a secret as long as possible, he ran down to the library, found the key in the lock of the one door, and turned it, just glancing in to see that he had beaten the housemaids, supposing any were up at this hour. The two keys in his pocket, he stood in the square hall waiting for the police, his mind in a turmoil. What in the world had happened? It must be murder, and yet—surely—had he been too quick to jump to conclusions, and had Youdale died in a heart attack and the pillow got across his face in a dying convulsion? The bed had not suggested any convulsion.

It had looked unusually smooth and trim. It suddenly struck Nicholson with horror that the murder, if it was a murder, must have taken place almost immediately after Youdale got into bed for the clothes to look so fresh and untumbled. His mind turned over all the events of last night as known to him. One thing seemed his duty. To keep Mademoiselle Le Brun's name out of the case if that should be possible. The dead man would have wished it, and he was his client, and he was lying stark and still upstairs, unable to lift a finger in defense of the woman he had loved. Nicholson heard the swish of gravel outside. Tukes was there to open the door with silent swiftness and to usher in a big, burly man, who stepped in without a sound.

The solicitor liked the look of Superintendent Claxton. He watched him have a few, almost inaudible words with the butler and then turn to himself with a low "Mr.

The Westwood Mystery 59

Nicholson? Will you lead the way? The doctor will be here almost at once."

Noiselessly, the three hurried up the stairs to the first floor. Nicholson handed the superintendent the key—and Tukes stood beside the door as though presenting arms.

The superintendent opened it without a sound. Tukes closed it after them as silently, and then stood by it, merely pointing to the bed. Claxton put his cap on the carpet, and stood hands on hips—a favorite attitude of his, bending down over the prostrate form. He tried to flex an arm. It refused to be bent.

"Dead right enough," he said to the two watching him. "Suffocated as you said, sir. I've seen men who'd been buried by shells. You found him, didn't you?" He looked over at the butler.

"With that pillow pressed down on his face?" he asked. "You lifted it?"

"Of course I lifted it!" Tukes said indignantly and yet defensively. "I twitched it away and it dropped from my hands when I saw the face under it. The color—the look at it—"

The superintendent nodded at him in sympathy. "Bit of a shock naturally." He turned to the bed again. "And to think of it being done almost within a stone's throw of us at the police station!" Nicholson liked the tone of suppressed fury in Claxton's low voice. "Well," the police officer went on, "the doctor'll be here in a jiffy. Still, I'll make certain that we oughtn't to try resuscitation." He just touched the back of one quiet hand on the bed with a burning match. There was no reddening of the skin. "No life there. Where's the telephone? The chief constable wants Scotland Yard to take hold, if it's murder. And it certainly is. No one ever held that pillow over his own nose and mouth—rammed it down with such force." He picked up the telephone tube. As he did so, Nicholson's eye was caught by something over the superintendent's shoulder. It was the door knob, and it was gently revolving. In two strides he reached it. Tukes had stepped forward when Claxton mentioned the telephone. Nicholson unlocked the door without making a click, and stepping out shut it carefully behind him. He saw no one. Now, it was not an easy place from which to vanish. On either hand fairly long stretches of corridor ran east and west. His own room had lain to the east. Lady Youdale's little group of three rooms was around a corner to the west, he believed. As he stood quite still he saw a door quivering. A door not far from his own. He was not sure enough whose room it was to venture to open it. And after all, some hint of the tragedy might have got about, or some sight of the superintendent in his neat blue uniform might have been caught. He contented himself with noting the door and then returned to Youdale's room. The doctor was just being shown in. Doctor Dowdall, who was the police surgeon, was also Youdale's own physician.

"No hope of doing anything here," he said laconically, trying an arm and finding it rigid. "What happened? You mean he was smothered with that pillow?" as the superintendent motioned towards it. "You mean it was deliberate murder?" The doctor was young and clucked his tongue against his teeth.

Claxton repeated that it was done almost within the shadow of the police station.

"But he didn't struggle," Nicholson said, puzzled.

"Apparently, he didn't even bite the pillow," the superintendent added. He introduced the two professional men to each other.

"There's a suggestion—I shan't be surprised if the post-mortem shows a narcotic of some kind." The doctor was examining one of the pupils. "Which would explain the whole thing."

The superintendent's glance met Nicholson's. To neither of them did it seem likely that the explanation would be so brief and so simple. The doctor had an urgent call and hurried off, saying that he would come back as soon as he was free.

The Westwood Mystery 61

"Yes, Scotland Yard are being asked to take the case up, which means that one of their big men will be here by car in next to no time." The superintendent was not sorry. The murder of Sir Adam Youdale did not strike him at all as the sort of thing to help him forward. He was a sensible man who knew his own limitations.

"When did you see him last, Mr. Nicholson?" he now asked, as soon as the doctor had slipped away.

Nicholson explained that Youdale had come up with him to his room, about half-past ten last night, had stood a minute or so talking, and then had left him, going on towards his own bedroom while saying something about turning in early, as he meant to be up early. He himself had heard no sound during the night. He had slept well.

"Anything in Sir Adam's manner to suggest that he was worried over his own safety—or was in fear of anyone—or anything along that line?"

Nicholson could assure him that, as far as he knew, death had come quite unexpectedly to the man lying before them on the bed.

He was standing on the landing when Tukes came up the stairs followed by a tall, well-set-up youngish man. Nicholson knew him by sight, as he did many members of Scotland Yard, for he had been called in not long ago on a lengthy will case, and had worked with one of the Big Five for weeks to prove his client innocent of what looked like fraud. He liked Chief Inspector Pointer, who, he knew, was considered a man who would never let the Yard down, either personally or professionally. Nicholson knew the accepted idea of many novelists that a detective should not look his profession. He thought again as he watched the lithe tall figure running lightly up the stairs, that it fitted this man's looks well. The indefinable air of authority of a man accustomed to think things out to the end, to make his own deductions—and plans. The strength of the detective officer's body, the resolute, grave look of his sunburnt, good-looking face all fitted, Nicholson thought.

62   *A Resurrected Press Mystery*

The two shook hands in silence. At the door of the dead man's room the chief inspector signed to the other: to precede him, and once inside and the door shut, turned to him first of all.

"The assistant commissioner told me to ask you to work with us on the case, Mr. Nicholson. As the family solicitor of Sir Adam Youdale your help might be invaluable."

"Anything I can do—" Nicholson murmured, with the mental addition of "with professional propriety."

With the chief inspector were two men in plainclothes. All three carried larger or smaller handbags which they set down on the carpet. Rubber gloves were pulled on first of all. Rubber soles next slipped over their shoes. A camera was produced, fingerprint paraphernalia likewise. First of all the usual photographs of the room from its four angles were taken, photographs of the dead man on his bed, photographs of what could have been visible from Adam Youdale's pillow. His fingerprints were carefully taken when this was done, and the room was immediately tested for other prints by the expert, while the chief inspector listened to the report of the superintendent, and then had a short talks with the solicitor. Major Pelham, the assistant commissioner, had vouched for Nicholson's trustworthiness and authorized the chief inspector to treat him with absolute frankness.

The question was, would Mr. Nicholson be equally frank? Pointer had noted the lack of enthusiasm in the other's promise to help the investigation. His glance seemed casual, but he could have drawn a very good sketch of Mr. Nicholson on copper—the chief inspector was an enthusiastic etcher in his spare time—with his neat frame, and his bald head of that type of baldness that is distinctly decorative, showing the bone configuration of a fine head that matched a scholarly face. Theoretically all people in a house at the time of a murder are suspect, and in practice are treated as such, but quite apart from his superior's guarantee, Pointer

The Westwood Mystery 63

would have been very much surprised if this man were a criminal. There is a look, there is a carriage, there is a type of face that is distinctly and always on the side of the law, in reality as well as in outward profession, and the solicitor belonged to this group.

"Who waits on Sir Adam, a valet?" Pointer asked finally.

"I think only the butler. I've never seen any other manservant around the house."

Pointer rang the bell. Tukes came on the instant. Yes, he was butler and valet.

"Is anything in the room out of the usual place, or missing, or has anything been added to it?" The chief inspector asked him.

The butler said no, that he had looked about him very carefully when in here with Mr. Nicholson, and could see nothing missing, or in the wrong place.

"Nothing? However trifling?" pressed the detective officer. From his tone the solicitor saw that he himself believed that something was different either to what it should have been, or to what it was ordinarily.

Tukes understood the inflection too—as he was meant to do. He rubbed his chin, which was for once not so clean-shaven as usual.

"Nothing different from usual that I can see, except that rose wasn't there last night when I brought Sir Adam in a glass of chartreuse. But, of course, Sir Adam evidently put it himself into water, and stood it by his pillow." Tukes went on to say that the vase was a pottery piece that usually stood on a shelf in the corner. He indicated the vacant place.

Remembering the bunch of yellow roses that mademoiselle had worn against her left shoulder, Nicholson could guess who had given this particular rose to Youdale and why he had placed it where it now stood.

"Was Sir Adam feeling unwell in any way?" Pointer persisted.

"No, sir. Not that I know of." Tukes looked worried. "I went off duty very early last night, having had a raging toothache all day. I only got up to superintend dinner, and after it I brought Sir Adam's glass of liqueur that he likes to have by his bedside; saw that everything was as usual in the room, the two windows open, and so on, and went off back to my own room."

"Then he wasn't in his room when you put the glass down?"

"He was downstairs having coffee. The time was around half-past eight or a little later."

"When did you see Sir Adam last?"

Tukes looked moved. His face quivered. Evidently the barrister had been good to his servants. "Around ten or a little past ten. He was talking to Mr. Nicholson in the library."

He was asked the stereotyped question as to whether he knew of anything which might be connected with this tragedy, or could explain it. Tukes said that he did not.

"Now about Lady Youdale," Pointer went on, when that was quite clear, "does she know of the tragedy yet?" The doctor came in as he put the question.

Tukes said that the household were sure something was wrong, but as her ladyship did not breakfast until eleven, the news, or disturbance, would not be likely to have reached her yet.

Pointer thanked him, told him that he would see him later, and turned to the medical man.

"Perhaps you would break the news to Lady Youdale," he suggested. "She ought to be told of it and questioned as soon as possible."

"I hardly know her." The doctor looked at Nicholson. "It's a task for the family solicitor."

And suddenly, to his own great surprise, Nicholson decided that he would tell Lady Youdale that her husband was lying dead—murdered—in his room. He had, unknown to himself, a great curiosity as to the mainsprings of all action. Not what happened to people,

The Westwood Mystery 65

but why it happened, and how they took it, chiefly aroused his interest in life. That was why he was a really good family solicitor.

"Perhaps you're right," he said now, and felt the chief inspector's casual glance just stray over him. Without another word, Nicholson went out into the passage and along it to the farther end. Turning the corner, he found Lady Youdale's maid hovering about. He thought she looked frightened.

"I want a word with Lady Youdale. Is she awake?" he asked.

"No, sir. I don't know what to do." She eyed him eagerly.

"Wake her at once," he directed. "Say that I want a word with her. You may add that something has happened to Sir Adam. No—don't ask me what. Do as I tell you."

Within two minutes Lady Youdale came out of her room in a wrap of some kind. At sight of her composed face the one that Nicholson had seen for a second at the library room door seemed a nightmare—it seemed monstrous to think that this woman held any key to the murder riddle. But none the less he had seen that distorted face, and so he kept his eyes on hers as she came forward.

"Can you come to Sir Adam's room, Lady Youdale? There's been an accident. The doctor is there."

"What kind of an accident?" she asked, standing: quite still.

"Please come to his room," he urged, and hurrying her on, he opened the door of Youdale's room and closed it behind her. The doctor stepped forward hastily.

"Lady Youdale! I'm so frightfully sorry! A ghastly thing to have happened." He looked at Nicholson as though shocked at his having brought the wife in here. But superintendent Claxton's eye met the solicitor's with cordial approval. As for the detective officer from the

Yard, he merely bowed and expressed his regret at having to ask her some questions as soon as possible.

She rushed to the bedside. "Adam!" she called sharply, and then again, "Adam!"

"Come into another room," the doctor took her arm; gently, "you ought never to've been brought in here."

"Is he dead?" She half-whispered the words, bending down over the white face, and to Nicholson, at least, her voice had more of excitement than of grief in it. Youdale's features had lost by now the strangely flattened look that the solicitor and the butler had seen most sharply.

"He is," the doctor said sympathetically, "must have been dead some hours."

"What did he die of?" she asked, staring at the still form on the bed.

"I'm afraid there has been foul play," Pointer said quietly. "We think that Sir Adam was killed."

"What with? By whom?" She spoke almost mechanically, her eyes on the chief inspector. Claxton promptly introduced him.

"Why didn't you ask to see me?" She stared reprovingly at the stranger. "Who fetched you? Why are you here?"

Superintendent Claxton said promptly and coldly that the chief constable had, immediately after he learned of the death over the telephone, put the murder of Sir Adam into the hands of Scotland Yard.

"When was my husband found like this? And by whom?" she went on.

While she talked her eyes looked about her. Nicholson wished that her gaze did not so suggest to him some one looking to see that nothing had been left lying about... but why should he mind, if it did? He had looked for possible clues. So had Tukes, and he did not suspect Tukes, then why that revulsion because Imogen Youdale peered about her so intently? His feelings seemed to him illogical, and he was ashamed of them, therefore. He told her briefly that Tukes had found Sir Adam and brought him—

The Westwood Mystery

Nicholson—that he had telephoned for the police, and the rest was not in his hands.

"You should have sent for me at once!" she said severely, then added grudgingly, "of course, I know, you thought you did it for the best."

"When did you see Sir Adam last?" Pointer asked her.

"Yesterday evening. Just after dinner." She turned to the doctor. "You're sure he's dead? That he's not just unconscious?"

"Quite sure." Nicholson found himself wondering if that was why she had come to the room. To be sure. It was a horrible thought, but it fitted. Fitted her manner now, and her face of last night.

"My uncle's here. He wanted particularly to speak to Sir Adam this morning. I must go to his room. It'll be an awful shock to him." Lady Youdale and the doctor left the room. "No, don't come with me! Don't come with me!" There was a note of true urgency in her voice. A note which Nicholson felt he best could understand. Lady Youdale must know about the papers sent to her husband, and knowing, must suspect—wonder—were they merely what Sturge had said they were?

He stood lost in thought, leaning against the mantel, waiting for the others to be done with the room. He heard, as in a dream, the superintendent and the chief inspector talking about the post-mortem and the inquest. Then Pointer turned to Nicholson.

"I think you said you locked the door of the library where the safe is; we had better go there first." They ran down the stairs. At the library door the solicitor produced the key, inserted it, and turned it. As he did so, he saw that Lady Youdale was just behind them. All three went in together. As Nicholson, who was last, closed the door behind him, a figure rose from a chair by the window.

"Mademoiselle!" Nicholson and Lady Youdale called out together. But in different tones. His expressed stupefaction, hers that this was just the sort of thing she expected.

"You locked me in." Mademoiselle was pale, but she was naturally that. Her eyes alone showed strain. Her pupils were enormous.

"What has happened?" she asked urgently. "I thought I heard unusual sounds, and came in here. What made you lock the door, Mr. Nicholson?"

"My husband has been murdered," Lady Youdale replied for the other, "and pray, what are you doing here in his locked study?"

Before the secretary could answer, Pointer introduced himself—was that in itself a warning, Nicholson wondered? Mademoiselle had made no outcry on Lady Youdale's words. She only stood quite still and rigid for a full minute. Her eyes, enormous in her white face, fastened on Pointer.

"He was found in his bed this morning, smothered by a pillow," Pointer answered.

"Who found him?" the Frenchwoman whispered, as though her throat were dry.

"The butler."

Again Léonie Le Brun stood as though even her breathing suspended. When she asked who had found Youdale, she had looked steadily at Lady Youdale, who had looked as steadily back at her.

Pointer meanwhile, who had Youdale's keys with him, went over to the safe. He put a key in it, and the door came open at once.

"It was open!" Lady Youdale gave an exclamation that sounded like triumph, and fairly sprang towards the steel door which had only been closed, not locked, into its place.

The chief inspector put an arm across the opening "Don't touch it, please."

"But it was unlocked and yet put so as not to show." She still spoke in a tone of hostile satisfaction. "Well, mademoiselle, what have you to say about it?"

The Frenchwoman's face was gray. Again the two women looked at one another and Nicholson saw that in

The Westwood Mystery 69

the features of Lady Youdale which strongly recalled last night's vision. He felt, too, that Mademoiselle Le Brun regarded her as quite a formidable opponent. They seemed to him, as they eyed one another, like two fighters warily walking round and round before coming to grips. Then the French girl said:

"That the will has been taken. That is what I have to say. I saw Sir Adam put it on the upper shelf last night, and now the shelf is quite bare. The safe has been emptied."

Nicholson now saw that on the handsome green-blue tiles of the fireplace was a heap of burned papers.

Pointer had already touched them gently and found them quite cold.

"The will did not mention you, Mademoiselle Brun," Lady Youdale said haughtily. "Mr. Nicholson here will tell me what further steps I must take, and so will the police, but for the moment, all I have to say to you is that you are to leave my house at once. Pack your things and leave immediately." .

"Your house?" Mademoiselle Le Brun arched her already well arched eyebrows. "Westwood is now your house? Sir Adam left everything to charity except what was arranged in the marriage settlements. But I forgot! Of course! This will has been taken. I suppose if it is not found the widow shares in everything?" She seemed to be thinking aloud.

"How about the money that my husband had in his safe?" Lady Youdale turned to Pointer. "He had a lot of French money in the drawers."

"How much? Do you know?" he asked.

"Over a thousand English pounds. I have no idea how many francs that would be at the present rate of exchange. It was all in thousand franc notes, he said, except, I suppose, the small change."

Mademoiselle Le Brun whirled around on her, opened her mouth, and then shut very tight its well cut, but thin, lips. The lips of a woman whose intelligence would always rule her heart.

"You are sure of the amount?" Pointer asked the widow.

"He spoke of it only yesterday. A thousand pounds at the present rate of exchange, was what he said. I ask you to please look and see that the sum is still there." She spoke temperately, but there was something about the way she drew in her breath that suggested a sort of dreadful pleasure at what she felt sure was coming.

"There should be around three hundred pounds in one-thousand franc notes," Mademoiselle Le Brun said now. "No more. Not nearly half the sum that Lady Youdale—imagined—would be there."

"And the remainder is where?" Lady Youdale demanded.

"The remainder of what?" Mademoiselle asked.

"That is all the money that Sir Adam changed. It represented a heavy loss. He was not sure enough of the pound recovering before he would need to use it. Perhaps he talked it over with you? Or mentioned the sum?" She turned to Nicholson. Lady Youdale looked at him keenly. Nicholson did not reply to them, for Pointer was asking him to count with him the packets, neatly banded. They came to just under three hundred pounds. "Three hundred pounds! And not quite even that much!" Lady Youdale made it sound like farthings. "Not three hundred pounds left! I put the matter in your hands, Chief Inspector." She spoke very gravely. "I insist, however, on this woman leaving at once. Whether you take her in charge or not."

"Be careful, Lady Youdale!" Nicholson said under his breath, and in genuine consternation, "you must be careful! Before witnesses—you mustn't—" He shook his head instead of finishing.

"It would be impossible to make an arrest on such a charge," Pointer was saying, "we must have proof, or a reasonable presumption, that the sum you mention was

The Westwood Mystery 71

there before looking for it, let alone before arresting any one for its absence." He looked steadily into her face that was now flushed. "The police and the Yard are in charge of the inquiry into your husband's murder, Lady Youdale, and everything that might even be remotely connected with it will be most carefully investigated. But I am afraid that I want the household to stay more or less as it is until the inquest." He looked inquiringly at the secretary, who bit her lip, her face grown quite white, again after the crimson that had flooded it during Lady Youdale's words.

Pointer had been looking around the room. It was a large one filled with books up to the picture rail. A north room, the one huge window was a solid pane of glass fixed in place; one that could not be opened. Above it were four large squares looking like part of the decorations, but on pulling down a rod beside the window to the depth wanted, the coverings slid back, showing wired open squares into the garden, admitting ventilation in plenty, for on the other side were smaller air bricks into the lounge. Youdale had had the room arranged to give him the maximum of silence and freedom from draughts, it now served the quite unexpected service of making it clear that nothing could have been thrown out or dropped out of the room—since the door had been locked.

On a table in the window recess was a glass tray on which were a bottle of sherry, and two glasses. One had been used. Lady Youdale, on being now asked about it, said she had no idea who had drunk the wine. Youdale himself, when alone, never used that table. It was, so to say, a sort of visitors' recess. Nicholson had not seen tray, bottle, or glasses there when he and Youdale had finally gone up to his room, and, as he had said, he thought from what Youdale said that his host was going directly on to his own room and bed when he left him.

No one could give any explanation, apparently, of the burned papers. Nicholson said that the tiles had been quite bare when he left the room last night. Evidently

72 *A Resurrected Press Mystery*

that departure had not finished the proceedings down here as he had thought. That glass of sherry... those burned papers... something seemed to have taken Youdale out of his room again.

The chief inspector turned to the solicitor and motioned him to follow him to the other end of the room.

"Could you give me the bare outlines of Sir Adam's career?"

Nicholson did. It ran: Winchester—Merton—Called to the Bar—North Eastern Circuit—A growing practice— Silk taken six years after—Went out to Tangier on a Board of Inquiry—Stayed on as leading British Member of the Legislative Assembly there with a small private practice among the British residents—Returned home two years ago, and went to Brussels, Berlin, and Paris as British Delegate on the Protection of Industrial Property and the Repression of False Trade. Descriptions—Was given a baronetcy about eighteen months ago—Is Legal Adviser to many important companies—Suffered severe financial loss in the Hatry crash—And worse in the Kreuger and Toll slump—Married about fifteen years ago a Miss Gurton, whose mother was a sister to Mr. Sturge the Chartered Accountant who is connected with the Rubber Trunk Company's affairs.

Pointer nodded when the other finished. Yes, this was what he already knew.

"And the errand to The Hague on which he was going?" he asked next.

Nicholson explained briefly that Youdale was merely holding a watching brief for the British Government in a Tariff Meeting being held there. By no possibility could it be connected with his death. Pointer had been told as much already, but he wished the solicitor to confirm this important point.

"Who is staying in the house at the present moment?" the chief inspector asked next.

Nicholson was just going to reply when there came the sound of a voice raised in expostulation.

CHAPTER FIVE

"Stand back, sir! If you please!" came a sharp order outside the library door.

"But I must spik to ze lady !" It was Monsieur Gaudet's voice considerably louder in tone than when speaking his own tongue.

Pointer opened the door at once. Gaudet was standing almost nose to nose against a plain-clothes man.

The Frenchman looked around him into the room. "Madame? Mademoiselle? Is anything wrong?" he exclaimed, bowing his good mornings, and clutching his overcoat around him from beneath which washed-out pajama legs ended in heelless Moroccan slippers of scarlet and blue.

Lady Youdale did not return his greeting, she stared at him coldly instead.

"I quite forgot that there were strangers in the house," she said to the chief inspector, "this man is the secretary's guest. She asked for him to come down and asked that he might spend the night here. Sir Adam had no objection." Her tone was rudeness itself. Mademoiselle for the first time showed perturbation. But Gaudet only looked at the lady of the house inquiringly and appraisingly through his thick lensed glasses.

"What is the matter?" he asked in French, "something has happened?"

"A moment," Pointer intervened in the same language. "I would like a word with you alone. In another room."

Something in Gaudet's glance around him suggested that he could bear to leave the apartment—and Lady Youdale. In the adjoining room Pointer asked for particulars as to who he was, and how he came to be in

74   *A Resurrected Press Mystery*

the house, explaining briefly what caused the necessity for the questions—and the need for full replies.

Gaudet seemed duly shocked, and expressed himself accordingly.

"Permit me to introduce myself—a very unimportant person, I am sorry to say." He handed Pointer a beflourished card on which was printed the name of Alphonse Gaudet of the French Colonial Service.

"I am a French postal official—postmaster—is, I think, the English word—out in French Morocco. On leave, I stopped over to see mademoiselle here. She and my mother are old friends. As the only train that was convenient for me yesterday was a late one, and I very much wanted to see some Arabic illuminated manuscripts of Sir Adam, he very kindly asked me to spend the night here at Westwood. It is a dreadful shock, this that has happened, since I said good night to him, safe and sound, last night. To learn that he is not only dead, but that he has been murdered, I permit myself to ask if the police have any idea of the criminal, or the motive of this amazing crime?"

Pointer studied the man without showing that he was doing so. There was power in those shoulders and those hands. Nervous as well as muscular power. The face, too, was interesting. The scholarly height of the forehead marred by odd bumps in the bone beneath, the bilious disillusioned eyes behind their thick lenses, the aquiline nose with the sarcastic nostrils. The mouth and chin were partly hidden by a square cut thick black beard, but the one suggested bitterness, the other ruthlessness. It was the face of a man hard on himself, hard on others, Pointer thought. Not one touch of sentiment would move Monsieur Gaudet, the detective officer believed. He might be capable of appreciating its beauty, or he might not be, but even if he were, it would be as something which would no more affect his decisions, his actions, than would a sunset which he might admire.

The eyes of Mademoiselle Le Brun rose before Pointer. Yes, they too had a little of this quality, just as they too conveyed the same impression to him of a clever, subtle mind behind them.

"We have no idea either as to the criminal, or his motive, as yet," Pointer answered the other's question.

"That, of course, is very trying for the inmates of the house," Gaudet said thoughtfully.

Pointer agreed. He asked if he might see the letter of invitation received by the Frenchman. Monsieur Gaudet professed himself as desolated that he had thrown it away after noting the date in his engagement book.

"Then it was mademoiselle who wrote you?" Pointer said promptly.

"I do not follow the 'then'," Gaudet said warily, "but she wrote me, yes. Passing on to me Sir Adam's kind words about hoping 'I would stay over the night and breakfast with them next morning.'"

"You heard nothing last night? No sound? Saw nothing that now strikes you as odd?"

"I heard voices that struck me, in passing, as intensely excited, but they were not in the room occupied by Sir Adam. I will show you which of the rooms I heard them in. One was a man's voice, one a woman's. Not Lady Youdale's and, of course, not Mademoiselle Le Brun's. Even at the time they struck me as suggesting something tremendously important to the speakers. As for Sir Adam, mademoiselle came to my room this morning to say that she wondered if anything was wrong with Sir Adam, she had heard footsteps and voices—then she remembered the safe, and said she would run down to the library and would return at once if anything was wrong. She did not return. I fell asleep. But finally I too felt a stir in the house that struck me as odd, and came to reconnoiter."

"When did mademoiselle wake you?"

"At quarter past six precisely. A clock was striking it as she came in." The reply seemed to come without any hesitation.

"Will you please return to your room now for the moment?" Pointer said next. "When we have finished an interview with mademoiselle you can, of course, talk together at your leisure. I should be much obliged if you will stay in Wimbledon until after the inquest, which will probably be tomorrow, or the day after."

"I am on leave." Gaudet shrugged his shoulders in very understandable ill-humor. "What a holiday! Certainly I will stay here until you no longer want my presence."

Pointer's last questions were his most important. In his talk with Sir Adam yesterday evening had anything arisen, or been noticed, however trifling, which now struck Monsieur Gaudet as odd, or which might be connected with the tragedy? Gaudet shook his head.

"Unfortunately, we are strangers. Our talk was of the most impersonal. Chiefly of Tangier and Morocco in general. I can be of no assistance, I fear."

"Will you show me the room where you heard the voices?"

Gaudet ran up the stairs with the chief inspector, and pointed to a door next but one to Sir Adam Youdale's.

Pointer thanked him, and when he had gone, turned the handle and walked in. He found a young man lying fast asleep in bed. Bending over him, Pointer saw that this was real slumber, profound and deep. The clothes were fairly neatly laid on a chair. Nothing in the room suggested desperate nerves strung up by a hideous deed.

He left the sleeper for the moment, and went down into the library again. He found Lady Youdale sitting silent and with closed eyes in an arm-chair, while mademoiselle looked out of the window, and Nicholson paced the floor. The solicitor had the feeling of being in a cage with two lionesses, and was thankful to see the chief

The Westwood Mystery 77

inspector appear in the door. With his entry a sound reached them from upstairs, a sort of shout of "Imogen!"

Lady Youdale sprang up. "My uncle!" She darted up the stairs. Pointer followed, and Nicholson joined him. They reached the bedroom just as Tukes came out with a murmured "Very good, sir." Inside, some one seemed to be haranguing the superintendent. Sturge, sitting up in bed, wild eyed, turned on Lady Youdale. What on earth, he demanded, did she mean by allowing workmen in the house on the very morning that he had told her he needed a long sleep? Had she no feelings at all?

"It isn't the workmen," she got in at last, "it's the police." And Nicholson for one, thought the lady had really compressed the opening up of the situation into a very compact nutshell.

Sturge gasped. "What's she talking about?" he asked the superintendent, but in lowered tones. Then, before any one could answer he sprang out of bed.

"Where's my despatch box with my papers?" he demanded, as though the police had probably stolen it themselves.

"Perhaps I had better explain," the chief inspector said quietly, but taking control as Pointer always did take control of situations, partly from training, but partly owing to that within him which would have made him a good leader of men anywhere, which had made his father for years the best coxswain in Devon. When he had finished, Sturge turned to his niece. "My poor child!" he said in remorseful tones, "I had no idea—who could have any idea of such an awful thing? But where are my papers? Good God, my papers!" He began prowling around the room, swearing that he must have those papers. "They're more than important, they're vital!" he wound up. Then waving Lady Youdale outside, he asked for further details of his nephew's death. "Youdale murdered! His safe robbed, and my despatch box with all my most important papers stolen!" He seemed to brood over it for a moment.

"It must have been something of Youdale's they were after," he said finally, "something connected with a case of his that's on, or coming on. And they thought I might be carrying it for him, keeping it or taking it away so they searched my room, and took my box off on the off chance! Look at the way my things have been searched!"

"I am," Pointer said dryly, and the superintendent, turning away from an inspection of a sock-strewn table, shot him a glance in which Nicholson fancied that he read amusement. As for the solicitor, the confusion everywhere was almost painful. It seemed impossible that one suitcase could contain the half, even though it was one of the rubber trunks which would extend almost indefinitely, about which there had been so much clamor.

"Damned bad luck for me that I stayed over last night! Damned bad! But I'll dress at once and see you as soon as I can get downstairs," Sturge was saying.

"Do you mind if I have a look round your room?" the chief inspector asked civilly.

Sturge stiffened. "I do," he said crisply. "Very much so. Unless you have a proper search warrant. And I should hardly expect that my rooms would be signaled out for that special attention."

"May I ask what makes you think that I haven't searched all the other rooms?" Pointer asked blandly.

Sturge had no reply ready.

"Do I understand that you refuse to let me look over your room? Your belongings?" Pointer asked.

"Not at all. I simply ask you to let me dress first." Sturge spoke in a more conciliatory tone. "I would like my room to myself meanwhile."

Pointer, and the superintendent, together with Nicholson, left him. Nicholson did not know what to make of Sturge's refusal. Legally he was in the right, but, just after his niece's husband had been murdered?

The three went down the stairs. The two officers withdrew into a room to discuss a few of the details of the

The Westwood Mystery 79

routine work to be done. Mademoiselle came up to Nicholson.

"Here is a list of all the papers that, to the best of my belief, were in the safe. I have put a cross to three, including his will, which I know was there—at least they were when he locked the safe in front of me last night and dropped his keys back into his pocket. I wrote it while I was waiting for you to open the door." Her eyes snapped at him, "What, by the way, did Mr. Sturge say about this dreadful murder? This absence of all Sir Adam's papers?" Nicholson did not reply. Pointer came on in at the moment and shut the door on the three of them.

"And now, mademoiselle, I would like to hear how you came to be locked in."

"Something woke me early this morning," she seated herself and faced him with the look of one anxious to tell all she knew, but not anxious for herself. "I can't tell you the hour, but the birds had just finished their calling—it isn't singing—I heard Tukes' steps go hurrying along to Mr. Nicholson's room—it was just below mine, I knew—I have good ears, and the way Tukes hurried along suggested that something was wrong. Then I heard both come running back to Sir Adam's room, and a moment later the sound of the telephone exchange being called. All that roused me thoroughly. I felt sure something was wrong. I thought Sir Adam was ill, of course, I never dreamed of what really had happened. I woke up Monsieur Gaudet, who has a room on the same floor as Sir Adam's, though around a corner. His room was the first one I passed on the way down from my own. He had heard nothing. I told him that probably it was all right, if so I wouldn't trouble to look in again. But if anything was wrong I would let him know. You see, my reason told me that possibly Sir Adam had merely sent Tukes along to Mr. Nicholson to find out if he were awake, and if he were, to ask him to come to his room to discuss something. Tukes always takes Sir Adam in a cup of tea at six every morning. He likes to look over his papers in bed. Well, I ran I down into the hall to ask the butler if everything was all right. His room is on the ground floor at the back and he would have to pass through the central hall. I stood by chance in the door of the library which I had opened. To my surprise, it was Mr. Nicholson who came out on the landing and began to run down the stairs. I had only slipped on this dressing-gown—I didn't feel quite up to meeting him—so I backed into the room and drew the door shut, thinking he would hurry on past, but he came on to the door. That screen there was between us, and he locked me in. So I waited for him to unlock me. I did not want to ring a bell and make a fuss, and I knew it could not be for long. Monsieur Gaudet, of course, as I did not come back, would think that everything was all right, until he too heard so many steps and voices and talking."

Nicholson stood biting his lip. He had made a damnable blunder, though a natural one. He had glanced in, but it had not occurred to him to search the room before turning the key. Thanks to his action, she had been left alone in here with Adam Youdale's safe; with what clues it had and with plenty of time to burn any papers she might want to destroy... He could not trust himself to speak, nor even to look at her.

"Now about this safe that we found unlocked," Pointer said. "Sir Adam had one key on his ring, the one I have; he is sure to have at least a duplicate, do you know where it is?"

"There are only the two keys. The other is in his rooms in the Temple, locked in a drawer, the key of which is also on his ring." She gave the name of Youdale's head clerk and his address and telephone number.

"Was Sir Adam in the habit of leaving his safe unlocked, even temporarily?" Pointer asked next.

She shook her head. "Without being fussy about it, I never saw him leave the room with the door open. But he could be very absent-minded." She glanced with a faint half-smile at Nicholson, "he would sometimes lay

The Westwood Mystery 81

important papers down, and quite forget them, if he were very preoccupied, so I can't say that he never left his keys about. Only—I never remember his doing so. Where I work, however, is on the other side of the hall. I can't be absolutely certain, of course. But I do know that he locked it last night—as I thought, and as I am sure he thought at the time—for the night. He said something about locking cares away until the morning as he did so."

"Any special cares?" Pointer naturally wanted to know. She said that she did not know of any special ones. But she looked at Nicholson, who refused to catch her eye.

"And when did you last see Sir Adam?"

"I left him with Mr. Nicholson here. I don't know when that was. I didn't come down again until this morning."

"You heard nothing during the night?"

"Nothing that I couldn't account for. Nothing downstairs in Sir Adam's room, but it's some distance away from mine and on the floor below, you know. I didn't fall asleep until late, so that probably I slept heavily the hours I did sleep."

"You won't, of course, object to my taking your fingerprints?" Pointer asked, taking out a piece of paper from a waxed envelope.

"You can get them from my room," she said wearily; and yet quite decidedly. "I see no reason why I should give them to you."

She had a right to refuse. She had a right to keep silence had she chosen. Few and scanty are the powers of the police in any murder investigation if people chose to stand on their strictly legal rights.

"You have no knowledge of or any idea as to the reason for this murder?" Pointer asked her.

"None more than you are certain to have yourself," she replied. "I have no inside information, if you mean that, nor have I learned of anything in my work as secretary, or inmate of the house, that can explain it."

82   *A Resurrected Press Mystery*

She spoke temperately, thoughtfully, reasonably. "There is nothing among these papers listed by you which are of sufficient importance, you think, to serve as a motive?" She shook her head. "Nothing known to me. Even his will is hardly a sufficient prize to account for his murder. He was more valuable living than dead." Very politely he asked her if she would mind having a woman from the Yard search her. After Lady Youdale's words about the money in the safe it would be a wise step in her own interests. She refused utterly, and with indignation.

"Place myself among the suspects, among the possible murderers of Sir Adam—certainly not! But certainly not! My father was Maitre Le Brun of the Paris Bar, monsieur, I, the daughter of a very much esteemed French lawyer to be searched like a common pickpocket! Impossible!" For the first time since Nicholson had seen her she looked really handsome.

"Believe me, if you could bring yourself to consent, it would be in your own interests," Pointer said gravely. "You must realize that, locked in here, in a room with windows that do not open, with an unlocked safe from which papers have disappeared, according to both you and Lady Youdale, your position is most unpleasant."

"I absolutely refuse!" she repeated. "I want to dress now. It is certainly high time." Her head was as erect as ever as she went out of the room, but something about the jaw told of strain.

"That looks as though she had them on her—papers— or will—or notes," Nicholson said under his breath. He had given up—definitely—his first idea of shielding Mademoiselle Le Brun. That intention had died when he found that, by his own doing though it had been, she had had access to that safe, could have been in the room all night as far as he, or any one else, knew so far. He would hunt with the hounds, without regard to the hare. His duty, as he thought it out, lay only with Sir Adam, with

The Westwood Mystery 83

his friend of many years who had been smothered within a few yards of his own room.

"Or wanted us to think so," Pointer was looking at his own shoe tips, "whereas, supposing she took anything or everything she wanted from the safe, she may have handed them to this Monsieur Gaudet when she went to his room—we shall find, I feel sure, that some one saw her coming in or going out of his room, or I don't think mademoiselle would have spoken of the visit at all." As he talked, the chief inspector rocked himself gently back on his heels, and then, hands in pockets, looked at his toes again as though a new precipitate might have been formed by the action. "Anyway, the only thing visible on her was a letter, or something of a similar shape in her dressing-gown pocket. Thick, and square, and flat. The size and outline of a thick letter in its envelope. That could clearly be seen as she held her gown about her, but nothing else, and I feel sure there were no bulky packages or long envelopes dangling round her."

Nicholson agreed.

Pointer walked over to the pile of burned paper on the hearth. "We'll have it analyzed, of course. A specimen of the paper you use for wills will possibly help to establish whether the will is among those burned flakes though I'm afraid that's too much to hope for. If it were on parchment—but in that case it wouldn't have been burned.

A figure passed the window. It was Monsieur Gaudet, smoking a thick black cigar. Pointer tapped on the pane and went round by the front door.

"Just this," he said, "could you give me an idea how long you have known Mademoiselle Le Brun, and when you first visited Westwood, if you have ever been here before?"

"As to the first I cannot say. We possibly met as children. Our mothers were friends. But I don't think so. I think we first met by chance after she went to Sir Adam as his secretary. He was then Mr. Youdale, the British

Legal Advisor and Member of the International Committee which watches over the safety of the British foreigners in that most unfortunate town of Tangier. I was in Tangier by chance and my mother and I called on her. Then, after Sir Adam had left the town, she wrote me in his name asking whether I would see to the carrying out of some small building alteration he wanted made—a repair really to the cistern. At that time my mother had settled in the town and I spent my leave there—when I got any. We in the French Colonial service are not like your men—I supervised the work as requested, and Sir Adam insisted on paying me an architect's fee. It was a most kindly thought."

There was a short silence. "I hope that this interest in mademoiselle has no especial meaning?" Gaudet asked then. "It is, of course, very terrible for her, this affair. And a great loss in more ways than one. Such appointments, in these hard times, are not easy to get. Especially when the employer has been murdered!" Pointer felt that Gaudet was choosing his words with care. "I hope he has remembered her in his will. Some trifle that madame his wife would never miss..." the Frenchman continued.

"The will is missing," Pointer said briefly. And at that Gaudet looked as shocked as he had at the news of the murder. "Missing! A will! What a calamity! Such uncertainty of mind until it is found! Especially here in England where you can dispose of your property so amazingly."

"Mademoiselle Le Brun thinks it is destroyed," Pointer said—a shot in the dark. Gaudet's face stiffened. The lines around his jaw tightened. His throat worked for a second as though he swallowed hard. He made no remark until a full minute had passed.

"Where was the will kept?" he inquired then.

"Mademoiselle thinks it was kept in the safe."

"*Eh, bien?*"

"The safe was found by us empty of all papers this morning. Mademoiselle, who was locked in the room for a little time, by chance, tells us that she thinks that no money was taken. Lady Youdale does not agree with this last notion. She thinks a good deal of money in French notes has disappeared." Pointer spoke judicially, without any emphasis. Gaudet started at each word.

"What a position to be in!" he said under his breath, and it seemed to Pointer that he was as angry with the woman as the position. Angry he certainly was. He changed the subject immediately and asked a few questions as to English inquest procedure. Questions that showed his alert mind. About the alleged loss of Mr. Sturge's papers, of which Pointer now told him, he asked, a few rather skeptical questions, but his real interest, the detective officer felt, was with the will of Adam Youdale.

It might mean nothing, except that Gaudet was more interested in the French girl than he, or she, cared as yet to acknowledge. It might be that a French prearranged marriage was in the offing, and that he was disturbed at the fear of a lost *dot*. Yet there was a quality in the man's anger as at a stupid blunder.

"Papers taken from Sir Adam's safe, papers said to be stolen from this Mr. Sturge... The criminal must have been a solicitor!"

Pointer made no reply to this malicious gibe, but thanked him, and returned to the library.

Superintendent Claxton had been questioning the servants meanwhile, and had just worked up to Tukes.

Claxton now had the butler come in with him, so that he could tell his story before the three of them. Nicholson listened to it while going over the list of lost papers, and jotting down any of which he knew, or could easily guess, the details. Mademoiselle had already marked those of which she knew the contents. A businesslike young person, whether a criminal or not. Tukes was of no help. He knew nothing about the little tray with the sherry and the glass on it. Youdale rarely rang for small things, just as he dispensed with the man's services for showing people out. As for his discovery of his master lying dead this morning, Tukes went into that in detail. He always got up and made Sir Adam a cup of tea at six o'clock, then brought it to him, drew his curtains and then went back to bed again until eight, when he made his appearance for the day. He had heard no sounds last night, but then, he had taken a sleeping draught on account of his toothache.

He had a list of all visitors to the house yesterday, including postmen and shop boys. But he explained that Sir Adam, if he met an acquaintance in the garden, would certainly bring him in without disturbing anyone in the house.

As to the burned papers, Tukes could only say he had not seen any when he looked into the room just after dinner last night, and he added, in reply to a direct question of Pointer's, that never before had he known any papers to be burned on those tiles, as the fire was gas, and in the lounge were two turf fires which were always alight at this time of the year, on which Sir Adam could burn any papers that he chose.

As to Monsieur Gaudet and Mademoiselle Le Brun, Tukes seemed to know of nothing here which could interest the police.

"By the way," Pointer said easily, as though dropping more important matters for the moment, "about Mr. Sturge—"

"Yes, sir. I've just this minute had to explain to him that he couldn't have a bath as there was something wrong with the main—like you told me to say to everyone, sir, when you turned it off."

"Did he talk to you at all about Sir Adam's murder?"

"Not a word. Too horrible to talk about, I think."

"You didn't speak to him except about the water?" Pointer pressed.

The Westwood Mystery   87

"Well"—a look of horror flitted just for a second over Tukes' face "I had to protest at the clothes he was going to wear."

"What were they?" Pointer stretched his arms a little as though glad of a moment's relaxation.

"Red tweed! A suit that's smart enough, I dare say. Mr. Sturge's age lets him wear clothes that would be loud on any other man. But today! This morning!"

"Where was it hanging?" Pointer asked, a question that made Nicholson wonder.

"Half in the grate, sir," Tuke said with a shake of the head, "that room of his was turned over and over like a Christmas pudding. Mr. Sturge says he left it in his suitcase."

"What did you suggest that he should wear instead?"

"His only other suit, sir. The one he came down in yesterday. A very neat pepper and salt affair. But he told me he never wore the same clothes two days running, no matter what happened. But I really couldn't put him out that other suit! Not in this house! It would have been an affront to Sir Adam's memory."

"Is he going to wear a mackintosh about the house, or his dress clothes?" Pointer asked.

Tukes, with a faint smile just flitting over his features, said that he had no idea what clothes Mr. Sturge was going to wear.

The butler rose—Pointer had asked him to sit—and was leaving the room.

"Who is the young gentleman in the room next to Sir Adam's bathroom?"

"That's Mr. Reginald Youdale." Tukes stopped. "Why, I ought to've said that's Sir Reginald Youdale!" he said slowly, as though the words sounded odd, "he's Sir Adam's only relative. Just down from Oxford. Going to be a barrister, too, like his uncle. Though I doubt if he'll ever be as great."

"Why not?" Pointer asked easily.

"Too easy going. Too soft, sir. Always being taken in, is Mr. Reggie. I mean Sir Reginald."

Pointer asked when the young man had arrived, and heard that he had apparently run down for a word with his uncle. That he was often at the house, Sir Adam being very fond of him. Tukes made for the door. But Pointer was not quite done.

The chief inspector asked him about his sleeping draught, in the tone of one who wants to get even unessential details correct in his mind.

Tukes said he had a bottle of syrup of chloral which he took now and then. It was a very mild prescription, he believed. Where did the bottle stand? On top of a cupboard in his bedroom. Yes, it was clearly marked. He took it perhaps once a month. He seemed surprised at the question as to whether he had slept well after taking it last night; in point of fact, he had not fallen asleep at once, not until he took a couple of aspirins which had helped to soothe his toothache. But he thought the pain had been too strong for the medicine.

A word to one of the men in the lounge and a bottle was now brought in. Tukes, very stiffly indeed, recognized it as his, in a tone that asked what the deuce it concerned anyone else. But on being told that, of course, the heaviness or lightness of the sleep of every one in the house last night was a most important thing to gauge, he made no objection to the chief inspector keeping the bottle for the moment. He, Tukes, did not want to have people think that he was a drug taker, he said plaintively, and the chief inspector assured him that they had no intention whatever of fastening this libel on to him.

A bell rang. Tukes said it was for him. Listening—a moment later they heard Sturge asking why his gas fire wouldn't light.

"And why did you want the gas and the water cut off?" Claxton asked as he shut the door and came towards

The Westwood Mystery 89

Pointer. His tone was that of a man who has wrestled long and vainly with a problem too stiff for him.

"For the same reason that Sturge wants them both to be working, I fancy," Pointer said, as a man feeling his way in a fog. "Difficult case this."

"And why does Mr. Sturge want the modern amenities of life? And why do you grudge him them? And why his intention of clothing himself today of all days in purple and fine linen?" Nicholson asked in his turn.

"Did you put them all together by chance?" Pointer asked. "For they belong together."

"As how?" Superintendent Claxton pounced at once.

"Well, Mr. Sturge's objections to having us search his rooms suggests a dislike of our going through his wardrobe. Everything else was more than open. It was, as you saw, flung about for us to inspect. I thought he might have some luggage or cases locked away in his wardrobe, but, according to Pukes, he only had the one big suitcase with him when he came as well as the small case which is said to be missing, and is said to contain important papers. That suggested that for some reason or other he didn't want his clothes inspected. It might be because of some torn suit, but since he has just asked for a fire and it's not at all a cold day, I fancy he intended drying something out."

"But why?" Nicholson wanted to know. "Youdale wasn't drowned."

Pointer was surprised at the question. It showed him once again that, where crime inquiries were concerned people usually seemed unable to see through the clearest of glass. Incidentally it showed him where Nicholson's strongest suspicions lay.

"The best I can do in the way of a reply is to say that it rained last night quite sharply after midnight, and that the countryside was still wet early this morning. So at least our weather expert told me at the Yard before I raced down here."

90   *A Resurrected Press Mystery*

"I still don't see how you thought of that water and gas beforehand." Claxton's tone was that of a man who has had some relativity explained to him by a neat theorem, and gives it up more than ever.

"Napoleon once said that the art of good generalship is never to do what the enemy wants you to do. Well, it's true of us detectives. Mr. Sturge wanted to be alone in his room. I couldn't prevent him writing nor tearing up, but I could prevent his washing anything or drying it out."

"Of course you took that bottle of Tukes' sleeping medicine," Claxton was on sure ground there, "to compare it with what the doctors will find was given to Sir Adam."

"If there's anything in Tukes's bottle of sleeping draught left to compare," Pointer said, "I rather expect that the chloral was all used up last night, and that poor Tukes had to put up with syrup and water, or sugar and water."

Claxton nodded his assent. "I don't think any of us three is much in doubt as to who we think is guilty. The question is the proof! As to the way that room of Mr. Sturge's was worked over!" He looked at the chief inspector whose glance told that he quite agreed.

"Been stirred up like a Christmas pudding," the superintendent explained to Nicholson in the tone of the expert to the amateur, "places and things opened out where no papers would ever have been hid. That room and the bathroom beyond had been staged, Mr. Nicholson, turned out for show, that's the plain truth."

"And that was why you said you were looking at the way Sturge's things had been searched?" Nicholson murmured, and Pointer with a faint grin said that it was.

"I wonder if Lady Youdale's maid has any special knowledge," Claxton went on slowly, "she professes, like all the rest, to know nothing of the murder, but a look in the back of her eyes made me think of a cat licking its whiskers when the family is hunting for the missing canary. But if she does know anything, she'll not part with it to us."

CHAPTER SIX

Lady Youdale opened the door at this moment, and came in.

"I've quite forgotten to mention Miss Luton to you," she said calmly. All three men pricked up their ears at that name.

"Her aunt is a woman who does chair covers and that sort of thing," Lady Youdale went on, "and as I wanted a new set, I asked Miss Luton to come down for a week and see to the measurements and cutting out. She helps her aunt, you know. She came down last evening. I met her by chance outside the gate and brought her in with me. I quite forgot to speak to Tukes about her. And my maid must have forgotten, too. I've only just remembered the poor thing and sent her down to get some breakfast in the morning-room."

"Are you speaking of the Miss Annabelle Luton?" Pointer asked, "who was acquitted about a week ago?"

"Yes." Lady Youdale seemed to think there could be but the one. "Sir Adam defended her, you know. He was very sorry for the poor thing, and wished me to have her here for a few days, until she could make her plans. She's quite good with her needle, I find."

Nicholson struck in with a kindly question as to Miss Luton's health, and Lady Youdale left them.

"Well, her being here isn't of any importance—she'd hardly murder the man who saved her. Though he did jockey justice to do it, in my opinion," Claxton said as the door closed. Then he flushed.

"I beg your pardon, Mr. Nicholson. I quite forgot that you were one of the solicitors for the defense. A thousand apologies." Claxton was so genuinely distressed that Nicholson's frown passed.

92   *A Resurrected Press Mystery*

"I assure you, superintendent, that, like Sir Adam, I am genuinely convinced of her innocence of the crime with which she was charged," he said earnestly.

"Well, of course, you know her. I don't. That makes all the difference. Anyway, as I say, she's safe even from suspicion this time!"

The superintendent hurried off to his police station, where he intended, among other things, to make very searching inquiries as to any strangers seen around the house, or whether any cars had been noticed stopping near there late last night.

Pointer asked Monsieur Gaudet if he might have a word with him, and while Nicholson was talking to Miss Luton he took the Frenchman through to the garden outside, and asked him if he had been in this part of the garden yesterday evening.

"I walked about the whole of the garden," Gaudet said quietly, "but that voice talking in the room beside us to Mr. Nicholson is the woman's voice which I heard last evening speaking in tones of intense emotion in that room I indicated to you. Which is probably what you also want to know." His eye was sardonic.

"Will you complete your good office by coming up with me to that bedroom, and see whether you can identify the man's voice too?"

Pointer and Gaudet slipped in through a side door, and a moment later the chief inspector opened the door of the room next but one to the murdered man's. The occupant of the bed was still sleeping profoundly. He had apparently not stirred since Pointer had stepped in before, but a cup of tea on a little tray suggested Tukes's kindly interest. The tea was lukewarm. Pointer put a hand on the sleeper's shoulder. "Eh?" asked a surprised voice, but with a sleepy smile. Then sitting up, Reggie Youdale stared at the tall young man looking down at him.

The Westwood Mystery 93

"Where am I? Who the dickens are you?" he asked, looking about him. "Oh, Westwood, of course." And the pleasant smile was wiped way.

"Sir Reginald Youdale?" Pointer asked.

"My name is Youdale. But you seem to've mixed me up with my uncle. He's the paramount chief of the tribe."

"I'm afraid an accident has happened to Sir Adam," Pointer, said gravely. Youdale bounded out of bed like a ball and began to ask question after question in horrified bewilderment, very genuine looking, very honest sounding. He had not seen his uncle last night. He had come back for a word with him.

"Come back?" Pointer repeated.

"I had been here only a couple of days ago," Reggie said hurriedly.

"On family affairs ?"

"We were discussing my future," Reggie said, after a second's pause. "Well, I came back last night for a last word—"

"Last word?" Reggie was not skillful—apparently—in choosing words that would pass through the chief inspector's sieve.

"Final talk-out," Reggie explained vaguely. "Lady Youdale told me that my uncle couldn't possibly see me. I really forgot that the Sturge meeting had been on in the afternoon, and I didn't know that Uncle Sturge had come along and that the two were probably going to talk half the night, but when my aunt explained, I went to bed, and hoped for a word this morning."

"You hadn't arranged to meet Miss Luton here last evening, then?" Pointer's tone suggested that everything which he had hitherto heard suggested this.

Reggie paled and looked as though Pointer had got in one on his solar plexus.

"Miss Luton—I—is she staying here? Oh, yes, of course she is—I—no, certainly not! I had no idea she was here when I blew in." He said the last with a fervor that sounded real.

94   *A Resurrected Press Mystery*

Outside, some one dropped a book and picked it up. It was the sound agreed on with Monsieur Gaudet, should the voice be the same as the one he had heard talking to Miss Luton last night. Reggie, unconscious of the signal and what it meant, again pressed for details, demanded to see the body, which had now been removed, and finally asked for Nicholson. The solicitor came while the two were talking. Pointer left them, after noting the apparently genuine friendship of their greeting. He wanted a word with Miss Luton. Reggie plied Nicholson with questions too. The latter told unreservedly of how Sir Adam had been found.

"He must have been drugged in some way," Reggie said with certainty. "Uncle Adam could put up as good a fight as I can. Those long arms of his could do a lot of punishing."

Nicholson said that the doctor, too, thought that Youdale must have first been made unconscious. He did not say whether anything had been found to bear out this idea, and Reggie did not ask. In fact, now that he had really grasped the fact that his uncle was dead, had been found smothered in his bed, Reggie seemed to grow more stony with every minute. His face was very white. He passed his tongue continually over his lips as though they were parched. Nicholson said he would leave him to dress, and held out his hand, with a few words of sincere sympathy, but the touch of Reggie's fingers startled him. They seemed to him icy as the touch of a dead hand. Greatly perturbed, Nicholson went on to his own room. What did this tremendous emotion on Reggie's part mean? Not all of it was affection for his uncle, great though that affection had been, for Nicholson was quite aware that it would take time for Reggie to grasp the fact that Adam Youdale was dead, for the heart seems to surround itself with a thick non-conductive element, or else with a vacuum chamber through which certain facts pass only with great difficulty. And death is one of these facts.

The Westwood Mystery

Nicholson was certain that Reggie felt that he knew who the criminal was, and it was that knowledge that affected him. Now there were not many people of whom that would be true. His 'Uncle Sturge,' as he called him? Hardly, Nicholson thought, for Reggie had never cared for Mr. Sturge. But what about Lady Youdale? Reggie, without being really fond of her, nevertheless. would be terribly shocked if the wife had had a hand in the murder of her husband, his uncle. Yes, Nicholson thought, that must be what the young man feared. If it were his aunt whom he believed so certainly to be guilty, the police would soon find it out. And Lady Youdale could not escape. She could not leave Westwood without the chief inspector knowing that she went.

Pointer meanwhile had had a word with Miss Luton. He saw a very silent, very still, young woman. Her face was known to him from her trial. Every important man at the Yard makes it his business to have a look at those accused of capital crimes during the trial if at all possible, so as to remember their faces should they be acquitted—and again come under the hand of the law.

He asked her about her presence in the house without learning anything different from what Lady Youdale had told him. Upstairs he found that the pretty room opening on to the loggia which had been given her, was tidied up in such a way as to show that she had only been put there for the one night. He found on inquiry that she was being moved to a room that had been the governess's in long past days. A glance into it showed nothing out of the way. It looked eminently suitable for the young person who had come to make new covers. The rolls of printed linen in the sewing room bore out the idea too. Pointer found nothing to suggest that Miss Luton's position in the household was not exactly what Lady Youdale had explained it to be. He went on out on to the loggia.

Nicholson, gazing out of Reggie's window, caught sight of the chief inspector's head, like a good-looking gargoyle apparently stuck on the angle of the house wall.

96   *A Resurrected Press Mystery*

Nicholson knew all about the loggia, with its stairs down on to the grass tennis courts. He had had tea there once. He made his way to the floor above Lady Youdale's bedroom. The door was standing open, the room was empty. Nicholson stepped through to where the chief inspector at once welcomed and silenced him with a cautionary glance. Nicholson watched him scan the mosaic floor as though hunting for something.

"Where the deuce did it roll to?" he heard the chief inspector say aloud in impatient tones, as though to himself, at the same instant that Lady Youdale's maid stepped out through the room that Miss Luton had had last night, and began looking about her.

"Her ladyship dropped a little gilt box here just now. She sent me to find it," she, explained, peering about her with what looked like genuine alertness.

"This it?" Pointer held out something small, round and gilt. "If so, I'm afraid I've dropped the cake of rouge out, and seem to've stepped on it."

"Where did you find it, sir?" The maid asked very pleased, Nicholson thought, as she held out her hand for the little object. "This is it."

"Just here, outside Lady Youdale's room," he replied. "I'm afraid it's got tracked about over the balcony, before I saw that I had stepped on the little red cake it held."

The maid said that that was no matter, and hurried off with the trinket. Nicholson looked hard at Pointer, who looked blandly back.

"Shall we go down into the library, Mr. Nicholson? I'd very much like you to be present while I look through the shelves there, in case of any missing papers." They went down together. Pointer stopped a moment for a word with Tukes.

"What does the rouge mean?" Nicholson asked as the other rejoined him and closed the library door on the two of them. "You didn't find it by Lady Youdale's door, but lying on the wooden steps leading on to the courts. You

The Westwood Mystery 97

didn't step on it. You didn't make those marks on the balcony."

"Granted," Pointer said almost gaily. "But some one trod on that little pan of rouge last night, and tracked it about. Above the third step down from the balcony only. There's not a mark or smear below the third step."

"Which means—?"

"That whoever trod on it was coming into the house, not going out," the chief inspector replied.

Nicholson said nothing. But he thought hard. Someone coming into the house... was it possible that Lady Youdale had a lover? In which case the marks would mean but little from a criminal point of view.

"Unfortunately, all three rooms that open off it are carpeted in heather-red carpeting, which won't show any marks of that rouge," Pointer went on. "Young Youdale has no marks on his shoes. I turned them over before I woke him. I've had no chance of seeing Lady Youdale's or Mr. Sturge's. Both, of course, even if their shoes were stained, could claim that they only stepped out for a breath of air. And in Lady Youdale's case I should accept that as a very possible explanation."

"Why not in his case too?" Nicholson wanted to know.

"The pan was on the third step down from the top, which happens to be the ninth from the ground outside. Some one came running up the stairs three at a time, leaped on to the cake of rouge and on at once to the loggia. Didn't go into any room for some little time—"

"Question?" Nicholson said, with a smile.

"The marks of rouge on the balcony show themselves as first vivid and thick, then pale, and finally almost non-existent. There are a lot of cigarette-ends below the balcony. My man says they're all the kind that Lady Youdale smokes. Considering she knew that she had dropped the rouge, I think it must have happened at night, when she couldn't see where it was and didn't have an electric torch, or didn't want to flash it around too much. Also, it was raining, and though the loggia has a roof, the steps have not. By the way, the cigarette-ends and marks all seem to show that whoever smoked and walked about very carefully kept as far as possible from the end on which Miss Luton's room opened. Also, Lady Youdale drew Miss Luton's windows shut from outside. Her fingerprints are on them, pressing them back flat— they open outwards."

"Why did Lady Youdale wait till you went out on the loggia before looking for the rouge?" Nicholson wanted to know.

"I had stationed a man outside to keep a general eye on the house. Apparently she didn't want to draw attention to the rouge and the marks—but when she saw me searching around, she thought she might as well know if I had noticed anything. Very clearly, I had not. Ah!" the chief inspector broke off to listen appreciatively to a bell. "I shouldn't wonder if that is Mr. Sturge asking for some ink. Tukes says there is none in either his or Lady Youdale's bedroom. I told him not to take any up. Let us hope that Mr. Sturge's fountain-pen won't be full enough."

"For what?" Nicholson found it quicker to ask questions than to use his really good brains.

"For blacking the soles of his shoes, I fancy," was the reply. "At least the tips of them. It would be the left toe that needs most attention, if I'm right in my guess."

The door opened. Tukes slid in and closed it behind him.

"Yes, Mr. Sturge rang, sir. Wanted some ink. I told him, as you said, that we are out of ink at the moment. Oh, yes, sir, I had emptied that in the library. He told me to send out for some."

"Say the police insist on knowing every order that goes out," Pointer said promptly, "and let me know if he still wants the ink. Don't let him guess that I know about it anyway."

Another minute and the man was back.

The Westwood Mystery

"Mr. Sturge says the ink is of no consequence, sir, and that I wasn't to mention it. He said he had found that his fountain-pen has still plenty in it."

The door closed. The chief inspector and the solicitor looked at each other with faint smiles.

"The rouge marks on the soles will probably be scorched over now," Pointer said. "Mr. Sturge is a very astute gentleman."

"Is he the guilty one?" Nicholson asked, looking hard at the other.

"I haven't the faintest idea," Pointer said frankly, "but I should be surprised if things were as simple as that. Why? I'll tell you later. Though you probably think the same, without, perhaps, giving yourself chapter and verse for the impression. But now about Sir Adam himself, is he briefed in any particularly important or serious case at the moment? I mean by that, the kind of case to which his death might make all the difference?"

Nicholson was sure that Youdale had no such case on hand. He knew the three in which the K.C. was appearing, but they were none of them ones where his removal would be sufficiently worth while for a murder. The head clerk would, of course, be able to furnish fuller information, but his home telephone, it seemed, was out of order, and it was still far too early to hope to reach him at Brick Court.

"And your own presence in the house?" Pointer asked next. That, too, the solicitor explained. Pointer listened with quickening interest to the fact that he was down here in connection with a new will, and that his visit was to pass as a purely friendly one.

"As I see it," Nicholson finished, after giving an idea of the contents of the old will as far as they were known to him, "it would not be to the advantage of either of the two women in the house to have murdered. Sir Adam, or to have caused him to be murdered. Lady Youdale loses the income he earned—from eight to eleven thousand a year—like all the rest of the world, Sir Adam's income has fallen off tremendously just lately, but those are the lowest figures."

"Unless she now marries a man with a larger income," Pointer said to that. His eyes just glanced at Nicholson in what looked like a very casual way, but Nicholson began to distrust the casualness of those dark gray eyes.

"At her age she's not likely to better her position much," Nicholson said bluntly.

"And mademoiselle loses a very well-paid, pleasant post," he added. "Her salary is two hundred and fifty pounds a year."

"Will you telephone to your office as soon as it opens for any notes on the will that you may have kept? Meanwhile, I'm expecting Sir Philip Crabberley, the Chartered Accountant who acted for the shareholders in the Sturge business," Pointer explained, for once unnecessarily; "he may be able to guess at what the papers contained that were sent on yesterday. Unfortunate that Sir Adam didn't mention the firm who sent them..."

Nicholson nodded. As it happened, Crabberley was a friend of his own.

The door opened. Sturge came in.

"Well, how, are things going?" he asked. "I suppose no trace of my papers has been found?" His face wore its usual expression of settled gloom.

"Not a trace," Pointer agreed regretfully. "But as you're here for the moment, do you mind if I take an outline of your foot in the shoes you are wearing? In case we find any prints on the flower-beds, it would be as well to have those of the inmates of the house. Otherwise one gets hung up."

Nicholson had hard work not to give a wry smile when he saw the smudges on the paper. As the chief inspector had expected, both tips had been thoroughly scorched with a cigar or cigarette-end, or the smoke from a candle. There were candles in all the rooms. Sturge annexed another morning paper and left on that; he either was or

The Westwood Mystery 101

seemed quite his usual dismally calm self, except that Nicholson thought that he was good deal paler than he remembered him yesterday.

Again the door opened. This time it was the superintendent who hurried in.

"Mr. Sturge's car was seen at a place not five miles from here, speeding along toward town last night. Close on half-past eleven. There was only one man in the car and he was driving. The constable couldn't see anything of his face, the pace was too swift, so swift that he noted the number down, as he himself was on a motor-bike, and had a good flashlight with him."

"Good man," Pointer said approvingly, "we'll put his name in the report with special commendation."

"Anything fresh turned up this end?" the superintendent asked, and was told about the pan of rouge and the request for ink, and the blackened shoes.

"Ah!", Claxton pursed his lips, "I'll tell you what I think," he went on handsomely. "Those papers Mr. Nicholson here has told about, the ones Sir Adam got last evening, weren't what he thought they were. What Mr. Sturge had told him they were. No." Claxton tapped his thumb nail decisively on his lower teeth, "they were something quite different. Important. Dangerous—to Mr. Sturge. He came down here to stop Sir Adam getting them, but failed to do so.

"He makes up his mind that at least Sir Adam shan't read them. He got the papers out of the safe, after murdering Sir Adam, rushed them out into some safe place, then came back himself by that same outside stairs, got into bed and slept until we woke him up. Simple! Yes, there we are!" Arrived at the solution of the crime, was his unspoken ending.

"The great trouble is this Rubber Trunk Company complication," Pointer said thoughtfully.

"Trouble? I should call it the motive." Claxton opened his eyes.

Pointer explained.

102   *A Resurrected Press Mystery*

"Mr. Sturge may have taken his own papers and those sent to Sir Adam, may have drugged Sir Adam, opened his safe with the key from his key-ring, may have taken the papers to some safe place and returned here, and yet be innocent of Sir Adam's murder. Frankly, I rank Mr. Sturge as at least an ordinarily clever man, if not more than ordinarily so. Well, it seems to me rather a mistake to murder a man on the only night that you're his guest."

"But the letter from Manchester with fresh papers only arrived late yesterday!" Nicholson reminded him. "And Youdale was leaving at noon today."

Pointer agreed that this did make a difference. Still, Sturge would, Pointer thought, have so arranged matters that Youdale would be murdered outside rather than inside the house. "He would know that we would know all about those papers," he finished.

"Know, but what about proving our knowledge?" Claxton asked. "Say Sturge got hold of the originals, as I think he certainly did, which were sent to Sir Adam—"

"Would they send valuable originals?" Pointer queried. "I should expect they were copies." Both looked at Nicholson, who could not say for certain, and until eleven o'clock it would be no use trying to find out which had been sent.

"There seems no question to me but that Sturge is the guilty man," Claxton said firmly.

"Very possibly he is the guilty man, but..." Pointer looked at his shoes, "but the trouble is, as I said, that if guilty of the minor crime, Mr. Sturge won't be able to give an explanation of his doings last night. As a rule, the inability to do so throws, very naturally, considerable suspicion on the man who can't, but here —with penal servitude by no means an impossibility—should he have misled Sir Adam about the company's accounts, and his knowledge of them—why, it's futile to expect frankness on his part. Supposing he's not the murderer, yet he can't—daren't—confess to having made away with those papers himself, and with having left the house to put

The Westwood Mystery

them into some safe hiding-place, or destroyed them." And with that Pointer seemed to dismiss Sturge and the papers from his mind for the moment. Then he asked Nicholson, "Do you know whether Mr. Youdale is a friend of this Miss Luton's who's staying in the house?"

"Not a friend," Nicholson explained, "but he spent a holiday on her father's farm, and when she was arrested, he told her to come to me. I don't doubt he feels, as I do, as his uncle did, profoundly sorry for that most unfortunate young woman."

"Lady Youdale says that her husband wanted her to help Miss Luton, did he speak to you on the subject at all?"

Nicholson said that Sir Adam had not, but that, knowing how he threw himself into her defense, he thought it highly likely.

"I ask, because Monsieur Gaudet claims to have heard Mr. Youdale and Miss Luton talking in very excited tones late last night. Talking in Mr. Youdale's bedroom."

Nicholson thought this over. "Very possible," he said finally, "it would be difficult to talk with her, as a friend, about her trial and not talk with intense feeling. As to her being in his room, she seems to have started on some sewing, or mending, last night, which may have been the reason for Reggie finding her in his room, and keeping her there in talk. He would never think of the hour or the appearance of things." Nicholson wound up with an affectionate smile. Even as he spoke Reggie's figure crossed the window, he walked like an old, old man, bowed shoulders, head sunk, dragging feet.

"This Monsieur Gaudet," Claxton said, turning away from looking after Reggie, "and this French woman— funny that it should be just the one night he came down here. But I don't see how he links up with Sturge," Claxton muttered half to himself. He sat down and began to make some notes.

Pointer turned to the solicitor.

"Why did you think mademoiselle was possibly not telling the truth when she said that she had not spoken to Sir Adam after she left you and him together last night?"

Nicholson was piqued. He was under the impression that his face was very difficult to read, and yet the chief inspector had done so with apparent ease. He was more than piqued, he was perplexed. What should he reply? Genuinely attached to his late client and friend, how could he best serve him? He would have liked time to consider his answer, to weigh consequences. Nicholson suddenly felt that to be on the spot in a case of this kind carries penalties, even for the innocent.

"Come, Mr. Nicholson, it's very evident from Lady Youdale's manner to the secretary that there's war to the knife between them, and war about Sir Adam. That being so, I don't mind telling you that I think all this part of the inquiry may be of capital importance. Besides, other things look that way. . . ."

Pointer's tone was thoughtful, groping. He was a man eager to advance himself by a sensational arrest, Nicholson felt that as well as knew it by hearsay. The chief inspector was as much a genuine seeker after the truth as any scientist with the added consciousness of the possible irrevocableness of any move on his part. There was natural kindness in the detective officer that made the solicitor feel that to the other, the clearing of the innocent was as important as the running down of the guilty. And in truth it was to Alfred Pointer the great compensation for much that was terrible in his work, though he rated that work as a high and honorable calling.

"That rose standing by Sir Adam's bed," Nicholson said in a low tone, "was one that mademoiselle was wearing last night. She had a cluster of them at her shoulder. Yellow roses. When I last saw Youdale, he wasn't wearing one, nor carrying one in his hand. It's too bulky for him to have dropped into his pocket, even if that

The Westwood Mystery 105

had been a likely thing for him to do. Besides, I should have noticed the bulge if he had. It's a big rose and long stemmed."

"And that accounts for the look Lady Youdale gave it," Claxton said with a faint grin.

"Ah, yes, that rose..." Pointer's tone suggested that a great deal about that rose was still untold. Nicholson glanced at him inquiringly, but the other only said:

"Are you quite sure?"

"Quite."

"Then we'll ask mademoiselle to step in for a moment. I fancy she's a quick dresser."

She was, and a trim one, too, they found, as she came down at once, dressed with most careful precision all in black. She looked older and plainer to Nicholson than he had ever seen her, but also he more nearly liked her then he had ever done before. It seemed to him as though genuine grief was at work here.

Pointer told her that apparently a rose that she had been wearing last night was standing now beside the bed of the murdered man. Nicholson expected her to break down at hearing this touching revelation of Youdale's love for her, but her face darkened.

"He should not have put it there," she said almost angrily. "Yes, he took it from the roses I was wearing." She addressed the chief inspector for the most part, but now and then her glance included the others as she went on, quite the mistress of herself:

"I think I had better explain the relationship between Sir Adam and myself." And she did so, with the same admirable lucidity that her compatriot had shown at the dinner table last night when talking of Morocco. All three men had experience enough of explanations to rate this one at its true worth. As a rule, explanations mean nothing except to the speaker, and often only mislead the listener. But in a few minutes Pointer was put in exact possession of the situation—true, it was only according to the secretary herself, but as it fitted in with what

Youdale had told the solicitor last night, Nicholson, for one, believed her. Her story was that Youdale had fallen in love with her when at Tangier when she first went to help him with translations of French legal documents and points of French legal procedure. She did not guess it at the time. Later, when she did, it had not annoyed her. Youdale was the most chivalrous of men, she said quietly. She herself had come to love him too, but she owed it to herself, to her dead father, not to do anything "foolish."

"You see, gentlemen," she went on quietly, "we were very poor when I was a girl. My father lost all his money in a building swindle of the devastated regions; there were so many such cases. And just because of it, he gave me the best education that a private secretary could have. I was sent to study Italian in Rome, and Italian law. French law, of course, he taught me. I came to England to study English and English law. In each case only sufficient law, it is true, to enable me to translate legal documents properly. Then to Spain and Spanish studies. My education cost thousands of francs. And he died just as I got my first post. A splendid post, thanks to him." For the first time a flush was in her face and her lips quivered, but only for a second, then she went on as calmly, as objectively, as before. "Apart altogether from my principles—hope I am too *Catholique* to do a wrong thing—do you think I would let my father have wasted what he could have so well spent on himself? He refused an operation, I found afterwards, because he wanted the money for me. *Parbleu!* He would not have needed to pinch himself from every comfort for me to become a man's mistress! That would have been quite inexpensive." Her eyes glowed. "I swore by his dead body that I would consider my hard-bought training a sacred trust, and never take the easy, instead of the uphill, path if I felt that he would have wished me to choose the harder way." She was standing now, her eyes aflame "*la rue qui monte*," she repeated. Her voice was quieter than usual, but she was talking her own tongue, and French can

The Westwood Mystery

107

make itself heard in a whisper. "My work has always been the kind I love. Thanks to my father, I have had no drudgery. Training such as mine, together with his name and reputation, obtains the best posts. No, whatever my personal feelings, I did not intend—ever—to sink below the position so painfully bought. My father had paid dearly, now it was my turn to pay. I told Sir Adam that I would never accept any other standing than that of his legal wife. At first I refused to consider marrying him at all, but a confessor in Paris explained to me that as his marriage was no marriage in the eyes of the Church, so there could be no divorce, and my position if I married him, though not what it ought to be, would not be bad. I told Sir Adam last night that if he got his divorce, I would marry him. I am telling you all this, because I do not want you to think that because he loved me, and I loved him, there was anything between us that should have troubled his wife. She does not love him herself, so why should she have minded? Her dignity was not injured. Her position not altered. Last night, therefore, when for the first time I agreed to marry him when he should be free, he asked me for one of the roses I was wearing, and I let him take one. It is most unfortunate that he put it by his bed." Again a cloud passed over her thin, mobile dark face.

"What did he do with it? I mean immediately he took it?" Pointer asked.

"He held it, twirling it in his fingers. Then he must have dropped it into a pocket—he could hardly wear it in his buttonhole, one of my roses! I should not have permitted such a lapse of good taste."

The constable tapped on the door. "Lady Youdale wants another word," he said, putting his head in. Pointer nodded, and the lady of the house came in. With a friendly smile she came swiftly up to Mademoiselle Le Brun.

"Mademoiselle, forgive what I said just now. It was the shock, the horrible shock. Of course, you would know

108   *A Resurrected Press Mystery*

what was in the safe better than I. I want to make it quite clear to all three of these gentlemen that I withdraw absolutely, any other idea. And that I fully accept your explanation as to how you came to be locked in the study. It really was your sense of duty that made you hurry there." Her manner was frank and friendly. No apology could have been fuller. Mademoiselle did not show up so well. She took the extended hand with an effect of holding Lady Youdale at arm's length. But she said some very cold and very stiff words of acceptance. Lady Youdale repeated:

"You do forgive me, don't you? I never really meant it! It was the frightful tragedy of the moment before."

Again mademoiselle murmured a perfunctory acceptance, and Lady Youdale turned away with the look of having planted a Christian virtue in the world. But she managed to shoot three very sharp, inquiring looks at the chief inspector, the superintendent, and the solicitor, before she left the four together again.

Pointer waited for Mademoiselle Le Brun to speak, but she stood rigid and unbending, looking down at the carpet. Something about her said that she would make no remark on Lady Youdale, however long they waited for it.

"Will you come upstairs and see if the rose beside Sir Adam's bed really is the one he took last night? It's hardly likely to be any other," Pointer agreed with a faint smile, "but we must have you identify it as part of the routine."

Nicholson, unasked, went up too. The bed was covered with a sheet. Mademoiselle crossed herself, went to it, and stood a moment with folded hands and closed lids, then she crossed herself again and turned away.

"Yes, that is the rose I gave him," and at that she hurried from the room as though from something very painful. Outside she said urgently to the chief inspector:

"I want to say something more to you."

In silence they went into the library again.

The Westwood Mystery 109

"It is this: surely you can keep it out of the papers," she said pleadingly. "I mean—that he put that rose of mine there. If it is possible my name must not be dragged into this dreadful affair."

"But Lady Youdale—?" Pointer asked doubtingly.

"I think I can persuade her to leave me out of it," she replied carelessly.

"I doubt it." He shook his head. But if he had hoped to get an indiscreet word from her in reply he did not succeed. He glanced at the two other men, who faded away.

"Mademoiselle," Pointer said, as Claxton drew the door shut behind himself, and he came close, "what was the reason that made you last night promise to marry Sir Adam should he get his divorce? Apparently it was only last night that you gave that promise for the first time. What was offered you in exchange for it?" The eyes looking into hers were very steady. Something like a look of fear flashed across her face, but it was gone in an instant.

"There was no question of any offer. I am not for barter," she said haughtily. Pointer joined Nicholson and Claxton deep in thought. What had been offered and accepted? Something definite, he thought, and, since she had only yesterday yielded, something that she might have long wanted Youdale to do for her, give her... He did not think her mercenary in the ordinary sense of the word. As Lady Youdale would be, for instance. Just as Nicholson had that type of legal face that is always for the law, so the Frenchwoman had that in her eye that always, in man or woman, means a refusal to consider wealth as one of the prizes to be striven for. But other prizes would move her. Which among these had Youdale offered her for the first time last night? He put the conundrum to Nicholson, who did not know, and could not guess.

"Then do you know what sudden thing has occurred to change the attitude of the two women to one another, or rather to bring it to a head?"

"What makes you think anything has?" Nicholson asked, with curiosity.

Pointer smiled.

"Something that happened last night I feel sure. Or yesterday, at any rate. Hating each other as they do this morning, I don't believe they would, or could, have lived in the same house together for years. No, I feel sure that they had practically not met, since something happened which told the wife how matters stood, or made her think them worse even than they are."

"Nor could any man have stood it either," the superintendent put in, "if they'd been ever ready to scratch each other's eyes out as they are now. Must have been that rose that did it! I wonder if that's why it was left beside the bed?" he added under his breath, but with the startled look of a man treading on something, half-hidden, which may be most valuable.

Nicholson, too, was struck by the superintendent's notion. He told of the opening by Lady Youdale of the library door when Youdale and his secretary were talking together last night.

"Sir Adam had her hands in his, and was pleading—successfully, as we now know—for her to come away with him, his face would have been enough, let alone the tones of his voice. I've seen him in court many a time."

So had both the superintendent and the chief inspector. Something in the latter's eyes told that Pointer had not cared for what he saw. Justice was being played with each time that he had seen and heard Youdale pleading for a client in passionate, moving words and pictures that had swept the jury along with him in an emotional rush.

"Then you can imagine how clearly his heart would have spoken in his face and voice," Nicholson said now, and the others agreed.

The Westwood Mystery 111

"I gathered from the arrangement of their rooms that he and his wife were leading quite separate lives?" Pointer said, or rather asked.

"Quite." The solicitor added that this had been true since they first went out to Tangier. Youdale had told him once that it had been at Lady Youdale's request.

"Pity," Claxton said honestly. "I mean these wrong people marrying, when the right ones are there all the time."

"I don't know if I've been able to make it clear?" Nicholson said slowly, "in the few minutes I've had to speak of his talk to me, with what great respect, as well as love, Sir Adam spoke of Mademoiselle Le Brun. I quite believe her statement of the condition of affairs between them."

"What about Monsieur Gaudet?" Pointer asked. "Do you know anything of him?"

Nicholson did not.

"Did he strike you as being in love with mademoiselle last night, or she with him?"

Nicholson could only say that he would not be surprised to learn that they were more or less engaged. But, on the other hand, there was a business-like tone— on the whole, he would rather be inclined to think that they shared some interest in common... they did not seem absorbed enough in each other for the first idea. They exerted themselves rather more than one would expect to be pleasant to others, to himself, for instance. He finished with his one-sided smile.

"Did Sir Adam defer to you in any way before either of them? Did he ask your advice at all?" Pointer asked.

Nicholson was struck by the question.

"He did. Mademoiselle rather commented on it."

"Ah!" Pointer was staring at his shoes. "Did she, or Monsieur Gaudet, harp on any one thing at all? Wills, bequests, or anything that might seem in your line?" the chief inspector went on. Nicholson shook his head.

"The talk last night was very interesting but travel talk chiefly."

"To my mind things look like it being Sturge," Claxton again struck in, "but there's no denying that this French girl could have done pretty much what she liked in here with Sir Adam's papers."

"She doesn't seem to have wanted to do away with the evidence of that used wine-glass," Pointer murmured. "Lady Youdale feels sure she's in the crime—or conveys that impression. What do you think, Mr. Nicholson?"

"She's a strange young woman," the solicitor said thoughtfully. "I don't think she'd stick at anything which she had decided to do. Even though she loathed the doing of it. I may be quite wrong. There's no use in pretending that I like, or trust, her. I don't. But Youdale did. And he was a very good judge of character indeed. I am almost a stranger to her and perhaps rather prejudiced against the French. I worked in France during the war, down in a hospital of ours at Cannes—" He stopped. This had nothing to do with Youdale's death.

"She seems to value your opinion, you say?" Pointer insisted.

"She has sometimes given me the impression that she wanted something out of me. But, as I say, I may have grossly misjudge her."

Pointer's eyes were on his shoes, his head bent deep in thought.

"Democritus said he would rather solve a problem in causation than be king of Persia," Nicholson murmured invitingly.

"So would I," Pointer murmured dreamily. "And this case presents some very odd features. Very."

"Such as?" Nicholson asked, while Claxton nodded as though he quite agreed, and also knew that they were connected with Sturge and his papers.

Pointer looked at the solicitor with one of his swift smiles that lighted up his face so pleasantly.

The Westwood Mystery 113

"I don't know if you ever read detective stories—" he began. Nicholson confessed that he was very much addicted to this way of spending an hour of relaxation from mental strain.

Claxton shook his head. "Don't hold with them. They give too many points to criminals," he said disapprovingly.

"Well," Pointer went on, "I'm rather partial to the type that say, when the detective picks up a pin, or finds a stamp on the bathroom floor, that 'had so-and-so known what that pin or that stamp really stood for, he would then and there have solved the whole mystery which was to occupy him for many weary days.' Or words to that effect."

"Yes, gives you a mental fillip. Well?" Nicholson pressed.

"Well," Pointer murmured, seeming to sink again into thought, "that's what I feel about some things in the bedroom upstairs. To wit, the dressing-gown, the bed-clothes, and the rose. You heard me ask the butler whether his master usually threw his gown over the end of his bed and he said that he had never known him to do it before... had never known him place a flower beside his pillow before—"

"But that was because of Mademoiselle Le Brun's promise last night!" Nicholson put in hastily.

"That's not the point, Mr. Nicholson. There'd be nothing odd about the rose if that were all. The point is, I know that the rose, and I think that the dressing-gown too, was placed in its position *after* Sir Adam was murdered."

Claxton, who had been making some notes of the questions that he intended to ask in Manchester, made a blot on the paper. "What?" he asked, staring hard, "what's that? How do you know?"

"By the measurements. You try it, Claxton, for yourself upstairs. Granted Sir Adam was killed in bed, as he probably was, no one could have leaned over and smothered him without moving that rose. Not a drop of water was spilled. Not a petal fell. Nor was the table moved away and then moved back. It's a very heavy one, and the carpet is new, with a very thick pile. Then the bedclothes—they were tucked in after Sir Adam got into bed. Which probably means that he was murdered. And that dressing-gown—I don't think that anyone could have got into bed with it lying as we saw it, though that I can't prove. It's amazing," Pointer was now talking to himself, "to take time enough for all that after a murder. A criminal may spend many minutes arranging something to prevent a crime being discovered, or with the object of misleading investigators. But neither of those motives seem to fit here."

Claxton's pen was still in the air.

"By Jove!" he muttered, "well, but, what about Lady Youdale, and a desire to implicate the secretary, or at least drag her name into the case? Subtle revenge."

"That might account for the rose," Pointer, conceded, "but why did she tuck her husband up?"

"She may have given him the sleeping draft, come in to see if he was asleep, and done it automatically, or moved by some woman's idea of regret." Claxton was thinking hard. "The draft may have nothing whatever to do with his murder. She may have left her husband drugged but not dead, and have had no notion of what ghastly thing was to follow."

"Quite possible." Pointer's tone was not convinced.

"But in my opinion, there lies the crux of this murder. I believe that, as a book would put it, 'understand them, and we have a straight clue into the heart of this problem.'"

"Sturge and the Rubber Company seem the safest line of reasoning," Claxton murmured, "and may explain all the rest."

"Certainly Sturge and his doings have our best attention, as they say in the shops when acknowledging an order," Pointer agreed.

The Westwood Mystery

Nicholson stared out of the window. Any one less likely to place a rose beside their defunct victim than Mademoiselle Le Brun, he could not imagine. But the wife? The rose had been given her husband by The Other Woman. It was a macabre touch, if so, but it supplied a new motive—jealousy. And jealousy, as the solicitor knew better than most men, could lead to dreadful things. Especially in women. And he had seen Lady Youdale's face...

.

CHAPTER SEVEN

Mademoiselle Le Brun wanted a word with the gentlemen. She was let in at once.

"I have something more that I want to say to you," she began, very gravely. "I ought to have told you at once. But—I wanted time to turn things over in my mind. I think you should ask Mr. Sturge what was in the bag which he carried away from here about midnight last night."

"Suppose you explain a little more," Pointer suggested dryly, while Superintendent Claxton had the air of one who hears that he has won a prize.

"I was on what we call the observatory. It was raining slightly. I was staring across a portion of the hedge which has been cut down—a wall is to be built there instead— when I saw Mr. Sturge run swiftly across the opening, on the other side, where the road is, carrying a small black bag like a solicitor's bag, which he clutched tightly in his arms."

Mademoiselle went on to explain that there was a lamp just at that spot. Across the gap in the hedge barbed wire had been twisted. No one could get in or out, but for a distance of four or five feet you could see straight out on to the footpath. Apart from his being there she had thought Mr. Sturge's manner odd, for he had paused a moment on the edge of the pool of light before hurrying across it, all but jumping over it. "I now feel sure that there were papers in that bag. Papers from the safe."

"What exactly do you think was happening?" Pointer asked. There was nothing that led so often to unexpected results as to ask people what they thought strange occurrences connected with a crime might mean.

118   *A Resurrected Press Mystery*

"He was taking those papers from the safe to a place of security," she said. "He may have handed the bag to a friend, an accomplice, or he may have taken it himself in his car... He put that in what we call the sheds. Sir Adam had four little lock-ups for friends of his who don't want to bother with the regular garage around the other side of the house. The keys to these lock-ups always hang in the hall."

"And what time was this?"

Unfortunately she had not the slightest idea, she said. It rained all the time that she was in the little look-out. She had not noticed how long she was there before she caught sight of Mr. Sturge with his bag, but she thought it must have been at least an hour, possibly more.

"But there's more than this that you have to tell," Pointer said quietly.

"What makes you think that?" she countered.

"I think you would have told us at once if what you saw—or heard—had only related to Mr. Sturge."

"You're right. Quite right." She spoke with a great show of reluctance.

"Yes. I heard a noise just a little before I saw Mr. Sturge running across that open gap. What I heard, I feel sure, was someone coming down the stairs from the loggia outside Lady Youdale's rooms. They're of wood, and unless you're careful they creak dreadfully. But there was a squeak first. The squeak of a door. The only door of the three, opening on to the loggia that squeaks is Lady Youdale's own room." She stopped. No one spoke.

"You see now why I had to think things over carefully before speaking to you," she added.

"No, I can't say that I do," Claxton put in bluntly.

She looked at him very gravely. "I am the secretary. Lady Youdale knew after last night that her husband had loved me. She might, if angered, spread terrible tales about me. She can ruin me. I was tempted to be silent. I— After Mr. Nicholson locked me in here, I was, of

The Westwood Mystery 119

course, in a terrible position," and her eyes rested on the solicitor with quite a glare.

"Why didn't you call out when I turned the key?" he said suddenly. "If you had done that, I should have come back and set you free."

"Ah!" she made a gesture with her hand, "if only I had! But I have trained myself so long never to speak without reflection that it betrayed me this morning. My impulse was to call out, but I never act on impulse. And when I had time to think what was best to be done, the opportunity had passed. I listened to hear you come down again, but you did not. Not until you came with the police. Nor did Tukes come by, alone."

It sounded a labored excuse. Surely innocence would have called to him, Nicholson thought.

"So having been locked in," she went on tranquilly, "being in such a false position, I am practically defenseless, should Lady Youdale wish to harm me. You saw how she spoke to me at first. Then she remembered, or Mr. Sturge recalled to her, that I might, by chance—as I did—know something, or have seen something last night, and had better not be antagonized, and so Lady Youdale came in again just now, and offered me tacitly silence in return for silence. I temporized. I was strongly tempted. But if you need me as a witness I will swear to what I have just said."

"We may not have to bring your name in," Pointer said. "If possible we shall not give you as the source of our information. Was there anyone else whom you saw leap across the gap about the same time?"

For a second she stood silent, then she said slowly:

"I don't know if I'm quite wrong, if I only imagine this to be important because of what has happened, but I saw someone standing by the gap staring at this house. At first I thought it was part of the old fence, then, as Mr. Sturge jumped across the lighted place, it hurried away, and I saw that it was a man, a young man I should fancy, from the way he moved. He must have been there before I went out on the roof and I think, quite without prejudice, that he was watching some one or something in the house. And watching most intently. Really watching. Not merely looking. I am sure he was using field-glasses. And there was a light on the lawn, which showed that one of the bedroom windows on the side of the house facing him had its blinds up. That would be Sir Adam's window. The library is on that side, too, but this wasn't a ground floor window."

"Could it have been the light from the room occupied last night by Mr. Youdale? That, too, looks on to the same side as Sir Adam's room?" Pointer asked.

Miss Le Brun said that it could have been Mr. Youdale's, but looking back now, from the peculiar rigidity of the man, and the care she believed he had taken not to be seen from the house, it seemed as though he must be connected with the crime and be watching Sir Adam's lights. It was too dark for her to say with any certainty whether she had, or had not, ever seen the man before. Certainly she did not recognize him. They asked her a few more questions, but without learning anything new. Then she left them.

"That watcher," Claxton murmured, "watching for Sturge probably. The lighted window Mademoiselle saw was, of course, just young Youdale's. Sturge would hardly light up Sir Adam's before murdering him. Yes, a helper of some kind... to take the papers away from Sturge and carry them to safety, should Sturge not succeed in getting clear away... or some watcher to whistle to him if any unexpected visitors arrived at Westwood. Young Youdale staying the night might mean a lot of young fellows flooding the house at the funniest hours—" He stopped. A constable tapped and put his head in at the door so simultaneously that it was as though he had tapped with his head. He looked towards his own superior, the superintendent.

The Westwood Mystery   121

"Mr. Sturge has bolted, sir!" he gasped, and then came in properly, saluted according to regulations, and said woodenly:

"I have to report, sir, that Mr. Sturge's room is empty. I think he must have escaped down the drainpipe when no one was looking.

Nicholson felt a desire to laugh. The idea of the austere form of Mr. Sturge down a drainpipe struck him as funny. But the superintendent's face was black enough for two. He and Pointer swiftly passed up the stairs to the room of Sir Adam's uncle by marriage. It certainly was empty, and Nicholson, following their gaze, saw the pipe to which the constable had referred just outside the window. It had very strong supporting bands. The pipe had been painted a deep red to tone with the bricks, and the scratches on the paint were visible even to the solicitor as he peered out. Sturge's. Open-air passage must have been accompanied by a good many abrasions, he thought.

Claxton began to question the man in the garden. One of the constables taking the measurements of the library windows outside, had asked him to hold a ladder, and Sturge must have profited by that momentary absence of the sentinel to get out of his window and through the barbed wire which had been cut and forcibly separated.

Lady Youdale expressed amazed grief and indignation at her relative's flight when Claxton promptly told her of it.

"He was afraid you would think he had anything to do with poor Adam's death," she repeated several times, and Claxton had hard work not to tell her that Mr. Sturge's latest act was hardly calculated to remove any suspicions of that kind.

Pointer left the superintendent to conduct the chase after the missing man. It was Claxton's constables who should have watched the house better, and he must hurry on with his investigations inside the house itself. He turned to Nicholson, who was coming down the stairs,

122   *A Resurrected Press Mystery*

and asked him if he could spare the time to look through the library cupboards with him.

"It will only be a brief, cursory glance over everything, of course."

The library, with its many cupboards below the books, was capable of holding a great deal of paper. To the relief of both men most of them were quite empty. Even of the four that were not, Pointer only glanced in at the first two. The dust inside told him that these had not been disturbed or added to last night. The third cupboard, it was also the third from the floor, was almost empty. A few papers, that looked like bills or invoices, lay on the shelves, but on top of all was a long sealed envelope. Without disturbing it, they could read the words on it in Youdale's characteristic writing, "My last Will and Testament," and below, his name. Pointer lifted it out very gingerly. The shelf beneath was very dusty.

"But—that's no hiding-place for a will!" Nicholson was quite shocked "It was certain to be found almost at once—"

Pointer did not reply. He was testing for fingerprints, and found that the paper of which the envelope was made would not retain prints. He stood a moment balancing it in his hands, and then gently replaced it exactly where he had found it. That done, he rang a bell and asked for Mademoiselle Le Brun. A word had told Nicholson what was going to be done, and when she entered both men seemed engrossed in going over some papers, chiefly old household accounts.

"Will you kindly glance over the cupboards to see whether, by chance, any of the missing papers or the will have been put in here?" Pointer spoke as though of quite a possible contingency. She looked at him as at a dull-witted child, but, with an air of humoring the imbecile, began the task in a half-hearted manner.

"Why should anyone put anything they had taken from the safe into an open cupboard in the same room?" she asked, as she just glanced at the shelves in the first

The Westwood Mystery   123

one, and then in the second. There she stopped, clearly in no mood to continue the search.

"Perhaps Lady Youdale might know better what is in them?" Pointer suggested, and the secretary at once said that she would ask that lady to come and speak to them. Obviously the Frenchwoman had no suspicion of what she was leaving behind her as she went out. Or had she? Nicholson was never sure of her.

Lady Youdale came in after a few minutes. Pointer explained that they wondered whether any of the papers that had been in the safe had possibly been put into one of the cupboards around the walls.

She, too, did not look charmed at the idea of helping in the search.

"I think that most unlikely," she said coldly.

"We've looked through the first one," Pointer indicated it.

Negligently she opened the second, gave a weary glance at the shelves, flipped something idly with the tip of a white finger and passed on to the third cupboard. Nicholson felt his pulses quicken as she opened it. She looked in, then, after a second's pause, closed the doors and opened the one next to it. There she remained quite still. Nicholson and Pointer stood where they could see her, and each was apparently deep in going through some dusty files in front of him.

"Mr. Nicholson"—she turned to the solicitor— "I wonder if you would be so kind as to get my little handbag which I left on the table by the window in the lounge? I daren't ring. The house is so upset."

Nicholson fetched the bag as she asked him. Lady Youdale, thanking him, passed for a moment back to the third cupboard. Then she hurriedly circled the room. Then she shook her head.

"That's the last!" She turned towards the door. "Well, I'll see if, there's anything in any of the lounge cupboards."

124 *A Resurrected Press Mystery*

"Just a moment, Lady Youdale," Pointer said. "I want that will, please." He had his back to the door and his hand out. She stared at him, her face turning whiter and whiter.

"You took a will from a cupboard there and slipped it up your sleeve. I want it, please."

"A trap! A police trap!" she hissed. "I haven't got it. I—"

He only held out his hand in silence. She looked at him. Then she slowly drew down from I her left sleeve the envelope which the two knew that she had taken. She had full sleeves gathered into loose wristbands that tied in a bow.

"Will you open this, Mr. Nicholson, please?" The chief inspector handed it to him.

"I wanted time to think things over," Lady Youdale now said in a more collected voice. "In some underhand way that woman has done the murder and is hoodwinking you all! My maid told me Adam had added a codicil to his will. She was one of those who witnessed it."

"A codicil which leaves Mademoiselle a piece of property. A small villa in Tangier. So that it is to her advantage to have it found." Nicholson knew the clauses of the will well. Only the addition was new and unexpected.

"That's why it was put where it was 'found.'" Lady Youdale spoke impatiently. "Well, what does it say?"

Nicholson read it out. The will itself, an old one, left her an income of a thousand pounds, including the income from her settlements. Then came provisions for any possible children. If childless, any other real or personal estate was to go to his only nephew, Reginald Youdale, to whom the whole was to revert on Lady Youdale's death. Should he predecease Sir Adam or Lady Youdale, the whole was to go to a Bar charity.

"There's roughly as much again as Lady Youdale gets," Nicholson said in answer to a glance of the chief

The Westwood Mystery

inspector's. "Judging by what Sir Adam said last night. It's merely a guess, of course."

Then followed the codicil of barely a month ago, leaving Youdale's villa outside Tangier to Mlle. Léonie Le Brun, who was at the time of making the codicil, his secretary. It was to go to her free of death duty, for which he made a provision from the residue of his estate. The gift was accompanied by some words of grateful thanks and appreciation for the splendid work that she had done for him in Tangier and elsewhere.

Lady Youdale listened with an impassive face, and without a word left the two men when Nicholson had finished.

"So neither woman knew," Nicholson murmured, replacing the paper in its envelope.

"And by leaving that will where he did, Sturge practically signed the crime." Claxton had joined them and a word had put him in possession of the latest turn of events. "Yes, he took the papers that concerned him, and carefully left the will where it would be found. So as not to inconvenience Lady Youdale."

Pointer decided that he must go to the Yard and have a word with his chiefs there. Claxton arranged to meet him in the assistant commissioner's room. As for Nicholson, giving up all idea of a holiday, he intended to return to his office, and get some of Youdale's papers. Pointer took him along in his car. But the two did not talk of the murder of Adam, rather of his prowess in the Courts, his forensic successes.

The chief inspector duly dropped the solicitor at Lincoln's Inn Fields and drove on to the Yard. Among other things, he had with him the linen slip taken from the pillow that had been used to smother Youdale. There was a small, yellowish smear at one end, that he wanted analyzed. It was on the upper side when the pillow had lain on the dead man's face.

When the time came for him to have his talk with Major Pelham, the assistant commissioner, he and

126   *A Resurrected Press Mystery*

Claxton, who had just arrived, went in together, and. Pointer gave a brief summary of the morning. One end of Youdale's pillow had been ripped open, and about a pound of duck shot poured in to weight it down, and prevent it slipping off the face. A canister with the same kind of shot stood on a shelf in a cupboard used as a gun cupboard, easily accessible to any one in the house. The seam of the pillow had been neatly sewn up again, with crossed stitches of yellowish thread. A needle with the same thread in it was sticking in the runner of the mantel. A woman staying at Westwood for the purpose of making new covers had left it there last evening.

"The odd thing is that she is Annabelle Luton," Pointer wound up. Major Pelham stared.

"Not the girl accused of drowning her baby? The same! By Jove!" Then he looked up keenly. "Does she stand for anything in this case?"

"Not as far as we know." Both men answered together. "Sir, Adam seems to've wanted to help her pick up her life again and got his wife to take an interest in her," Pointer explained.

"Certainly, she of all people would seem to have least interest in doing away with the man but for whom she would now be serving a life sentence if not already hung," Pelham said after another minute's pause.

"Nicholson is convinced of her innocence. As all the papers passed through his hands, we can be certain that nothing fresh has cropped up which would have meant a re-trial," Pointer agreed, and passed on to the stain on the pillow-slip.

"Mr. Barclay"—he mentioned one of the Home Office's best analysts—"says it's tangerine jam, probably home-made, as it contains no glucose or commercial products. Now tangerine jam is a preserve of which there is none at Westwood. But whether by chance or not, Monsieur Gaudet has a cardboard box in his room containing a few cakes brought with him from a French patissier in town. One of these was evidently filled with Tangerine jam of some kind, for there are smears of it inside the box, too slight for the analyst to tell whether it's the same or not, unfortunately. I've sent round to the shop, but they use it daily for some of their petit fours, and keep no track of the people to whom they sell the cakes, of course."

Pointer laid the pillow-slip carefully out on the table. The smear was but the tiniest affair in one corner. "It could have been made any time since the slip was put on the pillow, which is about three days ago," he continued, "possibly by the maid who put it on, but it's in a place where it also might equally have come off the hand that pressed the pillow down over Sir Adam's face last night."

He put the slip carefully away, and Superintendent Claxton took the field. He told the result of his talk over the various telephones just now. The Manchester stockbrokers were certain that Sturge could not have explained away the new points mentioned in the papers sent to Sir Adam yesterday afternoon, all of which told against Sturge. They had had two good men working for Sir Adam, and at the last moment one of them had come on a most ingeniously concealed trail which had finally, led to the unearthing of the transactions recorded in the papers sent on to the Shareholders' Proxy. What had happened meant deliberate fraud and embezzlement on the part of Sturge.

"So you see, sir," Claxton wound up almost triumphantly, "Sturge had an overwhelming motive for murdering Youdale and getting hold of those papers from his safe. He would be pressed for time. He couldn't wait a day. Early this morning Sir Adam intended going through them with him. As we told you, unfortunately Sturge has bolted without leaving a clue to his whereabouts."

"It certainly sounds a strong case..." Pelham tapped his fingers on his desk.

"And, of course," Claxton went on again, "It would be worth a murder—from his point of view. Had Sir Adam got going on those papers, there's no question but that it

128   *A Resurrected Press Mystery*

would have meant a long term of penal servitude for him."

Pelham nodded. "Why aren't you applying for a warrant for his arrest?" he asked of Pointer. "It takes the devil of a lot to satisfy you, I know, but it seems me that you're being a bit greedy here."

"Sturge, sir?" Pointer queried, looking at his shoes. "Maybe. But I have a conviction that things here are cleverer than they seem."

"Sturge is clever," Claxton spoke in the tones of a warm champion.

"Undoubtedly. Very," Pointer agreed. "But in a financial way. There's something odd—something about this murder that doesn't seem necessary, if it was Sturge. Why the rose?"

"That was the jealous wife. And a very neat touch, too!" Claxton sounded quite proud of it. "Just to drag the French girl into the mess. And give her, Lady Youdale, a chance to say in court all there was to be said and a bit over."

"The tucking in of the bedclothes?" Pointer asked.

"Due to Sturge wanting to be sure he didn't stumble over them. They're rather long."

"And the gown?" persisted Pointer.

"Oh, that! I think he had some idea of using the cords." Claxton was impatient. "After all, even a murderer may be careless as to how, and why, he sticks a pin in a pin-cushion!"

"Agreed," the chief inspector nodded, "but these pins all took time, and kept the murderer in the same room with his victim—in danger of discovery, that is to say.

"We certainly ought to have a provisional warrant for immediate use should Mr. Sturge reappear. The trouble is, sir, as I've said to Claxton, even if Sturge has had nothing to do with the murder, he can't explain his actions of last night. Or rather, he daren't. I'm with the superintendent in thinking that he got the papers, put them in safety, and then returned to the house. It's his

The Westwood Mystery 129

return which doesn't look to me like his being guilty of murder. For he escaped from the house afterwards when our inquiries frightened him."

"Thought he had better go while the going was good?" meditated Pelham aloud. "By the way, you were right in thinking that the butler's bottle only contained syrup. Any chloral must have gone into the glass of chartreuse which was heavily dosed. Here are the reports. But still, I don't see why you won't accept Sturge as the best candidate for a trial."

"All I've got to go on, sir," Pointer said honestly, "is the conviction that this is a clever crime, that being so, I want to know what the two cleverest people in the house were doing last night, what brought the Frenchman Gaudet to the house, what links them in the past. That's all. But until they're cleared in my mind I can't get up as much steam about Mr. Sturge as Claxton here would wish.

"Also there's Mr. Nicholson's odd feeling that they were trying to win him over to their side... some idea of something that interested both of them. And then there's whatever it was made her promise to marry Sir Adam last night—supposing he could get his divorce. He seems to have felt certain, or rather very hopeful, that Lady Youdale would set him free. He may have been right, or been mistaken, but I would like to know why Mademoiselle Le Brun suddenly said yes. I, don't think she says things without a very good reason for saying them."

"Oh, all that's just the rusty, creaky old quadrangle of husband, wife, mistress, and mistress's lover!" Claxton said with certainty. "You wait until I get more facts about the contents of those Manchester papers."

"Meantime, *I'll* get some facts together about the French secretary and her friend, Monsieur Gaudet." Pointer rose. The superintendent, as well as Major Pelham, knew that he had just arranged with the Yard's secret agent in Paris to get Mademoiselle Le Brun's dossier from Dijon. Where criminals were concerned, the Surete was the best medium, but when it is a question of French nationals in other countries who do not belong to the criminal classes, a private agent is the best way of securing honest reports.

"As for the man, since he's in the French Colonial service, try Captain Meredith at the F.O." Pelham wrote a couple of lines on a sheet of paper. "He's just back. The French colonies are his especial field. A moment!" Pelham had a word over the telephone, and, assured that the traveler was at work again, handed the envelope to Pointer.

"What about the fingerprint on the sherry glass?" he asked as he did so.

"Not identified yet, sir. It was left behind so carelessly that it hardly seems likely to have been made by the murderer."

"Besides, that would mean that the murder was committed by some outsider," Claxton said, as though dismissing the notion.

"You both agree that it's an insider?" Pelham asked. Claxton nodded. Pointer, more guarded, said that as yet they had found no evidence to point to anyone outside the circle of Westwood itself. "Though, mind you, sir," he added, "provided the person got in by day, and secreted himself, say, in an empty room, or behind Youdale's own curtains, which are never drawn except in bitter weather, there would be no difficulty about getting at chloral or duck shot."

"And the nephew, young Youdale?" Pelham asked. "We've learned only things that seem to put him beyond suspicion so far. Winchester. Oxford. Honors in Classics and Law. Too wealthy to need his uncle's money. Not in any financial difficulties. Even though he can't handle his mother's money for another eight years."

"Oh?" Pointer looked interested. "Who were the executors, sir?"

The Westwood Mystery   131

"Adam Youdale was the sole one. His brother left him full powers. If Reginald, for instance, married without his consent, Youdale could, it seems, have held up supplies pretty drastically. The young man's income would drop to a hundred a year in that case, until Youdale chose to lift the ban. Or until he reached the age of thirty. Eight more years. However, to go on with the members of the household. This Luton girl, who seems to've found a temporary haven; she sounds all right... besides, no motive..."

And the talk finished on a note of hopeful confidence that Sturge would yet be caught, and, "after the chief inspector had had a look round," Claxton's phrase, would be duly sent up for trial, accused of the murder of his nephew by marriage, Adam Youdale.

Pointer went on at once to the Foreign Office. He was shown into a room where a thin, dark man was bending over a map. Captain Meredith was what might be called an Observer of the Doings of Foreign Powers in North Africa. Meredith had served in the Foreign Legion, and had many a friend in the land.

He had all the facts at his disposal ready for Pointer.

"The name of Gaudet is given as a postmaster of Rufa, a God forsaken collection of mud huts. I've all the particulars of him here, that I've been able to lay my hands on at such short notice. He's been granted additional leave owing to chronic malaria. Rather wonderful that he should be willing to waste even a day out of France. All these malaria-soaked men usually make straight for a French watering-place, and then to their relations, without losing an hour. I've asked for his description to be wirelessed me in our private code."

"Is he an authority on things out there? Or does he write?" Pointer was thinking of Nicholson's account of Gaudet's learning.

"Not as far as we know. As I say, I've only a few notes on him. But I should know more if he were worth more attention."

"And Sir Adam Youdale—" Pointer went on, "when he was in the Legislative Assembly out in Tangier, was he mixed up in any important political cases? I'm groping for the possibility of a revenge—murder, or for something begun out there of which his murder is the outcome."

Meredith shook a regretful head. "I've just looked through the secret records. No possibility of a murder motive, I should say. You'll find the notes there." He handed a package to the chief inspector, who looked it through very carefully. Certainly there seemed no starting point in these dry facts.

"He had a private practice, too, I believe. Were any of his cases important at all?"

"Not at all," Meredith replied with decision.

"He owns a villa outside the town of Tangier. At least I infer so, since he's mentioned it in his will. I suppose he didn't tear it away from it's rightful. owner?" Pointer's tone of dejection made both men smile.

"I shouldn't think that anyone in Tangier ever refused to sell land," Meredith said to that. "This is where the villa in question is." He pointed with the end of his pipe to the map. "The part of the city, nearest it is the worst end of the *Bab Souika* region, all squalor and filth, but the villa is up on the cliffs along the Fez road, not far from the Riff and Bedouin villages, and so is certain to have a wonderful view. I'll have it looked into very carefully. Perhaps he built it over a place where there's the legend of a secret, buried treasure. Oh, I'm not joking," Meredith went on as Pointer stared. "Tangier, bristles with such stories, and very possibly a quarter of them are true. Tangier is a tangle to itself. I'll send a query by a private way to a man out there who'll be able to get at the facts in a short time. The town is his duty. But unless built on land where treasure is supposed to be buried, I can't see the villa as the motive for murder. It's a small house, though with what may be a lovely stretch of garden. But you shall know as soon as possible."

The Westwood Mystery 133

"Hidden treasure," Pointer repeated thoughtfully. "Gaudet told me that he had superintended some repairs out there for Sir Adam..."

Captain Meredith was on that fact like a terrier on a rat. He shook it and shook it again. Pointer could tell him further that it was especially to do with repairing a cracked cistern. Ah! *Cay est*, as he would say! *The* place in the east where valuables are hidden!"

Pointer stood lost in thought. Hidden treasure, hidden in a place where it could only be got out by disturbing the house itself, might explain a murder, if the owner of the house lived in it. But in this case with Youdale away in England, surely a report arranged to reach him that something, a crack in a wall—a leak a roof—needed attention, would have let mademoiselle suggest that Gaudet should superintend the repairs again. This would surely be all that was needed. Where then would the murder come in? Unless the treasure was something that would be known to have come from the villa, he could not see why Youdale should have had to die. He put the matter before Meredith, who nodded several times, and promised to find out who the previous owners of the villa had been.

Pointer thanked Captain Meredith, and returned to Wimbledon, but not to Westwood. He stopped his car at the *Sun in Splendor*, a hotel that had been a quaint hostelry in the old coaching days. Its proprietor, an ex-gunnery officer, liked it still to be called "Inn." Gaudet was installed here by his own choice. It was quite near Westwood, and he could walk over in a couple of minutes.

One of Pointer's men had searched his suitcase thoroughly, before carrying it to the inn for him, and Pointer himself had cast a glance in it. What that glance had retained was an impression of extreme care in the packing, care, that is to say, as to stuffing the sleeves of his one suit with paper, and laying more paper between each fold and around all the simple belongings. True,

Gaudet looked a man careful of his clothes... The man carrying the suitcase had heard all that, apparently, had passed between Gaudet and the secretary. It had been exactly what one would expect in two acquaintances caught up into the vortex of such a horrible crime. There had seemed nothing loverlike about their words, tones, or looks. Pointer had frowned a little as this report on the parting interview had been telephoned to him at the Yard. It struck him as too cool... too distant... too detached. But, after all, with self-controlled people who are merely friends, what more could he expect?

The Frenchman was reading the *Times* in the inn's square hall. he looked up pleasantly enough.

"Why are your papers this size?" he asked plaintively. "Some day I shall start an English paper, small and yet with proper political news in it, and I shall make my fortune."

"Like the *Wiener Journal*?" Pointer hazarded;

"Just so. Made up like a weekly. With the same standing, and with convenient handling. But can I be of any service?"

Pointer asked him some unimportant details about his visit yesterday. Then he himself said a few words about the case. The two were alone, out of range of any eavesdropping.

"Lady Youdale has retracted her accusation against mademoiselle—her words had amounted to that—that the secretary had any knowledge, or hand, in the money being missing from the safe, as she claimed that it was. She now states that the sum Mademoiselle Le Brun gives is the right one."

"Money! It was the papers that matter to Lady Youdale and her uncle," Gaudet said with a sneer.

"Unfortunately mademoiselle refused to allow herself to be searched by one of our woman searchers," Pointer went on. "That was a great mistake on her part— assuming that she had nothing on her that she wanted to conceal."

The Westwood Mystery   135

"You could hardly expect her to agree to such a proposition," snapped the Frenchman.

"I did expect it," Pointer replied smoothly, "in her own interests as much as to help us. With her intelligence she must have known that to be found locked in a room—however innocently—where a murdered man's safe was open, meant that there was only one thing to do."

"There is never but one thing to do," Gaudet retorted. "One thing for one person—yes. One thing for you—one for me—and evidently another for mademoiselle."

They parted on that. As Pointer walked away, he was thinking over his impressions. They were very clear, and only confirmed the hastier ones of this morning. Which was why the chief inspector had made the call. Monsieur Gaudet had about him all the thousand-and-one little signs that mean a man of the world, a man of affairs. The way he came into a room, as though he had done so innumerable times with many pairs of eyes on him. The way he shook hands. The way he spoke to the servants. The way he showed his visitor to the door. The way he bore himself, spoke, looked, all told the same story—that of a man accustomed to good society—moving easily among his fellows. Yet he was postmaster of an out-of-the-way little native hamlet. A solitary, therefore, by preference, and by years of life there. Nor was Gaudet an old man of whom one could think that once returned to familiar settings, old habits would reassert themselves. Gaudet's manners were polished by constant use. And that reference to the Viennese paper—Gaudet had taken it in his stride. Yet a Frenchman is usually the least well-read man in the world, outside of his own tongue.

And another thing was odd, though a much smaller thing. On the Frenchman's handkerchief were some tiny spots of blood. He had drawn it out just now to wipe his glasses, and had wiped only one lense, and then stuffed it back into his pocket with great thoroughness.

The specks did not suggest anything serious. They were such as would be caused by a prick. One of those

136   *A Resurrected Press Mystery*

pricks that a man can get only too easily when wrestling with his tie. But the Frenchman had not changed his tie since the morning when he had also wiped his glasses with the same handkerchief, which then had been spotless. Pointer knew that it was the same from an ironing defect of the corner which could not be identical in two articles.

True, the specks might mean nothing .. . even Pointer could not say to himself that the other had bundled it back with any appearance of guilt or uneasy haste. But— he had only wiped one glass, and he had not allowed even a hint of a corner to show as he replaced it in his coat. If he knew it was speckled, why not have put it along with his other soiled linen?

A good detective should not imagine things, some people hold. The idea amused Pointer. Imagination is the light, the sun. A clue is nothing until the imagination plays on it. A speck of blood from a prick on a finger means nothing in itself, but is immediately suggested a possibility to the astute chief inspector.

Returning to the house, he had a word with Tukes and the possibility grew stronger. He learned that Monsieur Gaudet had unpacked for himself the day before. He had not sent down any newspapers, or thrown any away, but this morning he had asked a housemaid for papers to be used in his packing.

In other words, Gaudet had carried more paper away with him than he had brought. This might mean nothing, except that he had packed hastily to come to Wimbledon, knowing that there he could do it more carefully, but if so, the little dots of blood meant nothing, and Pointer was not yet satisfied that they were meaningless. Supposing Gaudet wanted to leave something out of his luggage, what would he probably do with it? He had had plenty of opportunity to hand anything to Mademoiselle Le Brun, but, after the discovery of Youdale's murder, she would be a most dangerous guardian of anything that the police were not to see.

The Westwood Mystery 137

Gaudet's room had not yet been touched since the occupant had gone across to the inn. Pointer went to it now, and locked the door behind himself. His man had searched the bed and clothes as well as the room itself, but only in the ordinary way. Pointer was looking more closely. The mattress was covered by stout ticking with welted seams and fastening with strong tapes at one end. As Pointer untied these, he found a speck of blood on one. Just a tiny speck. He peeled back the cover for a foot or more, and, as he did so two tendrils of horsehair fell out too. He was right then. The mattress had been ripped and something sewn in. But he did not expect to find it here now. Simple and almost careless though the parting words between the French couple had been, according to his man's report, Pointer now fancied that they contained some hint as to what she was to do immediately after the man left the house, and the room should be free of police supervision. Yes, he found a place where a neat line of stitching showed that for the space of about a hand's length the end of the mattress itself had been ripped. The place had been sewn up again very neatly. But there were other marks, marks that showed where other stitching, larger and irregularly spaced, very suggestive of masculine work, had been cut open and replaced by this later, more careful work, when whatever had first been stitched into the hiding place had been taken away. No cavity had been left to show the size of the package or letters inserted. He had only one slight clue. The sewing looked to him like a woman's. He felt certain that Sturge could not sew like that. He himself could not have done it. The mattress was rose-colored, and the stitching was red silk, as he now found by undoing another inch of the original machining. The place had been closed again with silk that matched fairly well, but not exactly. It was possible that he could find where it had come from. He had one of his men, an ex-tailor, in to sew it all up again. The cover would hide the place for some weeks at any rate. He believed that mademoiselle had been the needlewoman, though she had not been seen going into or out of the rooms.

Pointer did her the justice not to expect that she would have been noticed. Nor would it have been difficult to escape observation. Westwood was a rambling house, there was much ground to cover. Once Gaudet's room had been examined, it was no longer watched. It was at the end of the passage, far enough from mademoiselle's room, one would have thought. But actually, a turn of the stairs and a cut through an empty bedroom would bring her to his door unseen except by some chance. It was she who had suggested to the butler which room to give Gaudet, saying that he liked a north room. There was another thing. When did Gaudet hide whatever he had hidden in the mattress? Presumably after the arrival of the police, though Pointer rather thought him the unseen turner of the door knob whom Nicholson had tried to locate. If his story and mademoiselle's was true as to her having stepped in to say that she wondered if anything was wrong in the house, he, in his turn, might easily have slipped along the passage when he heard low voices and the opening of Youdale's door by Claxton. There would be nothing guilty in his having done that, but if it was he, why had he said nothing about it? What had made him dodge back into obscurity when the solicitor tried to find out who had opened the door? Pointer could not see any other person in the house who fitted the incident as well as the Frenchman. Had he ripped his mattress then? On the whole he thought not.

A mattress suggests an unforeseen emergency. It looked as though Gaudet had sewn something into hiding after his interview with the chief inspector, and had left it to mademoiselle to retrieve immediately. A man had been outside the door of Gaudet's room all the time, for it commanded the passage and the back staircase. He had abstracted the key while the Frenchman was downstairs, but Gaudet had used a chair as a wedge while packing, and had moved the scutcheon so as to block the keyhole.

The concealment in the mattress had taken place then, probably. Pointer was perplexed. As with Sturge, if Gaudet was the murderer, why was the crime committed on the one night that he was in the house Why not earlier, or after he had left ostensibly? Suspicion would inevitably fall on every member of the household at the time of the murder. With mademoiselle as his friend or accomplice, he could be let in or out of the house at any time, on any date. Was Sturge's presence as a scapegoat the reason?

And the reason for the taking of the papers? If so, suspicion had fallen where it was hoped that it would fall.

CHAPTER EIGHT

Pointer decided to have another look round before putting up his shutters for the night. He saw Nicholson and Mademoiselle Le Brun hard at work sorting papers as he passed through the lounge and made his way at once upstairs to the French girl's room. He wanted to see if in her neat workbox there was a reel of the same silk as that which had sewn Gaudet's mattress up for the last time. There was no such color. He thought a moment, recalled something which he had seen, and to see a thing was, for Pointer, to register it, and ran down into the morning room. There on a table with some books was a native rush basket from which dangled tufts of red, yellow and blue silk. The red matched the sewing exactly. He tweaked a length out and laid it away with the inch or so that he had ripped. Then he returned to mademoiselle's room again. For his eye had caught sight of something there which interested him much more than any sewing silk. For, whether the silk used came from her own stock or another's, from her own room or elsewhere in the house, he already felt fairly sure that it was she who had done the stitchery in question, but what he was now looking at again was not expected. He had seen four yellow roses on a table. He bent over them and examined them closely. They were all alike in kind and in length. But the one by Sir Adam's bedside was much longer, and it was not a *Gloire de Dijon*. These were. Now in the paper basket of the library, under a sheet of paper, he had found another rose just as these, with its thorns cut off. While he believed that the rose by Youdale's bed was one of hers, the one in the paper basket meant nothing. Mademoiselle herself might easily have dropped it in, or it might have fallen from her bunch and been flung in by anyone. He had saved it merely as a matter of routine.

But now the castaway was no longer negligible. He went back into the room where mademoiselle and the solicitor were just finishing a few last notes. Claxton was there too. The superintendent had come up to the house for him, for Sturge was still at liberty, and he wanted suggestions. "Mademoiselle," Pointer began, without any preamble, "did you, or Sir Adam, cut the thorns off the rose that you let him have last night?"

She looked at sea for a moment, then remembrance came.

"I clipped them off as I always do before I give one. Why?"

"Because the rose upstairs in Sir Adam's bedroom has its thorns all on. But this withered little one that I found in the library waste-paper basket has its thorns cut off."

He drew out a very withered-looking yellow rose from an envelope. She stared at it in seeming surprise.

"But this is the rose that stood beside Sir Adam's bed. I don't understand. How did it get into the library basket?"

"Would you let me see the flowers you were wearing last night?" Pointer asked. .

"Certainly. A moment—they are in my room."

When she came in again, she held out the bunch that he had just seen.

"Here they are."

"How many roses did you have in all, do you know?"

"I had five. Four are here, the one that was in his room is in your hand."

Pointer looked at her with his quiet, inscrutable glance. "But, apart from its having all its thorns, the rose in Sir Adam's room is not this kind of a rose at all. It has fewer petals, and they are much fleshier. It has a darker, shinier stalk, darker and glossier leaves."

"Impossible!" mademoiselle said, almost scornfully. They went up to the dead man's room, outside which in

The Westwood Mystery   143

the corridor a constable still sat on duty. Pointer unlocked the door, mademoiselle hurried past him to the table by the bed, bent over the flower, and then faced around with rather a chagrined, deeply amazed look.

"But how humiliating! I was sure it was the rose I had given him! I have misled you. This, as you say, is not the same kind. I confess I am no amateur of gardening or of botany. I saw a yellow rose—I knew that I had given him a yellow rose—I took it for granted they were the same."

"In detective work, Mademoiselle," Claxton said heavily, "one must never jump to conclusions."   .

"True, Monsieur de La Palisse," she murmured ruefully. Claxton thought she was giving him the French polite address, and mentally added it to his vocabulary for the next time. when he should have to speak to a French confrere, but Pointer's eye acknowledged the hit at the superintendent's truism, as he carefully lifted the flower vase, after chalking around its foot on the wooden table top.

"May I ask, who gave you the roses?"

"Monsieur Gaudet," she replied at once. "In a way, I was his hostess, and he brought them with him from town. *Gloire de Dijon*, because we both come from Dijon."

Pointer spoke over the telephone. Within five minutes Gaudet was at Westwood.

The chief inspector asked him whether he knew how many roses had been in the bunch that he had brought Mademoiselle Le Brun yesterday afternoon.

"Five," Gaudet said at once. "Five *Gloire de Dijon* roses, small and short-stalked, for I knew she liked them best that way for wear."

"Was this one of them?" Pointer asked, showing him the little vase. Gaudet eyed it. He did not glance towards mademoiselle, and she seemed to make no effort to influence his answer.

"*Ma foi*," the Frenchman confessed after, peering intently through his thick glasses. "I cannot say. I think so—perhaps—but I confess that where flowers are

144   *A Resurrected Press Mystery*

concerned, I am no expert. I asked for *Gloire de Dijon*, and I supposed I got *Gloire de Dijon*. But no"—his voice became certain—"look, this rose has much too long a stem, and is too large... unless it has developed more petals since I bought it, and grown a longer stalk?" Monsieur Gaudet's ideas of plant growth amused the chief inspector, who was a Devon man.

On this, mademoiselle began to explain that there was some perplexing question as to what had become of the rose that she had given Sir Adam.

So she did not mind Gaudet's knowing. . . . The three men went downstairs together. Pointer stopped in the lounge, and rang for Tukes. When the butler came, he showed him a bowl of roses standing on a little table against the panelling.

"Most of these are *Mrs. Wemyss Quinn*," Pointer indicated. "That lovely, brilliant matron, but there are a few roses among them that are of a different kind, longer stalked, for one thing—more of the color of the old *Gloire de Dijon* but with thicker petals... some hybrid that's new to me..." He touched the roses that he meant.

Tukes looked faintly surprised at a detective officer having sufficient time in a murder inquiry to take an interest in roses, but he answered promptly that he knew nothing of those particular flowers except that Lady Youdale had put them in herself just before dinner. Then he added, "Those are the very ones about which Sir Adam and that gentleman who called in for a few minutes last night asked. His name was Manning, wasn't it, sir?" He turned to Nicholson.

Nicholson nodded. Again the solicitor was profoundly shocked at himself. He had completely and absolutely forgotten Manning's brief interruption. And for a simple reason. Nicholson had been urgently summoned down to Westwood. Arrived there, Youdale, his client and friend, had at once broached the question of a divorce, and asked him to try and get Lady Youdale to agree. Then had come the—to Nicholson—amazing discovery that Youdale was

The Westwood Mystery 145

in love with his secretary, and almost at the same instant the knowledge that Lady Youdale knew of this complication. His mind was engrossed with the situation arising out of these facts. When Manning came in and asked about Miss Luton's possible presence in the house, and was told that there was some mistake, that she was not there, and that Sir Adam would see to it that she did not come, Nicholson though intrigued by the tone of the interview believed that a question, unimportant, and not connected with the business in which his mind was working, had been asked and satisfactorily answered. Nicholson would have made a very poor newspaper man. His mind, when on a problem, promptly built a sort of caisson and lived within it until the problem was finished with.

Now, with a shock, he realized that Sir Adam had given his word to a lie... assured Manning that the unhappy girl he loved was not at Westwood, when all the time—unknown to Youdale, she was under his roof.

Did this stand for anything in the dreadful events of this early morning?

Pointer had already asked the butler to make him out a complete list of all callers at the house yesterday and the day before, both front and back door, including postmen and milkmen. Manning's name was on the list. The butler went on to say that, happening to be in the hall when Sir Adam was showing Mr. Manning out, he had heard the visitor stop by the bowl and exclaim that those were his roses, pointing to the ones that now interested the chief inspector, and he—Tukes—had explained how they got there, upon which Sir Adam had suggested that Miss Luton must have sent them to Lady Youdale in return for an invitation, and so saying the two gentlemen had proceeded to the front door.

Pointer drew Nicholson into the nearest room. Claxton followed. "Just what passed between Mr. Manning and Sir Adam? Can you tell me?"

146   *A Resurrected Press Mystery*

Nicholson could, though quite unconsciously. He made it sound very tame and commonplace, yet even so Claxton's brows went up.

"Odd!" he murmured. "Why should Manning mind her being here? Why should Sir Adam promise that he would see to it that she didn't come?... and so one of Miss Luton's roses that stood by the bed... Could Sir Adam have been carrying on with her as well?" Claxton asked Nicholson, who stiffened.

"Absurd!" the solicitor said almost rudely. "Youdale's sole interest in Miss Luton was, like my own, sympathy for a most unfortunate young woman who was placed, through no fault of her own, in a truly terrible position, doomed all her life to suffer from a most undeserved and awful suspicion, for, acquitted though she was in court, the suspicion will always remain that she did do it all the same."

Just for a second Pointer's grave gray eyes rested on Nicholson's face, flushed with indignation, but the chief inspector only said, "Well, we must go into this with Lady Youdale, at once."

"Lucky you spotted the difference in the flowers," Claxton said admiringly. "I'm a cockney myself, and, though I like my garden, I hadn't tumbled to the difference between mademoiselle's roses and that one."

Lady Youdale was asked about the flowers. She said that Miss Luton had brought her them. "As the nearest she could do to bringing them to Sir Adam," she wound up placidly. "Miss Luton was working in her boudoir if they wanted to question her. As to how one of her roses was beside Sir Adam's bed—he must have admired it, and placed it there himself." With a stony eye she watched the three file into the room she indicated as her boudoir. It adjoined her bedroom.

Miss Luton was on her knees, in what at first looked like an attitude of ecstatic prayer, but between her extended hands was a measuring tape and she was trying to get at the circumference of an easy chair. Around her

The Westwood Mystery

147

lay printed linen. Now Pointer had looked into that room—just a glance—already, early this morning, and the fragments of linen were now exactly as he had seen them then. Miss Luton did not seem to have progressed by as much as the length of one pin.

He asked her about the roses. They had come from Mr. Manning she told them, who considered them a new species, and was going to exhibit them at the coming flower show. When Lady Youdale kindly asked her to come to Westwood on the twenty-ninth, which she had misread as the twenty-seventh, she had brought half of them along as a little token of her gratitude to Sir Adam.

"Misread the date?" He questioned her on the matter. "She told him that she had read it hastily, and taken a nine for a seven." She had left the letter in Brixton she said.

"So that had you come on the day Lady Youdale set, you would have arrived after Sir Adam had left for Holland? I mean, supposing that nothing had happened to him."

"Yes. What of it, Mr. Pointer?" she asked defensively. He did not answer her. She herself had put forward the date of her visit. Seeing what had happened, this might be of capital importance. Pointer now referred to her own recent trial. He did it bluntly, as was his way when he had to do anything unpleasant, his idea then being that speed helped. What he was after was her feeling towards Sir Adam, which would be much more certainly and surely shown by talk about the case than by any direct questioning. She answered very guardedly and briefly, but, he nevertheless got an impression of red-hot resentment against the man who had so successfully defended her. A silence had followed to her last words, and Pointer was standing gazing meditatively down at his shoes when the door burst open and Reggie Youdale stepped in and closed it swiftly behind him.

"I will see you this once, after all," he said in doing so. Then seeing the chief inspector as well he stopped. "There

148 *A Resurrected Press Mystery*

is no reason why you should not do my chair covers next, as you wished." Reggie went on to Miss Luton. "I came to tell you so." And he left as abruptly as he had entered.

Pointer caught him up in the hall.

"Can I have a word with you?" he asked. "Certainly." Reggie looked apathetic indifference. "Where would you like it?"

"We've rather made the library our headquarters, if you really have no preference..."

Reggie's silence said that he really had not, and they went in together.

"It's about Miss Luton," Pointer began confidentially. "Why did she hate your uncle?"

Reggie drew in a breath as though he had been struck. His white face could hardly grow whiter, but it seemed to fall in.

"I suppose she dislikes anything and everything that reminds her of the—awful—experience through which she has just gone," he said tonelessly. "Besides—why do you ask me about Miss Luton? Ask her herself." His voice was low and flat.

Pointer stepped into the room where Nicholson sat. The solicitor was alone for the moment.

"Mr. Nicholson," Pointer said. The solicitor was just putting up for the night, and looked thoroughly tired out. "Mr. Reginald Youdale is a friend of yours, isn't he?"

Nicholson said "yes," and looked his inquiry. "What is wrong with him?" Pointer asked. Nicholson looked really surprised. Again he had been immersed in the work in hand and had given Reggie but a passing thought of sympathy.

"That's not natural grief," Pointer went on. "Something horrible has got at him. Something that he's too young—and possibly too soft—to withstand. It's eating his heart out."

Nicholson stared. Instinctively he had a tremendous respect for the opinions of the young man beside him, but surely these words were a little strong.

The Westwood Mystery 149

"And what was there between Mr. Reginald Youdale and Miss Luton?" Pointer persisted.

"Nothing whatever," Nicholson said blankly, adding, "as far as I know," but in a tone that suggested that that caution was merely a form of speech and that he, Nicholson, had no doubts as to his knowledge covering all the case. "He once spent a vacation down at her father's farm, so, when she was arrested on the charge of murdering her baby, he gave her my name as a solicitor. He's been profoundly sorry for her during the trial, as we all were."

"Including Sir Adam?" Pointer asked briefly.

"Certainly including Sir Adam," Nicholson said warmly. "Sir Adam believed implicitly in her innocence, and worked like a Trojan to get her off. Only he could have done it. I was afraid it would be guilty and a recommendation for mercy when I took up the case."

Mademoiselle came in at this moment.

"You, Mademoiselle, must have heard Sir Adam discuss the case often. Mr. Pointer wants to be quite sure that Sir Adam believed in Miss Luton's innocence."

She made no comment, but went on putting papers together and slipping rubber bands over them, ready for work tomorrow.

"You don't agree," Pointer said instantly.

"Certainly," she replied. "Only Sir Adam could have got her off."

"I don't mean that. I mean that you don't agree with Mr. Nicholson that Sir Adam really believed in her innocence," he said again.

"Officially, or should I say professionally, he was sure," was her reply.

"But personally?" he insisted, while Nicholson stared at her in amazement.

"What I think he thought personally is hardly evidence, is it?" she parried.

"It would be of value just now," he replied gravely.

"I wonder why? But since you say so, then—in confidence—purely between ourselves—Sir Adam was certain that she was guilty, but he was very sorry for her. He thought she was desperate. Sick of her life as it was, and seeing only one way to get out of it—marriage—which the child, the unwanted child, prevented."

"Marriage to Mr. Manning?" he asked.

Nicholson was silent. He could hardly believe his ears. He did not believe them. He did not believe that the Frenchwoman was telling the truth.

"Yes, Mr. Manning wanted to marry her," Mademoiselle agreed, as though answering the question. The solicitor could be silent no longer.

"Mademoiselle, you amaze me! Sir Adam and I had many a talk over Miss Luton, of course. And never once did he give me any reason to doubt but that his defense of her was founded on his sincere and honest conviction."

"We are talking of two different things," she said to that. "You spoke to him professionally, and professionally he was always certain of his client's innocence. But I refer to his private opinion. Which was generally quite another matter."

"You amaze me—in this case." Nicholson was aware of that absolute cleavage in Youdale between the barrister's and the man's opinions, but in the Luton case he felt certain that Sir Adam, like himself, really did hold the woman to be the victim of most unfortunate circumstances.

"Did Mr. Reginald Youdale as well as Mr. Manning want to marry her?" Pointer asked next. Nicholson stared again. Really, if Scotland Yard men went in for wild guesses and mad notions like...

"I think he alone can tell you that," came mademoiselle's slow reply.

"He's more likely to tell it to you, Mr. Nicholson," Pointer said. "And I came in here to ask you to have a talk with him. He needs help. Something is eating into

The Westwood Mystery

his heart, as I said. You might be able to get him to speak of it. And even that alone would be a relief to him."

Nicholson went to have the suggested talk. He felt as though the solid ground were shifting under his feet.

Adam Youdale—a disbeliever in Miss Luton. And his nephew suggested as being in love with her—a horrible mist seemed to blur his usually clear vision. He saw—dimly—shapes that he preferred not to watch.

"Poor Mr. Nicholson," mademoiselle said as the door shut after him. "You've shaken him up. He was so certain. But if he reflected, he would know that the last thing Sir Adam, or any good counsel for the defense would do, would be to let the solicitor who briefed him know that he was not certain of their mutual client's innocence. Mr. Nicholson was certain... Sir Adam appeared to be.... They worked in perfect harmony."

"Now about Mr. Reginald Youdale." Pointer, dropped his voice. "He came here late last evening, asked urgently for his uncle, but seems to have been willing to wait until this morning."

"After a word with his aunt—" mademoiselle said meaningly.

"Miss Luton we know was here yesterday evening too. Now that we are by ourselves, Mademoiselle, can you assure me that as far as you know, Mr. Reginald Youdale did not intend to marry Miss Luton, or that she did not think he meant to do so? And that his uncle opposed the marriage?"

Mademoiselle fingered the papers in front of her. Her face was troubled.

"Miss Le Brun," Pointer said as gravely as before, "you know that if you hold back information in a murder investigation, you may be charged with being an accessory after the fact?" And then he repeated his question.

"It's terrible," she said slowly. "Terrible! I cannot think she had anything to do with Sir Adam's murder. I know it sounds impertinent to a detective of your

152   *A Resurrected Press Mystery*

standing, but, to a logical mind, the criminal here is most certainly Mr. Sturge. But, of course, there is this other possibility"—she stopped as though lost in contemplating the new idea.

"There are several possibilities," Pointer said quietly. "Now about Miss Luton."

"Personally I think she was innocent of the charge they brought against her." Mademoiselle spoke firmly. "But you are not interested in my opinion. Nor in that other case. Sir Adam was perfectly certain that she was guilty. But it was a certainty based only on his personal belief, and for once, he was mistaken. I feel quite sure of that."

"And his nephew?" Pointer asked.

She sighed. "I hope I'm not leading you on to it false trail. As I say, feeling sure she was innocent of that other charge, I cannot easily believe her guilty of this. Though, of course, she may have been goaded to mad fury by Sir Adam. In that interview—"

"Which interview?" Pointer asked, frowning a little. "Will you please tell me all you know on this matter. Miss Luton's relationship to Mr. Reginald Youdale and to his uncle."

"He, Sir Adam, understood that Mr. Manning was going to marry her," mademoiselle said in her unhurried way. "We all thought that—during the trial, I mean. But when she came down here, after it was over, to thank Sir Adam, she met Lady Youdale—by chance, he thought. Sir Adam was angry. He was not in love with his wife, but there is a respect due to the lady of the house which he would never forget. He told me that he spoke brusquely and, intentionally, rather brutally to Miss Luton, letting her see that in spite of having been her defender so recently, he did not think her innocent, and fit to meet his wife. She flared up at him. I do not wonder! And told him that she was about to marry his nephew, Reginald. This was the first time that he had heard of there being any love affair between the two. He warned her he would

The Westwood Mystery 153

certainly prevent the marriage. At that, Sir Adam said, in telling me about it, she raved like a lunatic. He thought she acknowledged that she was guilty. I do not think her words necessarily meant or mean that..." Mademoiselle rolled her fountain-pen to and fro. "He said that she screamed out, and Sir Adam had a marvelous memory for words. 'You think I murdered my baby? Well, do you think that a woman who had done that in order to marry a man would let that man's uncle come between her and the marriage?' She said it with a ferocity that touched him. It showed such passionate feeling. But he also thought it an acknowledgment that he was right. Also he was shocked beyond measure to learn that it was for Reginald, not for Mr. Manning, that she had drowned her baby—if she had done it. As for me, as I say, I do not think her guilty—of that first crime. Of this other..." She bit her lip and shook her head slowly.

"She is evidently a woman of impulse," she added in a tone of regret. "Which is a pretty way of saying—an animal. But to go on with my account of this affair. Reginald Youdale was away at the moment. He was flying over to Paris for a day and had an accident in getting into the plane. Not at all serious, but he strained a ligament of his knee. He got back last night, apparently. I saw him and he said he had not seen Sir Adam, as Lady Youdale thought he ought to wait till this morning. Lady Youdale seems to be connected with Miss Luton's visit to the house and with Mr. Youdale's," she added slowly.

"Just what do you mean by that?" Pointer asked her.

"Nothing more than I say," she replied composedly. "But it is odd, is it not?" And she gave him a little nod as she wished him good-night.

Meanwhile, Nicholson had found Reggie pacing the floor like an animal trying to see some way out. He turned his ravaged young face to Nicholson and the solicitor was shocked at the change in it. Yes, the chief inspector was right, something was gnawing at the heart of Reginald Youdale. For a second the two looked at each other—across a deep gulf, Nicholson would have said, the gulf of some dreadful knowledge on the younger man's part. Nicholson went forward instantly. "Reggie, let me help!"

"I'm in the most awful difficulty," Reggie replied in a low, monotonous voice as though feeling itself had gone numb by now. "You're working with the police, aren't you?"

"We are working together to find your uncle's murderer. But I'm your family solicitor, Reggie, first, and foremost, and always."

Nicholson's warm handclasp affected the distraught young man deeply. He fairly clung to the fingers as he said with a deep sigh, "Then, in confidence, tell me what, in God's name, I ought to do. She's murdered my uncle, Nicholson! I'm as certain of it as I can be of anything. Murdered him because she saw, as I found out, that he would never have consented to our marriage, and I have to have his consent to get my mother's money, you know, if I marry before I am thirty." Reggie's words staggered Nicholson.

"I had a visit from him at the nursing home at Châlons," Reggie went on. "He only came over for the day. He told me that I must not marry Annabelle Luton."

"But—did you mean to?" Nicholson asked in amazement.

"Of course I did! That's why I told her to go to you. Because I loved her and wanted to help her so badly. I would have told everybody, only she wouldn't hear of it, before the trial. She absolutely forbade it. I never doubted her for a moment," Reggie went on. "You don't doubt people you love. But my uncle"—he passed a hand across his forehead—"he changed all that. His certainty as to her guilt, I mean. He told me I had no right to marry her, to bring that taint into the family, and I agreed with him."

The Westwood Mystery   155

"Well, I should hope so!" came fervently from Nicholson.

"Not at first," Reggie said defensively, "but his certainty—he's such a clever chap. Was. Good God," he broke out passionately. "I'm in the most horrible position. I feel as if I must jump under the next train and end it. She murdered her baby in order to marry me, according to my uncle, and now she's murdered him in order not to have him come between us. I told her last night I wouldn't marry her until he changed his opinion. I had to say something. She pleaded with me so, and I was foolish enough to say that as long as he took the stand he did about her guilt, so long I couldn't go back to the old feeling. As a matter of fact, I never could have anyway, but that was a damnable thing to say to a girl who was weeping on your neck, and swearing that nothing mattered but you."

"When was this?" Nicholson asked mechanically.

"Last night she was in my room—measuring for covers, she said. When I went up to it, she—it was horrible, Nicholson. Once I knew my uncle believed her guilty, he with his judgment, his knowledge of all the facts, I—well—something had changed entirely in me. I thought I loved her—I honestly thought I did. I wanted to marry her and go abroad with her to start another life— but his certainty as to her guilt—" Reggie shook his head. "She grasped it finally," he went on with a white smile, "and flew into his room to wait for him. She said she had an excuse—the covers. But someone—it was you, I now know, came with him. She slipped into the bathroom and out by its door, then she came into my room again, and again we had a scene. The upshot was that she went off simply demented against him. Raving like a mad woman." Reggie looked ill at the recollection. "I shouldn't have thought I could have slept after all that, but I did! Slept like a log! Now what am I to do? There's not a chance in my mind but that she did it—murdered my uncle, I mean. And if so, I can't let her escape. And yet—

156   *A Resurrected Press Mystery*

and yet"—his anguished eyes looked out of his set face—
"it was done for me. Because of my words about our
marriage depending on him entirely."

"You leave it to me," Nicholson said after, a moment's
deep thought. "You've told me the facts now. Don't brood
over them any more. If she is guilty, re-assured she'll be
found out. I shall say nothing unless I have to, and it will
not come through you in any case. The chief inspector is
as thorough and as astute a chap as they have at the
Yard. He won't let the right person slip through his
fingers, of that I'm convinced." And Nicholson proceeded
to speak further words of comfort to the stricken nephew.

But Reggie refused to be comforted. "A woman would
murder her own baby, such a jolly little chap too,
Nicholson, would do anything else."

Pointer meanwhile had asked for another word with
mademoiselle. She came down to the library at once.

"That watching man whom you saw, when Sturge
jumped across the patch of light. Could he have been Mr.
Reginald Youdale?"

Evidently the idea was new to her. She thought a
moment. "No," she said finally. "Mr. Sturge and he were
on the same level for a second or so, and he was taller
than Mr. Sturge and broader shouldered. Reginald is
shorter and much slighter in build."

"Could it have been Mr. Manning?" This was the man
whom, offhand, Pointer would have expected it to be of
the two. Again she thought before replying. Now she
nodded. "Very easily."

Pointer knew from Claxton that Mr. Manning too put
up for the last night at the *Sun in Splendor*. He also
knew that the young farmer had left around eight o'clock
this morning, as he had arranged when arriving, saying
that he was merely staying the one night. Claxton had
promptly ticked him off as an "outsider" whose
movements were of no interest. Pointer now went again
to the hostelry in question. He had a word with the
proprietor, and then left the questions to him. Captain

The Westwood Mystery 157

Yates came back in a short time and shut the door of his private flat carefully behind him.

"You're right, Chief Inspector. The man you're interested in was out until all hours. The night porter says Mr. Manning came in around one o'clock, and walked as though he had had a glass too much. Lurched a bit and stared with a stony glassy eye."

Pointer learned that no one had seen Manning go out, which meant that it must have been before eleven, and probably before ten, as the inn had but one main door, which was more or less closed at ten and locked at eleven.

"He does not seem to've lain down at all," the proprietor went on. "According to the chambermaid the bed was not touched, but the carpet was! He spent the hours tramping to and fro, with muddy boots evidently."

Pointer asked if he could see the room. Unfortunately it had been already done up. Pointer's keen eyes told him nothing. A try with fingerprint powder yielded many blurred prints but nothing clear, the only objects that might have retained one having been already in the too efficient hands of the chambermaid. He noted the room's position in the house—it was some distance from Gaudet's—and with that he had to be content for the moment. He walked the short distance to Westwood deep in reverie. The lighted window that mademoiselle had said she saw a man watching might well have been Reginald Youdale's, and if the watcher were Manning, and the light showed him Youdale and Miss Luton together, or if the curtains let their silhouettes be distinguished, it was possible that here was but a jealous lover watching his loved one talking to his hated rival. Pointer could guess very much how the interview in the young man's room had gone. Annabelle Luton would not have given up easily. She would have thrown her arms around Reggie, kissed him or tried to...

Pointer could imagine the young farmer watching a maddening scene. Again, as in the case of Sturge, as in the case of the French couple, Manning's actions were

158   A Resurrected Press Mystery

susceptible to two opposite interpretations. They might be those of innocence as far as the murder of Sir Adam Youdale went, or they might not. It distinguished this case to Pointer that, so far, this possible. double explanation seemed to run with all the facts as yet unlearned. Miss Luton might well be the criminal, but, if so, another hand than hers had placed that rose beside the bed. Some other person, coming on that murdered body, in that case, seemed to have tried to drawn the attention of the police to the criminal. But to whom did they think that the rose pointed? To Lady Youdale? To Miss Luton? Or to Manning? Pointer saw no light as yet on the three odd items to which he had referred when talking to Nicholson, and as yet no light came from them either. Possibly their meaning could only be read at the very end. Certainly, as far as Annabelle Luton was concerned, she seemed to have as big a motive to murder Adam Youdale as had Sturge. With both of them time would have counted. Both had opportunity too.

In her case the prize of security and wealth, and the position of a baronet's wife might be even greater.

Moreover, Miss Luton seemed to have made the opportunity for herself. That so-called misreading of the date, was it genuine? By it, at any rate, she had arrived at Westwood before Sir Adam left, instead of after it. But was it possible that Lady Youdale and she had arranged that mistake? Pointer, though he turned the thought over in his mind, could see no support for it, except the friendliness of Sir Adam's wife to the girl, her way of almost smuggling her into the house last night. And though there might be something intricate and deep here, so far the chief inspector rather fancied that Lady Youdale was merely helping to bring Reggie and Annabelle Luton together in order to spite her husband. Nothing would have galled him more, nothing would have cut him deeper—barring anything connected with mademoiselle than for his nephew to marry the young woman whom the French girl maintained that he

The Westwood Mystery 159

believed to be guilty. Yes, so far, Pointer thought that Lady Youdale had merely snatched at the chance of playing a spiteful game against the man who had shown that he wanted to be free of her. If so, what about Reginald He had opportunity but a weak motive. Merely that he could not marry before thirty without his uncle's consent and have the handling of his mother's money. Reggie would be handed over, metaphorically speaking, to one of Pointer's men, but the chief inspector did not expect to have to consider him as the criminal. Came Manning next. He also had opportunity to a lesser extent, unless he had a helper in the house, but had he any motive? Pointer could see no reason why he should murder Sir Adam. Rather the other way. The barrister's life stood between the marriage of his nephew and Miss Luton. No, Manning could be left to Superintendent Claxton as hitherto and Pointer at last could turn his steps towards the latter's police station and his own bed. Claxton called out to him as he was tiptoeing past the bedroom of his host, and Pointer gave him full details.

Claxton heard him in silence. Then he frowned rather wearily.

"Even so, they don't come up to Sturge in my opinion, I mean Miss Luton doesn't. Love's all very well, but money makes the most criminals. And a woman's threats never seem to me very reliable. True, she stood to gain more by Youdale's death—she gets a baronet as a husband, but Sturge stood to lose his liberty and his money... no, I still think it's Sturge. Don't you?" he asked quickly as Pointer was silent.

"The French couple are odd," Pointer murmured half to himself, "especially Monsieur Gaudet..." and he proceeded to give the superintendent a sleepless night by telling him of the ripped and re-sewn mattress, of the something hidden which had been taken away.

Claxton gave a grunt of disgust at the tangles in the case and implored the other to go to bed before he learned of a fresh one.

CHAPTER NINE

Pointer was early at Westwood next morning, but another visitor was there before him. He learned over the telephone that Manning had driven up just after seven, and asked for Miss Luton. The police had no power to prevent the interview or to listen to it, especially as she came downstairs and carried Manning off to the tennis courts, on whose asphalt surface they spent quite ten minutes in very eager conversation. That much Pointer knew. When he arrived Manning was waiting for him in the drive smoking his pipe and looking, on the whole, at peace with the world. A resolute face this, Pointer thought, narrow and obstinate, and the face of a man who was capable of bouts of violent temper.

"I hope you don't mind my coming to see Miss Luton," Manning said pleasantly, introducing himself, "she and I are engaged to be married, you know. Or rather, she wouldn't tell you so, it seems, because of not wanting to drag me into this dreadful business. We've been engaged for months. Capital and to spare was made out of it at her trial," he added with sudden passion, his eyes flaming, "it's enough to make one believe in the old Greek furies that she of all girls should have been in this house the night before last. But I want to get her out of it all. You've no objection, I suppose, to my taking her away at once? We'll be married by special license, change our name, and go out to a fruit ranch in Canada that I've already bought."

"You were down here the night of Sir Adam's murder," Pointer said, without answering the question of the marriage; "you called to see Sir Adam, I understand. Why?"

"To ask if Miss Luton was here. I wanted to see her. She wasn't at her aunt's—but Sir Adam didn't know of her arrival, and so I went back home next morning. There the papers told me of his ghastly end, and that Miss Luton was here after all."

Pointer decided that Manning was by no means as simple as he looked.

"But why did you object so strongly to her being under Sir Adam's roof?" Pointer went on.

"Jealousy," Manning answered, with that seeming complete frankness that masked a good deal—in the chief inspector's opinion. "Jealousy. Mr. Reginald Youdale was a good friend to Miss Luton and I always feared he would like to be something more. But it was all right. They are just good friends, nothing more."

"Sir Adam was as keen as you that they should not both be here at the same time, I understand," Pointer said to that. He was sorry for Manning, but this was a murder hunt. Feelings were of no account compared with getting at facts. Again that flame shone red in the young farmer's blue eyes, his strong yellow teeth showed a little as he said with studied calm:

"Very possibly. He too knew how charming Miss Luton is. He would not want his nephew to lose his heart to a girl who was going to marry another man."

"What did you yourself do night before last, Mr. Manning?" Pointer asked next.

"I came down here for a talk with Miss Luton," Manning said again, "missed her, spent the night at the *Sun in Splendor* near by, and went home by the first possible train next morning."

"Did you spend the night—all of it—at the *Sun*. Or did you go out at all?"

"I went for a walk, as I invariably do just after ten, lost my way, and got back rather late."

"At what time did you get back?" Pointer inquired next.

The Westwood Mystery 163

Manning named the hour that the hotel proprietor had given.

"Did you pass by Westwood on your walk?" Pointer asked, after a long pause. A pause which Manning bore without fidgeting.

"Close by. You see, I don't know Wimbledon, and at first I kept to the part of the common that lies this end. Then I strayed in deeper, and lost my way."

"Had you your glasses with you? Field-glasses of some kind, I mean?"

The pause this time was on Manning's side. "No," he said finally.

"Yet we have learned that you were seen watching this house through field-glasses around midnight, watching for a long time, Mr. Manning. Watching Mr. Youdale and Miss Luton talking together in his room. The curtains were not drawn, as they usually are. You stood against a tree just where there is a gap in the hedge."

Pointer glanced at his note-book as he detailed these bits. Manning changed color.

"You've caught me out," he said with an effort at a pleasant smile. "Yes, I did see Miss Luton, as you say, she and Mr. Youdale were talking over the case that's just finished. I didn't understand her presence in his room— as a matter of fact, as you know, she is taking the measurements for new covers for the chairs in the house—her aunt is to make them—and Mr. Youdale found her in his room and they got into talk. I didn't know this, and, of course—naturally—I watched them. I confess that having folding glasses on me, I always carry a pair, I'm a nature observer—I used them for a while until someone passed, and I realized that my being there might give rise to misunderstandings. Then I went on with my walk." Again there was a pause. "About our marriage?" Manning began. "I don't suppose you can stop it, and my taking her away afterwards?"

164   *A Resurrected Press Mystery*

"Oh, yes, we could issue a writ for her presence at the inquest, and should do so if she tried to leave this part of England," Pointer replied in a very official tone. Manning looked as though he would let the temper that showed in his face get the better of him.

"Mr. Manning," Pointer said quietly, "you, know the real facts of the case, as concerning Miss Luton, Mr. Youdale, and his uncle Sir Adam—know that there is a very good case possible against Miss Luton. Don't force me to take her into custody."

"You're not going to arrest her!" Manning said hoarsely, the color drained from his weather beaten face. "Not a second time! Not on another murder charge!" His face was twisted with pain as he spoke.

"Not as things are at the moment," Pointer repeated. He could say nothing more comforting. "But I really think you had better not try to help her to get away, Mr. Manning."

Manning looked at him. Pointer felt that something was given up in that moment. Some hasty notion of spiriting Miss Luton away. The door opened. Pointer had given orders from now on that there was to be no "guard" at the door. Miss Luton came in, a length of some gay flowering material over her arm. She let it drop in quite unprofessional carelessness, and stepped on it as she saw Manning's expression.

"Whatever is the matter now?" she asked in a hard defiant voice.

"Mr. Manning has been telling me that he would like to marry you by special license, and take you away at once," Pointer said to her, "but I told him it would be better to wait a while."

She looked at him bleakly. Pointer was profoundly sorry for her—if she was innocent. A blunder on the part of the law, and she might easily have again to fight for her very existence. "I had no idea you were to be married," he went on, "when I talked to you a little while ago; you did not refer to it."

The Westwood Mystery 165

"It was understood by everybody that we were to be married," she replied in a curiously even tone.

Pointer looked across at Manning, who reluctantly left the room.

"I understood that it was Mr. Reginald Youdale whom you were going to marry," the chief inspector said easily.

"Reginald Youdale!" The scorn in her voice would have cut through steel. "Who on earth told you such a story?"

"I heard it from more than one person."

"Then please tell the more than one person that it is a lie," she said through clenched teeth. "A lie! I wouldn't marry him—I wouldn't marry him"—her breath came in gasps—"any more than he would marry me," she finished proudly. Pointer was measuring her inner stature as she stood there. This was a woman capable, when sufficiently stirred, of a great deal, he thought. She was a woman of great vitality, and she had no work to interest her. She had kept house for her father at his farm. She was not interested in any form of country life, except golf and tennis, both taken up probably with the intention of bettering her social position. Given a character such as hers, with no other outlet, love would go deep, and run swift—love, and its reverse, hate. Her large powerful hands were clenched at her sides as she spoke. They looked quite capable of having held that weighted pillow on the drugged man's face until he ceased to breathe. A marriage to Reginald Youdale would have benefited her enormously. Besides lifting her into quite another world, socially; besides giving her wealth as well, it would have proclaimed definitely that her innocence, in the terrible charge once brought against her, was founded on a rock. She was sick of her old life, that had been amply brought out at the trial, here would indeed have been a fresh start. And one which this woman could have used. Pointer could visualize her in another ten years' time as a social leader, in spite of her old story. Yes, he could imagine how Adam Youdale's refusal to allow the marriage, supposing Mademoiselle Le Brun had told him the truth about the dead barrister's feelings—had been as vitriol on Annabelle Luton's high spirit and determination to rise. He now let her, go after Manning without another word. She had cared for Reginald, that much he was sure of from her look and tone. Was this then just a crime of sudden fury and balked ambition? Somehow, he doubted that.

He was wanted on the telephone. A "Mr. Waters" wanted to speak to him.

That meant Captain Meredith—for today. He changed his "phone name" daily. He was speaking through a man at the Yard who could rattle off the Yard's code as well as English. Pointer jotted down the extraordinary message and decoded it a moment later in his head. It was about Youdale's Tangiers villa. Or rather about the land on both sides of it. Meredith's informant, an Arab, who apparently earned his living by hawking carpets about the streets—told him that from secret sources, he knew that the land on both sides of the villa had been bought in small lots, and, though standing in other names, the real purchaser, each time, was a Mademoiselle Le Brun. Yes, that was the name on the Register of Owners. She started her buying about two years ago. And had spent smallish sums almost monthly since then. In all, she had spent around four hundred pounds up to date, getting the land at very reasonable prices. There was nothing whatever on it, and it was not cultivable. Probably she was buying it as a good speculation, the Arab had added, as she had forestalled the increase in values which is around there just beginning. Meredith himself now went onto say that he always kept his eye on the price of land. One got wind of strange happenings beforehand that way, and sometimes a fall, or a rise, was the only warning. That finished the coded message. In another half hour Pointer received a call on the 'phone from Paris.

From the Yard's agent there he received a detail account of Mademoiselle Le Brun's life. It bore out every one of her statements, adding nothing of any importance whatever at first.

"I asked you particularly to try and link up the name of a Monsieur Gaudet with her, or her family," Pointer said, when this part of the report was over.

"I know. Told me to dig down to China, if need be. The laugh at the other end came through with startling clearness. "I have found a distant link. Mademoiselle Léonie Le Brun was engaged to another citizen of Dijon, a Henri Jussin. That was before the father lost all his money. The engagement seems to have been broken off then, except that this same Monsieur Jussin acted as her proxy a couple of years ago when it was a question of receiving a small legacy, which looks as though the engagement still smouldered along underground, so to speak." Pointer listened to Jussin's description. It would have fitted Gaudet perfectly.

"Where does the name of Gaudet come in?" he asked.

"Jussin's mother is put down in the town records as being a Mlle. Gaudet of Saint Nazaire. Knowing your thirst for the last drop, I have ascertained from Saint Nazaire that a widow of that name lived there until recently, when she went out to join her son, who is the French postmaster at Rufa. They have no other relatives except this cousin Henri Jussin. Henri Jussin is in the French Colonial service. He is attached to the *Bureaux Arabes dans L'Oran*. As for the other, the postmaster, he's had extra leave granted him, after nearly dying of malaria, and is spending the first few days of it in England." That was all. Again it was enough. So Gaudet the postmaster of Rufa had a cousin Jussin who evidently resembled him exactly, as far as descriptions went, and who was in the French Native Intelligence Office. Pointer did some brain work, then he tried for Captain Meredith on the 'phone again, and after a little chase was put in touch with him. Did he know anything of a Henri Jussin? Of the *Bureaux Arabes*? "Did he not!" came a fervent reply, not in code this time. "As clever a chap as the

168   *A Resurrected Press Mystery*

French Colonial Service has. He's on leave somewhere. Have you run up against him? If so, I should be very glad to know where."

"I rather fancy I shall be able to let you know shortly, sir. But there's one very important question which will help to settle it. Has Jussin ever had malaria badly?"

"He's immune. Why?"

"I'll tell you when I see you, sir. Excuse my asking, but are you quite certain? The point's most important."

"I'm absolutely certain. He's been chosen more than once for that reason alone to act as the bearer of important messages to some Touareg chief. He can sleep on the ground, they say, and he's never even been inoculated."

Pointer thanked him, and said he hoped to be in at the F.O. very shortly. Putting down the instrument, he sent one of his men to get that speckled handkerchief away from Gaudet at the *Sun in Splendor* by hook or by crook. The chief inspector had it within ten minutes. It had taken no hooking or crooking to obtain. Immediately on Pointer's departure after his short talk with him yesterday morning, Gaudet had cut his finger sharpening a penknife, cut it in full view of the inn's one and only porter, and, after staunching it with his handkerchief, had gone to his room, tossed the stained square of silk into the soiled linen basket, and returned with a fresh square. All the Yard man had had to do was to pick it out of his basket. Pointer was delighted. So Gaudet, as soon as he had given himself an excuse in public for any marks on his handkerchief, had changed it for a fresh one. He whisked himself, and it, up to town at top speed, and within a very short time was handing it over to an analyst—for the blood of a man who has had malaria severely many times can always be identified. Gaudet was on sick leave, and Jussin his cousin was immune, Meredith said. The analyst would soon settle which cousin had come down to Westwood. He did. The man whose blood was on the handkerchief—it was all the

The Westwood Mystery 169

same blood, specks and broad mark of a staunched cut—had never had a serious bout of malaria in his life. So Pointer now knew, not merely suspected, that it was Henri Jussin with whom he had to deal.

And he duly passed on the information to Captain Meredith.

"Here's his picture, if you want to make sure. What gave you the—idea?" Meredith slid a photograph across to the other. "Well? Is he the man?"

"He looks like him." Pointer only glanced at the portrait. "But evidently he and his cousin are very much alike, for the most detailed description of Gaudet fits the man down at Wimbledon, but the blood test proves that it's Jussin." He explained about the handkerchief.

"Good egg!" Meredith went through the motion of clapping his hands. "That's better than any picture. Well, since it's Jussin down there, and he's under another name, you may be sure he's on something important.

"Would hidden treasure explain it?" Pointer asked. Meredith did not answer for a moment.

"In spite of the cistern repairs at the villa, I don't see Jussin on a treasure hunt," he said finally. "He'd melt every ingot in the world to make another step up his political stairway, but apart from that use, I should say that money doesn't exist for him. That's one of the reasons he's so respected. He's incorruptible. Let me have a look at that map again." Meredith bent over it with furrowed brow. Then he looked at a list of names and measurements that he had in a drawer, they had just been rushed to him, then he drew some outlines and juggled a little with a ruler.

"Look here, Chief Inspector, I had just got the information for you that a good deal of quiet buying up of land is going on apart from the secretary's little bits, I mean. It is whispered that the French government is going to buy a stretch close by, that has most unexpectedly come into the market, owing to the death of a wealthy Arab. They give out that it's to be a French cemetery, but what I see is this—" Meredith pushed his drawing across to the other. "Put all together, with just a few more plots added, and you get a splendid landing ground for sea-planes; and along a region that, as it happens, lends itself unusually well to fortifications. But the villa commands the lot. It and the bits owned by Mademoiselle Le Brun. So the government must have Youdale's house, or all the rest is of no military use whatever. As it's Jussin you've got down at Westwood, then this is much more in his line than hidden gold."

"And would be tremendously important for him to succeed in?" Pointer said slowly, half to himself.

"Rather! He's had such damned bad luck lately." Something in the grin that accompanied the words suggested that Jussin's bad luck was not entirely unconnected with the young man in front of Pointer. "Oh, yes, rather!" Meredith repeated, "when it's a question of plane-landings or fortifications, the French, like all of us just now, are going all out. Jussin, if he's been told to go after anything like this, could have the crown of France if he succeeded, and will be left to collect tickets on the Paris underground if he fails. He's a poor man. And keen as mustard."

"Did he ever have any job that took him much out into society?" Pointer asked.

"Very much so. He was French instructor at the Caid's College in Fez for a while, and then civilian aide-de-camp to the governor. He's more or less that still. His especial business is to meet Europeans, and natives, and explain them to one another. Sort of job that suits him down to the ground. He'd let himself be cut in pieces for *La Patrie*."

"I wonder if he would have smothered Sir Adam. Youdale for the same end?" Pointer asked promptly.

Meredith was heartless enough to give a chuckle, though he looked shocked at the sound himself. "I'd prefer not to say," he said. "If Youdale had promised this Frenchwoman the villa on his death, and if she was to be

The Westwood Mystery 171

trusted—from Jussin's point of view—and there seemed reason to fear that Youdale would change his mind, or that the secretary would have to wait until his death before she got hold of the place I wouldn't bet on Jussin's actions."

Meredith was making some notes as he talked. He was intensely grateful for the, to him, unimportant murder which had brought this possible field of action of Jussin's to light.

"And there's another little *dot* of news I've collected for you," he went on, pen between his teeth as he blotted some word. "I had a talk over the telephone with an old friend of mine, a French barrister. He says that the late Maitre Le Brun was the same type as Jussin. The kind to sacrifice not only himself but his nearest and dearest for France, for her prestige, for her extension. I mention it, because it may prove useful to know."

Pointer told him that it was. Miss Le Brun, who inherited her father's brains apparently, might well have inherited this attitude of mind. Indeed, it was hard to see how she could escape it. Given a father whom she evidently revered, who had sacrificed so much for her, his opinions must carry weight. Youdale had said that he would not part with the villa under any circumstances, yet she had bought the land on both sides as though expecting to get hold of it.

The chief inspector returned to Westwood thinking overall that he had learned. These were all only possibilities, of one thing Pointer was certain. He had never seen a man who, in his own quiet way, could be more terrible than Monsieur Jussin. He was of the Lenin type, capable of the most impersonal ferocity.

And, now that Pointer knew that the magnet might be political, the papers hidden in the mattress and taken out again, by the secretary, might easily be quite unconnected with the murder down at Westwood. The same was true of mademoiselle's refusal to be searched, if she had a letter from, or to, Jussin on her, which would give his real name and position away, let alone some indication of the reason for his presence at Wimbledon. On the whole, the fact that it was Jussin with whom he had to deal, only complicated matters. It suggested an adequate motive for a murder, but also an adequate motive for a great deal which, without it, was only capable of one interpretation.

Back to the papers that he had set aside for himself went the chief inspector. He finally disposed of all but one, a bill that had lain on the same shelf as the will, but which had either been put at the very back of the shelf, or had slipped or blown there. It was headed. *Anciente Thinges: Wimbledon High Street. G. Fullford* was given as the name of the proprietor, and the bill itself ran "To opening drawer-7/6." The date was some three weeks ago now. Tukes knew nothing about it. Neither did the housekeeper. Neither did the secretary. Neither did Lady Youdale. This general ignorance might be quite understandable, but it made Pointer all the more interested in the presumably small detail, which had needed the proprietor of an antique shop rather than a carpenter, or a handyman, to see to it. He was talking to Nicholson about it when Claxton came in. "It's the most amazing thing! Sturge's disappearance!" he muttered. "But of course with plenty of money, and plenty of time to make his plans, and knowing what might drop on his head any moment, he would have thought it all well out. I believe Lady Youdale knows where he is!" He looked interrogatively at Pointer, who nodded. He, too, thought that she did.

"Her husband's murderer!" Claxton said in shocked tones, to add: "But, of course, that would only make her all the more determined to hush it all up. It is a terrible position for her..." Claxton picked up the paper lying in front of the chief inspector.

"What's this? Ah, yes, Fullford's little shop. What interests you in it? Surely a man can't vanish into air? Sturge hasn't been seen... his car is in the car shed...

The Westwood Mystery 173

Who's Mr. Fullford? Oh, regular old antiquarian. Quite a decent old chap, but I don't see how he's going to help us."

"You mean you don't see his connection with Sturge," Pointer said quizzically. "Well, neither do I."

"I've had men questioning all the hotels and boarding-houses and apartment houses of Wimbledon and Putney Hill," the superintendent went on. "No suspicious characters can be traced as staying here night before last. It all comes back to Sturge, though I grant you there are perplexing bits—Miss Luton for one. And your French friends."

Claxton's tone of tolerance suggested that even in crime, the French must not be taken too seriously. It made Nicholson ask him whether he had been to see the French pictures in town yet.

Claxton stared at him. "Good Lord, no! The people here wouldn't like it. You've no idea how strict we have to be as to the shows we visit."

Nicholson decided in future to keep the conversation to the case in hand.

"I rather wanted a word with old Fullford anyway," Claxton now said. "My man couldn't get him on the 'phone yesterday. Mr. Fullford's the Wimbledon clock-winder and repairer. Day before yesterday was his day for seeing to the clocks here, Tukes says. Now, Fullford's a shrewd old fellow. Supposing there were anything to be seen or heard, he'd see or hear it. He might know something that would be of use... and this bill of his is a good excuse..."

Pointer intended having a word with the man who had opened the drawer without an excuse if need be... Nicholson was too busy to go, but he and the superintendent walked along together to the shop. It was quite nearby. The window showed only a stretch of petit point hung as a curtain across the back, and in front of it was a circular mirror set in pewter. The effect was unusual, and inspired confidence in the man who had

174   *A Resurrected Press Mystery*

arranged it. On the door a card was tacked. It ran, in tiny copper-plate writing:

> "Mr. Fullford is away on his rounds until further notice. A man attends to collect letters and take orders Wednesday morning. Other times, all inquiries to Mrs. Gay, 2 Pugh Cottages, Mile Lane."

Claxton decided, in view of the walk to Mile Lane, that he had some pressing work to see to, but he gave the chief inspector careful direction and in due course Pointer reached the little house. The reference to a drawer that had been opened of which no one seemed to know, might be merely a little bubble floating on the surface that would burst emptily as soon as touched, but it might mark the place where something really important lay hidden.

Mrs. Gay, when found, proved to be a singularly lugubrious lady, who looked after Mr. Fullford as much as he permitted. Pointer got an idea that he was not a grateful subject for fussing. The antique dealer lived in two rooms above his shop, the remaining two being let to a Mr. Jenkins, the man who, when its owner was away, attended to the shop on Wednesday mornings. Jenkins was an auctioneer in a small way. As to how long Mr. Fullford would likely be before he returned, Mrs. Gay, after a pause which suggested extreme punctiliousness with regard to hours, let alone dates, said that it "depended." Sometimes he would be gone for a week or longer, sometimes only for a day or two.

Finding that he could learn nothing from her, Pointer returned to the shop and rang the bell. Mr. Jenkins was in and opened the door. He confirmed Mrs. Gay's words that when Mr. Fullford left, there was no knowing when he would return.

"His idea is to go hunting around until he finds enough things that take his fancy, and then bring them

The Westwood Mystery   175

home and sell them before going out for another find. That way he doesn't have to tie up his money in a lot of stuff that no one wants. Safety first is old. Mr. Fullford's motter."

"We found a bill of his for opening a drawer. Would there be any counterfoils, do you think?"

"There'll be a duplicate," Jenkins said proudly, and pulling out a stubby book he turned up the number stamped on the bill that Pointer handed him. It proved to be only a duplicate. There was no added word.

"Does he keep no notes of his work anywhere?"

"Keeps a regular working diary, does Mr. Fullford. Here in this drawer. I'll show it yer. Mr. Fullford wouldn't mind. On the contrary. Fearful shock this murder of Sir Adam will be to him. And a great loss in business too. He sells quite a good deal to Sir Adam, first and last."

"Any idea in the neighborhood as to who the criminal is?" Pointer asked. Local gossip was sometimes of value, however undocumented it was sure to be.

Jenkins leaned forward mysteriously.

"You'll know more than you let on, sir," he said, nodding his head. "But I think we all say the same. What about a certain relation of his wife's? Eh? Rubber Trunks are tumbling headlong, they tell me. And you can't sell them at no price at all, I hear. Ah, this is the book."

Pointer turned the pages of the diary written in the microscopic hand which got more into the inch than most people could get into three. They found an entry, corresponding to the number and date on the bill—some three weeks old. It ran:

"Sir A. sent for me to open a secret drawer in Sheraton frame I sold him. Half hour's work. 7/6."

Then below, as though added later on in the day, came in still smaller writing:

"Papers inside. Sir A. very excited. Forgot to pay me. Memo. To charge to his next account.

There was no record after this in which Youdale's name appeared. Pointer had Jenkins copy out the entry for him and sign it. He asked him further to lock away the book until Mr. Fullford's return, of which he wished to be informed at once. "Not a word to anyone, Mr. Jenkins, please—Mr. Fullford will probably be ringing us up," the chief inspector added.

"Not he!" Mr. Jenkins interrupted. "Never reads anything in the papers. Says they're all lies and poison to the system. Says if you want to live long, as he does, living long is his hobby, you want never to open a newspaper. Always screws his eyes up a-passing hoardings." Mr. Jenkins wrinkled up his own to show him what he meant. "Won't hearken to a boy shouting 'all the winners' if he can help it. That's his hobby, too. Hating newspapers."

This was unfortunate. Mr. Fullford would have to be asked by the B.B.C. to return. But Jenkins promptly put a hole through that hope too.

"It'll be no use broadcasting for him neither," he went on with relish, "never goes near them. Never goes to movies or talkies. 'Rubbish' is what he calls them. He says to me often, 'Quiet is the hardest thing in the world to get, and the easiest to lose. Like independence.' And then he always goes on to say that people seem determined to throw both away. He holds on to his. An organ recital is Mr. Fullford's idea of having a really snappy time."

Fullford sounded like a sensible old gentleman, but not a very accessible one. He had no family, Jenkins said. He put his age at about seventy.

"At the beginning of life, according to him," Jenkins said with a laugh, "provided you leave newspapers alone."

"Is he a talkative man?" Pointer asked.

The Westwood Mystery 177

Jenkins shook his head. "Dissipates energy, he says. He's a man of one idear, is Mr. Fullford, to do nothing that would bring him early to his grave."

"Still, he must speak to people about the things he wants to sell, or how does he sell them?" Pointer asked.

"Prices is always penciled on the back," Jenkins explained. "'Take it, or leave it, but for Gawd's sake don't haggle,' is another of Mr. Fullford's motters." And, on that Pointer left him.

Back at the house, he went carefully over all the pictures or rather over all the frames. He knew that hiding places in them were quite frequent in the latter seventeenth and early eighteenth century, when safes were unknown, the times disturbed, and the distance from a bank often formidable. He decided that there were three possibles. On the back of one, an intricate piece of carving on very thick wood, he found a little label with the number 3080 on it in what he felt sure was Fullford's own writing. Back to the shop and Mr. Jenkins he went again. Jenkins was keen to help.

"Lot No. 3080," he murmured, going to a cupboard. "That'll be in this book, then. The thirty refers to the year. The eighty to the sale itself. Oh, Mr. Fullford has wonderful method!" It was plain that Jenkins had a great admiration for the gentleman who meant to see his century out. They found number eighty quite easily. It read:

Bought Atcherley sale, March 10th, £50.

Then came:

"Without pedigree. Modern artist. Frame c. 1800. I believe Sheraton, though maybe earlier. Possibly Chippendale in a rather ornate mood."

Below was hastily entered, as though Mr. Fullford considered this unimportant:"

178   *A Resurrected Press Mystery*

Family say late Mr. Atcherley bought picture and frame in a secondhand shop in Sydney, Australia."

Jenkins went out of the room to see if he could find any further notes or letters referring to the picture. But he found nothing more.

"Has Mr. Fullford any especial friend?" Pointer asked. It promised to be a slow business, this learning what the secret drawer in the frame had held, and yet it might be important, that re-sewn mattress might have held for a brief moment the contents of the secret drawer instead of political papers.

Mr. Jenkins decided that he came most under that heading. "Not that I'm his class," he added frankly. "Mr. Fullford is an old gent. A scholar. Why, he can read Latin as easily as you can English, sir. Knew what that motter around the mirror in the show-window meant as soon as he saw it. 'Look at yourself,' is what it means, he told me." And with vicarious pride Jenkins pointed to the *Bezee u selve* hammered on the pewter. This proof of Mr. Jenkins' classical learning passed without comment.

"What about customers of his?"

Jenkins shook his head. "Selling one thing at a time, his customers are pretty scattered. Sir Adam was his most regular one. Besides, he's done very little business lately. Like everyone else. The times is so bad, that the only inquiry I've had the whole this month when I've been minding the shop for him, was from one gent. And he never turned up. Something about a Raybun he'd asked for. I couldn't quite make out what the object was. These 'phones—" and Jenkins lost himself in comments on the telephone's vagaries.

Pointer left with a list of houses where customers of Mr. Fullford lived. As for the man who had asked about Raybuns, he had given his name as Myers, said he was staying at the *Sun in Splendor*. Pointer left the shop and walked on to the inn. This man, this Mr. Myers had asked about a Raeburn probably. It happened that that artist

The Westwood Mystery 179

was the chief inspector's favorite portrait painter, perhaps because his decision, and power, and simplicity appealed to the same qualities in the detective officer, and just because of his liking for his work, he had noticed that Sir Adam had a really noble example on his walls. Now, if this Myers were interested in Raeburns, he might well have come down to Wimbledon merely to see Youdale's, in which case it was possible that either Sir Adam himself, or Mr. Fullford had acted as his guide, since he had rung up on the matter, and there was no note of any purchase from or sale to him of such a picture among the antiquarian's books.

There was just the possibility that Mr. Myers might have heard some word of reference to the Sheraton secret drawer and its contents from Mr. Fullford, or even from Sir Adam himself, supposing him to have gone to Westwood to look at the Raeburn there. Pointer could not afford to miss the remotest chance of learning what that drawer had contained that had seemed to excite Sir Adam. There were many people at Westwood with which the papers in it might be linked.

There was Sturge, if an enemy had hidden some all-important paper there and then notified the owner of the frame of its presence... there was Miss Luton... with the same proviso, and there was the French couple... The place of purchase by the last owner probably meant nothing. Sir Adam had never been to Australia, but that, too, was a possible clue.

True, an immediate inquiry over the 'phone to Tukes was no help. The butler knew of no such named visitor presenting himself at the house. Nor of the picture in question being shown to any stranger. But that meant little. There were many visitors whose names Tukes never learned, as Youdale himself had brought them down with him. So after a word now to the police station over the 'phone, as to sending men out near and far among Mr. Fullford's customers, should he himself draw blank, Pointer stopped at the inn.

CHAPTER TEN

At the *Sun in Splendor*, he learned that Mr. Myers, too, had left yesterday morning. He had never stayed there before. He had occupied one of the cheapest rooms in the inn, and had conducted himself throughout his stay of one week as though by no means wealthy.

He learned in answer to further questions that the man, on arriving, had said that he was merely down for a week's rest. He left by train around ten o'clock, which would mean that he would not see any notice of Sir Adam's death before his departure. Not that that notice might have meant anything to a stranger in the place.

He learned further that the man seemed in just the same spirits on leaving as when he came.

"Always fault-finding," the proprietor said with a weary lift of his eyebrows. "Bustle here fancied he was an American from his accent."

"That's right, sir." The porter spoke up for himself with the freedom of an old servant. "The flower-bed outside his window was being worked over, an' a lot of rubble and gravel was being dug in." Bustle was addressing Pointer now. "When I brought him some whisky after he had unpacked, he growls at me:

"'What's that mullock doing there?' And when I explained, he said as he wanted boards laid over it immediate, as freshly turned-up earth gave him malaria."

Mullock... that was an Australian word, surely? *Mullock*... that frame was bought in Australia.

"Between ourselves, you don't think he might have been an Australian?" Pointer asked the proprietor. Yates seemed a man who would be a good judge of other men. But the ex-dragoon officer looked a shrug.

182 *A Resurrected Press Mystery*

"That's what Mr. Fullford said," the porter chimed in again. "He happened to be passing in the lounge when Mr. Myers was ordering something or other in the American bar. The door between was open, and as he passed, Mr. Fullford jerked his head in the direction of the voice, and said 'Australian.' I says, 'No, American.' He shakes his head as he passes on and says, 'No, no! Australian!' in his positive way. I chaffed him about it, 'Come, now,' I says, 'you may know all about clocks, but you aren't a collector of Aussies, surely.'"

"And like most of the things Fullford is certain about," Yates struck in, "I shouldn't wonder if he weren't right. Besides, the fellow's manner wasn't American—not friendly enough."

"You've a good opinion of Mr. Fullford?" Pointer asked.

"Very," Yates said heartily, "and I've a still better one of his opinion. You can tie to what Fullford says. Always." And with that he was called away on business.

Pointer regretted the absence of Fullford more than ever.

"He's a character," the porter said with a grin. "Many's the time people staying here have gone into his shop—so they tell me afterwards, and want to buy whatever little thing he stuck in the window, looking-glass just now, ain't it? Yes. Well, more than four people have wanted to buy that glass, and instead of quoting a price, he hums and haws and says he hasn't got anything else to put in its place, and what would the window look like without it? And he's got fond of it, and the long and the short of it is they come away. I don't think he cares about selling to people he doesn't know."

"He knew this man Myers, didn't he?"

The porter shook his head. "That's what I said to him. 'Mr. Myers has been asking the way to your shop, Mr. Fullford,' I said, 'why not stop and have a word with him?' That was when he would have it he was an Australian.

The Westwood Mystery 183

But he says, 'Never go to meet a new customer. Always let 'em hunt you up.' And with that he goes out."

A new customer. That was a disappointing piece of news.

"And did you ever see Mr. Myers speaking to anyone in the inn?" Pointer asked Bustle.

"Not except for a few words he exchanged in the lounge with a gent, a stranger too, who spent last night here. Mr. Myers hadn't any matches on him, and he asked the other gent, who was smoking in front of the fireplace, for a light. They just exchanged a few words about the weather and the outlook for cricket after that."

"What was the gentleman's name?" Pointer asked. The porter said he knew his room number and would find out as soon as the bookkeeper returned.

"Was Mr. Myers a cricketer, apparently?" Pointer wanted to know.

"He said he liked to watch a good game, but didn't play himself. Said as he found golf took all his spare time. And the other gent now, he said as he was never happier than when he was going out to bowl. Ah, there's the bookkeeper."

Pointer walked over to the desk with him and learned that the stranger's name was Manning. He made quite sure of this, and then was told that the time of the only—observed—exchange of words had been just before seven o'clock.

Within a minute or two Pointer was speaking over the 'phone to the hotel in town which Myers had written in the inn's register as his home address. They knew nothing of the name there, nor did a careful description of the man mean anything to them. So the address was false... Pointer now expected that the name would be too... The question was, did he link up with Manning, with the picture frame from Sydney, or with the Raeburn, in which he seemed interested that hung in Youdale's bedroom. Hung just where Pointer himself would have put it had he owned it, facing the bed.

"I'd like to see Mr. Myers' room," Pointer said next. It was very near to the one that Manning had occupied, he found. Both were on the ground floor. Both opened out into the quadrangle made by the tennis courts and flower garden. The boards laid down still lay under the window well on to the grass. The inn buildings ran around three sides of the quadrangle, the fourth was divided from some open land by a railing and a gate, the latter never locked.

Anyone with a ground floor room could, should he so desire, come and go by his window, practically undetected. Also, had they wished it, Myers and Manning could have continued their talk on cricket versus golf in each others' rooms—also undetected.

Pointer's eyes were filmed with thought as he took all this in. He asked to be left alone in Myers' room. His interest was especially in the window. The boards outside showed nothing. The woodwork of the window itself, however, had various scuffed places where a man had clambered in at least once, and Pointer thought more than once. He did some measurements. Quite apart from any description of Myers, when he had finished, the chief inspector was certain that he was small and youngish, but of at least average muscular strength.

Next he took his "powder puff" and dusted the window for fingerprints. Mr. Myers was beginning to interest him. A minute later he interested him vastly more. The powder showed several fingerprints on the polished oak frame made by someone who had grasped it while leaning out, or swinging himself over the ledge, and the clearest was identical with that on the stem of the sherry glass in Sir Adam Youdale's library. So Myers had been the visitor, or a visitor, night before last, and had not come forward. And did he link on to Manning? Pointer had another chat with the hall porter and asked him to talk both Myers and Manning over with every member of the staff. Inquiries made personally by the chief inspector would of necessity be formal compared with Bustle's chatter, and the latter might learn with ease what all the

The Westwood Mystery 185

most skilful questioning of the detective officer could not draw out.

Back again at Westwood, he studied the Raeburn very carefully. He felt sure from its luminous beauty that it was an original. The back, and the stretcher, showed no marks of tampering. In other words, he felt sure that the picture was what it purported to be, and as it had been sold to Youdale.

He would, of course, have expert judgment on this, but meanwhile he took it as a fact.

Nicholson and Superintendent Claxton came in together as he was replacing the picture.

"We've got the motive right enough now that made Sturge kill Sir Adam," the superintendent said grimly. "Right enough!" He turned to the solicitor with the air of a man careful not to shoot his neighbor's bird.

"By some dreadful mistake," Nicholson said, "the papers connected with the Rubber Trunks Company that were handed over to Youdale day before yesterday were originals, not copies."

"So that the murderer, by getting them, got rid of all proof." Claxton could not hold his fire longer. "From a criminal's point of view, it was well worth a murder to secure them."

This made a great difference. Pointer had always felt that a murder for the sake of securing copies could only be a murder to secure time, and as, apparently, Sturge had made his arrangements for concealing himself so well that he could disappear swiftly, it hardly seemed worth it.

"Well, Pointer, ready for a warrant now?" Claxton asked gleefully.

As a matter of fact, there was a warrant out for the arrest of Mr. Sturge in connection with Sir Adam Youdale's murder, but the superintendent was speaking of Pointer's agreement with his own conviction that Sturge was the murderer.

The chief inspector was wanted on the telephone.

186   *A Resurrected Press Mystery*

The porter had learned something. One of the waiters had seen Myers out walking in a lane on the common with another guest at the hotel, a Miss Green. It was evening, and he thought the two were talking in very lover-like attitudes, arm in arm he fancied, though he would not swear to that, as it was growing dusk when he caught sight of them. They did not see him, for they took a side path, before he got up to them. He heard the lady say "I think it's a beautiful name. Oliver—so steadfast! So true!" Miss Green, said the porter, was a silly looking woman, with a perpetual ingratiating smile.

"Age?"

Oh, the usual age. Fortyish, he would say. Or a little under. She had a couple of very good rooms at the *Sun*, and seemed to have plenty of money. She had stayed there for a fortnight, leaving a few days before Myers' week was up.

"Was she a lady?"

Well, he would be surprised to learn that she was anybody in particular—Bustle had a quaint way of talking—but she seemed all right. Her address, as given in the hotel book, Pointer now found to be a pretentious and very expensive hotel at Queen's Gate. It happened to be one whose head waiter was quite a friend of his.

He 'phoned to him, and learned that a Miss Green lived there. She had been away for a fortnight just recently—to visit friends, the lady had said. Got back about four days ago. What was she like? The description that followed fitted the Miss Green of Wimbledon too closely for there to be much likelihood of mistake, especially as the fortnight away from town agreed too. The chief inspector arranged to drop in as soon as possible at Queen's Gate. He had to have lunch somewhere, he would have it there. And with him would go the *Sun's* porter. That good man was to keep out of sight, and if the lady, when she appeared, was the Miss Green he knew, he was at once to send Pointer in a newspaper. If she was not the Miss Green who had stayed

The Westwood Mystery

187

at the *Sun*, a telegram instead would be handed to the chief inspector.

Miss Green was not in at the moment of his arrival, but the porter said that she rarely stayed long. She was one of the "in-and-outers" according to him. Primed by the head waiter, and anxious apart from that to stand well with a chief inspector from the Yard, the man was most anxious to be of use. He readily arranged to give the porter from the *Sun* a seat in his own booth where he could look out but not be seen himself.

Pointer's first inquiry was as to Miss Green. According to Higgins, the head porter, she was a woman who probably had suddenly come into money. She tipped as only a person unaccustomed to money or service would tip, with a lavishness quite unaltered by the quality of the service itself. He had an idea that she might be a lottery winner. She was a pleasant-spoken little thing, but—well—the kind you often find keeping lodgings or little newspaper shops... She seemed to have no friends. And as he felt sure of her respectability, he gathered from that, that she had not been in a position to make them. "She talks as though she had heaps, poor, soul," he went on, "always telling me and the head waiter about the 'delightful evening she had with friends last night,' or the dinner she's going to. Just now, she's back from a fortnight in the country with 'dear friends of mine. They live in such an interesting old manor house.' She's always getting flowers sent her—by herself, I think. A little gray mouse who'll never see forty again."

Pointer asked about a man called Myers. The porter did not know the name, but when Pointer mentioned that he believed that he and Miss Green were friends, he called the head waiter.

"What about the bloke you told me of who dined with Miss Green last night? I was off duty and didn't see him."

The waiter had the man's name instantly. "Myers. Yes, for the first time since she's been here, Miss Green had a visitor last night, and he looked to me as though he had been drinking hard. Or just off a sick bed. Not fit to be up in either case. But Miss Green had made such a point of the dinner, ordered it so regardless that I let him pass."

"Look here," Pointer said on that, "I think the man may be wanted by us. Can you give me a description of him?"

Few men can equal a head waiter when it comes to memorizing faces, but this man had nothing salient about him.

"Good-looking enough in a sort of way," the head waiter allowed, "but a mean type. Very insinuating manners—to Miss Green at any rate."

Pointer asked for the waiter who had had charge of the table. He had been within three paces of the two throughout the many courses, for Miss Green had insisted on a seven-course meal.

"I rather thought he could have borne to see less of me," the man remarked with a faint grin. He was an elderly man with an eye as keen as a bird's. But his description of Miss Green's friend included nothing outstanding or peculiar, dark smooth hair, dark smooth face. Blue eyes. Poor teeth. Small but good figure. Very well dressed. Manicured hands. Second-class table manners but first-hand knowledge of expensive wines. Miss Green and he had talked in low tones. He especially had adopted quite a lover-like way of bending forward and looking at her while he talked hard.

"He was trying to persuade her to do something she didn't quite like, and yet half did like. Sort of looking at the cold water in the tub on a winter's morning was what she made me think of," and the waiter smiled a thin wintery smile himself.

"Did you hear what they, talked about?" Pointer asked him.

"I did my best," the waiter said frankly. "Miss Green isn't the kind of lady one thinks of as getting much of that sort of thing. As far as I could make out, she wanted to

The Westwood Mystery 189

see over his home, and he wouldn't have it. Kept saying, 'It's not fit for you, my darling. Wait till I come for you.' And all about their trip together somewhere off on a sea voyage. Which meant they were going to get married evidently. And the way she listened to him!"

"Hark, the herald angels sing!" threw in a young waiter who had assisted at the table. The men laughed.

"Just, that way," the first one went on. "He said he was coming for her this week, or possibly next. She hasn't given up her room yet, so I fancy it will be next week. And any day will be a day she'll regret, in my opinion."

At that Pointer was told that Miss Green had returned.

He saw a woman with a weak, silly face, expensively but badly dressed, and expensively but badly made up. Stopping her, as she crossed the lounge, he produced a sealed envelope.

"Miss Green, I believe? Captain Yates of the *Sun in Splendor* wondered if you could let him have Mr. Myer's address."

Pointer spoke low, and half-shepherded, half-led the way to the empty drawing-room. "I won't keep you a moment," he went on, "but it seems that Mr. Myers left an Australian railway bond behind him, and the proprietor is asking all the people who happened to be at the inn last week if, by chance, they knew where he lived. He seems to have left the address he gave in the hotel register."

The, door of the drawing-room opened. "Your paper, sir," and it was held out to the chief inspector, who took it with a nod, and laid it beside him. Miss Green simpered a little and pulled at her long earrings.

"Well, of course it's rather awkward. Mr. Myers is an author and—well—"

"Even authors don't like to lose money," Pointer suggested.

"Of course not! I didn't mean that. Very well, then, I'll give it to him when I see him."

190   *A Resurrected Press Mystery*

"Oh, but that may be weeks off." Pointer looked blank disappointment. She shook her head and smiled, a smile that showed all her gums.

"I shall be seeing him very shortly." She held out her hand. Pointer did not lay the envelope in it. "I'm sorry," he said instead, "but that won't do at all. You see, the proprietor's liable by Act of Parliament for its safe custody—in reason. If you'll be kind enough to address it, and hand it to one of the porters here to register it off at once, I should be quite satisfied. But I think Captain Yates wouldn't feel comfortable otherwise."

Miss Green, who looked as though she would need someone to think for her even in small things, grew flustered.

"He's leaving where he is now. This wouldn't reach him in time... but if it's financial, he's just been frightfully swindled by someone in whom he trusted."

Pointer gave a cluck of sympathy. "Are you by chance engaged to him?" he asked with a pleasant smile. She bridled and flushed.

"I am. Of course, I haven't known him long, but with some people one feels at once as if one had known them all one's life, doesn't one? And besides, he's the kind of man who needs a wife. He's no one to look after him. And of course it all has to be so hurried—this frightful disaster he's had... such trust to be abused seems too cruel. But the world is full of wicked people. We all know that..."

"Look here," Pointer put in. "Just register this letter on to him. It'll reach him quite safely then, wherever he is."

"Oh no, it won't," she said almost in a whisper. "I told you he's leaving—very suddenly. I'd take it myself, only—of course, he wouldn't hear of my looking him up. He made me promise I wouldn't. You know what a bachelor's house is like," she giggled. "Dreadful disorder, I expect!"

The Westwood Mystery   191

"He shouldn't have told you where he lived, if he didn't want you to pay him a surprise visit," Pointer, said in as silly a tone as he could manage.

She looked mysterious but made no reply. Pointer was certain on the instant that Myers had not told her but that she had come upon some paper or letter giving the address. But he could not suggest that, even to Miss Green, without her perceiving that she was being questioned.

'Still, if he's leaving, a registered letter will be sent after him," he persisted.

She looked at him with watery, helpless eyes. Had she stated her belief in so many words that Mr. Myers intended making a moonlight flitting, she could not have said it plainer.

"And if not," Pointer went on, "Captain Yates will have done his duty. So will you. If you just send it to him by registered post." She obediently disentangled a pair of glasses from much beadwork about her neck, and, going to a table, wrote for a moment, then she called the head porter, and gave him directions to register it at once, and bring her back the registration slip as soon as he had done so. Pointer had already given his instructions. A copy of the address would be taken, and when, in a very few minutes, which Pointer spent in making himself agreeable to the lady, for fear lest she should use that convenient but sometimes diabolical invention, the telephone, the man brought her a slip which she put away carefully, he also turned to Pointer.

"Beg pardon, sir, but I gave you the wrong paper just now. This is yours." Pointer took the exchange with a nod, and said good-by to Miss Green. They had been talking of Myers. He had learned nothing more. Which told him that, under the excuse of being a writer who wished to keep frenzied admirers at bay, Myers had told her very little about himself.

"You don't know if he saw the Raeburns after all?" he said lightly as he was leaving.

192   *A Resurrected Press Mystery*

"I never heard him mention them. Are they friends of yours?" she asked ingenuously, and Pointer's last sight of her was as she stood twisting her beads around her throat and biting her lip, worried already, at what she had done. But it was too late. On the paper handed him at the last moment was O. Fox, Esq., 7 Elizabeth Street, S.W. I. He drove there at once and found, as he thought, that number seven was a building of offices. The name of O. Fox was on the board. Fourth floor. Pointer had a word with the commissionaire who acted as caretaker for the whole premises Who was Fox? What was his work?

"Home-made jams and jellies, sir," the man replied at once. And Pointer thought of a smear of tangerine jam on a pillow slip. "Just has one room where he and his typist work. She only comes up twice a week, for a few hours. Nice girl."

"And what's he like?" Pointer had shown the man his official card, and the old soldier was eager to help.

"Don't like the chap. Though he's very smooth-spoken. But she's gone on him, poor kid. I wouldn't trust him myself with a dead cat. He's the sort that always does you in the eye. Always. As he did, Mr. Davies, the man he bought the business from. Now Mr. Davies was a horse of quite a different color!"

Pointer asked him for a description of Fox, and came the usual unhelpful generalities.

"And the secretary?"

"Miss Drury?" He gave a description of a young slim, fair girl who looked only seventeen but might be twenty or even more at a pinch.

Pointer was told about the sale by Davies of his business and his house, and of the furniture in both cases for a mere song. But Davies had come a cropper, and had to get from under.

He came in here the other day," the commissionaire, went on, "and told me that even so, he couldn't collect the money owing him from Fox without threatening to County-Court him."

The Westwood Mystery 193

"Do you know Mr. Fox's home address?"

Owing to the chance of its being Davies's, the man did. Mr. Fox himself had never given it him, and, from certain precautions taken, the man had the idea that Fox believed he did not know it, and for that reason the commissionaire had not volunteered the information that it was duly entered in a little notebook in his room. He wrote it down now for Pointer.

"How's he been in his manner lately?" the chief inspector asked next. "Seem cheerful? In high spirits?"

The man gave him a shrewd look.

"He looked something awful yesterday. He only came in for a minute in the late afternoon with a wad of papers under his arm as big as a suitcase. I fancied he was going to pack up with them, but they were all on the floor of his office this morning. Then I thought he was going in for these 'ere crosswords—until you came along, sir."

"Is he in the office now?"

"Hasn't turned up all today, sir. I wasn't surprised. He looked so white and liverish yesterday. Spent the afternoon drinking, too, unless I'm much mistaken. Had a dinner on, and changed here, like he often does. But never sleeps here. Came round for his things in his suitcase later on, and went off home."

That would have been Miss Green's dinner.

"Does he ever go away for a day or more at a time?" Pointer inquired.

"Just been away for a week, sir."

"What about his letters and parcels?"

"Left here for the typist to look after."

"Has she been just as usual?" Pointer asked.

The man thought so. "Cheerful little thing always. Smiling and gay."

"She hasn't done anything different from usual lately?" Pointer pressed. "Nothing, however trifling, during this week. Has she sent out any telegrams, for instance?"

194   *A Resurrected Press Mystery*

The man did not know of any. "Unless you're meaning her will?" he added. "That wasn't sent out. But she had me and one of the cleaners witness it for her. Told us what it was we was signing, of course."

"You've seen nothing to make you think this Mr. Fox was leaving?" Pointer asked next.

"Ah," the commissionaire leaned still more comfortably on the newel post, "I was just coming to that, sir."

Pointer nodded encouragingly.

"I've seen him talking, just before he went off for the week, to two men, who I happen to know as buyers of small businesses. My belief is he's going to sell it again. Miss Drury don't know nothing. I fished a bit, in talking to her, while waiting for the cleaner to come all witness her signature. No, she don't guess nothing, I'm right. Besides, these men, they came on a day she wasn't up at the office, and I heard them talking about going down to the house where the stuff is made, and they named one of the days when she is at the office Fox is doing her, you bet!"

Pointer went into the question of the dates when the business brokers had been seen. It was a fortnight ago, a fortnight before Youdale's murder. It all fitted, as far as times went. But what could be the connection between Fox, who called himself Myers in Wimbledon, a man running a little jam business, and Sir Adam Youdale? Youdale was not being blackmailed, that was certain from the inspection of his pass-books. How had the fingerprints come on the sherry glass?

Pointer went over the office, though it yielded nothing except fingerprints that matched those on the window frame at the inn, and the sherry glass at Westwood. But it showed that a genuine business was being done, and nothing else. Then he drove out to Tollard Road. He learned at the house that Mr. Fox was away until evening, so was Miss Drury. Pointer, who had not yet

The Westwood Mystery 195

named his business, promptly became a fruit grower; who had an appointment with Mr. Fox.

"I'm a bit before my time. Roads are so difficult to gauge—but Mr. Fox said he'd be here. He must be coming back. I'll wait for him. Naysmith is my name."

Mrs. Goodge looked doubtful. Not of her caller, but of Fox's return. "I think he must have forgotten the appointment, though I've never known that to happen before. He's a wonderful head for business. Such a memory! But he and Miss Drury are off on a picnic... They said they was going for the day." By this time she had shown him into a room.

"Did they go in his car?"

They had.

"Then I might overtake him. I've a good goer myself. What's the make of his?"

Mrs. Goodge had no idea.

"What's its number then?" the caller asked chattily. "If I pass it on the road, I'll stop them."

Mrs. Goodge had seen the car a hundred times, but she had no idea. Yes, she knew where he garaged it. Pointer explained that question by wanting some petrol.

"Well, I hope he's not overlooked a rather important appointment I'd arranged between him and a customer of mine." Pointer seemed worried."'It was arranged for next week. Perhaps just now he's other things to think of?"

"Ah, so you've heard?" Mrs. Goodge looked at him so archly that Pointer ventured on.

"Wedding bells in the air? I have. When's it to be?"

"Very shortly, sir. And that in love with one another, it's pretty to see it! I mean, you expect it with a young lady, but with a gentleman like the Commander, well, it's a sight to charm, that it is!"

Pointer left a few minutes later. His silent search of the room he was in had shown nothing, except the corroboration of fingerprints once more. A few minutes after his apparently rather disgruntled departure, he was at the garage used by Fox, and getting the number of

196   *A Resurrected Press Mystery*

Fox's car. Also a technical description of it. Mr. Fox had just had it overhauled, he heard, that is to say, the sparking plugs cleaned and the tires tested. Which bore out the idea of a day in the country.

There was a telephone near the garage, and from it Mrs. Goodge received a message from a stranger who said he was a hotel porter at Richmond speaking for Mr. Fox, who had suddenly developed a sore throat. Mr. Fox said that in going off for the day just now, he had quite overlooked two things. Would Mrs. Goodge. therefore please go to his office in Elizabeth Street, and ask the commissionaire for a packet, coming by registered post? It should have arrived this morning, but should it by any chance not be there, she was to wait for it and bring it back with her to Tollard Road. For himself and Miss Drury, would not return before ten o'clock. As he was very keen on the parcel, he thought the best thing would be for Mrs. Goodge to take a day off, do any shopping she wanted, spend the evening at a picture show, and get a meal out for herself—Mr. Fox would stand for both a good seat and a dinner at the Lyons just around the corner from the office. If by any chance the package did not arrive by the nine o'clock evening post, then Mrs. Goodge was to give it up, and come back to Tollard Road. The second thing he had forgotten was an appointment with a gentleman, name of Naysmith.

"Tell him he's called, and is coming back," Mrs. Goodge said into the telephone.

She heard the self-styled porter evidently talking to someone standing beside him. She caught "The lady's saying, Mr. Fox, that—" and the rest was mumble-mumble until the porter's voice reached her again clearly.

"Mr. Fox says he'll 'phone to him, and head him off. He knows where he can catch him." There followed a repetition of the first request. Mrs. Goodge faithfully memorized it. She had already told Naysmith that she was alone in the house—As it happened, Kathleen had seized the opportunity of a day in the country to give the

The Westwood Mystery   197

little maid a holiday too—and Mrs. Goodge had a hundred and one things she was longing to see to. Off she went after, as she believed, locking up well. In came Pointer, who had had a good look at the front door lock, and had managed, while talking, to shut it on himself on leaving. As he thought, Mrs. Goodge only looked to the back door. He had search warrant to be used if necessary, but he did not want to alarm Fox. The front door yielded to a resolute push on his part, a small dab of a preparation in which cobbler's wax played an important part at top and bottom, had done the work of holding it apparently shut. Two of his men were with him, and the house was searched room by room, foot by foot, inch by inch, and yet with amazing swiftness. And in a cupboard, where kindling was stored under the stairs, a cupboard that seemed quite unused, since there was gas throughout the, house, was a newspaper bundle. In it were packages tied with tape. Packages taken, as the contents and docketing showed, from Adam Youdale's safe a week ago. But there were no papers connected with Sturge among them, except ones relating to well-known matters of the Rubber Trunk Company, which had been fully ventilated weeks ago. Yet, bar them and the will, apparently all the contents of the safe were here. Intact. But there were other things they found, though not in that cupboard. In Fox's own bureau they found an envelope marked "Tickets for our honeymoon. Rome." The envelope was sealed. Inside was but one ticket—for South America. There were absolutely no personal records whatever, let alone any link with the murdered barrister, bar the papers from his safe which had apparently been left wrapped up in the newspaper so as to be ready to be stowed in a suitcase or dropped in a bag, or car. Probably they had only today been placed in that cupboard. No link but them with Youdale and at Westwood no link to be found with Fox but the fingerprints on that sherry glass, though the burned litter on the hearth stood in all likelihood for papers that would have led the hunt here at once. But for the moment it was at the ticket to South America that Pointer was staring.

He put it back again with a worried frown. He was worried for the slim, fair-haired girl. She had just made her will. Fox might know nothing of that, but it showed that she had something to leave... the commissionaire thought that she was devoted to Fox, anything she had, would probably go to him. True, the housekeeper here was convinced that Fox was devoted to Miss Drury too, but against that was Miss Green's fond belief that the man was going to marry her. Did he mean to marry the older woman really? It was possible, only too possible, Pointer thought. He stared at his shoes. Where had Fox and Miss Drury gone today? Supposing Fox stood for something in the murder of Adam Youdale, where does an unsuspecting girl who has made a will, and is with an unscrupulous scoundrel in whose favor she may have made it, run the most danger? They had taken a picnic basket, Mrs.. Goodge had said. Miss Drury had run back for an extra warm wrap. If Fox had chosen the New Forest or some such inland spot, Pointer doubted if he or anyone could save the girl. Supposing his fears were right.

But there was a chance that the seaside would be much more useful to any sinister purpose... the Cliffs— the sea—the sands. The river would be packed today... nor did he think, from the description of Fox's pale face and small smooth hands, that he sounded a river man... no, in his place, Pointer would choose the sea... In a stride he had the telephone, his men were sent to the nearest instruments around, duplication would not matter, time might be all important. Every seaside place was asked to let the Yard know at once if a car of the number—he gave it and the description as an additional help, had arrived there today. All possible speed in searching for it was to be made. He began with Brighton as the best and most crowded spot for Fox's possible purpose, and a town which he probably would know. In a very few minutes,

The Westwood Mystery 199

Pointer was told that the car he wanted had been parked in the Brighton pier garage just forty minutes ago.

He ordered the police to watch the cliffs and the beach for Fox and Miss Drury. Fox by himself would have been almost impossible to find, but the company of the pretty fair-haired girl improved the searchers' outlook—as long as the fair-haired girl was with him. *Ominous proviso.*

Her photograph stood in Fox's room, and Pointer itemized the features in the police way, which makes identification as nearly certain as any description can. Then he consulted his notebook. High tide would be in a little over two hours from now. And dusk would be a little later still. If he was right in his fears it looked as though Miss Drury might have a very close shave... there was a train leaving for Brighton shortly. It would beat any car. He telephoned to the station, and by their keeping it back for a couple of minutes he just caught it. Meanwhile, Scotland Yard sent out further instructions for an especially careful watch to be kept of all boats for hire, and along the sands and cliffs this evening, and for the detention of either one of the couple at sight. Those two people, neither of whom Pointer had seen, but one of whom—if things were as they looked—he hoped to save, and one whom he might yet be instrumental in hanging.

Danger hour would probably be at, and after, dusk, but a swimming accident could happen at any time.

And then came a recollection that if the old antiquarian, Mr. Fullford, was right in what was probably but a careless guess, even if correctly understood and reported, Fox might come from Australia, and be able to swim like a fish. A dangerous accomplishment possibly, for the companion of Miss Drury today.

One thing seemed clear. The man who took the papers from the safe and burned the others must have known that the owner was dead. Only Sturge would have reason enough to kill for the sake of getting possession of them, but with anyone else as the murderer, it would seem that they were but secondary, and that the actual, primary motive must lie in what had been destroyed. Well, motive did not have to matter to the police. Any more than the prosecution has to prove it in order to secure a conviction. It would be the first time, however, that Pointer had ever made an arrest where he did not understand the whole story, and often a good many other stories as well, that had got caught up with the larger one. But now it was a question of the possible safety of Miss Drury. He could not wait to get his case clear against her companion.

Arrived at Brighton, he was told that the car was being watched, but that no one had claimed it. That no couple answering to his descriptions had been seen in the town, except at one shop, where there was a sort of idea that a man and a fair-haired girl had bought some fruit.

A careful search of sands and cliffs was going on, but, so far, without result.

CHAPTER ELEVEN

Kathleen Drury was always down to breakfast before Fox. Today she was unusually early. She had slept badly. Last evening she and Oliver had had—she hesitated, they were called tiffs, weren't they? But in her heart she knew that this had been no ordinary tiff. It was not open enough. It was too mysterious—to her. In a tiff, someone exploded, the other followed suit, then one or other apologized, the other followed suit there too, and everything was all right again. But yesterday evening he had come back, looking like a man who had had a dreadful shock, staring eyes and blotched, chalky cheeks. He said that he was ill and must go to bed at once, and that if anyone asked for him, Kathleen was to say that he was away in the country—he was quite incoherent for a few minutes, then he pulled himself together and flung away to bed, only to ring a moment later and order all the latest editions of the evening papers to be brought to him, and to be furious beyond all reason because one paper had been forgotten. Kathleen had had a shock. He had, treated her like a stranger, or worse still, almost like an enemy. It was at her that he had sworn when the paper he wanted was omitted from the others. After reading them through, he seemed in a better mood, and even apologized for having been so 'nervy.' But somehow, Kathleen felt as though she no longer mattered. It was an odd feeling, quite impossible to account for, but quite clear. When she had questioned him about his week's trip, he had looked so terrible that, frightened, she had pretended that she meant something else—the city dinner that he had just attended—so he had told her.

202   *A Resurrected Press Mystery*

"Oh, that," he rubbed his hands, and laughed a little under his breath, "quite promising. Quite a hopeful proposition, Kit."

This morning a letter came for him, among a number for her. As a rule all his letters went to his locked box at his office. This one was in a long envelope, so carelessly fastened, that it was only held by the tip. Deep in her own uncomfortable thoughts she ran a finger under the flap, and then, forgetting to draw out the sheet inside, a circular of some kind probably, she stood gazing into the fire. What had happened to him? And to her? For since his return she seemed to be meeting a stranger, and one whom she rather disliked. Had Kathleen been older, she would have known that it had only been glamour and a sort of lovers' moonshine that had ever captivated her. That she had never loved Fox. But she thought that she had, and now when that feeling seemed to have passed as swiftly as a morning mist, she did not know how to account for it. They were going to be married so shortly, and here she was, actually feeling as though she did not care whether she saw him again or not.

He came in at that moment. She dodged his kiss. "I've got a cold," she said, and was horrified at herself for the fib. But she knew how he avoided people with colds. Instantly he dropped the arm he was holding and sat down at table.

"By the way, Kit," he began, "do you think that little niece of Mrs. Goodge's can carry on while we're on our honeymoon?"

"As far as the cooking is concerned, she could run the show alone," Kathleen said indifferently. Somehow the word honeymoon had lost its beauty—entirely. Just as he seemed to her to have lost his good looks this morning.

"Did you give her your book of recipes? That tangerine jam is taking on well."

"I've written down all my recipes as you suggested," she told him, "so that at any time she can turn to them."

He leaned forward and took her hand.

The Westwood Mystery 203

"My darling girl, I want to apologize"—he began in his voice that she had thought so hearty; now it seemed to her merely very loud—"I drank Burgundy last night, and even one glass upsets me frightfully. Goes straight to my liver. And then I backed the wrong horse!"

Looking into his magnetic blue eyes, she felt her doubts, her dislike, swept away.

They had a delightful meal. When it was over, she opened her letters and suddenly remembered his. It was still lying where she had finally laid it on the mantel.

"This is for you. I opened it by mistake, but didn't read it," she said, handing it him.

"Doesn't look anything very vital," he murmured, taking out the letter, which was in printed characters. It ran:

"By every sign and token, the murder of Adam Youdale is your work. You fool, to think that the police will not connect Westwood with Tangier!"

Kathleen was busy scribbling down some figures, and did not see his face. Mrs. Goodge, coming in with matches, got its full effect. For a second it was not human. Then, shaking, he covered his face with his hands.

"Oh, my head!' he moaned. "My head! What can one do for neuralgia like this? It's been tormenting me for days—and just now, it's unbearable." For a full minute he sat there, his features covered, while the two women fussed over him. Mrs. Goodge laid a hot cloth on the nape of his neck. Kathleen begged him to try some antipyrine. Finally he looked up, his face shining like a piece of melting suet, Mrs. Goodge described it to herself.

"It's better. Now what about a letter, Kit, that you were going to show me?"

"Why, you dropped it on the fire. It was only a circular probably." He shot her a glance of dislike and suspicion. But she was bending over the coal scuttle, and Mrs. Goodge was putting some things on to her tray. Neither saw it. Kathleen was thankful that his attack was passing so swiftly. She helped him to a strong cup of black coffee, which he made stronger still with something from the sideboard.

"I need a day in the open air," he announced, when he had drunk it. "What about a day in the country? It's glorious just now. Don't say no," he wheedled, and with that he got Mrs. Goodge to rush around and put them up a lunch basket, while he took Kathleen off with him in his car to shop for some extra touches and a very good luncheon he bought. A cold fowl and little *bouchées* of fish in mayonnaise, and *babas au rhum*. Laughing like a boy, he bought two bottles of champagne at a price that made her gasp.

"Good for my head," he grinned, as he drove home with her again, "and you won't find a headache in the whole bottleful." He would hardly let her stay to change into some warmer things, and when she asked for extra time to put on more festive raiment, he showed something like ferocity. Something that frightened her. Then he begged her to forgive him, and seemed again to be in the same boisterous spirits, ragging Mrs. Goodge, and roaring with laughter as they stowed the food with difficulty into his car.

"Nobody can say I've not done my best to prepare for a happy picnic!" he said to Mrs. Goodge, in a loud almost angry voice, then burst out laughing.

In the same spate of hilarity they set off, but after a few minutes, Fox seemed to change utterly, and fall into a peculiarly dark and forbidding silence. She felt oddly unhappy, oddly unwilling to go for a picnic. But it was too late to back out now. Suddenly he turned his face, a smiling one again.

"What about Brighton? It's so warm, and there's splendid bathing to be had down there? Always' lots going on..."

The Westwood Mystery 205

She was too relieved to see him cheerful again, to care where they went. She noticed that he did not have to turn the car. Evidently the road they were on led to Brighton.

The rest of the drive was quite gay. They picnicked merrily enough, though, as she pointed out, he had brought quite twice the number of things that they could eat. But he only laughed and said it would come in on the way back. Arrived in Brighton, they parked the car, and Fox, who evidently knew the town well, took her by a roundabout way down to the beach. They had a delightful walk, he was a more fascinating companion than she had dreamed that even he could be. He talked of other walks, in other countries. He told her tales of the East. Kathleen listened spellbound. There were caves outside Gibraltar, and he described them.

"By the way, there are some fine caves down here too," he went on, as though just reminded of that fact. "One in particular. It's called the 'Smugglers' Pocket,' which is well worth seeing." He led the way, it was a scramble over boulders at the end, to what looked like a crack in a cliff. Following him, she squeezed through into a large twilight cave where the sound of the sea came only like distant thunder.

It was delightful on this hot day, and fairly dry.

"The tide never comes in here," he said, going at once to the further end. "Spray gets blown in, of course, through the opening if there are storms outside. I remember as a kid spending whole days playing pirates in here with my brother. As we were motherless, we had a good deal of liberty."

"Motherless?" Kathleen echoed in blank surprise.

"My mother is really my step-mother," he said hastily, "but she's so fond of me she hates to tell anyone. I always have called her 'mother.'" That explained what had puzzled Kathleen a little. His infrequent allusions to his mother,. his habit of forgetting to include her in any plan for the future.

He had insisted on taking the hamper with him, and now they had a second lunch, Kathleen making coffee on the little spirit lamp. It was all very amusing, and after it, he told her more stories, more accounts of the countries that he had seen. She thought that she had never enjoyed anything more.

Finally he led her up the very, steep slope of the cave, and clambered on to a sort of jutting step of rock.

"I say, this shelf is nice.! I'm going to lie back and have a rest. Now you climb up here this way"—he swung her up behind him to a still higher shelf—"and I'm going to stretch out here for a quiet half-hour. Comfortable, darling?"

She assured him truthfully that she was.

"Then I'll just close my eyes, they ache so, and have a nap. It will do me all the good in the world." And in a second he seemed to fall asleep. She sat on, half-dreaming herself. Thinking of how charming he really was, what a lot of the world he had seen... She had said that she wished she could see it, and he had suddenly laughed outright and said that perhaps they might manage a longer honeymoon. Gradually she too slipped from semi-dreaming into real sleep, for he had put his coat around her, and she felt quite cosy.

It was dark in the cave when she woke, cramped and stiff. She roused him, and he looked at his watch, striking a match. Then he laughed. "It's early yet. It's only dark in here, not outside. Do let me have another nap, darling, it's doing me a world of good. Just change your position and sit quiet a little while longer. This is better than any medicine for me—" He was off again on the instant, or seemed so. She changed her position dutifully. Of course she must let him have his rest. He was really out of sorts evidently. Again she dozed off, but only fitfully, and woke to a swishing sound below them at the other end of the cave. She wished she had her cigarette lighter, but Oliver had borrowed it and forgotten to return it. She wanted a light. She wanted suddenly to go, to get away from the

The Westwood Mystery 207

booming of the water, which seemed to have grown louder and now was rather terrible to endure. But she sat on patiently. He would wake of himself any moment. Finally she heard a sound that brought her to her feet without any regard for Fox's slumbers. The sound of water lapping at her feet. Lap—lap—it must be just below them!'

"Oliver," she called, stooping down and shaking him. He was very slow to rouse. She herself could not get past him for fear of slipping on him. "What's the matter?" he asked finally and very sleepily. "Oh, Kit, why did you wake me?"

"The tide's not going out, as you thought, but coming in, and coming in here," she said tensely. "Where's my lighter? Strike it." He did so, and they saw a spread of water reaching from below them away to the further end.

Oliver gave a cry. "Good God, it's the Devil's Hat. Kit"—he turned to her with an air of desperate, resolute calmness—"don't lose your head, my darling. I've made a mistake. Not only about the tide, but about the cave. It isn't the one I thought. But it's quite safe up here. The only danger is the floor shelves so steeply near the mouth... can you swim?"

"I've told you twice I couldn't," she replied, her teeth chattering. The darkness, the wash of sea below her, the loud roar of the water outside, all terrified her.

He took her hand and pressed it.

"Fortunately I can. Like a fish. Now don't be alarmed. There's no danger, but we don't want to spend the night here, do we? Very well, I'll swim out through the entrance to some boats I saw quite close. You didn't see them? But I did. Not two minutes away. I'll get one, and come back with the boatman, and we'll pick you off this like a rose from a hedge."

"But can you get a boat through that narrow entrance?" she asked, doubting, but soothed by his air of complete mastery, complete certainty in his own ability to meet the situation.

"If you know the trick, it's child's play. It only looks narrow because it winds so. Sorry to have been so stupid, sweetheart, but we'll have you out of here in five minutes. Now I must strip for the swim to my underclothes. I'll leave the others here piled up, and we can take them off when we come for you."

In the darkness she heard the sound of his clothes being pulled off and apparently folded. How slow he was! But at last he gave her feet a final pat.

"Now I'm off to get to the boat. Br-r-r, but it's chilly and deep. Mind you stay quiet, darling. Promise me you won't stir from where you are."

"My lighter!" She reached down for it.

"'Fraid I must keep it, darling, to see the opening out of here."

"Of course! How silly of me. You won't be long? There's no real danger?" she asked, struggling for his own composed manner.

"Not the slightest," he assured her. "But as you can't swim, and the floor sinks so steeply, the boat is the only way. Back in five minutes." And he was off. She heard him slithering, and saw him use the lighter for a second as he clambered down. Then it was out and the only sound was the splash of his body pushing off. It didn't sound very deep.

"Are you wading?" she called hopefully.

"Treading water. It's well over my head. Ah, there's the opening! Why, it's bright sunshine outside. Shan't be a minute. But mind you don't budge."

"Oh, I won't," she assured him fervently. She heard the splashing sounds grow fainter, then only the booming, which seemed to fill the cave. It grew worse with every minute. So did the sound of lapping water. The five minutes of which he had spoken seemed very long. They really were very long. Then she knew that a quarter of an hour must have passed by, and with that knowledge the booming grew very dreadful and the lapping of the water very horrible. She took off her stockings, tied them

The Westwood Mystery 209

together, put a pebble in the toe of one, and lowered it. To her horror, the water was not one stocking's length from her ledge. She waited, calling "Oliver! Oliver!" Her voice was lost in the roar of the water. She put her hand down—the water was up to where he had been lying. She felt behind her, there was no higher ledge, nothing but the rock wall. Something had happened to Oliver—he had hurt himself—or the boat had overturned... Fortunately he had said that the water never came up to her ledge. But it was up to it now—it rose instep deep—ankle deep—knee deep—waist deep—and then, icy with chill and terror, abandoned in that dark and awful place she saw a light—the beam from an electric torch. It swept about —around—it was on her. "Oliver! Oh, thank God?" she had called and screamed until her voice had given out. Now she could only croak. There was no boat, but Oliver was swimming back to her, an electric torch fastened somehow to his head. Like a beautiful star it shone over the dreadful water. Then she saw that it was not Oliver Fox, and that whoever it was, was not swimming, but walking, his head just above the level of the water. It must be the boatman whom he had sent, himself injured.

"You can't swim, of course, or you wouldn't be there," said a pleasant voice. "It's Miss Drury, isn't it?"

"Yes. Is he badly hurt?"

"He's quite safe on shore came the soothing answer, "and if you'll sit on my shoulders I think we can do it without even swimming."

"But—it's deep—by the entrance," she managed to get out. Pointer said nothing more, gathered her up like a child, for she was past holding on to him, and carried her out, out of the cave that had been meant for her tomb, out to where, the other side of the entrance, a boat really was waiting. A minute more and she was being assisted up the beach. There was a car... a house... a nice woman who helped her into bed and told her to drink this, not to

210   *A Resurrected Press Mystery*

worry, that everyone was all right... Then came sleep, deep and profound.

Fox had walked out of the cave, clambered up some rocks, located the biggest, found an electric torch where he had left it yesterday, buried under a little mound that he had marked with some stones, found below that again a package wrapped in waterproofing containing an outfit which he proceeded to put on. He had not meant to use them for another week, but that letter... of course Kit had read it... all women were liars and deceivers or she might even think it a silly joke for a moment, but on reflection... no, she was a sudden danger to him. He shaved off his mustache in the darkness with a safety razor and some shaving cream, and stuck on a much bigger, darker one. There was a path up the cliffs from the boulders. He found it with difficulty, but he had "arranged" some stones so as to catch his eye if need be, just touching the edges here and there with a line of phosphorous. Cautiously he climbed to the top. He did not want to spoil his clothes, and stepped out on to the hard road with a sigh of satisfaction. All had gone according to plan. A bright light fell on him. Blinking, he moved aside. It moved too. A hand was laid on his shoulder. A whistle sounded. He tried to wrench himself free—he fought like a madman. The whistle blew again and again. Men with other lights came running.

"This is him, sir," said a voice. Another second, and a tall, bronze-faced man was scrutinizing every feature of the face before him.

"Might easily be. With a false mustache"—Pointer tweaked it—"ah, just so. Baxter, what cave is nearest to us now?"

"There's a girl in the cave," interrupted Fox hastily. "I don't know, and don't care, whom you're looking for! Not me, I know that! But hurry. She can't swim and the cave's under water. Rising fast." He panted the words out breathlessly. "Down there... just by the path, I clambered

The Westwood Mystery 211

up... I left her to get help. She can't swim. I got swept out to sea myself nearly. Hurry!"

Pointer was already down the path with a man in a dark blue serge suit—Baxter, a Coast-guard. They had been "working" all the dangerous caves since Pointer arrived in the town, but this one which Fox had selected was far off and known only to a few people. Their electric lamps found the entrance from Baxter's boat. In a trice Kathleen was out and handed over to Mrs. Baxter's care. Then Pointer walked down to the police station, where Fox was being detained.

"Your name is Fox, I understand," Pointer said now. "Or at least that is the name you are known by, as well as Myers. You are detained in connection with the murder of Sir Adam Youdale at Westwood."

"It's absurd," came the instant reply, while the man's face showed green white. "I don't know the man. My name is Fox all right, and I'm a maker of jams and preserves. Doing quite nicely, too. I'm not a criminal. And that young lady you found in the cave is my fiancée. There's nothing against either of us. You got her out safe and sound, of course?" He may have thought his face looked eager, but it only showed wariness.

"Why did you change your clothes, and shave off your own mustache before putting on a false one?" Pointer asked, as though mildly curious. Fox looked like a cornered wolf for a moment. Taken back to London, he refused to speak, except to insist on his innocence. Searched as he had at once been, several letters were found on him which showed that he was contemplating flight in the very near future, so near that it was all but the present, and was collecting his funds together for that purpose. His passport and a bank deposit, which seemed to have just been made, was in the name of Outram Carfax. So was a special license for his marriage to Mary Elizabeth Green.

Pointer walked on to his own home in Bayswater that night, thinking over the events of the day. They had rather rushed him. Fox must be the guilty man surely, for there had been that in his eyes that spoke of a man who believed that there was no hope for him. He protested his innocence truculently enough, but he never once had asked what possible motive he could have for murdering Youdale. A very curious omission, that, in the experience of the chief inspector. A message was sent to Tangier asking for particulars of all the non-political cases in which Adam Youdale had appeared. The chief inspector meanwhile pored over the political papers of which Meredith had given him copies. Thanks to the notes of the F.O. he found nothing to lead him to Fox. Towards dawn, a reply came from Tangier saying that owing to changes in the Courts there, it would take some days to obtain the copies asked for, but when procured, they would be at once sent off to the Yard. Pointer sent a message to *The Tangier Resident*, the English paper of Tangier, which promised to look through their files for him. As for Manning, no connection seemed traceable between him and Fox, though the young farmer had lived all his days in a little country place where every incident of his life was noted.

Questioned, he had at once told of the few words interchanged with what he claimed was a total stranger at the *Sun in Splendor*. But the fact remained, that both men had been out that night, that one had left his fingerprints on a glass in Sir Adam's library, and that the other had acknowledged, when he could not deny it, being on the ground, and watching through a field glass what he claimed was the room next to Youdale's, but which might have been that of the murdered man.

In fact, as far as was known, Manning had acted just as an accomplice of Fox's might have been expected to act, and there was only his assertion to show that, as far as he was concerned, what was known was all that had taken place at Westwood in the night when Adam Youdale was smothered.

The Westwood Mystery 213

As for the papers taken, they were perplexing, Pointer thought. They all concerned Sturge and the Rubber Trunk Company, but they seemed of no importance, and certainly would have been of no use for blackmail. Then why had they been taken, kept, and apparently placed ready to be carried on by Fox? One thing was fairly clear, they could not concern Fox, just as there seemed no reason why Youdale's death should have benefited him.

The inquest was at eleven. Fox had asked for a solicitor and had chosen a man who had acted for him in the purchase of the jam business. He came beforehand to ask the police what they had against his client. Pointer was vague. He did not intend Fox to have a chance of cooking up a good excuse.

"He tells me he was never near Westwood," the solicitor said finally. Pointer smiled faintly. Claxton, who was relinquishing the idea of Sturge as the murderer, and relinquishing it with pleasure, since that gentleman still remained hidden, smiled also.

"I should recommend him to be more candid with you," Pointer said. "Tell him we can prove that he was there."

The solicitor, his name was Slazenger, returned to Fox and eyed him rather keenly. If Fox really was the murderer of Sir Adam Youdale, what a magnificent advertisement for Slazenger. He would get the best—that is to say, the most expensive counsel to defend him when he went for trial, and for a second, so quaint are the ways of the mind, he found himself picking on Adam Youdale as the best man for his purpose, an Acquittal in the face of almost proven guilt, for the fact that Chief Inspector Pointer had made the arrest was a guarantee that it would be well documented.

To Fox, Slazenger opened with a homily on the duty of arrested men to themselves to be frank with their solicitors, especially when they had a noose around their necks. Fox yelped at that, and began to swear again that he had never been near Westwood.

Slazenger tossed his cigarette away with an air of flinging the case from him.

"The police know that you were there," he said firmly. "They weren't bluffing—as you are. I suppose it's fingerprints, but whatever it is, they are sure of their facts. And it's no use trying to deny facts, Mr. Fox. What we have to do is to meet them with a reasonable explanation."

Fox was silent, staring at him with something almost resembling foam on his lips. Slazenger, watching him covertly, and entirely without sympathy—apart from the right and wrong of the question, Slazenger considered that a criminal was a fool, and as such to be despised—wondered at the look on the other's face. Things must be bad indeed. Fox must have killed the K.C., and have no sort of defense... Still, Slazenger's name would be advertised...

"Now this young lady you took down to Brighton yesterday," he went on. "You say you lost your head and rushed to get her help. Well, Mr. Fox, what's the use of telling me that when I learn from the local police that you changed your clothes and shaved off your mustache and put on another one, disguised yourself, in fact, before you climbed to the top of the cliff? What's the use of telling things that don't hold water?" Slazenger asked contemptuously.

Fox writhed. His face was drawn and haggard.

"The explanation I have—I mean about Westwood—sounds poor," he said huskily, his eyes moving to and fro on the wall behind the solicitor, who promptly decided that Fox was not able to twist the truth into anything plausible.

"Let's hear the facts first," he said bluntly, "and then your explanation."

Fox swallowed hard. He certainly did not look like a man telling the truth, the whole truth and nothing but the truth.

The Westwood Mystery 215

"I've got a complete explanation of everything," he said now.

"Oh!" said the unsympathetic Mr. Slazenger wearily, in a tone of deep disgust.

"One day, I'll go into dates with you. Later, it was roughly a fortnight ago, a bloke called at my house on a Saturday afternoon. I was in. He said he wanted to get on to a picture which Davies's father owned. You know all about Davies's father being a picture dealer in a small way?" Slazenger did. "His name is Fullford. He keeps an antique shop in Wimbledon. Well, he looked at the pictures which I took over with the house from Davies, and seemed tremendously struck with one of an old gal in a muslin cap and mittens. Said he thought it was a Raeburn which had had the signature painted over by some restoring fool. Said he was commissioned by a Monsieur Broukère, a Belgian millionaire, to pick up any Raeburns going. On Monday, a fat little dark chap turned up who said he was Monsieur Broukère. He looked at the picture for pretty well a solid hour on end. Then he said he would buy it for five hundred pounds if it was guaranteed a Raeburn. I asked him whose certificate he wanted. He said he would take Sir Adam's written statement that be believed the picture to be a genuine Raeburn. He would arrange with him to see it, he said, as he was a pal of his. The only thing was, that the greatest secrecy was to observed about the whole affair on account of the tax on pictures taken into Belgium. Then he said I was to bring it down to Wimbledon, take a room at the *Sun in Splendor* there, and wait for a telephone message from him. I was to go prepared to spend a week, for which he agreed to pay. He did so there and then. I did as he said. When I got there I had a telephone message from Broukère to say that he had a bad cold. Finally, after kicking my heels about for just on a week, I got a message from him to say that I was to bring the picture with me to Westwood at eleven-thirty p.m. I was not to go to the front door but to enter by the first long French window to the right of it, which would be left standing open for me. Mr. Broukère said he would be there waiting with Sir Adam, and that if Youdale passed the picture as genuine, he would pay for it on the spot and take it away with him."

"Well, I'd have refused such a proposal from anyone except to go to Westwood, but I knew Sir Adam—by reputation—" Fox added hastily, "so I took the picture along at the hour named, after trying to have a word with Fullford. But he was out. I found the nearest window standing open and the light on. I went in. The room was empty, but it looked very comfortable, and on a brass tray was a note to say that should Sir Adam and Monsieur Broukère be detained, they were trying to get a special lens by which to examine the picture, and might be delayed, would I wait for an hour, and if by that time they had not come, I was to know that it meant they couldn't secure the apparatus that night but would be bringing it down early next morning. I was to return to the hotel and wait for an early morning telephone giving me the hour at which to bring the picture once more. Meanwhile, would I help myself to some sherry to pass the time? Well, I waited, had some sherry, and finally after an hour's wait went back to the *Sun*. By the way, I had a room that let me get in and out of the window without bothering to pass through the inn door. There was a little wicket gate just opposite that was merely latched at night . . . so I went back and waited for the message. None came by ten next morning, and I decided to teach Broukère a lesson. He mustn't think I was going to stay at his beck and call for the sake of a measly five hundred, which was a tenth of the picture's real value probably."

"Let me see"—Slazenger mused aloud as Fox paused at this—"those pictures—I think they have not yet been formally purchased from Davies?"

"Not completely," Fox said sulkily, and in saying so gave his reason for being only too glad to make the sale in

The Westwood Mystery

secret. "But, as I say, I went back home, and.. on the way to my office saw the late morning papers,. and learned that Sir Adam had been found murdered, and well—I decided to say nothing whatever, to lie low and wait on events. Of course, I knew they couldn't touch me, as I was—" This was said in an almost comic tone of bravado.

"But you decided not to come forward with your story," Slazenger finished with a grin. "Sensible resolve. Have you got that note on you?" Fox's eyes flickered uneasily.

"No. Fact is I fell asleep after my glass or two of sherry, and when I woke up I never thought of looking to see if I had it. I must have left it in the room. On the table probably."

"Pity," Slazenger said with due gravity. "It might have made a lot of difference if you could have produced it."

"The police must have it," Fox said to that. "Unless they want to keep it dark. Just to get me in their grip."

"Ever been in trouble with them before?" Slazenger asked suddenly, and watching him narrowly.

"Never," and an odd, gray tone floated under Fox's skin, making him look older and almost wizened.

"Liar!" thought the astute Slazenger, "so he has been! Wonder what for?" Then he recalled that the police had his client's fingerprints and would probably tell him honestly if they had any previous conviction against Fox. Also, something might come out at the inquest this afternoon.

The inquest was an eagerly awaited function. Sturge was not there. His name was bandied about freely, but it was known that the police had made an arrest, 'under sensational circumstances,' said the press, who went on to relate how Mr. Fox, the detained man, had been in the act of setting out to swim the channel when he had been arrested.

At the inquest only formal evidence was taken, formal evidence from the doctor as to the cause of death, which was by smothering with a pillow after taking a powerful, but not fatal, sleeping draft. Then came evidence of the fingerprint on the glass of sherry and on the window frame at the *Sun in Splendor*— the same prints as Mr. Fox's fingers gave when tested. Mr. Fox had been disguising himself when arrested, and on him was found a passport, and evidence of a bank account in the name of—etc., etc...

Fox, questioned, told the same story as he had told Slazenger, and it was received with the same degree of belief. The inquest was adjourned for a week, Mr. Fox being detained as before.

So the police had nothing up their sleeve, Slazenger decided, after a talk with Claxton. But they would, of course, leave no stone unturned to find out the past of the man who called himself by so many names, and they, like Slazenger himself, evidently believed that the true story of Fox's past would not exactly redound to that man's credit.

Fox contented himself with demanding the presence of Mr. Fullford who, he said, would certainly bear out what he had just told. If so, this would be tremendously in the detained man's favor, and the coroner hoped that the antiquarian would be ready to give evidence when the inquest sat again. So did the police. So did Pointer. And to his joy, on going to answer a telephone call some three hours later, he was told that Mr. Fullford was speaking, that Mr. Fullford had just learned of Sir Adam Youdale's murder, of Fox's detention, and of the story that he had told, a story in which the antiquarian's name was mentioned. Mr. Fullford, whose voice sounded very faint and weak, said that he would be at the Wimbledon police station in half an hour. Meantime he wished to say that there was not a word of truth in the account given by Fox. The real story was quite another matter, and would be in the hands of the police as soon as he, Fullford, could get to them.

CHAPTER TWELVE

Pointer hurried to the police station with Claxton and Nicholson. The superintendent was feeling very pleased with the way things were going. He had not been too open in his hunt for Sturge, and that was perhaps just as well, though only this morning further confirmation had come to hand showing how great was the peril hanging over the head of the financier, how great, therefore the reason for him to get free at all costs. Still, Fox, with his midnight entry, his fingerprints, his alias at the inn, his silence, even though he knew that Youdale had been found murdered, all looked much more like the real criminal, so Claxton now thought. As for the chief inspector, he wondered, as he walked along, what, in the story that Fox had not told, would explain the tucked-in bed, the dressing gown, and the rose.

He found Mr. Fullford to be an elderly, thin man, who looked very frail and ill. The antiquarian was seated when they went into Claxton's private room, and as he rose with difficulty, Claxton sprung forward with a shocked look and pressed him back.

"Good Lord, Mr. Fullford, what have you been doing to yourself?" he asked in concern

"I didn't do it to myself, superintendent," was the reply in a quavering voice "I've been poisoned! You should have seen me a couple of days ago. Then I did look an ill man."

"What's that?" Claxton asked in professional, as well as private, horror.

Fullford nodded his white head.

"Fox thought he had finished me. That was why he told that story. But I'll go into that later—" he stopped and ran a trembling hand over his face to steady himself.

He looked very ill indeed. Claxton murmured something to a constable, who hurried out. A doctor, and meanwhile some brandy, would be sent in.

"Yes," Fullford went on, half-closing his eyes, "he wanted, or rather he needed, a man who would serve as a link between himself and Sir Adam. He had to have an excuse."

"Look here, Mr. Fullford," the superintendent now recollected himself, "that is Chief Inspector Pointer from Scotland Yard. He's in charge of the case, and this gentleman is Mr. Nicholson, who represents the murdered man's interests."

Fullford bowed politely.

"Have you any objection to my being present?" Nicholson asked promptly.

Fullford shook his head.

Not in the least. On the contrary."

"Any objection to one of my men taking down what you tell us? It may save fatigue," went on Claxton. "I'll get a man who'll take it down in shorthand, then write it out in longhand and bring it round to you to sign. Will that do?"

Fullford said it would do excellently. Sipping some brandy and water which was brought in, he began:

"A man I know, a chartered accountant, name of Burns, was talking to me of another man called Davies, a picture dealer who went smash. He mentioned that the man, though frightfully poor, had a few pictures that he wouldn't part from, and one of them was said to be a Raeburn. Burns gave me, among a lot of details, the address of the old gentleman. It was 545 Tollard Road. I have a memory for numbers and it stuck. The other day, I happened to hear of a dowery chest going cheap at a house in Tollard Road, and I went to have a look at it. It's price was too fantastic for me. On leaving, I remembered about Davies and his canvases. My garrulous friend had mentioned that Davies's son had had to sell the house. I decided to see if the pictures were still there, and if so,

The Westwood Mystery 221

whether I could have a look at them. Well, I met a man—it's the Fox who murdered Sir Adam, as I now know."

Pointer hoped that this was more than a pious belief. Fullford looked to him the type to hold fast to any idea which he had once got into his head.

"I told him that I understood that old Mr. Davies, who had owned the house some three years ago, had also owned some good pictures, and that, if they were still in the house, I should like to see them. I handed him my business card, and I noticed he read it very carefully. He asked me in, and showed me everything he had in the way of pictures. They weren't worth sixpence the lot. The supposed Raeburn was a copy of an oleograph. I told him so in decent language, thanked him for letting me see them, and left." Again Mr. Fullford sipped his brandy and water, and eyed a constable, who stepped in and whispered a word to the superintendent. The word was to say that the doctor was outside. When the constable had left the room, Fullford, who evidently did not intend to let an effect be spoiled, put his glass down. "And that, gentlemen," he said solemnly, "is the first, last, and only time I ever met or saw the fellow. As for his telephoning to Jenkins—I take it that was just a clever attempt to lend an appearance of truth to his story. But I've a lot more yet to tell you about my one and only talk with him. I'm never likely to forget it, for more than one reason." For a second, exhausted, he lay back against his chair. The doctor came in. He was the police surgeon, and had taken the same oath as the police around him. It had only been in fear of putting the old man off his tale that had kept him waiting outside. Now he felt Mr. Fullford's pulse, and nodded approval at his brandy and water.

"The sooner we have you in bed, my friend, the better," he said genially. "Better still to lock you up. I know you, Fullford. You'd roll off your death-bed to do something you had set your heart on doing. Your real illness is mule-headedness."

222   *A Resurrected Press Mystery*

There was a general smile, in which Fullford joined. Then after another sip, he resumed, "It was I who mentioned Sir Adam's name first to Fox. I had just been shown a room full of awful rubbish, when by the door I saw what at a glance I took to be a photograph of Westwood, so I said something like 'Is that a snapshot of Westwood from the back?' Fox said 'Do you mean Sir Adam Youdale, the KC.'s, house at Wimbledon? Oh, of course you come from Wimbledon, don't you... No, that's not his house, as far as I know.' By this time I had seen for myself that it wasn't. I went on to another room. Half-way round it, Fox asked suddenly if I knew Sir Adam. I said I sold him things now and then. He was eyeing me closely, and, I thought, had half a mind to say something more about Sir Adam. But he didn't, and we stuck to business. But before I left, he asked me where my shop was, and then, if it was near Sir Adam's place. I told him, 'quite near.' Again I thought he wanted to say something, or ask something, but he only fingered his chin."

They had all seen Fox doing that very thing.

"After that, he dropped Sir Adam. I don't think he referred to him again, but he seemed quite interested to hear that I was just off on one of my rounds which took me into the country, sometimes for days—sometimes for over a fortnight or even longer. Well, I said good-by to him and the stuff on his walls and never expected to hear from him again. But the morning before Sir Adam was found murdered, the morning before I set off on my round, that is, which date, as I told you, I had mentioned to Fox, a parcel came for me. In it was a pot of sloe jam. Now Fox had talked a lot about that jam to me as it happened. He was just putting it up by some old family recipe of his. Something unusually good he told me. I had acknowledged to being partial to sloes, and when I saw the pot, with no label or note, I felt sure it came from him, and thought it very decent indeed of him. I found it delicious. But fortunately for me, I only took a spoonful, as I don't care for jam for breakfast, and fortunately for

The Westwood Mystery 223

Mrs. Gay, I took the pot along with me in my suitcase. On the way down to Canterbury, where I was bound for, I was about as ill as a man can be and live. The very thought of sloes sickened me for days. I nearly flung the pot out, but I brought it back home with me. Oh, yes," in answer to a move of Claxton's, "I have it at home. I've locked it up safely. Of course I didn't connect my illness with the jam at first, why should I? I thought it was a lobster salad. But when I heard some men in the compartment talking about Sir Adam's murder—asked them for a paper and read the news asking me to come forward, and referring to that murderer's fantastic tale, well, I saw the whole thing clear."

"What's your idea about the poisoning?" the chief inspector asked him. Mr. Fullford looked a very shrewd judge of all that came his way, Pointer, thought.

"Fox wanted to poison me," was the instant reply, "so as to be free to tell any lie he liked. I can see how much to his advantage it would be, both in talking to Sir Adam and in explaining things afterwards to you, if he could make me have said, or done, anything he, liked."

The men nodded. They all saw that quite clearly. "You think he used your name as a sort of introduction to Sir Adam?" Pointer pressed.

"Undoubtedly. I don't believe a word about Monsieur Broukère or that mysterious invitation to come in by the window. He knew or guessed that if he met Sir Adam in the garden, as though walking up to the house, Sir Adam would naturally take him in, if he mentioned me in some way—"

Suddenly Fullford's eyes flashed He almost stood up for a second. "I have it! All this talk of his about a Belgian and a Raeburn! It was Fox who posed to Sir Adam as having heard from me that Sir Adam was the possessor, as he was, of a fine Raeburn, and asked whether he might be allowed the privilege of seeing it."

224   *A Resurrected Press Mystery*

"By night?" Pointer asked thoughtfully. Fullford's thoughts were following along the ground traversed by his own, more or less.

Mr. Fullford looked at the chief inspector for the first time, in the sense of really seeing him. He nodded his approval of the question.

"Quite a fair objection, even with special lighting, but if Fox told Sir Adam that he had to leave that night or early next morning...? I can imagine that Fox would find it easy to think out some suitable lie." Fullford's thin lip curled.

"At any rate, that, I think, is how Fox was taken up into Sir Adam's bedroom and could see for himself what the room looked like. There are ample hiding places, supposing he slipped into the house later on, and hid until Sir Adam was in bed."

"He would have been able to dose that chartreuse if he was hidden in the bedroom," Claxton nodded in agreement with the sketched plan of the murder. Fullford was merely putting into words the most obvious explanation of the events of that dreadful night which had led up to the finding of Sir Adam's dead body in the early morning.

"And have you any notion as to the motive, Mr. Fullford?" the superintendent went on hopefully.

The antiquarian looked at him with far away eyes. "I think the police generally know the answers to the questions they ask," he said with a hint of a smile. "Certainly, if you don't, I don't. And that, I think, is all I can tell you." He made as if to go, but though he looked as if bed were a necessity, since he had told them so much, and was there, they detained him a moment longer.

"About that secret drawer that you opened for Sir Adam," Pointer suggested. Here was what the chief inspector, and Nicholson, and Claxton, too, for that matter, hoped might furnish a clue to the mysterious motive the link between the K.C. and the jam maker.

The Westwood Mystery 225

Mr. Fullford looked as though he thought it rather hard lines to have to stay up for such unimportant details.

"Oh, that! Well, I don't think there's anything to tell. I had sold Sir Adam a picture in a frame which is, I think, without a doubt a genuine Sheraton. You know you can generally tell by—"

A cough from Claxton and a scratch of the pen from the constable clerk recalled the antiquarian, from what promised to be an interesting talk on how to detect genuine Sheraton. "Well, I happened to see one at the Victoria and Albert Museum which reminded me very much of it. The museum one had the secret drawer open. I had a look at Sir Adam's next time when I wound his clocks. I see to them once a week. He has a genuine Tompion, and one which I really think is possibly—"

Another cough from Claxton, another scrape of the pen from the clerk.

"Ah, yes, where was I?" Fullford murmured, looking a little cross at being driven back into the straight and narrow path so firmly, "yes, about Sir Adam's frame. When I inspected it carefully with my glass, I found a line of what might be cleavage which is practically impossible to detect unless you know it's there. Sir Adam was tremendously interested when I 'phoned him about it. He was away at the time, but as soon as he came back he summoned me to open it if it really existed. I did. Inside were a lot of papers."

"Yellow? Old looking?" Claxton and Nicholson asked in one breath.

"Not at all. Quite newish looking. Well, I think that's all there is to tell, except that Sir Adam took them out, and opened them, and seemed immensely struck. I don't think I ever saw a man before really stand with his mouth open." Fullford's eyes were once more distant, and seemed to see far-off objects, faraway scenes. "But Sir Adam did. Then he said: 'Impossible!' And gave me a rather odd look."

For all he had spoken of it as unimportant, now that he was actually telling it, old Mr. Fullford quite warmed to the recital. "Yes, quite unpleasant. As though he thought I might be up to some trickery or other. I stared at him, I remember, quite hard in my turn, perhaps my jaw dropped too, for he seemed to pull himself together, and stepping to a table in the window, began to look through the papers as though intensely keen on them. He forgot me altogether. Dropped off this planet, in fact, for the time being. I stood waiting a minute or two, for I didn't know whether he wanted the drawer put back or not. I had to cough as often as you have just now, Mr. Claxton—"

Claxton grinned apologetically.

"Before he heard me. Then I he looked up like a man in a dream and murmured: 'I wouldn't have believed this if it had happened to anyone else.' But really these old drawers in picture-frames of that period are by no means uncommon. I asked him if he would like the drawer screwed in again or merely replaced; there are a couple of wooden screws that look like part of the foliage which hold it shut. He didn't hear me. He only stared over my head and asked if I believed in destiny—what some people used to call Providence. I was asking him just then about the drawer, and finally he got it, for he said, 'Oh, as you like, Fullford, as you like,' and repeated his question about believing in Providence. I said it all depended. When things went well I did. When they didn't I called it Fate, and cursed it; and said I would screw the drawer in again. He only said that there was no more foolish saying than that murder will out, but that for once it seemed to be true, and by that time I had the drawer in place again, and left him to his papers and his old saws."

By this time Mr. Fullford had run down like a piece of machinery, only will-power was keeping him able to talk at all, and the doctor now took him in charge, forbidding him to speak another word, for the time being.

The Westwood Mystery 227

Claxton accompanied the two back to Fullford's shop, and there duly took over the pot of sloe jam, which was promptly sent off by dispatch rider to the Home Office analyst's bureau.

Meanwhile Nicholson was going over the evidence just received piece by piece, shaking each out and examining it, and then laying it aside, like a careful housewife with the washing back from the laundry.

"Papers—old family papers—some old case in which Youdale was interested..." he muttered. And in which Fox was interested? That would be it! 'Murder will out,' Youdale said. Whose murder?" He was asking the questions now, but the chief inspector did not answer. A little later Pointer was seated in front of a pile of papers which represented the cases in which Sir Adam Youdale had figured in England. The Tangier ones were not yet to be had.

The telephoned analysis of the sloe jam reached him before he was nearly finished. Enough arsenic to kill a regiment had been put into the jam after it was cooked, and after the pot was filled. The whole had been rather roughly stirred so that it was distinctly patchy. A hurried performance, the analyst thought.

"But effective," Fullford said, when Pointer stepped into his shop to tell him the result of the test. The doctor had rung him up to say that Fullford could be questioned in moderation now. He had had a very narrow shave from death, but the medico thought that, with great care as to his diet, he should get well in time. Mr. Fullford was still looking very ill indeed, and Pointer felt that but for his own determination, he would look still worse.

"I want dates and hours, if you feel up to them," Pointer said.

Fullford said he felt quite himself again, and asked for his business diary.

Pointer made his notes, and then said, "And now about the rest of the people at Westwood, Mr. Fullford.

228   *A Resurrected Press Mystery*

Are they, any of them, customers of yours? Take Lady Youdale to begin with?"

He learned that everyone except the servants, Miss Luton and Monsieur Gaudet, who had been at Westwood when Sir Adam was murdered, knew the antiquarian slightly, and had bought things from him, even Sturge.

"Now, the last time you were at Westwood, what time did you leave?"

But Fullford could not give a guess, beyond saying that he would put it somewhere between one and three o'clock. He said that he had heard nothing unusual, and had seen absolutely nothing out of the way.

"You attend to the clock in Sir Adam's bedroom?" Pointer went on, but on this occasion Fullford said that he had not opened the case. He wound the little eight-day clock on the mantel and for once did not open the big wooden-cased clock which he had seen was in perfect condition the week previously. He agreed that, provided he knew how to take off the various hanging parts, a man could have hidden in that case, and replaced the detached pieces before leaving the room. Pointer knew by careful measurements that Fox might have been able to squeeze himself into it, supposing he had left the door ajar for fresh air.

"Did anyone in the house know anything of clock-making, or how to detach those parts, do you think, Mr. Fullford ?" Pointer asked finally.

"It wouldn't take any special knowledge," Fullford said, "any man with good eyesight could do that job. Just a matter of unhooking and hooking again."

Pointer arranged with him that, supposing he felt well enough, he would come to Westwood next morning, and show him the secret drawer in the Sheraton frame. "As I think I had better not be seen calling for you, I'll ask Mr. Nicholson to do so."

Mr. Fullford said that he would need no one to come for him but would be at the house by ten o'clock tomorrow morning.

The Westwood Mystery 229

"Don't thank me," he added. "Jenkins is getting on my nerves with his talk about a mistake having been made, and it being Mr. Sturge who murdered Sir Adam. Mr. Sturge is no murderer!"

"What makes you so certain?" Pointer asked as he was just on the moment of leaving.

"Because I know him a bit. Mr. Sturge isn't a criminal. I don't care what people say. He's one of these people who can't help being clever with figures, and he's been a bit too clever, that's all," Fullford said wisely. "In his line of business it's just a question of putting some naughts on one side and taking them off the other—just to make things balance. Look at the government budgets these years past. If that isn't crooked, what is? Same thing. A passion for balancing books. Mr. Sturge may have juggled with figures a bit, but a criminal, except in the same sense as they are? Oh, dear, no!"

Pointer was amused at the old man's certainty. Fullford saw it and looked put out.

"Fortunately you know better, you know all about Fox, and so can't be shaken," he went on in a more mollified tone, "but these village idiots who talk as though Mr. Sturge had crept into Sir Adam's room, weighted his pillow with duck-shot, sewed it up with yellow thread, dropped it over his face after drugging him, and then stolen some papers that had been sent to Sir Adam—well, they're silly. Mr. Sturge would no more murder anyone than would the Bishop. Not actually steal either—at least, I think so. Much more likely that Sir Adam left those papers lying around—he could be very absent-minded on occasions, and that Mr., Sturge pounced on them and then got away. Oh, he'd do that! But not murder. Nor, as I say, downright theft, such as opening a safe and taking a man's keys to do it first."

Pointer said it must be pleasant to feel so sure of the innocence of anyone, and left Mr. Fullford to rest up still more.

230   *A Resurrected Press Mystery*

By ten next morning, Tukes had been sent in to the other end of Wimbledon to a bank whose manager Pointer knew, with a letter asking that good citizen to detain the butler, under some pretext or other, for an hour. The pretext being a hunt for some money which Pointer claimed to have found had been deposited in the bank by Sir Adam Youdale. By the end of the hour the manager was to hand the butler a note saying that they were quite unable to trace any such deposit with them and to ask for further details. The chief inspector "happened" to be in the garden when Mr. Fullford, looking pale and wan enough in the morning light, came slowly up from the gate.

"Going to see that all my children are acting properly," Fullford announced as the chief inspector opened the door for him.

"Will it bother you if I come too, and ask any questions that occur to me?" Pointer said.

Fullford, playing up well, replied that he would be delighted to answer anything in his power. Nicholson, too, "happened" to be passing in the hall and came along.

"Just want to see if a picture-frame is all right in here," Fullford said airily, going into the dining-room and up to a fine landscape on a side wall over the dinner-wagon. He took out a little velvet covered wooden mallet, in case "things stuck," as he said vaguely.

At that instant a shot rang out. It shook the windows and the crystal chandelier trembled to it. In a second Pointer had the window open.

"Don't leave the room on any account!" he called to Fullford, and was in the act of rushing out when Mademoiselle Le Brun almost stumbled into his arms. She was very white and shaken looking.

"He aimed at me! Did you hear the shot? He's there! Among the rhododendrons. He's still there." She shook violently.

Pointer was out of the window in a flash. So was Nicholson. So was the man on duty in the house. The

The Westwood Mystery 231

rhododendron clump, to which she had pointed, was close to the house—which explained the loud report—but out of sight around a corner. The servants had rushed out, and were scuttling around like frightened hens.

"Oh, he's hiding in the hollow tree," squeaked one. "I saw his arm go up—a red-brown suit on—just like Mr. Sturge had on."

The clump of rhododendrons, twenty feet high some of them, were planted on a mound of three steep rubble steps with the oldest and tallest trees at the foot and the smallest on the top. The other side was cut down sharply to a tiny pool at the foot. They found the hollow tree, it was one of the middle ones but very large of girth for its species. A ladder was brought. There was no one inside, but a rifle was there, warm to the touch and with a blackened barrel. It was a beautiful gun, a twelve bore, hammerless ejector, light in weight and superbly finished. Such a gun as would cost at least a hundred pounds, and one that had been well cared for—up till now. It had the name of Adam Youdale on its plate. Pointer looked the ground over, very carefully while the ladder was hurried up. Once the chief inspector knew that no man was inside the hollow tree, he gave a glance to his subordinate that meant that the other was to carry on in the detective officer's absence. Pointer hurried back to the house. Mademoiselle Le Brun, meanwhile, had collapsed into an arm-chair.

"A glass of water," she panted, "with brandy in it—quick—please." She pointed to the next room. Fullford found no water there, nor brandy. He rang the bell, but the servants were all outside, and Tukes away. He remembered that in the morning-room there usually stood a jug of water with two glasses. As he poured one out and searched for some brandy, he heard the chief inspector come sprinting in from outside.

"Where were you exactly, Mademoiselle, when the shot was fired?" Pointer asked her. Fullford brought in his glass of water and she drank it eagerly. Then rising, and looking her collected self again, she took the detective to a spot, where she said that she had first heard a rustle. Thinking it a cat or dog she had turned to walk towards it, when she saw a gun-barrel pointing straight at her from the rhododendrons, a shot rang out, and turning, she ran for the house. There was no one beside herself in the garden at the time. The line of the shot, as Pointer now saw, precluded the idea that it was anyone in the house, standing in doorway or at a window, who had been aimed at. He sent a code word to the police station, then he took her with him to the cloak-room on the ground floor, where, in a large cupboard, hung a rack. On it three guns were usually kept. A sixteen-bore, and a twenty, beside the twelve found in the hollow tree. The twelve-bore was on the lowest rack and therefore the easiest to reach. The closet was always locked when Sir Adam was away from home, but if he was in the house, the key would usually stand in the lock. The window of the cloak-room opened on to the lawn and was directly in front of the rhododendrons.

So that anyone in the garden could have got the gun; for no one thought of locking the cupboard door, so explained mademoiselle. Pointer said nothing, but he had locked that cupboard within an hour of being in the house. One of his first questions to Tukes had been whether Sir Adam had any firearms, and if so where they were kept. Tukes had mentioned the gun-cupboard and Pointer found the tally correct, locked it and taken the key. Pointer's men had since verified the guns by Sir Adam's gun-license. The cartridges were on a shelf inside the same closet. There was a perfectly fitting key in the lock now—a duplicate of the one Pointer had. Yet Tukes had said there was no other. Nicholson now returned from his fruitless search of the bushes. He rather wondered at mademoiselle's pallor. The spirit in her seemed so strong that he had expected her to ignore danger to mere flesh and blood.

The Westwood Mystery 233

"No," she now replied in answer to another of Pointer's questions, she had not heard any window open, she had only heard the slight rustle and then seen the gun-barrel—pointing straight at her.

"Why should anyone want to shoot you?" Pointer murmured.

She said that she could not imagine. But, of course, she had seen Mr. Sturge running across that lighted gap... she still thought there was the real criminal...

Pointer shook his head.

"The only thing you possess of any value—excuse my bluntness—as far as we know, is that villa in Tangier that Sir Adam left you in the codicil to his will."

She started as though he had touched her with red hot metal. "Impossible. Quite absurd!" she said vehemently. "You forget that the Rubber Trunk Company's papers were stolen, that Sir Adam was murdered to get them... for this poor Fox is but Mr. Sturge's cat's-paw in my opinion."

"We have those papers now," he objected.

"Exactly, and I am not shot at until now," she retorted impatiently. "The reason for the attempt to shoot would be that I know something..." Her face flushed as though at a sudden and good idea.

"Suppose it was because I was walking to investigate that rustle that I was shot at and missed? Suppose it was someone, in confidence I will be frank and say, suppose it was Mr. Sturge who, fearing lest I discover him, fired over my head, just to frighten me away from coming closer? I was not hit. Perhaps it was only meant to do what it has done, send me running into the house?"

"And the police running out?" Pointer asked dryly.

She shrugged her slender, sloping shoulders "That! One cannot always achieve every object at one and the same time! I think whoever was in those bushes wanted to get rid of my inconvenient curiosity quickly, and did the one thing that would accomplish that."

"And how did, whoever it was, come to have Sir Adam's gun in his hand?" was the counter-query. "No, Mademoiselle, the fact that a gun had been taken beforehand, by some means we have yet to find out, and that you were fired at, means I feel sure, that we must consider that villa left to you as of more importance than we first thought."

Pointer smiled inwardly at the exasperation on the Frenchwoman's face.

But behind that exasperation was a hint of repressed fear.

"But that is impossible," she cried again, "quite impossible."

"I'm afraid it's by no means impossible," Pointer said slowly.

"But you've got the man who murdered Sir Adam, what interest would that little house in Africa be to him? Or to anyone? It's value is not worth one room of Westwood, for instance."

"Then why were you singled out?" Pointer persisted obstinately, "and how was it that one of Sir Adam's own guns was used? Taken from a locked cupboard?".

Mademoiselle made a sudden gesture. "I remember noticing this morning, without giving it a second thought, that the gun-closet was unlocked."

"I was told that no other key in the house would unlock the door, certainly none of the keys my men tried would do it."

"I believe a duplicate key was always kept in the tobacco-jar on the mantel, under the tobacco," she said, as though thinking back to some chance heard word. "Tukes had no idea of its existence, but Mr. Sturge might easily have been told for he sometimes came down for a day's shooting with Sir Adam, over Sir Hercules Robinson's coverts near us."

Pointer did not take up the matter further. He glanced at the glass of water. "You fetched that for Mademoiselle, I suppose?" he asked Fullford. The old

The Westwood Mystery 235

gentleman nodded, he looked put out by something in the talk.

"Suppose you unfasten the hidden drawer for us now?" Pointer said to him. Nicholson wondered at his asking for it in front of mademoiselle. What did this mean?

"Hidden drawer?" she repeated as though vastly surprised and interested, and staring at the furniture behind her.

Mr. Fullford stepped silently to the picture-frame, and touched what looked like a rose-bud in the carving; it turned in his fingers, holding on to a spray of raised foliage as though it were a handle, he pulled a long box-like drawer of nearly a foot in length, about two inches deep and two wide, came out. It was quite empty.

"Not screwed in?" Pointer asked Fullford shook his head "No. Only fastened with the turn-pin at the end." Pointer took the drawer from him and examined it.

"Marks down the side here where someone with long nails and a very slender hand recently pulled something out." Even as he spoke he lifted mademoiselle's right hand with his left. The first and middle finger nails were black. Pointer looked at her, she at him, and there was in her dark eyes the unmistakable look of a plucky person summoning all her courage to meet an emergency.

"Come, Mademoiselle, confess," he said lightly, letting her hand fall back on her chair, "you knew all about this drawer, and wanted to be the first to see if anything was hidden in it? Well, Mr. Fullford could have told you it was empty."

Fullford nodded as he took the drawer back from Pointer and began to replace it with one swift careful motion. It took only a second to do.

"You are right," she smiled at him, "but a woman's curiosity—it is always her strongest point, is it not?"

"Not with you, I should have said," Pointer replied in the tone of one paying a compliment.

Mr. Fullford suggested that unless Pointer had anything more that he would like him to do, he would go back home. The chief inspector thanked him and suggested that Nicholson might see Mr. Fullford safely to his shop.

When he was alone with the Frenchwoman he looked at her with an air of concern.

"Mademoiselle, that French friend of yours, Monsieur Gaudet, who attended the inquest this morning, he's free of observation now, and I don't feel any too sure about him. He comes from Tangier, or around there... it looks to me as though this really had been an attempt on your life with the villa behind it as the motive... hidden treasure, say?..."

"Oh, but it is too absurd," she snapped. "It is ridiculous! How should he know where the guns were kept and the cartridges? What interest can he have in a villa such as you can buy by the dozen out there?"

"I'm afraid you're saying that because he's a friend," Pointer said doubtfully, "yes, I'm afraid you're shielding him because he's a compatriot. He's been down to Westwood a couple of times, and he stayed here over a night... Sir Adam might easily have shown him his guns..."

Mademoiselle looked as though she would have liked to slap the pleasant face gazing at her with such kindly concern on it. "There's no one else," Pointer repeated. "I think you are making too little of it. I still think that villa... we certainly shall keep our eyes on this Monsieur Gaudet very carefully after this. And do be careful of yourself, Mademoiselle, too. Don't meet him without witnesses present. Avoid lonely places. We'll do our best to shadow you, but you mustn't be fool hardy."

Mademoiselle pressed her finely cut lips tightly together, and left the room without a sound, and yet with the effect of slamming the door behind her.

CHAPTER THIRTEEN

"I wonder if it was Sir Adam who unscrewed that secret drawer?" Nicholson said on his return from seeing Mr. Fullford home. "The old chap seems very certain that he screwed it up again, and it isn't the sort of thing about which one would be likely to make a mistake."

Pointer said nothing.

"It looks to me—" Claxton was with the solicitor, he had hurried to the house in reply to a description of the shooting affair, "as though Fox had a go at it when he was here, we all think those papers may have concerned him, and if so, he very likely thought they were still in their hiding-place, and that he could get them. He may have looked here before trying the safe. But this shooting at mademoiselle—her idea, Mr. Nicholson tells me, is that it was Sturge trying to frighten her away from coming closer and recognizing him. That seems quite a good notion, except that it doesn't answer the question as to how he came to have that gun in his hands. It looks to me more serious than just an attempt to get away. What do you think, Pointer?"

"Have you seen the place yet where the person stood who fired the shot?" Pointer asked. Claxton said that he had not. Pointer took him out to the knoll of rhododendrons.

"Someone stood here close beside the tree, right enough," the superintendent thought.

A telephone rang. The superintendent was hailed to the 'phone.

"Anything about the marks that doesn't tally with her story?" Nicholson asked curiously. He knew that more had passed between her and the chief inspector than he understood.

238 *A Resurrected Press Mystery*

"You don't shoot yourself, do you, Mr. Nicholson?" Pointer asked, and both men laughed for a second at the awkward form of the question.

"No," Nicholson said, "I've never fired a gun in my life. Why?"

"Well, there are many ways of doing everything, but the man who wants to hit what he's shooting at puts his weight on his left foot with the heel of the right slightly raised. On uneven ground, the left foot is always lower than the right—unless the shooter is left-handed. This is a right-handed gun, and the blur of a glove on the trigger shows that the oil was wiped off by a right-handed person. True, when you're shooting straight up into the air, as was done in reality here, you do throw your weight on the right leg for a second, but, take it from me, standing as this person stood, you couldn't have hit a barn in front of you, nor a stationary balloon just overhead."

"You think the shooting was just as she thought, to prevent her coming closer?" Nicholson asked

"I think mademoiselle can shoot, in the sense that she can load a gun and fire, but that's about all," was the reply with a faint smile.

Claxton had snapped out a telephone message in record time, and overheard the last remark.

"Ah," he murmured, "now, what would she be trying tricks of that kind for? Of course, being a French girl, she wouldn't know anything about how to choose a good place. Who was she firing at?"

Nicholson looked so horrified that Pointer's smile widened for a second. "No one," he was able to reassure the solicitor. "I think she wanted to create a diversion, and made a bad choice of locality."

"I wonder why she chose it, then." Nicholson, had a great respect for Miss Le Brun's brains.

"The answer, I think, is because time counted, and the rhododendrons were the nearest cover to the house, which was out of sight of most of the rooms. As it was,

The Westwood Mystery 239

one of the maids caught a glimpse of the gun being flung into the hollow tree-trunk and thought she saw a brown coat sleeve."

"Just like a woman to fling a valuable gun into that old stump," Claxton said with a shake of the head. "But what was the idea behind her shooting? If it was her, as you think."

"I think she saw Mr. Fullford and Mr. Nicholson together when she was in the town. I think she noticed the little bag in Mr. Fullford's hands in which are his velvet-covered hammer and so on. I think, knowing of the secret drawer, she wondered whether by any chance we were after it. When we got here, she was in the cloak-room getting the gun and loading it. She rushed out of the window into the nearest cover, fired a shot, toppled the gun into the hiding-place, and then, pale and shaken lest we had opened the drawer, of which she thought us ignorant, rushed in to get there first. She sent Fullford for some water."

"Fullford ought to've spotted that as an *'Anciente Thinge,'* ". Claxton muttered, in disgust.

"Fullford was certain that the drawer was empty, and so had no qualms about not doing what I asked of him— not leaving her alone in the room. Meanwhile she took out the papers that were there, and hid them on herself."

"Is she in with this Fox?" Claxton asked suddenly. "I always did say you never can tell what foreigners are up to."

Claxton had fought in France with a French army corps on one side of him, and a Belgian contingent on the other, and since those days he posed as an authority on all international questions.

"I have an idea that she's outside the crime," Pointer said. "I may be quite wrong, but I don't think she's anything to do with Sir Adam's murder."

"Then what was she after?" begged Nicholson.

Pointer replied that he thought that mademoiselle had discovered the secret drawer for herself, had no idea

240   *A Resurrected Press Mystery*

that Youdale knew about it, and had used it, during the search of the house, to put away there some private papers that she did not want the police to read. Not, as he so far thought, papers connected with the murder in any way. And in any case he had been notified to be very careful in his dealings with her. France was rather on edge at the moment.

Nicholson would have liked to ask further questions, but he quite realized that he must be content with what was handed out to him. It was more than anyone else would have got, outside of the police, and he knew it. He also knew that he must set to at once on some work that was waiting for him, and reluctantly he hurried off.

"The papers she hid there had to do with the Tangier villa," Claxton asked when they were alone.

"I think they were the papers that she took out of the mattress in which Gaudet sewed them temporarily," was Pointer's only reply.

Claxton was silent a moment. "I wonder what she'll do with them?" he said finally.

"Not hand them back to Gaudet in a hurry," Pointer said to that. "I hope she will either post them somewhere or else keep them with her, in her handbag. In which case, Claxton, I'm rather afraid that before long you'll hear of a case of that most regrettable crime of bag-snatching having taken place here in Wimbledon. Personally, I shouldn't be surprised if her bag were grabbed the first time she sets foot outside the garden." The two men exchanged an understanding look as Pointer hurried off.

He had an appointment with Miss Drury. It would be painful, but it might lead to something. It was far more painful to her than to him, for, as he saw it, he was doing her the greatest possible service. The fact that she had escaped death seemed to him less than the fact that she had escaped marrying such a brute. Kathleen at first utterly refused to believe what he had to tell her, until she heard of the false mustache and above all of the

The Westwood Mystery 241

complete set of new clothes in which Fox had arrived at the top of the cliff. That broke down her wall of insistent loyalty, a wall all the more elaborate outwardly, because she was conscious of some crumbling process going on inside it, which needed careful shoring up to keep it in its old position.

But when her first passion of grief, almost of despair, at having fallen in love with such a man had worn away, she seemed to have no knowledge of Fox that would assist the police. But Pointer was sure she must know something—something which hurried Fox up in his plan to get rid of her. This sudden disposal of the girl, so soon after Youdale's murder, even though he believed himself to be unsuspected, struck the chief inspector as only to be explained if Fox dreaded or feared Kathleen, or her knowledge. Yet Kathleen insisted that she knew nothing whatever, of his past life beyond the story of the purchase of the house and business

"Had he received any letters the morning of the excursion?"

"Only a business communication of some kind," she replied blankly. "I can't tell you what was in it, for though I opened the flap, I didn't look at the contents. I suppose it was some request for payments, he was always in difficulties about money."

He questioned her in detail about that envelope, but evidently there was no joint in Fox's armor known to Miss Drury.

An appalling case this, he thought, as he drove down to Westwood again, it was like trying to force your way through soft bog. Could that envelope she had opened have held anything of importance? Anything that had frightened Fox? He might have thought that she looked at the contents given a letter of sufficient importance. Fox had dropped it on the fire, Kathleen had said in reply to one of his many searching questions, but who knew enough to send such a note? Was it a threat, or a warning

242 *A Resurrected Press Mystery*

to get away? Who wanted to befriend him? Who knew enough to do so? Did Manning? Was he the link?

He found Nicholson holding forth to an impressed Claxton on an enlargement of his idea that the papers which Youdale had taken out of the hiding place in the frame must have vitally concerned Fox, and must therefore be the ashes which they had seen piled on the hearth.

"I believe we shall find that Fox figured in one of Youdale's early cases, and that those papers would have changed the jury's finding could they have been brought forward at the time of the former trial?"

Nicholson rubbed his chin till it crackled. "A man can be tried again for murder, if new facts come to light that were not available at the time of the first trial. Supposing Fox had been the accused, Youdale the prosecutor... and the man had got off for lack of sufficient proof, and Youdale found that proof the other day and at once sent word to Fox to come and explain the papers found..."

Claxton's nod said that Nicholson was expressing his thoughts too.

"That's rather a new risk in our profession, Nicholson went on ruminatingly. "My life insurance will be raised next... the idea that because your client leads you up the garden, and the truth comes out later, he's going to murder solicitor and barrister in order to prevent their re-opening the case."

Pointer gave a half smile of agreement. He heard a voice in the hall. It was Miss Green asking for him. He tossed the match he had just used to light his pipe down on to the green tiles of the hearth, and turned as the lady was shown in. She looked the caricature of the woman to whom he had spoken in her hotel. Disheveled, weirdly garbed, she insisted on having a word with the man in charge of the case, by which she only too clearly meant holding forth in one continuous jet of exclamations and

The Westwood Mystery 243

lamentations, but no questions brought out any useful information

Under the plea of getting her to write everything down, they promptly handed her over to the care of a plain clothes man Pointer stooped and picked up the match that he had tossed down. Where it had fallen was now a brown scorch-mark. He examined the tiles. He would have sworn that they were china, but obviously this must be some form of enamel, or was there some varnish used to keep them glossy? He rang for Tukes. The butler told him that the tiles were originally brown, that Lady Youdale wanted green ones to go with the woodwork, but as she had decided on this just before Sir Adam's last return, and as Sir Adam disliked any work in the house while he was there, the old tiles had been provisionally painted over with enamel.

"Wonderful, isn't it," he wound up, "no one would guess the tiles hadn't always been that color."

"But scorch-marks show," Pointer objected. "Aren't they impossible to remove."

Tukes agreed that they were, and that that was the great objection to this simple way of changing a color-scheme. As it happened, Sir Adam was extremely careful with his matches, and the tiles had escaped without a mark, up till now.

Claxton waited impatiently for the talk to be done, and the man to leave the room When the three were alone together he said, "Going on with what we were talking about, it's ten to one we find Fox was once had up on a charge, very serious charge—murder, likely enough."

"Of a woman, I fancy we shall find," Pointer said, deep in thought, "smothered in her bed, with a weighted cushion probably."

"Just so." Nicholson was deeply interested. "I wrote an article for The Solicitor's Journal only last month on the well-known tendency of criminals to repeat the way they commit their crimes."

244   *A Resurrected Press Mystery*

"If they get off with it once, they think they can again, and again," Claxton agreed. "Natural enough reasoning, I suppose."

"I think it's more than that." Nicholson felt himself the expert here on this one little phase of the subject of crime. "It's psychological. I think when a man commits a crime with a heavy penalty attached to it, he acts automatically, as it were. The first crime makes such an impression on his mind, cuts ruts so deep, that when he is again under similar conditions of strain and anxiety his mind acts in a precisely similar manner. Provided the second occasion permits of similar things being done. You know," he turned to Pointer who was standing deep in thought, "you have felt all along that that rose by the bed, the dressing-gown and the tucked-in bed-clothes were excrescences on this murder. Well, in my belief, and I can see now in yours too from what you've just said, Fox found, or placed, that rose, that gown, that neat bed for his other victim, and on this his second murder, his surface mind, being all absorbed with thoughts of danger, and risk, and fright, his subconscious self would cause him automatically to go through exactly the same actions as on the previous occasion."

"That's a very possible explanation," Claxton said warmly, "extraordinary how, many crimes are signed, as we call it. Even in small affairs." Claxton had a lecture to deliver to his constables tomorrow, and he intended to incorporate this view and embellish it with some recent crimes that bore it out.

A telephone rang. Claxton listened with every appearance of pleasure and turned to Pointer.

"Your idea has clicked, Sturge has been found! I've been concentrating on the Wimbledon poorer parts, where every house takes in a couple of lodgers, and it was through his ordering so many papers, as you thought, that we've got him. He gave out he was a reporter ill with 'flu and has stayed in his rooms pretty well all the time, but read every rag that was printed. Yes, we've got him

The Westwood Mystery 245

now, and we can find out from him whether he was acting in collusion with this Fox. Though I doubt it."

"I doubt if you'll find out anything at all from him," Pointer replied as so often before, "he can't speak—to you. However innocent of the murder, he can't confess that he made away with damning papers any more than mademoiselle can tell us about Gaudet's papers. I don't think he'll say one word, except to protest his innocence. I rather wonder he doesn't allege loss of memory."

Which was exactly what Sturge was doing. He insisted that his name was Smith, and that he was an out-of-work reporter whose memory had temporarily left him owing to overstrain. All his past was a blank, he averred, and the position resembled a deadlock, as far as he was concerned.

"I want a word with mademoiselle," Pointer went on.

"Connected with Sturge?" Claxton asked with interest, eyeing the other closely.

"Connected with the fact that the tiles in here are painted."

"Important?" Claxton asked wonderingly.

"Very," Pointer said, with something rather grim in his tone. "And for that reason I want to see her alone. I'll talk to her in the morning-room, so that if, or rather when, I learn something from her I can pass it on to you at once."

He rang the bell and asked for mademoiselle. She had not yet left the house. Sir Adam Youdale's papers were still not finished with.

Pointer closed the door after himself and went up to her where she stood by the window.

"Mademoiselle, something was taken from the library before I saw it on the morning when Sir Adam was found murdered in his bed. Something very important. All important in my opinion. Something which would have pointed straight to the motive and the murderer. To put it still more concisely, something that would directly link Fox and Sir Adam together."

246   *A Resurrected Press Mystery*

"I took nothing from the room," she said almost angrily, then, watching his face, she repeated it more insistently still, for the look on it sent a chill through her.

"I know something was taken away," he spoke as quietly as ever, but with his eyes like points of steel, "I know it, Mademoiselle."

"I took nothing away," she repeated.

"You had something that looked like a letter in an envelope in the pocket of your gown," he reminded her.

"That was a letter that I wrote to—a friend. My own private affair. I wrote it to pass the time after that Mr. Nicholson locked me in."

"Did you write it in pen, or in pencil?"

"With my fountain pen. Why?"

"Where did you blot it? The top sheet of the blotter was quite plain when I saw it Mademoiselle, I want that top sheet. I think that you wrote a letter to Monsieur Jussin, the cousin of Monsieur Gaudet, who is using his name for the time being, doubtless concerning his mission over here to get that villa for the French Government. Listen, Mademoiselle, your handbag was snatched from you about an hour ago by what looked like a tramp. You carried it wound tightly round your wrist with a steel chain, but one tramp held you, and the other got the bag away, and both made off in a tumbledown car. You haven't reported the loss to us because you did not wish the police to be brought into the affair. The handbag was brought to me. It contained the papers which Monsieur Jussin sewed into his mattress and which, when he left here for the inn, you afterwards hid in the secret drawer of the picture frame. They are papers showing that he came down here to get that villa from Sir Adam, by any possible means"

"Except violence!" she said swiftly. Then her head drooped a little. Pointer did not agree with Nicholson that she was plain. Quite the contrary It was to him a face though cold, of very noble possibilities. Now the coldness was gone for a moment.

The Westwood Mystery   247

This was no longer Portia. This was only a young woman uncertain for once of what path to take.

"Oh, Mr. Pointer, I miss him so! I mean Sir Adam. I almost wish now that I had been foolish—that we had gone away together—" She bit her lip. It was trembling. "It stings to have schemed against one you love who is dead." She raised her beautiful eyes to the chief inspector, lambent and full of pain they rested on his before she let them fall again. "I wish we could have been frank and told him why we wanted that villa. But he was not an easy man to manage. If he thought he was being driven, he would refuse to budge. But oh, how it all sickens me now. As for my French friend—I used to think that rather than be Sir Adam's half-wife I ought to marry him as his mother wished, but I know now that I should never have really done that. I know now that all the time it was Adam.

"But for that reason I want to be very careful not to harm him. His career is everything to him. He will have the villa now, of course, but please let him have it free of those ugly details—these quite unfounded suspicions."

"What I want you to understand," he said quietly, "is that he can't be injured by your being absolutely frank with me now. We know the truth, and all of it, as far as he is concerned."

"I was afraid of this," she murmured in a low, distressed voice. "And I helped him unwillingly to hide the papers. But what would you? One owes a debt to one's country. My father would have wished me to help him."

Pointer nodded his agreement to both statements. "I must see that blotting-paper," was all he said.

She jumped up "I will show it you, but you will find you are wrong. I confess that I did take the top sheet with me—I always do, when I write private letters, and by chance I have it still. It has the imprint of the last words that Sir Adam wrote. Had I known he was dead when I wrote my note I would never have blotted it on his lines. I saw him write the sheet that he blotted. I know what he

248   *A Resurrected Press Mystery*

wrote. It concerned a dog license. You will find that only his writing is on the paper except blottings from my own letter to Monsieur Gaudet. I prefer to continue to call him that. I will fetch it for you." At the door she hesitated. "You are mistaken in thinking it will help you, why are you so sure?"

"I'm absolutely certain that a leading clue, a link between Sir Adam and this man Fox was left here in the room. As I have found none, it must have been taken away before I got here. It can only have been done by you. Taking your assurances as honest, as I do, Mademoiselle, then the clue must be on that blotting sheet, since you say you took nothing else out of the room."

"I cannot follow your reasoning. But in any case, you will find you are mistaken," she said confidently, and he heard her run up the stairs. In a moment she was back in the room, and handed him a blotting-paper folded in half in an envelope.

Opening it, he saw, as she had said that there was no other writing but Youdale's and her, own on it. Pointer held it up in front of the mirror. Her writing was the closer, and overlaid the other, but he could make out words and bits of words.

"There is nothing here to do with a dog license," he said quietly, "it is the evidence I knew must have been left in the room."

She stared at him.

"But I saw him write it and blot it late in the evening! It's his writing. I haven't tried to made out the words, because I knew them—or thought I knew them..."

Pointer did not seem to be listening. His thoughts were following his own lines in truth.

"Come into the library for a moment with me, please," was his only reply. There he asked her to initial the sheet of blotting-paper with an indelible pencil that he handed her. Looking utterly at sea, she did as he asked, and then left the three men together again.

Holding the blotting-paper to the mirror, the three read, here and there, a word in Sir Adam's neat characteristic writing. Nicholson jotted them down. Pointer would have the paper photographed, and that photograph enlarged, for the present, the jottings would help. The words were "old frame—you sent back to Sydney—concealed—changed your name—Fox to Honesty—Public Pr—new facts not then available—Tangier—tr—murde—Alderley—",

Some of the words were made out with great difficulty, but fortunately mademoiselle's pen-writing was light, and her words nearly dry when she closed the blotter. The remainder of Youdale's writing could not be deciphered, or were words of no peculiar significance.

"That must be his real name! Honesty with a capital H can only mean that." Claxton was speaking. "Or at least it's the name he went under when Sir Adam knew him."

"And Alderley is on the list of interviews which Sir Adam had within the last three months—" Pointer said.

But he spoke almost absent-mindedly. "They are all firms of repute, and as I had each firm asked whether their business could in any way however remote, explain or be even distinctly linked with his death, I let their assurances that there could be no possible connection pass for the time being. I think we'll have a word with Mr. Alderley first of all."

But he learned over the telephone that Mr. Alderley was in a nursing home having his appendix removed, and that his head clerk was out. He asked to be at once informed of his return.

Nicholson had drawn in his breath sharply. "My brother-in-law heard Youdale defend a man in Tangier of the name of Honesty. It's the kind of name that sticks in the memory. It was Youdale's first murder trial, the man was accused of the murder of his wife, and Youdale got him off. I never asked for details. I wanted you to have a word with him, anyway, Chief Inspector, because he tells

250   *A Resurrected Press Mystery*

me that he belongs to the same golf club that Fox does, or did. If you like, I'll ring him up, and see if we can't get him to come here at once. He may know something, but I feel sure he hasn't connected Fox of the golf club with the man he saw tried and acquitted out in Tangier, while he was on a pleasure trip there."

Nicholson was ringing up as he spoke. His brother-in-law was busy, but at Nicholson's urgent request freed himself, and promised to go in an hour's time to Scotland Yard, and ask for Pointer.

The three of them motored up to town and at his room Pointer found a message from Tangier. The photograph of Fox had been identified as that of an Australian from Sydney, name of Honesty. He had been a purser on a boat, but he had married one of the second-class passengers, and used her money to open a bar in Tangier. At first it was a success, but Honesty started for some ammunition-smuggling which went wrong. Also he lost heavily on a cargo steamer in which he took shares. His wife's money vanished. Then an aunt left her about six hundred pounds. The wife was a chemist's daughter of Sydney, name of Trevor. She had the money, which the aunt left her, forwarded to her by way of a check on Cook's. When the check arrived, she endorsed it, and sent her Arab servant to cash it, giving him a note to the bank manager, whom Honesty had previously notified that she would send for the money in just that way, and would want it in cash. The next day she was found smothered in her bed, a weighted pillow over her mouth. She had first been given a sleeping-draft. Honesty was arrested, but he claimed that it was the doing of the Arab servant, who had disappeared that same night. Full particulars and papers of the trial should reach Pointer tomorrow.

And then, hard on the heels of the wireless came Nicholson's brother-in-law. At first it seemed as though the two new pieces of information were merely overlapping, but finally he mentioned something new. It came after many details of no importance, for in that trial

The Westwood Mystery   251

the young solicitor's interest had centered entirely on Youdale. He had barely glanced at the accused man, had seen nothing of his face when he did glance, and had not recognized Fox as the same man when he met him in the golf club. "There was an advertisement in the *Times* that someone called my attention to, a firm of solicitors asking Oliver Honesty to communicate with them, something to his advantage. I'm afraid I don't remember the firm's name, except that they were a small old-fashioned firm—"

"Was it by any chance Alderley?"

"That was it, Alderley!"

"The date?"

After thinking rather helplessly for a moment, he shook his head. "Around a month ago, or possibly two, within the last quarter anyway."

"Was there anything on at the time," Pointer asked him, "in the political or sporting world that could fix it?"

"By Jove, yes! The Oxford and Cambridge boat-race was coming off that Saturday. Yes, that was the day. Quite certain!"

That would make the day in question, when the advertisement had appeared to be March 15th. A Times was immediately forthcoming, the advertisement was found on the front page. Pointer was more than ever sorry that Mr. Alderley could not be questioned. He decided to try the solicitor's clerk, a very capable-looking man. Nicholson now carried his brother-in-law off with him. And Claxton, too, had to hurry away on business connected with Sturge. But they both returned in time to hear the next piece of evidence.

The head clerk, his name was Mowbray, looked at the advertisement in question and nodded meaningly.

"Yes, sir. We put that in. Put it in twice weekly for six months, and more, before he saw it. Mr. Trevor, his father-in-law, had died. I would have communicated with you when I read of Fox's arrest, but I didn't quite venture to do that."

"I wish Mr. Alderley was here," the clerk said, "but he has instructed me to be quite frank with you—as far as I know the facts. I don't know them all. There was a touch of—well—caution—about the way the whole business was put through, that I noticed at the time... But then we see a lot of caution in my profession. Yes, Mr. Alderley advertised for Mr. Honesty because of a legacy left him by his father-in-law. By Mr. Trevor. Mr. Trevor felt that he had been unjust to him. I believe I'm right in saying that he was the main instigator of the trial of Honesty for his wife's death. Well, he evidently saw that he had been wrong and left a thousand pounds to his son-in-law because of that trial. We advertised daily for months and at last Mr. Honesty appeared. He satisfied Mr. Alderley as to his identity, and would have had the thousand paid over to him in due course but—well—it all depends now, doesn't it?" he finished vaguely. The obvious ending being that if Mr. Honesty was hung, the legacy would not pass into his hands.

"Any reason why the money hasn't been paid over yet?" Pointer asked.

"By Mr. Trevor's will it was only to be paid three months after being claimed by Mr. Honesty. Mr. Trevor, quite naturally, had a great fear of an imposter claiming the money. He evidently felt that, owing to his peculiar position, Mr. Honesty might find it hard to establish his identity, and conversely that an imposter would find it, or might find it easy to impersonate him. I take it that was why the delay in the handing over of the money."

"Was there any difficulty about the identification?" Pointer asked.

"None whatever," Mr. Mowbray, said promptly.

"Have you any note of the charge made to Mr. Fox Honesty by your firm for the work done for him, so far?" Pointer asked next. It must have been very difficult for Fox to establish himself as Honesty. How difficult, the solicitor's fees would probably indicate.

The Westwood Mystery 253

The clerk looked surprised, and shot the chief inspector a reluctantly admiring glance.

"Yes, I have a note of it with me," he confessed, "just in case I was asked what work we had done." He stated the amount. Nowadays a solicitor can charge pretty much what he likes, but, even so, it was a stiff figure for what sounded like a brief interview, and a couple of letters. Pointer inquired the reason.

Mr. Mowbray twiddled a fountain-pen. "I wish Mr. Alderley were able to be here," he said finally, "but he wants to help you in every way, and it's really Mr. Trevor who was his client, not this Mr. Honesty; the extra charge was for arranging an interview between Sir Adam Youdale and the claimant to the legacy. Yes, that's why I didn't see my way to come forward before. I felt that I must wait for Mr. Alderley to handle anything so important. But as it is, these are the facts. Mr. Trevor, foreseeing, as I said, the difficulty of identification, and evidently very much on his guard against deception, wrote a personal letter to Mr. Alderley which accompanied the will. In it he stated the test which, if possible, supposing Sir Adam to agree to do it, was to completely satisfy Mr. Alderley about the handing over of the money. Some question as to something that passed between the two of them during that trial in Tangier, I fancy. At any rate, if Sir Adam said the answer was correct, then all responsibility was taken off Mr. Alderley. The extra charge was for arranging for an interview at Sir Adam's chambers in Brick Court, and for obtaining from him a written deposition that the claimant before him had correctly answered the test question suggested by Mr. Trevor."

Pointer asked to see a copy of the will leaving Honesty the legacy. It only occupied a couple of lines.

Pointer seemed lost in thought as he put it away with other papers.

"Your firm were this Mr. Trevor's solicitors of old, I suppose?"

254   *A Resurrected Press Mystery*

"No, but Mr. Alderley was some sort of connection of Mr. Trevor's, and Mr. Trevor had left a very urgent private letter for him asking him to undertake the task of finding Honesty, for which purpose a hundred pounds had been put at the firm's disposal. When that sum should be used up, the legacy to Mr. Honesty could be tapped for further supplies if necessary. The whole estate of Mr. Trevor, when death duties were paid, only amounted to some forty pounds over and above the thousand and this hundred."

Pointer asked some more questions, none of which brought out any answer of importance. Mowbray was thanked and allowed to go back to his work. Pointer next rang up Sir Adam's head clerk. He had had several talks with him, which, so far, had amounted to nothing. But he was now asked to supply the fullest possible information concerning the visit to Sir Adam, on a certain given date, of Mr. Alderley the solicitor, with a client of his, a Mr. Honesty.

"Ah!" came the head clerk's voice over the telephone, "so that's coming into this, is it? But I don't see how!" After which involved exclamation, he proceeded to say that he was at the chief inspector's absolute disposal.

CHAPTER FOURTEEN

The head clerk of the murdered barrister knew all about the identification of the man called Honesty. Youdale had few secrets from him. He promptly gave a very accurate account of the transaction. Nicholson and Claxton were as interested as was Pointer in hearing the exact question chosen by his father-in-law as a test of identity.

"But, gentlemen, I don't see the connection," the head clerk murmured when he had finished. "I mean, there can't be any between this scene and Sir Adam's murder! He *did* identify Honesty. Now, if he had been unable to do so or not sure—but he helped the man to get the legacy!"

Nicholson was in the same perplexed state of mind. How did the chief inspector expect to get his proofs of Honesty's guilt here? Yet he felt sure that Pointer was following some consecutive train of reasoning. He would have put the question outright to Pointer but for the fact that the latter, on leaving Brick Court, hurried away to New Scotland Yard.

"And in my opinion the rose, and the dressing gown, and the tucked-in clothes are 'repeat performances' due to the same strain." The superintendent since his lecture had quite adopted the scientific outlook, "the criminal's brain repeating itself automatically, when engaged in similar crime," he explained airily, to Major Pelham's secret amusement, for they were in the assistant commissioner's room. "Mr. Fullford is having an interview with Honesty," Claxton went on. "Honesty asked for him. Fullford was more than willing. I fancy that, quite apart from his regard for Sir Adam, he wants to have a word with the dear fellow who made that jam. He promised to let me look him up when I get back and hear what he has to say. Should Honesty say anything important, he's going to telephone it here."

But no message came from Fullford, and Pointer was in a hurry to get back to Wimbledon. Claxton went with him, wondering at the speed of the car. Was Fullford in danger?

They found Fullford looking pale and wizened, waiting for them in his shop. He shook his head sadly.

"Hardened liar, I'm afraid, intends to bluff it out."

Pointer glanced at the telephone drawn close up to the other.

"I shouldn't be surprised if Honesty asked for me again," Fullford answered the look. "He must know he can't get away with that tale! Ah!" The instrument rang its bell. But it was Claxton who was wanted. His sergeant was speaking from the police station. Fullford looked at him inquiringly, his old hands caressing a blunderbuss he was polishing, compared to which they were youth itself. Claxton's face grew set as he listened. He turned away and looked at Fullford.

"I don't know what you said to him, Mr. Fullford, but Fox—or rather Honesty—has just killed himself."

"I'm not sorry—in a way," Fullford said judicially "In a way I am! He deserved hanging, of course. How did he do it?"

"Why did he do it?" pressed Claxton severely.

"Probably because he knew the game was up," Fullford suggested indifferently. "Once he knew that I really was alive. He hoped I might be dead, after all, and that you were only bluffing. But when he saw me in flesh and blood, evidently he threw up the sponge."

Pointer leaned forward and lifted Fullford's hand from the gun. The eyes of the two met. Fullford, with a slight smile, left his hand in that of the chief inspector, and leaned back in his chair as though more at his ease. On the instant the room shook to the noise of a thunderous report, the air was full of the smell of powder. Pointer had seized the antiquary and dragged him to one side so that

The Westwood Mystery 257

the shot from the second gun, which was leaning against the old man's chair, well hidden, went through into his body, not, as Fullford had intended, through his brain. He had so placed it that a touch on the trigger with his foot, even with a shoe on, would fire it.

They laid him on the floor. Pointer tried to staunch the great wound in his chest, but it was no good. Fullford was suffering no pain, but he could not last more than a few minutes with a gap like that in him.

"How did you guess?" he asked faintly, looking up at Pointer.

"I am bound to remind you," the, detective officer said gently, "that anything you say may be used."

"At the Judgment Seat, if there is one," Fullford finished in his ghost of a whisper. "But why suspect me? Who am I that I should have any motive to kill the great Sir Adam Youdale? The fluent barrister."

There was mockery in the tones, all but inaudible though they were.

"I haven't had time yet to prove it," Pointer said, bending down. "But since I've learned of how Honesty's wife was found murdered in Tangiers, a rose beside her bed—tucked in by a loving husband—her gown ready for use, and find this to be a replica of it, as close a one as was possible under the circumstances, many things pointed to you, Mr. Fullford."

"But why? What motive?" scoffed Fullford, his dark eyes looking amazingly youthful and full of spirit.

"I think you must be Mr. Trevor, the father of that Mrs. Honesty."

"He's dead," came in a murmur.

Pointer could have replied. "No, that he was now dying," but he did not say anything.

"How did that devil kill himself?" came from Fullford. Pointer looked at Claxton and nodded. They could safely tell Fullford.

"He had a picture with him. In the back of it a safety razor blade must have been pasted in. He cut his jugular.

258   *A Resurrected Press Mystery*

What did you say to him, Mr. Fullford?" Claxton too was on his knees, bending over the little man. Fullford seemed to be better able to speak now than at first. It was but the last flicker of life before it should leave his body, and both the men with him knew it. So did Fullford.

"And your interview with Honesty—he killed himself after it?" Pointer murmured. "What did you say to him?"

"I let him think I was the father of another, girl, or rather woman, who had thrown in her lot with his." Fullford spoke exultantly now. "I had found out a good deal about her. Australian she was. And there was that woman in Malaga... and there was this Miss Drury... And I spoke as though the Arab servant whom he had flung into the sea had by a miracle got free from the stones tied in with him and had told of his assault on him, and was only waiting to tell it again. Oh, I made him see that the end was very close, and not a pleasant end. But I'm glad he didn't wait for his trial. I know now that I might not have lived to see it out, or he might have got off. Though I tried to make this impossible. I tried to make a ring fence around him without a gap or a crack that he could crawl through—loathsome reptile that he is. He murdered my Flora"—the dying man's voice came with surprising firmness, "and Youdale knew it. Knew it, and for the sake of scoring a success, of proving that he could cajole a jury, and twist falsehood around till it looked like truth, he got him off. Let him go scot free. But I swore that he should pay. That both should pay. Well, both have paid and my task is over. There's nothing for me to live for now. The doctors warned me a month ago that I'm a doomed man anyway, which was why I couldn't wait any longer."

There was silence while he drank some water. "Tell me," he asked in a lower tone. "You believed my account when I claimed that Fox was lying about there being a picture..."

"Well, I had my doubts just then," Pointer said. "You see, you could invent that excuse of the picture deal, but could Fox? I doubt if he knew what a Raeburn is. It's not

The Westwood Mystery 259

in his line at all. He would have invented—so it seemed to me—something to do with business of some sort... not a picture. It struck me at once as being far more in your line of knowledge. But, Mr. Fullford, it won't make any difference to you what I think. Why not let us have the true story... come..."

Fullford closed his eyes in what was the equivalent of a shake of the head.

"If you don't know it, you shall never learn it."

"I think we can guess it. You hid in the old clock in Sir Adam's bedroom, sitting on a stool taken from the cupboard in his bathroom, an old milking stool originally, that had been painted white. You took off pendulum and weights, of course, for the time being. When Tukes put the liquor glass beside his bed, you drugged it with chloral that you had taken from Tukes's bottle. He had often talked of his sleeplessness to you, and there is an old clock in his room that he got you to regulate for him. It was probably on that occasion, some time last month, that you took the chloral, and filled up the bottle with plain syrup. Before getting into the clock case, you sewed the shot in the pillow, stitching it shut as you would the end of a bandage—"

"Ah!" murmured Fullford to himself.

"The door of the case opens in such a way as to be in complete shadow when the lights are on in the room. You probably kept the door ajar all the time. When Sir Adam fell asleep, you smothered him, put a rose from the lounge by his bedside, with the idea of duplicating as much as possible the scene of your daughter's bedroom when she was murdered."

"The roses in the lounge gave me the idea," murmured Fullford almost sleepily now. "I thought it would help to point the way back."

"You waited until Fox, as he now called himself, fell asleep over his drugged wine. You must have drugged the sherry you put out for him, I think, and taken it away

260   *A Resurrected Press Mystery*

with you afterwards, leaving Sir Adam's undoctored bottle in its place"

"Full marks—" murmured Fullford

You took the note from his pocket purporting to be written by Sir Adam, and when he woke—woke owing to something you did to him, poured down his throat probably—" Here Pointer looked questioningly at the dying man, who merely murmured "Probably," in reply, without amplifying the word.

"When he woke up and left, you went down into the library again, opened the safe with Sir. Adam's key, which you took from under his pillow, emptied the safe, leaving the will in a cupboard of the room, and leaving, as you thought, a straight trail for the police to follow on the blotting pad in the room and in the little chit of paper left with the will. You had brought with you some burned papers, probably in a paper bag which you emptied on to the hearth tiles together with the match that had lit them. These were to look like the incriminating papers which Fox had burned, and because of which he had murdered Youdale. The imaginary papers whose equally imaginary finding in the secret drawer by Sir Adam, you later described on your return after Fox's arrest. Last of all, you took from the safe in the library the Rubber Trunks Company's papers, merely because you wanted some link with Westwood to put in Fox's house, and these were neatly tied and fastened up. You hid them in the Tollard Road house, where you felt fairly sure that he would not look for them, going to the house probably in some disguise, though since Fox himself admitted you the time when you went to look at the pictures, you may have gone as you are. You expected, of course, that we would at once search all his rooms, and find proofs that he had been to Sir Adam's safe."

"Which is what you did do," came from between Fullford's bloodless lips. "You gave him rope enough to hang himself, though just why the delay... but it's all right now... I don't mind going. I was only afraid of dying

The Westwood Mystery 261

before I had got him and Youdale." The voice dropped with alarming suddenness.

"Mr. Fullford," Pointer's lips were at his ear, "you left some words traced from Sir Adam's writing on the blotting pad, so as to look as though he had blotted a letter there?"

Fullford heard him with ease.

"Of course. I wrote out every link so as not even the thickest numbskull of the lot could miss it. I didn't know you would be given the job, or I shouldn't have made things quite so plain."

So, as Pointer fancied, Fullford had no idea how nearly his scheme had gone wrong—owing to the inadvertent suppression of the blotting paper. The master clue.

"And I sent a letter to Fox telling him you had the Tangier end of the string in your hands," Fullford went on. "I wanted to stampede him into doing something foolish."

So that was why Fox had rushed down to Brighton with Kathleen Drury. Pointer had felt sure that the letter which the girl had opened accounted for the urgency of her peril.

"You pretended to die, so as to leave him a thousand pounds that you were sure he would never get? So as to have it on record that he and Sir Adam had recently met, and that he could not claim not to know where Sir Adam lived?"

Fullford had to wait a second before he could get strength enough to answer. He was almost free of his body now, and glad of the fact. He was very weary of this life.

"Partly. I didn't know where he—Honesty—had hidden himself. But I knew he would crawl out of the grave to get a thousand pounds."

"But if he had died?"

"The money was to be handed over without question to whoever brought the remainder of a torn piece of paper

262   *A Resurrected Press Mystery*

enclosed under a separate covering letter to Mr. Alderley."

Pointer did not press for further information about this piece of news. He suspected that Mr. Alderley might not be so ignorant of Fullford's identity as he was expected to appear to be—officially, or rather, professionally.

"But what made you suspect me?" Fullford whispered urgently. "That sewing? Not enough surely."

"I could find no one else who knew both men, except you, Mr. Fullford. And it was you who suggested that Mr. Fox was an Australian. And you who, according to your own books, had opened the secret drawer and—according to your own account only—had watched Sir Adam take some papers out of it, read them, and make very leading remarks. Today, you even have on the shoes you wore when you sat on the stool inside the clock."

"They were freshly cleaned this morning. How do you know they are the same?" Fullford actually tried to have a look at his shoes but he could not lift his head.

"There's a roughness on the side of the left heel that marked the stool leg, and there's white paint scrapings on the inside of the arch of both shoes."

"But you found Fox's fingerprints on the glass. That was pretty neat," Fullford said in an exultant whisper.

A silence fell. Pointer thought that the man was dead. But suddenly he opened his eyes—wide.

"I drove her to that marriage," he said in a clear voice. "I mean, my Flora. She didn't really care for the brute, and just before the wedding, she told me she was afraid of him. But I wanted to marry again just then—it came to nothing—my marriage idea—so I pooh-poohed her fears. Shoved her off with her mother's money—into her coffin. And when she was murdered, it all came back to me, her terror of the man, for it had been that, that last day—she suddenly felt he was after her little fortune. Flora was no beauty. I had my doubts about his love, too, but I thought he'd make her the average husband, and Flora didn't ask

The Westwood Mystery 263

much of life." A spasm crossed his face. "And when she was murdered, I knew what I'd done. I swore that her murderer shouldn't escape. I did my best to get him hung in Tangier, but Youdale with his damned charm and winfling tongue was too much for me—and justice. So I swore that he should pay too. He had flouted justice for the sake of scoring a triumph. I would flout it too." A grin twitched the mouth around which the blue shadows were settling fast.

They were the last words he spoke, and in themselves summed up the reason for the whole tangle surrounding the murder of Sir Adam Youdale. Even as he spoke them, Fullford died as suddenly, as easily, as though he had stepped through a door and softly closed it behind himself.

"I still don't see why that heap of charred paper spelled Fullford."

Major Pelham balanced his paper knife on his forefinger reflectively.

"Why, sir, as soon as I found that that heap of charred paper couldn't have been burned where it was found, it said that probably everything else found with it was a sham, too," Pointer explained, "like a sign with IMITATION on it in front of a case of jewelry. There was no other place in the library where papers could have been burned... granted a faked scene, what about the missing documents from the safe, the fingerprint on the wine glass? They were all linked with it, and so all fell away into nothingness, as far as clues went. The papers found in Fox's house in Tollard Road meant nothing, either—Fox's story was possibly true.

"I never was satisfied with the automatic theory of that rose and dressing gown and those bed clothes, whereas if everything was a delusion and a snare. they fitted the idea of revenge... of someone who knew of that old murder case... Mr. Fullford's name, and his alone, was closely mixed up with Youdale's, and slightly with Fox's. No one else that I could find knew both... touched both...

264   *A Resurrected Press Mystery*

That was fairly certain, and seemed to me very significant. Then, too, his dose of poison—well, he was a very ill man indeed, the doctor said. The marvel was that, if anyone wanted to poison him, he should still be alive, for the doctor said that a full dose of arsenic would have done for him. Yet he certainly had taken poison. If his story was true, the dose was an amazing piece of good fortune for him. But if it wasn't true—it pointed to some medical knowledge on Fullford's part. His writing flashed into my mind at that point, of course. It was so typically the chemist's writing. And that will which left the money to Fox and yet which made him repeat a caution of Youdale's which showed that Sir Adam was really perfectly sure that the man was guilty."

"So he was of that young woman—Annabelle Luton," Pelham broke in. "Was she, do you think?"

Pointer could only say that mademoiselle believed her innocent and mademoiselle was a good judge. He continued along his single rail.

"A chemist, next to a doctor, would find it easiest to arrange for a false death certificate during an epidemic—"

"In Tangier!" completed Pelham. "Quite so."

"I all along felt that the time was badly chosen if it was Sturge—"

"I've just had a talk with him, by the way," put in Pelham. "He swears he saw Youdale lay the envelope with the papers down on the lounge table and leave it there. He, Sturge, pounced on them—naturally—that's his word, not mine, slipped out of the house down the outside stairs with them in a bag that night, after a talk with his niece, put them—somewhere, he won't say where—and came back to what he had every reason to think was a normal household. He assures me that he nearly died of heart failure when he learned next morning what he had returned to!"

Even Pointer gave a grin at Pelham's tone.

The Westwood Mystery 265

"Apparently Fullford was most anxious to have the crime at once linked with Fox, and yet he chose that one night!" The assistant commissioner went on.

"I don't think Mr. Fullford had ever heard of the Rubber Trunk Company," was Pointer's explanation "He strikes me as the sort of man who is so completely wrapped up in his one all-engrossing purpose, that he would have no idea of what was interesting the rest of England. He never reads a paper, for one thing, and he rarely pays any attention to the talk around him, unless addressed directly to himself. But his illness, which was a mortal disease, would make him want to hurry his scheme through as soon as he had found Honesty again."

"Why so long over that?" the assistant commissioner wondered.

"Probably collecting the thousand pounds, sir," Pointer suggested rightly. "Supposing I was right, and that Fullford, the only man who touched Fox and Youdale, was the criminal—there must be some reason for the murder of the one and the effort to hang the other. It must be a strong one The murdered woman's father would fit Mr. Fullford, as far as age went; he had been a chemist, and the writing and the sewing of that pillow fell in with this idea. Mr. Fullford fitted so many things. He could come and go as he liked. He knew the butler's bedroom as well as Sir Adam's. He could detach pendulum and weights of that clock without a scratch. And it was after an interview with him that Honesty killed himself."

"I still don't quite see why you were so sure something was missing from the library" The ivory knife was balanced now again and swung to and fro.

"No man would have faked all the accessories so carefully and forgotten to put in the main clue. I had found my way to Fox, it was true, but not thanks to the gentleman or lady who had put those ashes on the painted tiles. I knew there must be something else—a clue directly linking Fox with Youdale, and giving some motive..."

"So all that tale of papers in the secret drawer was false. The drawer was empty?"

"I don't think he ever showed it to Sir Adam," Pointer thought aloud—and rightly. "I think he found it out for himself, and at once decided it might come in handy in just the way he used it. I think mademoiselle noticed some unevenness in the frame after he put the drawer back, which made her investigate closer, or else happened to hear, or read, of this other frame on exhibition in the South Kensington Museum, the one that set Mr. Fullford himself on the track of the hiding place. Knowing that Monsieur Jussin was coming down with very valuable papers on him, she, I think, decided not to refer to it for the present. Merely a vague feeling that as long as Jussin was in England they might need a safe hiding place in a hurry."

"Where is she, by the way?"

"At a Sacred Heart Convent. Now that she has the money that the villa will fetch for a dowry, she intends to take the veil there. And if she does, she'll make a Mother Superior in a thousand. Jussin will get the sole glory of securing the house for his government."

There was a pause. Pelham was thinking things over, before turning his mind to another case.

"Miss Luton and Manning were married this morning. Lucky for her the job was in your hands. Manning told me to thank you for what you did and how you did it. Pretty damnable position for the other man—Reggie Youdale Manning himself isn't any more thankful than he is."

There was another pause

"I'm glad you weren't able to save the chap— Honesty," Pelham said finally. And Pointer's look said that for once the chief inspector too was quite satisfied that a man accused of a murder which he did not commit should not have been set at liberty.

The Westwood Mystery 267

"But I'm glad, too, that Fullford didn't get away with his double vengeance undetected," Pelham went on. "To think of him being the Devil in the Car. He nearly stampeded Fox into trying to murder Miss Drury!"

"Oh, Fullford wouldn't stop for a trifle like that," Pointer said dryly.

"Especially when he believed you were hard on the fellow's heels. Well, well so Claxton's scientific theory of crime repetition has come out in the wash!" Pelham gave a laugh.

"I don't say the theory is wrong, sir, but it didn't apply here. It would only apply to a successful crime. Granted that Honesty had got away with his first murder, or his earlier murder, without rousing any suspicions, then one might expect him to repeat it. But he was all but hung. Nothing saved him except Sir Adam's incredible skill in cajoling, almost hypnotizing, a jury into agreement with whatever he chose to say."

"Yes, Youdale was rather proud of his skill in that line. Well, he paid a quite unexpected penalty for it." Pelham began to push the papers away from him. "Lucky you placed the missing clue, Pointer, and were right, both as to its existence and its significance. The Missing Clue Case is how I shall think of this in future," and Major Pelham offered the chief inspector one of his best cigars as a mark of appreciation.

THE END

Other Resurrected Press Books in *The Chief Inspector Pointer Mystery* Series

Death of John Tait
Murder at the Nook
Mystery at the Rectory
Scarecrow
The Case of the Two Pearl Necklaces
The Charteris Mystery
The Eames-Erskine Case
The Footsteps that Stopped
The Clifford Affair
The Cluny Problem
The Craig Poisoning Mystery
The Net Around Joan Ingilby
The Tall House Mystery
The Wedding-Chest Mystery
The Westwood Mystery
Tragedy at Beechcroft

MYSTERIES BY ANNE AUSTIN

Murder at Bridge

When an afternoon bridge party attended by some of Hamilton's leading citizens ends with the hostess being murdered in her boudoir, Special Investigator Dundee of the District Attorney's office is called in. But one of the attendees is guilty? There are plenty of suspects: the victim's former lover, her current suitor, the retired judge who is being blackmailed, the victim's maid who had been horribly disfigured accidentally by the murdered woman, or any of the women who's husbands had flirted with the victim. Or was she murdered by an outsider whose motive had nothing to do with the town of Hamilton. Find the answer in... **Murder at Bridge**

One Drop of Blood

When Dr. Koenig, head of Mayfield Sanitarium is murdered, the District Attorney's Special Investigator, "Bonnie" Dundee must go undercover to find the killer. Were any of the inmates of the asylum insane enough to have committed the crime? Or, was it one of the staff, motivated by jealousy? And what was is the secret in the murdered man's past. Find the answer in... **One Drop of Blood**

AVAILABLE FROM RESURRECTED PRESS!

GEMS OF MYSTERY
LOST JEWELS FROM A MORE ELEGANT AGE

Three wonderful tales of mystery from some of the best known writers of the period before the First World War -

A foggy London night, a Russian princess who steals jewels, a corpse; a mysterious murder, an opera singer, and stolen pearls; two young people who crash a masked ball only to find themselves caught up in a daring theft of jewels; these are the subjects of this collection of entertaining tales of love, jewels, and mystery. This collection includes:

- **In the Fog - by Richard Harding Davis's**

- **The Affair at the Hotel Semiramis - by A.E.W. Mason**

- **Hearts and Masks - Harold MacGrath**

AVAILABLE FROM RESURRECTED PRESS!

THE EDWARDIAN DETECTIVES
LITERARY SLEUTHS OF THE EDWARDIAN ERA

The exploits of the great Victorian Detectives, Poe's C. Auguste Dupin, Gaboriau's Lecoq, and most famously, Arthur Conan Doyle's Sherlock Holmes, are well known. But what of those fictional detectives that came after, those of the Edwardian Age? The period between the death of Queen Victoria and the First World War had been called the Golden Age of the detective short story, but how familiar is the modern reader with the sleuths of this era? And such an extraordinary group they were, including in their numbers an unassuming English priest, a blind man, a master of disguises, a lecturer in medical jurisprudence, a noble woman working for Scotland Yard, and a savant so brilliant he was known as "The Thinking Machine."

To introduce readers to these detectives, Resurrected Press has assembled a collection of stories featuring these and other remarkable sleuths in The Edwardian Detectives.

- The Case of Laker, Absconded by Arthur Morrison
- The Fenchurch Street Mystery by Baroness Orczy
- The Crime of the French Café by Nick Carter
- The Man with Nailed Shoes by R Austin Freeman
- The Blue Cross by G. K. Chesterton
- The Case of the Pocket Diary Found in the Snow by Augusta Groner
- The Ninescore Mystery by Baroness Orczy
- The Riddle of the Ninth Finger by Thomas W. Hanshew
- The Knight's Cross Signal Problem by Ernest Bramah

- The Problem of Cell 13 by Jacques Futrelle
- The Conundrum of the Golf Links by Percy James Brebner
- The Silkworms of Florence by Clifford Ashdown
- The Gateway of the Monster by William Hope Hodgson
- The Affair at the Semiramis Hotel by A. E. W. Mason
- The Affair of the Avalanche Bicycle & Tyre Co., LTD by Arthur Morrison

RESURRECTED PRESS CLASSIC MYSTERY CATALOGUE

Journeys into Mystery
Travel and Mystery in a More Elegant Time

The Edwardian Detectives
Literary Sleuths of the Edwardian Era

Gems of Mystery
Lost Jewels from a More Elegant Age

E. C. Bentley
Trent's Last Case: The Woman in Black

Ernest Bramah
Max Carrados Resurrected:
The Detective Stories of Max Carrados

Agatha Christie
The Secret Adversary
The Mysterious Affair at Styles

Octavus Roy Cohen
Midnight

Freeman Wills Croft
The Ponson Case
The Pit Prop Syndicate

J. S. Fletcher
The Herapath Property
The Rayner-Slade Amalgamation
The Chestermarke Instinct
The Paradise Mystery
Dead Men's Money

The Middle of Things
Ravensdene Court
Scarhaven Keep
The Orange-Yellow Diamond
The Middle Temple Murder
The Tallyrand Maxim
The Borough Treasurer
In the Mayor's Parlour
The Saftey Pin

R. Austin Freeman
The Mystery of 31 New Inn from the Dr. Thorndyke Series
John Thorndyke's Cases from the Dr. Thorndyke Series
The Red Thumb Mark from The Dr. Thorndyke Series
The Eye of Osiris from The Dr. Thorndyke Series
A Silent Witness from the Dr. John Thorndyke Series
The Cat's Eye from the Dr. John Thorndyke Series
Helen Vardon's Confession: A Dr. John Thorndyke Story
As a Thief in the Night: A Dr. John Thorndyke Story
Mr. Pottermack's Oversight: A Dr. John Thorndyke Story
Dr. Thorndyke Intervenes: A Dr. John Thorndyke Story
The Singing Bone: The Adventures of Dr. Thorndyke
The Stoneware Monkey: A Dr. John Thorndyke Story
The Great Portrait Mystery, and Other Stories: A Collection of Dr. John Thorndyke and Other Stories
The Penrose Mystery: A Dr. John Thorndyke Story
The Uttermost Farthing: A Savant's Vendetta

Arthur Griffiths
The Passenger From Calais
The Rome Express

Fergus Hume
The Mystery of a Hansom Cab
The Green Mummy
The Silent House
The Secret Passage

Edgar Jepson
The Loudwater Mystery

A. E. W. Mason
At the Villa Rose

A. A. Milne
The Red House Mystery
Baroness Emma Orczy
The Old Man in the Corner

Edgar Allan Poe
The Detective Stories of Edgar Allan Poe

Arthur J. Rees
The Hampstead Mystery
The Shrieking Pit
The Hand In The Dark
The Moon Rock
The Mystery of the Downs

Mary Roberts Rinehart
Sight Unseen and The Confession

Dorothy L. Sayers
Whose Body?

Sir William Magnay
The Hunt Ball Mystery

Mabel and Paul Thorne
The Sheridan Road Mystery

Louis Tracy
The Strange Case of Mortimer Fenley
The Albert Gate Mystery
The Bartlett Mystery
The Postmaster's Daughter
The House of Peril
The Sandling Case: What Would You Have Done?
Charles Edmonds Walk
The Paternoster Ruby

John R. Watson
The Mystery of the Downs
The Hampstead Mystery

Edgar Wallace
The Daffodil Mystery
The Crimson Circle

Carolyn Wells
Vicky Van
The Man Who Fell Through the Earth
In the Onyx Lobby
Raspberry Jam
The Clue
The Room with the Tassels
The Vanishing of Betty Varian
The Mystery Girl
The White Alley
The Curved Blades
Anybody but Anne
The Bride of a Moment
Faulkner's Folly
The Diamond Pin
The Gold Bag
The Mystery of the Sycamore
The Come Backy

Raoul Whitfield
Death in a Bowl

And much more!
Visit ResurrectedPress.com
for our complete catalogue

About Resurrected Press

A division of Intrepid Ink, LLC, Resurrected Press is dedicated to bringing high quality, vintage books back into publication. See our entire catalogue and find out more at www.ResurrectedPress.com.

About Intrepid Ink, LLC

Intrepid Ink, LLC provides full publishing services to authors of fiction and non-fiction books, eBooks and websites. From editing to formatting, from publishing to marketing, Intrepid Ink gets your creative works into the hands of the people who want to read them. Find out more at www.IntrepidInk.com.

CPSIA information can be obtained at www.ICGtesting.com
Printed in the USA
LVOW12s2136070515

437716LV00014B/165/P